TAKE CARE OF US : THE FINALE

TAKING CARE BOOK 3

GIANNI HOLMES

Editing by
EAL Editing Services
Ann Attwood Editing and Proofreading Services
Proofreading by Barbara Ingram

❀ Created with Vellum

WARNING

This book contains sexual content that is intended for a mature adult audience.

ACKNOWLEDGEMENTS

Thanks to all the wonderful supporters who held my hand while writing this series. I appreciate the enthusiasm with which you've greeted this series and sticking through it all.

To...

Author S.M James who's always there in the middle of my doubtful moments and for not letting this writing journey feel alone.

Author K.M Neuhold for being so willing to read a 100k+ manuscript without batting an eyelash and providing me with her feedback.

Anna K Neal for supporting this series from the beginning when it was nothing but a discarded manuscript.

Thanks for believing in me even when I don't believe in myself.

Claudia Polydoro, your big heart makes the world a better place. So free with your virtual hugs and uplifting words.

And if I forget anyone, blame my absent-minded brain, but I thank you all the same.

Gianni

Families are the compass that guides us. They are the inspiration to reach great heights, and our comfort when we occasionally falter.

Brad Henry

A good boy and daddy take care of each other.

1

OWEN

"Ugh. Come on!" Oscar cried in frustration, running ahead, then turning so he could face us while walking backward to the parking lot. He waved his arms wildly at the crowd around us dispersing in every direction since the fireworks had ended. I almost felt bad for missing most of it, but then I glanced at Declan beside me and had no regrets at all.

I still couldn't believe he had asked me to move in with him permanently. The thought of it was intimidating, but appealing at the same time. I hadn't lived with anyone except my kids since James left.

"The night's still too young to go home," Oscar continued, eyes dancing with energy. "Tomorrow you guys will be back in Cincy." A hand waved toward Declan and me. "And we haven't spent time together in forever. It's the Fourth, and the only ones going to bed right now are babies and old people." His eyes flicked over to me. "No offence meant, Dad."

"Hey, why isn't James included in the 'no offence' speech?" I protested, gesturing at my ex who just laughed. "You do know we're the same age, right?"

"Yeah, but James is cool," Oscar answered, eyes going wide as he gave James a smile that I couldn't fathom. It was almost as if he knew something about James that I didn't, which was likely given they'd had almost two years to get to know him. "Just ask Auggie! He can tell you how cool James is."

"Leave me out of this, Oscar," Auggie grumbled, but I could see the color rise in his face. *How interesting.* I was definitely being left in the dark about something, and now my curiosity was piqued.

"As I was saying," Oscar remarked. "It's still too early for bed. Let's go somewhere, like a bar or a club. It's kind of been a stressful last couple of days, and I think we all could let our hair down." Another sly look in my direction. "Of course, Dad—"

"Knock it with the old people jokes, Oscar." I scowled at him.

Declan snagged me by the waist and pulled me into his side. My scowl melted at the hot look he gave me. *Jesus, right there in front of my kids.* He had no shame at all. *I* had no shame either, because at the look he gave me, I wanted to strip for him and ask him to mount me like a filly in heat. He tipped my chin and gave me a swift kiss.

"Oscar's just jealous because *you* got the hot young billionaire boyfriend," he said with a playful smile.

Silence ensued for a couple of seconds before Auggie dissolved into laughter. James joined him, but Summer still had on her frowning face from earlier. I seriously needed to have another conversation about what was going on with her. I had never seen her so disagreeable before, and she had been giving Declan the cold shoulder all day.

"I am not jealous!" Oscar denied, stuffing his hands into his pockets.

Auggie hooked his arms around Oscar's neck and ruffled his twin's hair, still laughing. "You deserved that! Stop referring to their age difference, will you? I thought you wanted to go to a club."

Oscar pushed him away and finger-combed his stylish hair back into place. "I do. Maybe James can help us come up with an appropriate place. You know somewhere not so depraved that Dad and Mr. Billionaire will object to it."

Declan and I glanced at each other, and I was pretty sure he was thinking about the depraved things he'd done to me last night in our hotel bed. On the chair. In the tub. Oh God, if only they knew of the things Declan did to my body, but it was our little secret. I had no problems with my kids believing me to be a decrepit man who did not function sexually. Anything that made them sleep better at night. I sure as hell didn't worry about who they were shagging here in Columbus—as long as they were having safe sex.

"Actually, there's a club that would be perfect," James replied. "Lucky Gents. It's not too rowdy, light on the hook-up scene as most people go there for the dancing and drink."

"Sounds perfect," Oscar said. "All agreed?"

"Why not?" James said with a shrug. "Summer?"

I held my breath, waiting for her response. James was trying so hard, but Summer remained at such a distance. I hated seeing her so clearly unhappy and maladjusted.

"Sure, I can hang around for a few," she replied.

"I guess we're in then," I answered, glancing at Declan for his confirmation. "Right Da-Declan?" I flushed at almost slipping and calling him *Daddy*.

He grinned at me, my slip-up not flying over his head. "Sure. The club sounds fun. Plus, I have it on good authority that your dad twerks better than he slow-dances, so this I want to see."

"Oh God, please no!" Auggie protested. "I'm going to need to load up on shots before I see this."

"Yeah, keep that in the sanctity of your bedroom, please," Oscar agreed. "And just to clarify, I am in no shape or form jealous because Dad scored someone like Declan."

"Mmm-hmm."

I shook my head as Auggie continued to tease Oscar about having the hots for Declan. I couldn't help feeling smug as hell about it, because there was a smidgen of truth to Auggie's words. Oscar was used to attracting the hot guys. Now I had one of my own.

We had three separate cars that we piled into. Since Summer drove, Oscar decided to travel with her to avoid Auggie's teasing. Auggie went with James, and Declan and I had Silas on standby as usual.

"Are you sure you're up to going to the club?" I asked Declan as we followed James's car to wherever this Lucky Gents was located.

"I'm fine," Declan answered. "Plus, I couldn't waste

the opportunity to hang out more with your kids and get to know them better. It's all working out fine, don't you think? They're a lot more accepting than I'd have thought."

I groaned. "Except for Summer. I'm sorry about that."

He squeezed my thigh nearest to him. "Hey, two out of three ain't bad. I'll just have to work on my charm a little bit more when it comes to her."

I frowned, fretting as I remembered my conversation with Summer when we had picked up snacks for everyone just before the fireworks began. She wasn't happy about my relationship with Declan at all. Unlike the twins, she didn't care about him being wealthy. She had plainly told me that she didn't believe we suited.

The light had gone out of her eyes when I'd gently informed her that I was in love with Declan, and our relationship was too serious to break off. I was trying to be understanding, but it was also disappointing that she couldn't see how happy I was.

I was relieved to find that Lucky's wasn't crowded. I had anticipated the club being packed as people continued their celebration of the Fourth, but as we located a table inside, James explained that a hot new club had recently opened up on Parson's Avenue which would be seeing most of the night's action.

The club was decent, although smaller than I had anticipated. I liked the mixture of soft purple and pink lights and that the music wasn't deafening. Thanks to Declan, we got in on bottle service and were promptly taken to a VIP section with our own real estate upstairs, where we had an excellent view of everything below.

I wasn't too thrilled about the way our seating arrangement turned out. Somewhere along the line of getting situated, I ended up between Auggie and Summer. Declan sat opposite us with James and Oscar. I stamped down the urge to ask for a switch since we were all sitting together anyway.

"Maybe coming here wasn't such a good idea after all," Summer said, frowning at me. "This doesn't strike me as your kind of vibe, Dad."

I placed an arm around her shoulders and squeezed her in an affectionate hug, trying to cheer her up. "This isn't my first time at a club, Summer," I informed her gently. "In fact, after our initial meeting, that's where I ran into Declan again and we became a thing."

She made a face. "How much of a thing can you guys be? Look at him."

I did glance at Declan who was chuckling at whatever it was Oscar was saying to him. I had expected them to hit it off well, because Oscar was the fun kind of guy. He would make the best out of any situation. I was pleased that as the more hesitant and suspicious one, even Auggie had taken a liking to Declan.

"He fits right in," I remarked with a shrug.

"If he was *Oscar's* boyfriend!"

I frowned at her words, but before I could reply, Auggie leaned forward and across me to pinpoint her with a glare. "Knock it off, Summer. Instead of nitpicking, try to get to know him, will you? Why are you so angry with everybody lately?"

"Hey," I gave Auggie a gentle shove back into his space, "she has a right to feel the way she does. Give her the time to adapt, okay?"

Summer rose to her feet abruptly. "I should phone Penny and let her know where I am."

"Summer…"

She was gone without responding.

My phone vibrated, and I plucked it from my pocket, already knowing who it was even before I checked the message.

Declan: *Everything okay?*

No, everything wasn't okay. I was worried about Summer and all the changes that she seemed to not be dealing well with. Maybe I was worrying too much, and like I told Auggie, she would come around soon. She had to.

I flashed a smile in Declan's direction and nodded to him that everything was fine. He didn't look like he believed me, but Oscar tugged at his shirt dragging his attention away.

Although we were on bottle service, I didn't have much to drink. I noticed that neither did Declan. Summer rejoined us, looking chirpier and even joined in the conversation which made me relax.

We were at the club for close to an hour when Oscar got to his feet. "Who's going below to dance?"

To my surprise, Auggie unfolded himself from the lounge chair and stood. "I'm game. Need to shake off some of this alcohol in my system."

"Dad? Declan?" Oscar asked.

With a shrug, I rose to my feet. I might as well make

the most of the night. It wasn't every day that I got to hang out with my boys like this. After the scare of Declan's surgery, we definitely could do with some relaxation and fun.

"Dec?" I asked, when he didn't get to his feet.

"Go ahead," he told me. "I like to watch."

He smirked at me, and heat flamed my cheeks at what he was alluding to. That night still made me hot and bothered when I thought about it. Declan wasn't the only one who enjoyed watching. I liked the way he watched me too.

"If you're not dancing, neither am I," I protested, about to sit when Oscar looped his arm through mine.

"Come on, old man. Let Auggie and I show you how it's done."

Declan laughed as I protested being pulled along with Auggie and Oscar to the first floor where all the dancing was taking place. I completely understood why James had brought us here. There was no pressure of coupling on the dance floor. Sure, there were couples who were dancing together, but there were just as many single dancers and groups of people who looked like friends, so I didn't feel odd to be dancing with my sons.

"I know you didn't drag me down here just to dance." I scowled at the twins as we picked up on the rhythm with no real semblance of a dance move. "Couldn't you have chosen a more suitable place than the dance floor?" I shouted, emphasizing how impossible it was to speak to each other with all the loud music around us. The music was definitely louder on this floor than where we had been seated. The glass must have blocked out some of the noise.

"We just want you to know we approve!" Oscar yelled back at me. "Your guy's pretty cool!"

"And hot!" Auggie added, prompting a scowl from Oscar. "Seriously though, Dad, I like him, and it's obvious he's in love with you."

"Yeah, plus you'll never hurt for money!" Oscar added.

"I'm not with him because of his money!"

"I know, but just saying it doesn't hurt, you know!" Oscar replied. "How about we shut up now and let's do that move Dad taught us for our first dance."

"Oh nooooo!" I cried, backing away, but they smashed me in the middle between them both, hands on my shoulders. I was trapped.

2

DECLAN

My eyes trailed Owen as he reluctantly followed the twins who wouldn't let him escape their clutches. I gave him a wink when he threw me a desperate look. I wouldn't miss this for the world. Owen dancing in a nightclub, knowing my eyes were on him, watching him everywhere he went.

Like a drunken man seeking out the last drop of whiskey in a glass, I didn't take my eyes off him as they settled in on the dancefloor. Instead of dancing to the vibrancy of the music that bounced off the walls, all three men shuffled from side to side while they engaged in an animated conversation. More than once a set of eyes turned to where I was seated, and I had enough imagination to know they were talking about me.

The twins were alright. They seemed to like me as far as I could tell. Unlike their sister whose dagger glare I could feel on me even though I wasn't looking in her direction.

"What the hell are they doing?" I cried, laughing when the twins smashed their shoulders into Owen's at the sides, trapping him in the middle. They were trying to coerce him into dancing which he was hesitant to do at first, before he shrugged and gave in.

Watching Owen dance with his sons filled my heart with both joy and ache. I enjoyed seeing him so relaxed and carefree enough to not care about those who were watching them. He didn't dwell on how out of sync they were, especially at first.

Damn, seeing them hurt. Why couldn't I have had a relationship like this with Charles? It was way too late to develop this sort of bond that Owen had with his kids. The love between them all was this big magnetic field that sucked up everyone in its path, and I was getting pulled right in there with them.

I hoped to forever be sucked into it. This was family. This was what I wanted for Charles and myself. Maybe with everyone coming together, he and I would be better at interacting. Maybe we could learn from them.

"You love him, don't you?"

I tore my eyes away from Owen reluctantly to focus my attention on his ex who had mostly been quiet. I had been prepared not to like James, knowing he had recently tried to get back together with Owen. He'd kissed Owen, which I didn't appreciate at all, but while hanging out with their family, it had come to my attention that James was not just an ex. He was also an integral part of this family. The boys respected him, sought his approval, and Owen supported them, which meant I had to support him.

Whether I liked it or not, James wasn't about to disappear overnight. He was the father of Owen's kids, and he would be around. The best thing I could do was to try and get along with the guy.

With this in mind, I tried not to think about the kiss, hoping by now he would have gotten the drift that Owen was mine.

"He means the world to me," I answered, unashamed of my feelings for Owen. A man didn't cower behind his feelings when he was confident in them, and I had so much confidence in Owen and me.

"You know, I had my doubts," he continued, eyes trailing to where Owen and the twins were still dancing together. "I kept telling myself that you must have an ulterior motive, but having you spend the day with us, I see that you genuinely care about him."

"So do you," I pointed out, baring the elephant in the room. "You want him back."

At least he had the decency to glance away from Owen and looked uncomfortable. "I'm not going to lie about that," he replied. "He's the father of my kids. We had great years together, and I was a fool to fuck it all up."

"But that's all in the past," I added, clarifying things. "Owen's with me now."

James held up his hands. "No need to get possessive. He's made it clear what his choice is, and I respect that. You're a lucky guy."

I nodded, some of the tension easing from my shoulders. "I am lucky. I don't think even he understands just how significant he is in my life, but I'll make damn sure I show him every day."

"You do that. You're young, but you seem mature. Owen might need a bit of a... umm... firm hand at times."

I frowned at his ex. "No offence, but I think we can handle our relationship just fine. I know exactly what he needs, and if there's something he craves, he can communicate that to me."

At least he should know he could communicate that to me, but he still hadn't mentioned anything about his manuscript. What if he had other things that he was keeping from me? I didn't like that thought at all.

"Just don't hurt him," James added. "He deserves for things to go well for him after everything, and as you can see, he's well-loved by his family because of how much he's sacrificed for everyone. We would not watch from the sidelines while you hurt him."

It took every bit of maturity that I had in me not to tell James where he could shove his concern. Once more, I had to remind myself that he was a part of the family and that he was just worried for Owen. I could appreciate that without getting huffy and possessive about him pushing his nose in my business with Owen.

"Noted," was the only thing I said to him while I returned my attention to Owen on the dancefloor. They were still in the same position, laughing and moving to the beat of the music. I couldn't be angry tonight when I was seeing pure unadulterated joy radiating from him.

A man bumped into Owen from behind. I frowned as

Owen tried to side-step the guy and return his attention to his sons. The man, tall, wide in the shoulders and completely bald had no intentions of being dismissed, however. Oblivious to Owen, the stranger brushed up against him. Once more Owen moved forward to avoid him, not giving him a second glance. On the dance floor, it would have seemed like just the regular bumping into each other of two people dancing on a crowded floor, but it wasn't even too crowded to begin with. From my vantage point as well, I could see that clearly the stranger had his sights set on Owen.

I stiffened, the second the guy's arms came down to rest on Owen's hips and he whispered in Owen's ear. Owen spun, stepping away as he eyed the stranger up and down. I rose to my feet, the music, the people dancing fading as I zoomed in on the scene below. Nothing mattered, but the confrontation that was happening as the stranger persisted despite Owen's blatant attempt to shake his head in a refusal to dance.

A hand clamped down on my shoulder before I could move off. I scowled at James whose grip tightened.

"Don't. The twins will take care of it."

I was about to tell him the twins weren't responsible for Owen, I was, but true to his word, Auggie stepped up to the guy. Even from my position, the anger radiating off him was evident. Whatever Auggie said to him, the guy made another remark and leveled an obscene gesture at Owen, grabbing his crotch before he slinked away.

I couldn't tell the last time I was this furious. It was worse than the night Ridge had interrupted our date. I trailed the harasser with my eyes from Owen to the bar and had every intention of confronting him to apologize for harassing Owen.

"Look, the boys took care of it," James said quickly, as if sensing my intention. "Let it go. No harm was done."

I shrugged off James's hand. "I'll be the judge of that."

Summer, who had mostly stayed to herself, had her jaw slack as she watched me head for the stairs. I didn't take my eyes off Owen who had a puzzled look on his face, as if he couldn't fathom what the hell had just happened. I was grateful at least the twins were still there with him. Auggie looked just as furious as I did, and every so often he glanced over at the bar.

I came up behind Owen and slid my hand over his tense shoulders. He stiffened for a second before he inclined his head and saw that it was me. His whole body turned mellow.

"You okay?" I asked him, trying to divorce my anger from the situation. This was all about him and what he needed.

"You saw all that?" His cheeks were ruddy as if he was embarrassed by the encounter when he had no need to be.

"I told you I'd be watching you," I answered. "What happened?"

"It was just a misunderstanding," he replied, but I could tell he was lying.

"Misunderstanding!" Auggie fumed. "That dude clearly doesn't know what 'no' means. He fucking pissed me off with his attitude. What a jerk!"

"Auggie, it's alright," Owen said, trying to calm down his son. "Come on. We're not going to let him ruin the evening, are we?"

Auggie ran a frustrated hand through his hair. "I should go get a drink."

"Stay clear of the bar!" Owen called after him fretfully. "Oscar, go after him and see he stays out of trouble."

Oscar scowled. "Maybe I'll go give him a helping hand."

"Oscar!"

He ambled off, and I grasped Owen's shoulder before he could go after them. "Auggie's smart. He won't do anything stupid."

Owen turned troubled eyes in my direction. "I've never seen him like this before. I don't know what got into him."

"The same thing that got into me," I said on a growl. "I didn't like watching that fucker put his hands on you."

Owen's eyes widened as he gave me his full attention and caught wind of how pissed I was. He cupped the side of my face and kissed my cheek. "Relax. It's fine. I was fully capable of handling it even before the twins intervened."

"Now I need my hands all over you to forget about that asshole mauling you," I said, holding him against me. "Dance with me? I do owe you for that dance Ridge interrupted."

He smiled at me. "Yes, you do."

As if waiting on us to find each other, the music changed to a song I was familiar with. Kelly Clarkson's

Piece by Piece filled the club, the lyrics so apt for us that I chose to believe this was fate's way of letting us know we belonged together.

"Know this song?" I asked him as we swayed together. We were probably off sync with the music, but I didn't give a shit. Slowly the creep was being erased from my mind, Owen was in my arms, and I didn't wish to let him go. Not now. Not ever.

He leaned closer to me, his chin on my shoulder so he could speak directly into my ear. "I don't think so."

"Hmm."

I didn't say anything else as we continued dancing together, definitely out of sync with the music, but completely in sync with each other. The words of the song washed over us, and I hoped Owen was paying attention. Despite the way James had left his heart tattered, I'd put everything back together piece by piece, and I'd never leave him—never betray him the way James had.

He made a strangled sound in his throat before his lips pressed to the side of my neck, and I knew he noticed the significance of the song.

"I love you so damn much," he said in my ear.

With a groan, I stepped back only to cup his face and kiss him. His hands came down on mine, holding me firmly to him as if he never wanted me to let go. I didn't have the words to say because my mouth was too busy seeking his, but I showed him with every slide of my lips over his that he didn't have to worry. Come hell or high water, I would never let him go.

3

OWEN

"Okay, guys, I think I'm about ready to turn into a pumpkin," I said a while later that night, making no attempt to camouflage my yawn this time. I had been ready to leave the club since half an hour ago, but had tried keeping up with everyone else. The twins had this endless surge of energy, and as young as he was, Declan was right there along with them.

I didn't want the night to be over yet, which was the reason I had fought the yawns and fatigue. I liked watching Declan hang out with my kids. I enjoyed hearing their mingle of laughter as they debated sports, cars, and even food. I had been content to chime in only every now and then, which was fine with everyone else.

I loathed being the party pooper to call an end to tonight's gathering, and from Oscar's groan, he wasn't ready to quit. Despite that asshole who had tried hitting on me, the night had turned out fairly well.

"It's barely midnight," Oscar murmured. "And I'm not nearly hammered yet."

I scowled at him. "You shouldn't be getting hammered at all. Impairs your ability to think clearly. That's when people usually make shitty choices."

He groaned. "And the fun Dad's gone. Yeah, Declan, you should really take your old man home."

Dutifully, Declan rose to his feet. He'd been so comfortable where he was that I felt guilty for pulling him away from the conversation. We'd spent so much time together, and maybe being around others closer to his age would be a breath of fresh air.

"You should stay," I said, before I could think twice and be selfish about him leaving with me. "You don't have to leave now because I can't keep my eyes open. Finish your bottle with the twins."

He glanced from Auggie and Oscar to me. "Of course not. If you're ready, I am too. Besides, how would you get to the hotel?"

"I can drop Dad off," Summer, who had been quiet for most of the night announced as she got to her feet. "I should go home anyway. Penny will be up until I get back."

"I can't let you go to the hotel alone," Declan protested. "We're out together. What kind of boyfriend would you think I am?"

"One who's having fun," I answered, kissing his cheek. "Seriously, Dec, stay. I'll see you back at the hotel."

He still seemed uncertain, but I wanted him to stay. It was important for him to get along with Auggie and

Oscar. With me not around, they might be able to connect on even a deeper level. They might eventually be friends, which would mean the world to me.

"I promise I'll let you make it up to me," I told him, before I kissed him briefly. "Just stay with the boys, Dec."

Although he nodded, he wasn't completely in agreement with my suggestion. "Okay, but I won't be out long. I'll be there shortly."

"I won't wait up," I assured him on another yawn. "I'll probably be fast asleep when you get back."

By the little smile tugging at the corner of his lips, I knew he wanted to say something kinky, but he refrained because of our audience.

"I should get going too," James said, climbing to his feet. "I'm just as tired and should get a move on. I have a client to see tomorrow afternoon."

Declan touched my arm. "I'll walk you out."

I didn't need him to come with me, but I nodded, giving him something. He already felt ambivalent about letting me go back to our hotel alone. The least I could do was allow him to accompany me to Summer's car.

I hugged Oscar and Auggie who promised to keep in touch. Summer and James led the way without talking while Declan and I brought up the rear. The music had gotten louder as the night deepened, so we didn't bother to attempt a conversation until we were outside.

The sudden quiet and calm of the night was a huge difference. My shoulders slumped a little at the energy I was losing fast. I seriously needed a bed soon. As though sensing my fatigue, Declan wrapped an arm around my shoulders, and we bumped into each other as we walked.

"Are you sure you'll be okay on your own?" he asked me, slowing down to put more space between us and Summer and James.

"I won't even realize you're gone," I answered. "Pretty sure I'll be knocked out as soon as I get to the bed. I may not even make it to the bed before I crash."

"Damn, I should have realized you'd be tired and called a halt to the night earlier."

I wrapped an arm around his trim waist and squeezed him with the little energy I had left. "You were having fun. I liked that. I really enjoyed tonight Declan and the way you hit it off with the twins. That's why I think you should stay a little longer and enjoy the night."

"Plus, it will give them a chance to grill me about my intentions without you being present. That's the only reason I'm staying—to get this over and done with."

I lost the battle suppressing another yawn. A damn big one. "Sorry, I'm really tired." I glanced at him sheepishly. "Besides, didn't they already give you the third degree?"

"Hah. I think that's more like the first. Don't worry. Your boys don't scare me. I'm only too happy to stay behind and be very open about how much I'm in love with their dad."

By this time, we had arrived at Summer's car. James had his started, waiting on us to get closer as well.

"Well, it was nice meeting you, Declan," he expressed, then nodded at me. "Owen, we'll keep in touch. Thanks again for coming and lending your support. I really appreciate it, and if there's anything at all I can do for you, don't hesitate to call."

Declan's arm tightened around my shoulder. I'd never had anyone showing the slightest gesture of possession over me before, but... I liked it. That he wanted me enough to not want anyone else to have me was a good kind of feeling.

"It was nice meeting you too, James," Declan returned.

James drove off with a honk of his horn. He must have addressed Summer while we were lagging behind, because he said nothing else to our daughter.

Summer didn't exchange pleasantries with Declan, which I found extremely rude, but I didn't want to make the situation worse by addressing it in the open, so I filed it away for now. I would have plenty of time on the road to talk to her about her attitude.

"Text me when you get to the hotel," Declan told me. "Don't fall asleep without doing it."

"Okay. I won't forget."

"Good Boy."

I melted under his praise, and I was determined to keep that promise to him. To be his Good Boy. Until I was bad. Then he could make me be good again.

He cupped my chin and kissed me, too short and a little bit too sweet. I grasped fistfuls of his shirt front barely refraining from rocking back against the car and pulling him into me to grind against him. The sound of an engine coming to life burst through my lustful haze. Summer was beginning to show her impatience.

"I swear I'm going to wring her neck," I groaned, releasing Declan's lips. "She's being impossible."

He gave me another peck on the lips. "It's fine. Don't

be too hard on her. She'll come around eventually when she sees that I have no ulterior motive."

I didn't bother to inform Declan that I feared her not coming around at all. That would be horrible. I didn't want a wedge to be driven between my daughter and me.

Always the perfect gentleman, Declan opened the car door for me, and I got in. He closed the door firmly then leaned forward, resting his arms on the lowered window.

"It was nice to meet you, Summer," he told my stubborn daughter. "I hope to see you again soon."

"Yeah, I guess," was her response, before she put the car into reverse. "See you around."

"Don't forget to text," were Declan's final words as Summer backed out of the parking lot.

I fully expected Summer to complain about Declan being too young for me and to come up with a million reasons why I should dump him, but she said nothing. That in itself was a bigger disappointment, because it was impossible for me to know what was going through her mind. I didn't want to be the one to bring up the topic, but I didn't have a choice.

"So, what do you think of Declan now that you've had the chance to spend some time with him?" I asked. "Still think he has an ulterior motive for being with me?"

"We barely had a chance to speak," she answered, her voice low. "He spent all the time buttering up to Auggie and Oscar."

I frowned at her. "Uh, from what I remember of the night, Summer, he tried to engage you several times, but you knocked down every attempt he made. You were not being very likeable, whereas the boys were quite the opposite."

"Well, Oscar and Auggie are clearly dazzled by his looks and wealth," Summer answered, her voice rising. "Thank God, I'm into women so I'm not easily convinced."

"What do you need to be convinced of, Summer?" I demanded, annoyed and trying my best to rein it in, but it was so damn hard. "Declan's a good guy. Or is it that you don't think he could possibly be in love with someone like me? Because I'm *old*?"

"I did *not* say that!" she argued. "You're an awesome Dad."

"I'm also an awesome *man*, Summer!" I snapped. Not liking the tone of my voice, and recalling everything Declan had taught me about remaining calm in stressful situations, I took a deep breath. Then another. And still another. "I know you want to see me as just Dad, but that's not all I am. I'm a man too. I have *needs*, which I ignored to give you guys the best life I could. If I had to do it over, I wouldn't change it for the world. I don't regret neglecting my needs to ensure my kids were well taken care of, because you are always priority. But the fact is that I have desires I never thought would be fulfilled again. Then Declan came into my life, and he satisfies those needs, Summer. He makes me feel like more than just a dad. He makes me feel like a live flesh and blood man with desires and passion. He makes me believe in my dreams again. Why is that so wrong?"

She didn't respond, and I could only hope that she was giving what I had said to her some serious thought.

Before the words came out, I hadn't even contemplated the full extent of what Declan had brought back into my life. An identity I had lost along the way, because being a good parent had consumed me. My entire life had revolved around that identity. Of being a parent. Of being Dad.

Declan hadn't just given me a sexual awakening. Moreover, I didn't want just any man to fulfill my sexual needs either. I wanted only him. Declan had spoiled me for other men. I had never known such love and care from anyone else, even my own kids. Sure, they loved me, and I was confident about that. But, they took me for granted too, and they had expectations of me. Declan allowed me to just *be*.

For the rest of the drive to the hotel, we didn't speak. When she parked, we sat there for a few seconds, both of us struggling to find the right words to say.

"Look, Summer, I know it's hard for you to see me with someone," I said, choosing my words carefully. "You've never seen me with anyone in a romantic light before. Maybe if I had dated openly when you were younger, it would have been easier for you to see me with someone else now, but I didn't want to date anyone then. My priority was ensuring that my kids were okay and had my undivided attention. But now you're all grown up, and you have your own lives. It is lonely being by myself, Summer, and to have someone like Declan come along and offer not just companionship, but so much more— it's more than I've ever dreamed of, especially after James walked out on us."

Summer inhaled deeply, and to my alarm, a sob tore

from her throat. "Dad, I'm sorry," she sniffled. "I know I am being awful about the whole situation. I guess things are just tough right now with James and Penny."

"I know, honey." I reached across the console to hug her. "I know. And you take your time to come to terms with all of it. Don't let us pressure you into anything. But it would sure be good to have your blessing on my relationship. I'll never be truly content if I don't know all my kids respect and are okay with my choice."

"You're right," she said on a sniff, and pulled away. "I just need some time. You're so right."

I smiled, glad to see that she had found some clarity at least. I brushed her hair from her face. "Are you going to be okay?"

"Yes, I'll be fine. I love you, Dad."

"Love you too, kiddo." I groaned as I unlocked my seatbelt. "Go home and get some rest. Before you start your classes, you come on back to Cincy, and we'll spend some time together, okay?"

"That sounds great, Dad."

"Good night, Summer. Drive safely."

"I will. Good night, Dad."

I watched her drive away before I entered the hotel, feet dragging from both emotional and physical fatigue.

4

DECLAN

"Shit, I can't believe I got Owen's boys drunk," I groaned, slamming the car door shut behind me. I had just ensured both Auggie and Oscar were safely tucked inside James's house after calling a halt to the night. I'd had the vague impression that without the others, we would continue with some amount of drinking, but not to the proportions that we had indulged in.

I hadn't anticipated Owen's boys being as cool as they were, but they had turned out to be amazing shot buddies. I had quickly lost track of how much we'd had to drink, and that *never* happened to me. I was usually the one who kept tabs on how much Ridge had to drink.

Between our chatting and them ribbing me about their father, I had been lost in the moment. There had been questions which I answered patiently even when they got repetitive, and then there were the tests. Hell, they'd tried to test me, both going to the restroom at the same time while leaving me alone in our booth.

No sooner had they gone than a guy our age approached me and tried to hit on me. I hadn't let the twins be any the wiser that I knew they had paid the guy to flirt with me to see how I would respond. All it had taken was a hundred slipped under the table for him to spill about the identical twins who had cornered him and asked him if he wanted to make an extra buck.

When that ploy hadn't worked, they had outright asked my opinion on guys around the club that they supposedly had interest in. There had been some good-looking men of course. I was sure as hell not blind to see that, but none held a candle to Owen.

"This might sound odd, sir," Silas said with a chuckle as we continued on our way to the hotel. "But, it's good to see you less than sober for a change."

I righted myself in the back of the car and leaned against the door. "I guess it's obvious, huh?"

"Well, I don't think you could walk a straight line if asked."

"I'm not *that* drunk," I muttered. "Just a little off kilter." I took in a deep breath at the liquor sloshing in my empty stomach. Not a good sign at all. "Perhaps we should find a coffee shop around here somewhere. I can't let Owen see me like this. What will he think?"

"He'll think you had a good time with his kids, sir," Silas replied. "I bet that would make him happy. I doubt he'd be upset because you're a little… uh… tipsy. He knows this isn't something that's likely to happen too often."

I groaned, wiping my face with the palm of my hand. "But I'm supposed to show him how responsible I am."

"I'd say he already knows that. Being responsible doesn't mean you can't let loose and have fun sometimes. I think you're the only one who expects you to be in control twenty-four-seven. I know it works for the dynamic between you two, but you've got to take a breather and relax every now and then. Besides you did the responsible thing and brought his boy home."

I sighed, contemplating the truth behind Silas's words, but at the same time hesitant. "It's a lot tougher when you're the younger dominant one in the relationship, Silas," I confessed to him, something I wasn't certain I would even say to Owen. "It's like I have a whole lot more to prove— that although I'm young, I can be *all* he needs."

"Hmm, you want to know what I honestly think?"

A dangerous question, but I had started this, and I would see it through. "Go ahead. Tell me."

"I think you worry more about proving yourself than Owen does," he answered. "You have nothing to prove to anyone. Even I see the proof in what you do for him every day without even thinking about it. I've watched you, and I've watched him. The care, patience, and love you show him are a result of how you feel about him. Nothing will change that. Owen already sees you in everything you are to him. If you have a moment of weakness, he'll just be strong for you."

I digested Silas's words. He was always in the background that sometimes I forgot he was there taking in every little action, hearing every word that we said to each other. There was nobody else I trusted more about this topic than him.

"You know if you ever decide to stop working for me you could become somebody's therapist," I stated, only for his soft laugh to follow.

"I'll keep that in mind."

Fifteen minutes later, Silas and I separated as he came off at his floor. After advising him to take the day to rest tomorrow and we'd head out to Cincy in the evening, I rode the elevator the next three floors up.

I entered our suite as quietly as I could in an attempt not to wake Owen. Closing the door softly behind me, I kicked off my shoes and made for the bathroom where I brushed my teeth, splashed some water onto my face and stripped down to my underwear before I padded to our bed.

Guided by the soft light I had left on in the bathroom, I skirted the bed to the vacant side and slid in with a groan. My body buzzed pleasantly from the alcohol still in my system, and as much as I'd had no intention of waking him, I spooned close to Owen, wrapping an arm around his hip and burying my face in his neck. I was a fool to have spent so much time away from this. His broad back bracketed my chest and just the solid feel of him in my arms was enough to send tingles through my cock.

"Good to know you still work," I mumbled at the stirring in my groin. Unable to help myself, I pressed my pelvis to his ass. Owen shifted, pulling his knees up toward his chest and shoving his ass directly into my crotch.

"Fuck!" I groaned, clinging to his hip and waiting for the feeling of wanting to strip him of his shorts to pass.

My cock was hard, but I knew having had so much to drink, I was in no way up to my usual standard of performance.

"Hmm," Owen moaned in his sleep and wriggled his ass against my crotch again. He shuffled, restless, and I remained still, hoping I hadn't woken him. "Dec?"

No such luck. He sounded so sexy when he purred my name in that half-asleep manner of his.

"Shh." I rubbed his upper thigh. "I'm here. Go back to sleep."

Instead of doing that, he shuffled, turning over so he was facing me. His eyes were sleepy, but the more he blinked the more the expression cleared.

"You got back," he said, sounding surprised as if he didn't expect to see me so soon.

"Sorry I took longer than expected."

A lazy smile greeted me. "Does that mean you enjoyed the time you spent with the twins?"

"Yeah, they might have gotten me a little bit drunk though," I said on a groan. "But they were the worse for the wear. Don't worry, I had Silas drop them off at your ex's before coming here."

He sighed and leaned forward, resting his head on my pillow instead of his. "Thank you for looking out for my kids."

"You're—"

I didn't manage to get the words out, because he leaned forward and captured my lips with his. One of his hands rested on my shoulder as he sighed into my mouth. I let out a moan and shifted, lying on my back, taking him along with me so he was half-lying on my chest.

Running a hand down his muscled back, I reached down to secure a handful of his ass. *Perfect.* I could fall asleep like this. Except, Owen might have started that kiss innocently, but the way he was devouring my mouth, he meant to carry it further. I had unleashed a beast that had no intention of stopping any time soon.

"Somebody's in the mood," I groaned when he kissed my jaw and down my neck. His breath was harsh, uneven, and hot against my skin. I was surprised at how quickly he became horny when he had been sleeping only a couple of minutes before.

He paused and peered up at me with a mischievous smile. "Sorry, I was having a sexy dream when you slipped into bed. Now I figure the real thing will be even better."

I squeezed his ass, nudging him with my cock to show him how hard I was. "Do you mind getting on top?" I asked him. "I might be a little out of sorts from drinking with Auggie and Oscar."

Owen groaned and shifted to the edge of the bed to grasp the lube from the top of the nightstand. He shuffled out of his shorts before rolling back toward me. "Let's not talk about my kids right now," he murmured, straddling my hips. "We've been with them all day. Right now, I have a mission to accomplish."

I chuckled at the need in his tone. "Yeah? What kind of mission?"

"I'm going to ride you so good, Daddy."

Fuck. My toes curled under at the rawness of his words. I brought my hands down hard on his ass. "Then get on with it, Boy. You want my cock, it's yours. Help yourself."

He moaned and shifted his hips in an undulatory movement. "Thank you, Daddy."

Owen leaned forward and kissed me again, tongue waltzing with mine, our whispered breaths the interlude to our foreplay. I might not have my equilibrium back a hundred percent, but I refused to be the passive partner even with him all set to ride the fuck out of me.

"Tell me about that dream you were having," I moaned, as he lowered his head to my neck, kissing me wildly with a trail of wet lips, teeth, and tongue. His beard was abrasive wherever it rubbed against my skin, and while I usually hated being marked during sex, this was different. Owen had already marked me where it truly mattered. My heart.

"There was a lot of kissing," he replied as he kissed across my collarbone. "A whole lot of moaning and fuck-ing." He tilted his head to give me a grin. "I think I'll do better to show you."

"Go right ahead."

I tried to stifle my moans when his lips enclosed my right nipple which turned out to be a brave but futile attempt. I'd shared my kryptonite with him last night, and now he used it against me in the most delicious way, eliciting gasps and moans I couldn't contain.

"You know what you should do?" he asked, slowly swirling his tongue around my tight nipple.

"What?" I croaked, my soul unraveled by the atten-tion he lavished me with.

"You should get these pierced," he said, removing his

mouth to grip both nipples between his thumbs and forefinger.

"Fuck!" I grunted, squirming beneath him. *Goddamit, I usually have him squirming, but tonight he has me by the balls.* The hell of it was that I didn't even want him to let go. "You want my nipples pierced?" I eventually managed to croak out.

He nodded. "It would be hot as fuck. Think of how much more fun I could have with them. You'd love it."

"Maybe," I answered, though the suggestion had already taken root. I filed it away at the back of my mind to examine it closely when my brain wasn't so frazzled from the best nipple action I'd ever had. This wasn't a fetish I had shared with many. Ridge was my closest friend, and even he didn't know I could get off just by having my nipples sucked.

Owen followed the faint line of my happy trail, kissing as much of my skin as he could on his way to his destination. When he got there, he moaned, burying his face into my groin.

"I'm so glad you woke me," he said on a sigh. "I would have missed this."

"I didn't intentionally wake you up," I answered. "Now stop stalling and take my cock out to play. It's ready for your wet hole to smother it."

"Hmm. My mouth or my ass?" he asked, peeling down the waistband of my underwear. My cock sprang out and I groaned from the relief of being restrained by my boxers.

"Does it matter which?" I growled at him. "I'll take both."

"Good answer."

I reached down to slap his cheek gently. "Less talking. Put those lips to good use, Boy. You're keeping Daddy waiting."

"Sorry, Daddy."

He wrapped a hand around the base of my cock and circled the head with his tongue.

"That's it. That's my Good Boy."

He moaned, loving the praise. He sucked the entire head into his mouth, letting loose a stream of saliva to run down my shaft. He chased the wetness, lips swooping down to take in more of my length. I gasped, grasped a handful of his hair, pressing his face down to my pelvis while I thrust upward. He was already prepared for the move, swallowing down my cock instead of gagging. He was becoming so good at this.

"Holy fuck yeah," I grunted, but the words came out as a mashup of run-on syllables. "Yeah, Boy, let me fuck your face good."

Between the alcohol still in my system and the light-headedness of Owen sucking on my dick, I was close to bliss. My hips thrust with no sense of stability or rhythm. I was all over the fucking place, hips grinding, cock plunging in and out of his mouth.

When I couldn't take anymore without spilling down his throat, I pulled his head back. "Enough of that now. Why don't you put your pretty mouth up here and your ass onto my cock?"

Owen didn't need to be told twice. With one last lick, he reached for the lube and squirted some onto my cock, smoothing the slick down my length. He squirted more onto his fingers and reached behind to prep himself. I leaned back against the pillows, my chest rising and falling hard as I watched him, straddling my hips, eyes half-mast, moans torn from his lips as he massaged the lube inside, getting himself ready for me.

"That's it. I'm ready," he remarked.

"Sure? Let me see."

He moved closer to my chest as I reached behind him to grab his ass cheeks. Spreading with one hand, I used the other to stick one finger then two inside his hole. They slid in easily, so I added another third, and he started rocking on my fingers.

"God, can't wait to feel your fist up my ass!" he gasped.

I chuckled, pulling out my fingers and giving his ass one last squeeze. "Not tonight, Boy. Now deliver what you promised us."

He shuffled back down my body, easing up slightly as he sank down. The first attempt was a bust, my cock sliding right past his taint and up his crack. He reached behind to grasp me by the base and keep me steady while he sat, his hole connecting with my tip.

It was fireworks all over again as my cock breached his hole. Instead of fading, the feeling intensified as he continued sliding down my cock. By the time he sat fully on me, my eyes were tightly closed, and I was grinding my teeth together from the pleasure racking my body.

"Fuck, don't move, Boy." I croaked out when he shifted. "Give Daddy a second to adjust."

Owen chuckled, and I cracked an eye open to find

him looking on in amusement. "I thought *I* needed the time to adjust with *your* cock being in *my* ass and all."

I reached up to run my hands up his furry chest and grip his nipples. "Smartass." I rolled the points between my fingers and smirked when a shudder rippled through him. His mouth fell open as he gasped.

"Now fucking move your ass up and down my cock," I instructed him.

I tried to pretend at first that he wasn't unraveling me with every clench and release of his hole as he worked his hips up and down. I didn't have to pretend for long, as soon I couldn't even decide who was fucking whom. Owen's ass crunched into my pelvis, as he fucked us both good, his movements hard and deliberate.

And when he took just the tip of my cock into his hole and worked his hips in shallow pumps before slamming his ass back down completely over my cock, I couldn't tell who moaned louder and who cussed harder.

"Do you like that, Daddy?" he asked, leaning backward with his hands planted behind him, bracing himself as he continued gliding. His dick flopped up and down with each motion, droplets of precum dotting my skin. "Having your cock all up in my tight ass?"

"Yessss!" I hissed at him, running my hands up his hairy thighs. "Show me how you can ride that cock, Boy."

"Oh yes, Daddy. Like this?"

He shifted forward, hands pressed into my chest while he moved harder up and down my shaft. I couldn't resist him. I gripped him by the neck and pulled him down to kiss him. Sex had never felt this good. Drunk.

Drunk on him. He was in my blood, the alcohol that could never be flushed out of my system.

I canted my hips, shifting him upwards which was no mean feat given his size. I reached behind him, and grabbed his ass cheeks, planting my feet firmly on the bed. I thrust upward hard, and he gasped into my mouth. I couldn't have stopped even if I wanted to. Harder, each thrust became more manic, more needy, craving something more. Fuck I wanted… Oh holy fuck, I needed.

"Fuck! Fuck!" I yelled. My shout filled the room, and I squeezed his ass, thrusting upward hard one last time as I filled him with my seed.

Owen released my mouth, straightening as he fucked himself through my climax. Jaw slack, I watched him, the way his skin flushed, the bead of sweat trickling down his neck as he reached for his cock. With just a few strokes, he sank down on me and gasped, head thrown back, muscles bunched, the vein throbbing in his neck as he pumped his cum all over my stomach and chest.

"Oh God, Boy, you've completely wrecked me," I said on a groan as he slipped forward to lie on top of me. He was breathing hard, legs trembling, body shaking from the powerful climax he'd experienced.

I wrapped my arms around his large frame, not minding that he was crushing me into the mattress. If he didn't get off soon, he would suffocate me, but for now, for a few minutes I could hold on to him and pretend I didn't have to let him go. I would never let him go.

Never.

5

OWEN

I tried to cling to the delicious dream that lingered in my memory, but it was already too late. I was rudely awakened by something I couldn't yet fathom. Disoriented and all, I yawned. Turning over, I stretched out a hand, seeking out Declan's warm body, but I encountered nothing but the soft silk sheets we had tangled in after making love some hours earlier.

"Dec?" I mumbled, raising my head to seek him out. It was no fun waking up alone.

I frowned when I didn't make out his frame. And then I heard it. Someone being sick in the bathroom. I clutched the sheet my hand had encountered, squeezing tight as I fought down the instant alarm that went off in my head. *Declan doubled over in pain, me standing outside the bathroom while he threw up.* Oh God, not again.

"Dec?" I called, springing out of bed. The sheet tangled around my left leg, tripping me up. To save myself from sprawling to the floor, I flailed frantically, finally untangling my leg but ended up hitting my shin into the nightstand. Shards of pain shot up my leg, and I almost went down. It *fucking* hurt.

"*Shit!*" I cursed, ignoring the pain to limp to the bathroom. If he was getting sick again... Damn, we weren't even in Cincy and close to his doctor.

The bathroom door was partially opened, and I didn't even consider knocking lest he kicked me out like he had done before. I had no intentions of leaving this time though. He was stuck with me forever.

"Declan?" I dragged in a painful breath at the sight of him naked, hunched over the toilet, emptying his stomach. I was ready to hightail it back to the room to grab his phone and call Dr. Dover when the stench of alcohol assailed my nostrils, and I realized what ailed him. He wasn't sick then. *Thank God.* He was just experiencing last night's Oscar/Auggie effect.

When his next heave came up empty, Declan flushed the toilet and rose to his feet.

"Jesus, what's with you and wanting to watch me puke my guts out?" he growled, ignoring the sink for the glass-enclosed shower. He adjusted the faucet before ducking beneath the showerhead and into the direct line of spray.

"I was worried about you," I admitted, speaking louder so he could hear me above the running water. "I thought..."

He wiped the water from his face to peer at me. "I promise I'm fine. I've just been reminded why I never get drunk. Your sons did push my limits though, and if that wasn't enough, someone insatiable decided to use me in the most carnal way afterward."

I chuckled, moving to where his toothbrush was and squeezing toothpaste on it for him. "Then what would you have said had I not been half-asleep while riding you?"

He slid the glass enclosure open when I walked over to the shower, taking the toothbrush from me.

"Thanks," he said, then indicated something over his shoulder. I followed his gaze over to where my phone was on the counter. "You left your phone in the bathroom last night? You should get it on the charger because it wouldn't come on when I tried."

I returned my eyes to him guiltily. "Um, I think it's broken."

"How?"

I felt horrible for destroying the expensive phone he had bought me. "I was using the bathroom while texting you when I got home. It fell into the toilet. I told you I was tired."

He made a face. "I touched your toilet phone?"

"I hadn't used it yet," I replied. "I was trying to get my zipper down when it fell."

"That doesn't make it any less gross." He sighed, eyeing me. "When we return home, I'll buy you a new one."

"That's not fair to you," I protested, still feeling awful about the expensive phone I had been so careless with. "I'll take it in for phone repairs or I'll replace it. With something less expensive. I seem to have a habit of losing them one way or the other."

"Don't worry about it." He stepped back under the spray of water. "Why don't you get into the shower with me?"

I stripped out of the underwear I'd slipped back on after we'd had sex. I could feel him watching me as he brushed his teeth, but I had gotten used to his eyes making love to me, so it didn't bother me anymore. Not like it had done at first when I had been so self-conscious about everything.

Our shower routine was rote. Brushing our teeth, taking turns to get lathered with soap, passing the shampoo bottle between us and reaching places on the other's body that was hard to get to. There was nothing sexual about it, but the deep intimacy of the moment wasn't lost on me. We didn't even need to communicate to say what we needed. Declan and I moved to the beat of old lovers.

I startled when he snagged me around the waist and pulled my wet body against his. A quick hard kiss landed on my mouth.

"What's that for?"

"For almost breaking your neck to get to me because you thought I was sick," he replied. "I'm sure I heard you hitting into something."

"Yeah, I might not have the best coordination when I just wake up."

He snorted. "Nothing wrong with your coordination when you climbed on top of me last night. In fact, I'd say pretty damn good coordination."

I tried to be cool for about two seconds before I broke into a grin. "Knocked your socks off, didn't I?"

"Hmm. I wasn't wearing any, but definitely knocked my boxers off."

"Yeah, for once I think you were louder than me."

"That's debatable. Have you ever listened to yourself when I'm deep inside you?"

I hadn't. I usually was too busy basking in everything he was making me feel. He slapped my ass when he turned off the showerhead, and I stepped out of the stall ahead of him.

"Want to test that theory out again?" I asked, running my gaze over his naked body. Why couldn't I get enough of him? The last forty-eight hours had been full of sex, and still I would gladly position for him now if he was game.

"I need to replenish first," he said on a groan, rubbing his tummy. "I'm running on E."

He snagged a couple of towels from the towel rack built in under the sink and handed me one while he knotted the other about his waist.

"It's kind of late to order breakfast, isn't it?" I asked as we made our way back into the bedroom.

"What time is it?"

I pressed the middle button on his phone to check the time and smiled at his screensaver— a picture taken of us in São Paulo, kissing before a colorful graffiti of a tree on Batman Alley. "Ten minutes to eleven."

"We have enough time to eat. I've given Silas the day off to rest since he'll drive us back to Cincy this evening."

"Sounds good."

"Where's your charger?" I asked him. "Your battery is almost empty."

He groaned. "I think I left it at home."

"Okay, I think I have mine."

I searched through my bag and came up with the charger that now existed without a phone. When I returned to plug in his phone for him, using the outlet beside the bed, he leaned over to kiss my shoulder.

"Thanks."

I straightened and snagged the towel from my waist to blot the remaining droplets of water from my body. On second thoughts, I threw the towel at Declan's head and dropped onto the bed, spread out on my back.

"Dry me off, please."

I peeked up at him to find him fighting back a smile. "You're turning into quite the bossy Boy, aren't you?"

"Depends." I stuck my tongue into my cheek and spoke around it as Declan moved up between my legs. "Do you like it?"

"There's very little about you I don't like, Owen," he answered, touching the towel to my chest.

"What? That sounds like there *is* something you don't like."

"Hmm."

I placed my hand over his, stalling his movement. "Hmm? Just hmm? You're supposed to reassure me that you love everything about me, even if it's bullshit, so now I'm curious. What don't you like?"

He peeled my hand away from his and continued patting my stomach dry. When he reached my groin, he paused and looked up at me. "I think you still keep secrets from me."

I gave a bark of laughter. "That's crazy. My life's been an open book for you. You're usually the tight-lipped one." *Speaking of book, damn he's right. I still haven't told him about my manuscript, but that's not technically lying.*

He patted between my legs, drying my cock with the utmost care. "Are you telling me that there's nothing about you that you're keeping from me?"

He kept looking at me expectantly as though waiting for me to spill all my secrets to him, but I didn't keep secrets. Just the one. *Should I tell him?*

I opened up my mouth to blurt out my one remaining secret, but no sound came out. I glanced away from him, willing the vulnerability to pass. I couldn't tell him. I'd try to be tough, but if he didn't enjoy my novel I would be crushed, and I wasn't ready to give up on that dream yet. Soon. If I wanted him to read it, then I should finish it first so he could read the entire story.

Yes, that was exactly what I would do. Finish the novel first, then get his opinion if it was worth pursuing. I would have to make it clear to him though that I intended to seek out publishing opportunities on my own. I didn't want him to interfere and sway minds into accepting my book just because they were aware of who I was sleeping with.

"I won't keep secrets from you without a reason," I said carefully.

He frowned at me, none too happy at my response. Even though displeased, he didn't walk out though. He kept drying my legs down to my feet. He never lost his gentleness, although I could feel the tension that had crept up on him.

"You shouldn't have *any* reasons to keep secrets from me," he responded, carefully getting in between my toes. "Don't you trust me?"

"Of course, I do."

He straightened, dropping the towel on my chest. "Then why keep secrets?"

I sat up on the bed. "You want me to believe you have no secrets of your own?" I asked in disbelief. I wasn't buying it at all. When he couldn't respond, I shook my head and got to my feet. "See? That's exactly what I thought."

"If it wasn't for you, I wouldn't have to keep it a secret."

I blanched at his accusation. "Me? What did I do?"

He headed for the bathroom with the towels, and I assumed he was going to hang them. "Let's drop it. Get dressed so we can get something to eat."

I didn't want to drop it. I wanted him to explain in detail what he had meant by his secret being my fault. My book secret was hardly anything grand. Either I had potential, or I sucked. What kind of secret could he be keeping from me? As open as we were to each other about having these secrets, I didn't like it one bit that I hadn't the vaguest idea what he was hiding from me.

We dressed in silence and fifteen minutes later we left the hotel to locate a restaurant where we could eat. We were on our own since Silas had the day to himself, but we made do, walking three blocks before we found the restaurant Declan had pulled up from an app about the best place Downtown to eat. I hadn't been aware of how hungry I was until we were ushered to our seats and handed menus.

Lucky for us the restaurant had a late brunch going, so we were able to order breakfast which was equally as delicious as it looked. As hungry as I was, in no time, I'd polished off my order, then made with a start on Declan's as well when he could only manage a few bites. He downed four cups of black coffee all the while swearing last night was his final episode of getting drunk.

"Until you hang out with Oscar and Auggie again," I said on a chuckle, pleased we could bypass the vexing topic of secrets. "The both of them together can be pretty persuasive."

"I noticed. They got you on that dance floor last night despite all your protests. What was that dance you were doing together?"

I swallowed the hash browns I had stolen from his plate before answering. "When the boys had their first dance in middle school, they were afraid they didn't know how to dance, so I decided to teach them a dance move they could do with their friends. Let's say it didn't go so well."

Declan laughed. "That's cute. There should be a Father-of-the-Year Award. I bet you would win hands down. I've never known another parent so involved in their kids' lives. I went to school with a bunch of trust fund kids whose parents couldn't wait to drop them off at boarding school."

"That sounds awful. I can't even think about doing

that to my kids. I think I needed them just as much as they needed me."

"Well, it wasn't all that bad," he said with a shrug. "At least being away from Charles wasn't that bad, and over time I met Ridge and we became close."

I frowned at my plate, wondering if I'd ever hear Ridge's name without feeling that unease in my chest about how close he had been to Declan.

"Were you really upset last night with that man on the dance floor?" I asked him, because I needed the reassurance that I wasn't the only one who felt this wave of possession.

"If by upset you mean, did I want to knock his teeth down his throat? Then yeah. Every single one of them."

"You're just as bad as the twins," I grumbled, but it was mostly to cover up the way my heart fluttered and I turned to mush at his words. No wonder he thought me a big softie incapable of standing up for myself. While I did try to avoid confrontations, I knew when enough was enough.

"So now you know that you have all five of us ready to defend your honor," he said with a humorous smile.

"Five?"

"Pretty sure James wouldn't be far behind," he stated. "Guilt's eating him up when it comes to you and the kids. I think if you asked him to give you a kidney, he would go for it."

"Oh." I had no idea how to respond to that because Declan was observing me carefully. Sometimes he seemed comfortable with the idea of James being in my life because of the kids, and another time, it was almost as if he was overcome with jealousy at the past I shared with James. Yesterday I had been nervous at first with everyone being in the same place, but he hadn't once scowled or growled at James, so I took it that since meeting, he had come to the conclusion that James didn't do it for me anymore.

"I wouldn't let him," Declan answered. "Not when mine are still available."

I shook my head at him. "Jesus, talk about being intense. After your recent scare, I don't exactly want to talk about illness at this point."

"What do you want to talk about?" he asked, leaning back into his seat.

I shrugged. "I dunno." Definitely not about me taking one of his kidneys. No talking about our secrets either. Those were conversations for another day.

"How about safe words?" he suggested.

I glanced around our vicinity and sat forward to be closer to him. "You want to talk about safe words, *here?*"

"Why not? No time like the present. We need to agree on one before we do all the things you want to explore. That's the rule. You did say you want me to fist you, didn't you?"

"Ahem."

I closed my eyes at the waitress who had appeared at our table. *Sweet heavens another one.* With all the people who were hearing tidbits about our private sex life, they could start a fan club about us. I didn't dare look at her to see how much she had heard of our conversation. Declan didn't even seem flustered when she presented him with our bill, and he handed over his credit card.

"Jello," I said, when the waitress moved on.

"Huh?"

"That's what my safe word is," I told him. "Jello. Now we can stop talking about it until we're somewhere private."

He grinned at me. "There's one more thing. Would you be open to visiting a BDSM club?"

"A BDSM club?" I squawked.

"Yes. Of course, as just an observer. I'm no longer a member, but Heath would be more than happy to accommodate us, and I can always check on Ridge's progress while we're there."

I stared at him, undecided if he was being serious. I had never thought about that sort of thing before, and I would have never expected it to come up in such a laissez faire setting. He just said it like it was an everyday thing to drop in at that kind of club. I didn't even have any idea what one looked like.

"What does Heath have to do with a BDSM club?" I asked, frowning. "Is that what's supposed to cure Ridge of his addiction, because I don't think that's the way it works."

"Heath's a Dungeon Master," he explained. "When Ridge and I went there for the first time, he saw how green we were and took us under his wing."

Now I was even more confused than ever about Heath. "So, you've… uh… you and Heath?"

He shook his head. "No. As much as he was older, Heath wasn't my type. Too dominant. He was quite taken with Ridge though. They were both taken with each other and a more perfect match—other than ours of course—I've never seen. I'd never seen Ridge so happy in all his life."

"And, of course, you won't tell me what happened between them."

"Not my story to tell, love. Maybe one day you'll hear about it."

6

OWEN

S pending the day along the Scioto River wasn't exactly how I'd thought to pass our last afternoon in Columbus. After our meal, I had anticipated returning to our hotel room for perhaps another round of sex. I wouldn't have admitted that to Declan for the world, when he suggested we go for a walk, and I had agreed. Walking along the Scioto Mile, however, which stretched between Broad Street and Rich Street, I quickly got sucked into the natural beauty of the place.

The green space open to the public was a bustle of activities with its boulevards, bike trails, and pedestrian paths, but at the same time, giving us the feeling that we were in our own private oasis. We went from watching the kids enjoying the fifteen-thousand-square-foot inter- active fountain to me coaxing Declan to get wet along- side me, because why not? I felt so happy my heart could burst. That might have been the reason for my crazy suggestion which I would probably regret later when I wasn't all pumped up with happy juice, but right then I wanted to get wet in the fountain. And I wanted to get wet with Declan. Not in our usual kinky way either. Just for fun.

"Come on, only the kids are getting wet," he protested when I tugged on his hand. "Look, all the adults are simply watching from the sidelines."

"Who gives a damn? Adulting is overrated anyway. I'd bet they want to get wet too, but are afraid to make the first move. Let's start a revolution!"

I probably sounded ridiculous trying to persuade him to do something totally out of character for him—hell, out of character for me too. Once the idea seeded, however, I couldn't get it out of my mind.

"You're crazy," he said on a laugh. "There're more interesting ways of getting you wet."

"I'll hold you to that later, but for now, the fountain!" When he didn't budge, I pouted. Man, did I put a lot into a full pout while I gave him my best wounded eyes. I was trying to recall what Summer as a child had called "pretty please with the puppy dog eyes" and trying to imitate that look to a T. It usually got me good.

"You think a pout's going to work on me?" Declan roared with laughter. "Boy, Daddy's made of sterner stuff than that."

Damn. I was determined not to leave the fountain until we were both soaked. Didn't he realize this was a memory of us that I wanted badly? When I was old, gray and shit, these memories would get me through the years.

I crowded closer to him, clutching the front of his

shirt and sucking up all the air around him. "Then do it because I ask, and it would mean a lot to me."

I watched his resolve crumble and tried not to show how smug I felt about it. "Shit," he muttered. "You're exploiting my weakness, aren't you?"

"Huh?" I widened my eyes innocently. "I don't know what you're talking about."

"Bullshit." He kissed my nose. "Alright. Let's go get wet."

We were soaked in less than a minute. The kids found it hilarious that two grown-ups had joined them in their watery foray, and despite Declan's scowl at first, he eventually ended up smiling at them splashing us.

"I can't believe I let you talk me into doing that," he groaned, when we emerged from the fountain, our clothes sticking to our bodies. Our shoes squished with each step we took.

"Admit it. You had fun." I grasped his hand, intertwining our fingers as we continued our walk. As wet as we were, the sun was hot enough that we would be mostly dry soon.

"Maybe," he conceded.

I stopped in the middle of the promenade and kissed him, placing my free hand on his shoulder. Our lips had barely met when Declan ended it.

"Not a good idea," he said, gesturing to his groin. His semi couldn't be hidden behind the wet material of his pants stuck to his body. Neither could mine.

"Ah, there's a swing where we can park our asses and cool off," I pointed out.

We ended up lounging on the swing, people-watching, but mostly enjoying the beauty of the scenery. A few years ago, the Scioto Mile had been little more than a lifeless urban highway which was later developed into the new riverfront promenade and park we could now enjoy.

Whether it was Declan gently pushing the swing with his feet, or the warmth of the sun—quite possibly a combination of the two—I got comfy enough to doze off. He woke me with kisses pressed to my face, and I opened my eyes to find myself leaning heavily against him, my head on his shoulder. He had slipped his arm around me at some point to settle me much better against him.

"Damn, I didn't mean to fall asleep," I murmured, hating that I immediately thought of Oscar's age inappropriate jokes last night.

Declan didn't look the least bothered. "It's fine. I loathed waking you, but we should probably get back to the hotel and prepare to get out of here. We're mostly dry now anyway."

We walked back to the hotel in silence, me still disoriented enough from sleep for Declan to decide holding my hand wasn't just a show of affection, but necessary. I was relieved when we walked into our suite, and I headed straight for the bathroom to take a leak.

I was stripping out of my still damp clothes when Declan called to me from the bedroom. "Babe, come here a minute, will you?"

My heart never ceased to do somersaults when he let loose with one of his endearments. Hauling on the complimentary hotel robe, I entered the bedroom to find him already shrugging into dry clothes. He was frowning at his phone, fingers busy tapping away at the screen. We had left his phone behind while we went out so that it could be charged.

"Something wrong?" I asked, observing his frown.

Instead of responding, Declan sat on the bed, snagged me around the waist and pulled me into him.

"I love you," he said.

While it wasn't uncommon for him to tell me this since he was quite open about his feelings for me, I found the timing to be rather odd. He had all but avoided my question.

"Why do I feel like there's a but behind that?" I asked, peering over my shoulder at him.

"No buts."

Without another word, he handed me his phone, and I frowned at over twenty missed calls he had from Auggie and Oscar. They must have exchanged numbers sometime last night, but the number of missed calls didn't escape me. He had a right to be alarmed.

"Maybe they were trying to get to me, but couldn't?" I offered.

"Only one way to find out."

Declan redialed Auggie's number and pressed the key to activate the loudspeaker.

"Declan, thank God!" Auggie answered at the beginning of the fourth ring. "We've been calling your phone and Dad's for over two hours without response!"

"Sorry about that," Declan replied. "Your father's phone isn't functioning, and we left mine behind while we went out to eat."

"Is Dad there with you?"

His hands tightened around me. "Yes, I have you on speaker so he can hear you."

"Shit!" Auggie cursed. "Can you take me off speaker, please? I want to talk to just you."

I startled at his request. "What? Auggie, what do you have to say to Dec that you can't say to me?"

"Dad—it's just… please, just let me talk to Declan."

"What's this about?" I demanded from Declan since I wasn't getting anything out of Auggie.

He shrugged. "I swear I have no idea. Let me talk to him. That's the only way we'll find out."

I didn't like it one bit, but I nodded my consent. As he deactivated the speaker, I tried to pull away from Declan, but he wouldn't let me go.

"Behave," he ordered, squeezing me before talking into the phone. "It's just you and me, Auggie. What's going on? You're freaking out your father."

I loathed not being able to hear Auggie's end of the conversation, and there was little I could do, but rip the phone out of Declan's hand, and I didn't see that going over well. I waited, taking in Declan's body language and had no idea what to think. When he went stiff, I really began to worry.

Something was wrong.

"Oh my God!" Declan expelled and when I squirmed, his hand tightened even more. "Where are you guys now?"

"What the hell is going on?" I hissed at him. "I deserve to know."

He ignored me to listen to whatever Auggie was saying

to him before he answered. "I can understand why you'd think that, but we can't be sure. I'm not willing to take that chance. I'll call my driver, and we'll get there in ten."

This time I couldn't stand it anymore. I tore myself out of Declan's arms, frustrated and angry at both him and Auggie. How dared they talk over my head like this? And after Auggie had known him for only twenty-four hours.

"Thanks for calling me. I'll break it gently to your dad. See you in ten."

Declan barely hung up the phone before I leveled accusing eyes at him. "What the hell was that all about? Why'd he want to talk to you and not me? When I said I wanted you to be close to my kids, it wasn't so you could all keep secrets from me."

"Owen, come here." He patted his thigh when I remained indignant. "Please, it's important."

"Can't you see I'm freaked out?"

"I know you are, but let me do this properly. It's already hard enough having to tell you this."

Still feeling malicious toward him, I stalked over to the bed because I figured it was the way I would hear what was wrong sooner. He made me sit on the bed, reversing our position so he stood between my legs. When he cupped my face, and I raised my eyes and saw the torn look in his eyes, a deep fear took root inside my stomach and dug in.

Oh god, I knew that look.

"Declan…" His name came out on a groan. "What is it? Is it Oscar?"

His grip on my jaw increased in pressure. "No, it's Summer."

"Summer?" My heart skipped a beat. "What's wrong with Summer?"

"She's missing. Auggie—"

"*What?*" I exploded, trying to get up, but he pushed me back gently to sit. "What do you mean Summer's missing? If this is some kind of joke the twins orchestrated to—"

"Your boys aren't that insensitive, Owen," he answered. "You know that. According to Auggie, she didn't make it home last night. Her girlfriend didn't realize until this morning and thought Summer was staying at James's as well."

My heart sank, a wave of despondency crashing over me, but it didn't stop. It kept beating and beating against me. "Summer's really missing?"

"Yes, but we'll find her. I swear we'll find her."

I heard Declan's words from far off. I tried to make sense of them, tried to cling to the hope they offered, but their significance slipped by me. *Dear God, no.* I couldn't breathe. I'd forgotten how to. Icy fingers of dread trailed over my skin and poked its poisonous talons into my heart.

"Owen!"

I blinked up at Declan, surprised he was so close because his voice sounded much farther away. The next thing I knew, I was flat on my back on the bed, my heart racing as I stared up at the ceiling helplessly.

"Breathe, baby, breathe." Declan's worried face appeared above mine, hand stroking my face.

His fingertips felt cold or maybe it was my skin. That would make sense since I felt so numb inside.

"Missing?" I repeated the word which felt strange on my tongue.

An image flashed through my mind of a sleepy three-year-old Summer entering my bedroom the night James had left us. I remembered tucking her back into bed that night, packing my large frame onto her much smaller bed to keep her company until she fell asleep, and all the while hoping I didn't break her bed.

"We'll find her," Declan kept saying over and over.

He lay beside me and pulled me into his arms. I was too pliant to resist. He could have done anything he wanted with me and I probably wouldn't have noticed. I was still trying to fathom what this 'missing' meant, but I was at a loss to speak much less to ask questions about what had happened. How could my daughter who had argued with me last night then dropped me home be missing?

With a distressed sound, I grabbed at Declan, willing him to anchor me lest I turn into a basket case. I couldn't freak out more than I already was. I had to get a grip and find Summer. I had to find my daughter.

"Declan, let me up," I croaked. "We need to talk to someone. Find out what happened. She can't be missing."

He gripped my chin. "Regardless of what happens, Owen, we're in this together. *We'll* find her."

But he couldn't make such a promise, could he?

7

DECLAN

I watched Owen like a hawk as we piled into James's house and hugs of comfort were exchanged all around. It had taken twenty minutes to get there instead of the ten minutes I had assured Auggie of, but Owen had taken the news extremely hard. It was that reason Auggie had explained why he called me instead of his father. He wanted me to break the news to Owen that Summer hadn't returned home after she dropped off her father last night. There was no evidence at all that she had slept in her bed.

While on the drive over from the hotel, I had filled in Owen on everything I knew, which was very little.

"Summer's girlfriend Penny stopped by earlier," Auggie had explained to me. *"Summer didn't sleep at their apartment last night. Ringing her phone goes straight to voicemail. Penny's afraid she's missing since she's never done anything like this before. We called the police to look into it, and they just showed up. They're talking to Penny now."*

There was one thing I hadn't mentioned to Owen, though, because I definitely didn't want to downplay what Summer's disappearance meant, but Auggie hadn't been convinced Summer was missing. Just to us.

"She was really acting strange last night, and maybe she did this because she's upset. The way she's been behaving lately, I can't say that it's inconceivable for her. Dad might not want to hear this, but Summer's always been spoiled, and I think she'd pull a stunt like this if she wasn't getting her own way."

I could understand why Auggie felt that way, but at something so frightening as going missing, I pushed his interpretation of what happened to the back of my mind. We had to find Summer first and ensure she was alright. Only then could we deal with why she had gone missing, but I wasn't willing to just write off the disappearance as a deliberate attempt by Summer.

Seeing how broken Owen was at the news, I knew exactly what I had to do if we were ever going to get back that smile on his face. We had to find his daughter, and fast, before he worked himself up to a heart attack. Earlier, when he'd all but passed out on the bed, he'd freaked me out.

"Still no word?" I asked James as Owen and his two sons embraced in the living room.

A young woman I'd never met before was sitting on the couch. She glanced up at us, her eyes red and puffy. At the blotchiness of her otherwise snowy white complexion, I gathered she had to be Penny, Summer's girlfriend.

Beside Penny, there was a cop with a notepad out. He had been sitting, but as soon as we entered the living room, he rose to his feet. While Owen was hugging the life out of his twins, I walked over to the cop and extended a hand in greeting. I knew how these situations often played out, and I wasn't beyond throwing my weight around to get results.

"Officer, I'm Declan Moore," I introduced myself, watching for a reaction from him at my name, but I got absolutely nothing.

"I'm Officer Pike," the cop replied, shaking my hand. "And your relation to Ms. Long is?"

At that time Owen appeared at my side. He leaned into me, and sensing he needed my support now more than ever, I slid a hand around his waist. I could feel some of the burden of his body shift away.

"Officer Pike," Owen stated, having overheard the officer's name. "I'm Owen Long, Summer's father. Declan's my partner. What can you tell us about my daughter's disappearance? Is someone trying to locate her?"

The cop glanced down at the notepad he held and frowned. "I'm still gathering all the sides of the story to make sense of what happened to your daughter. Since you were the last person to see her as far as we can tell, do you mind me asking you a few questions?"

"No, I don't mind. Anything to find her."

"Good, then why don't you have a seat?"

Owen hesitantly sat, and I perched on the arm of the sofa, taking one of his hands in mine. His sons flanked us immediately, Auggie's hand resting on Owen's shoulder. James wasn't too far either although he gave us a little distance.

"About what time was it when she dropped you off at the hotel?" Officer Pike asked.

"It was some minutes after one," he answered. "I remembered because I had to text Declan that I'd arrived, and I took notice of the time." His face blanched, and he sucked in a deep breath. "I shouldn't have let her drive home alone at that hour. I should have asked her to stay, but she doesn't live far away, so I thought it would be okay."

I squeezed his hand at his obvious distress, but before I could answer, Oscar beat me to it. "Dad, don't blame yourself. If that's the case, we're all guilty for letting her go off alone."

"And I'd have offered for her to stay here, but we know she'd never agree to that," James added.

The cop cleared his throat, commanding our attention. "Can you say what state she was in when she left, Mr. Long?"

Owen buried his face in his hands. "She was upset," he said on a groan.

"Why was she upset?"

"She's been dealing with a lot," he answered. "She recently left home, and I'm not sure if she's been adjusting properly." He inhaled deeply, his shoulders shaking as he sent James an apologetic look. "To top things off, she recently was reunited with James who'd left us when she was little. She didn't take it well. Then... then she learned about my relationship with Declan, and that only seemed to make her mood worse. We talked about it on the way to the hotel last night. She said she needed time..." Owen trailed off as he glanced around the room with a frown. "She said she needed time," he repeated. "Oh my God, do you think she just upped and left without telling anyone? Was that what she meant when she said she wanted some time to process everything?"

The officer closed the little notebook he had with him, and the look on his face said it all. He didn't think Summer was in danger.

"That's what it seems like to me, Mr. Long," he said, getting to his feet. "Based on what you've just told me, plus Penelope's admission that their relationship ended a couple of days ago, I'd take a guess that Ms. Long decided to take some time off."

"Time off from her family?" Owen asked in dismay. "Why would she do that? We're all very close. We would have helped her through whatever she's going through." He then paused and turned his attention to Penny. "Did the officer just say you and Summer broke up? *Days* ago? But when I called, you said nothing. She said nothing."

Tears spilled down Penny's cheeks. "I'm sorry. She didn't want to let you guys know yet. She told me she was better, that now the pressure of a relationship was gone, she was happier. If I'd known she would do this, I wouldn't have tried to hide it."

"Well, let's not get ahead of ourselves," I announced, trying to rein in the emotions. "As much as this is the most palatable way of thinking of Summer's disappearance because it means she's more than likely okay, we don't know for sure what happened. She's still missing, and we need to find her."

"Mr...." the cop trailed off helplessly as he tried to remember my name.

"Moore," I answered. "Declan Moore."

"Mr. Moore's right," he said, nodding at me. "Even though we have a theory that she left on her own, we can't rule out other possibilities."

"Other possibilities?" Owen asked.

"Yes, other possibilities," the officer answered. "Like an abduction. Or..."

"Or what?" the voices echoed in the living room asking the same question.

"Now this is only precautionary," Office Pike announced, and I wished I could stop the words that would come out of his mouth, because I could sense they would do nothing but add tension to the situation. "I have to ask, does anyone have reason to believe Ms. Long is a danger to herself?"

"Danger to herself?" Owen echoed. "Are you asking if my daughter is suicidal? Of course not!"

"Owen," James protested. "I know it's hard to think about it, but if she is—"

"I know my daughter!" Owen snapped, letting go of my hand and glaring at James. "Sure, she can get moody, but that's just her way of dealing with things when she's having a tough time. Summer is *not* suicidal!"

The police officer didn't seem convinced as he turned to Summer's girlfriend. "Penelope, you've been living with Ms. Long for a while. What's your general impression? Do you have cause to believe she's a danger to herself?"

Penny stalled, her face becoming even whiter. Her

face was puffy from all the crying, and now the tears kept streaming faster as she sobbed.

"Penny," Owen said in a pleading tone. "We both know Summer better than anyone else. Tell them. She would never hurt herself."

Penny wrapped her arms around her body. "I-I don't know," she sobbed. "I'm sorry, but I don't know if she would. We've had some terrible arguments, and she's said stuff, but she always said she didn't mean it when we made up. One minute she would be the Summer I knew from before we moved here and another she would be so sad. I'm sorry, but things have been so hard between us lately, and I just couldn't get through to her. She would accuse me of not loving her enough and th-that—" She sobbed harder, incapable of continuing.

"No!" Owen protested. "Come on, you *do* know. Summer would never do that to us. She wouldn't!"

He stormed out of the living room, and I yearned to go after him, but I needed to speak to the cop some more. I glanced over at the twins and indicated toward their father. "Go to him."

They were off the second I said the words, and I breathed easier knowing they would be there to comfort him through the difficult time he would be having, accepting that maybe Summer needed more help than we all thought. Maybe this went a lot deeper than me being too young for Owen. Maybe there were other things at play here, and everything that had happened made her snap.

"I should get going," Officer Pike remarked. "I'll stay

in touch. If there's any new development, reach out to us."

"I'll walk you to the door, Officer," I announced even though it was not my place. James didn't make a fuss. Like Owen, he looked like he was on the edge too. As I walked the officer out of the living room, I saw him go over to pat Penny's shoulder.

"Can you say what exactly will happen now, Officer?" I asked the cop when we were standing outside.

"We'll go through the standard stuff of course."

"Can you give me a rundown of what that is? We'll not be waiting for forty-eight hours to declare her legally missing, will we?"

"Of course not," he assured me. "Contrary to what popular television would have people believe, someone should be reported as soon as possible."

He went on to explain that Summer's information would be logged into the National Crime Information Center, Missing Person File where it would remain until she was found, then the record would be removed. A broadcast would be sent to all the law enforcement agencies in the state, and a press release would be issued, including the posting of her information on electronic billboards.

"And from then on, it's just sitting and waiting for someone to recognize her and contact the police?" I asked. On the one hand, I was relieved they would actually be doing something, but on the other, I was frustrated that it only included the routine stuff. No one seemed as if they would be in active pursuit of her, which was a dismay. I couldn't stand aside, twiddling my thumbs, hoping for her to be spotted and recognized.

"This is all precautionary," the cop answered. "Speaking quite frankly, Mr. Moore, the circumstances surrounding her disappearance suggest Ms. Long willfully left on her own. We suspect no foul play is involved, and I anticipate her reaching out to someone after she's had some time to settle her thoughts."

I nodded, accepting that from the police end, that was all I would get out of them. I removed my wallet from my pocket and took out a business card, handing it over to the man.

"If there's any development, this is how you can reach me," I stated. "Their father is in a fragile state right now, and I'd appreciate breaking any news to him that you may have."

There. That didn't sound so ominous when put that way. The last thing I needed, however, was for some cop to use his very routine speech to relay bad news to Owen.

"You're *that* Moore?" the cop asked in surprise, staring at the card. "The financial Moore guru?"

I nodded. "Yes, that's me, and you can bet I won't be sitting around waiting for someone to call. I'll use every resource I have to find that girl."

He slipped my card in his pocket. "Then good luck. Either way, I hope we find her soon. Have a good afternoon, Mr. Moore."

He shook my hand before he got into his squad car and drove away. His car hadn't cleared the driveway as yet when my phone was in hand. Like I had said, there was no way in hell I was going to sit idly by, waiting for someone to get in touch about Summer. I would move heaven and earth to bring her home to her family.

"Declan, what's up?" Charles asked, answering the phone on the second ring. "When are you getting back from Columbus?"

"Change of plans, Charles," I informed him. "Something came up, and I'll need you to be in charge while I handle it. Owen's daughter is missing, and this is what I need you to do for me."

8

OWEN

Missing Person Notice

The Columbus Division of Police is asking the public to help them locate nineteen-year-old Summer Marie Long.

She was last seen driving a red 2012 Honda Civic from the Hilton Hotel on 401 N High St to Sheridan Avenue at approximately 1 A.M.

She is Caucasian, five-foot-four, weighs 116 pounds and has a slender build. She has long blonde hair, blue eyes, and a small butterfly tattoo on her left shoulder.

She was wearing a purple top, black jeans, and boots.

Anyone with information is asked to contact the Columbus Division of Police.

L ying in bed, unable to sleep, the missing person's notice of Summer kept going through my mind. I had read the report so many times that I was able to recite it without even thinking too hard about it. Missing for almost forty-eight hours, and no one still had a clue where she was.

Everyone had been so certain that she had gone off on her own and would get in touch once she had her head clear. Declan had given me his personal phone so I could keep trying to reach her, but her phone remained off. I had left her so many voicemails asking her to call me on this number but nothing. The twins had done the same. Penny had tried and even James.

The general consensus was that she was okay, but if she was alright, why wouldn't she have tried to get in touch with me? If she had checked her phone, she would have seen the missed call. She would have seen I was trying to reach out to her, so the conclusion I came up with was that my daughter didn't want anything to do with me.

Swallowing the sob that rose in my throat, I burrowed down under the covers, closer to a sleeping Declan. I didn't want to disturb him, but I needed the reassurance of his presence beside me. I didn't know what I would have done, had he not been with me throughout it all. He kept me busy, ensured my mind was engaged, but at night, there was very little he could do. He had distracted me earlier, enough for me to fall asleep, but I felt like I had only dozed off for a few minutes.

Declan lay on his stomach, his face turned in my direction. One of his arms was around my waist, anchoring me to the bed, as though he was afraid I would slip away where he couldn't keep an eye on me. The pale moonlight, spilling through the curtains caressed his skin like a lover jealous of my attention. I reached a hand out to chase the light away, claiming what was mine and no one else's.

Being this close to Declan was usually comforting. He'd held me while I slept fitfully last night. Tonight, I couldn't make myself fall asleep again, no matter how much I tried. I would close my eyes only to see Summer in a dangerous and sometimes deadly situation. I hated that my mind went there, but I was terrified she was alone somewhere and hurt. I refused to lose hope, but it was also hard to be optimistic when I knew absolutely nothing about her disappearance. It was almost as if she had been abducted by some alien and had been sucked into another dimension, car and all.

With a sigh, I conceded that I wouldn't be getting anymore sleep for tonight. I carefully removed Declan's hand from my waist and shifted out of the bed without waking him. He deserved his sleep, especially if he was going to continue doing an amazing job of keeping me sane while I worried. I stood there at the foot of the bed and watched him, thinking about how much I would have been driven up the wall if not for his presence.

I'm afraid of losing you.

I startled at the unexpected thought that sprang to mind. Since accepting that Declan loved me, I never contemplated about losing him. James had left. Technically, the twins had left, and now Summer had left. Why should I believe Declan would stay?

And yet, I had to cling to that belief. It kept me from falling further apart.

With one last lingering look at his frame in the bed, I slipped out of the room and closed the door. James had offered us the guest room to stay, since we all wanted to be in the same location when the police contacted us with whatever news we would get. Oscar had to return to work, so he was back at the house the twins shared, which was a forty-five-minute drive away, but Auggie, who had saved up his vacation time, had taken an emergency vacation to remain behind.

I made my way down the stairs, being stealthy, so I didn't alert the whole household to my wakefulness. I already saw the concern in everybody's eyes as they watched me like I was going to fall apart. Again.

Auggie was supposed to be camping out in the living room, but when I peeked inside, I only found the discarded sheets, half-lying on the floor and the rest on the air mattress James had gotten on short notice. A quick sweep of the living room revealed that he wasn't there, so I followed the only light that was on downstairs to the kitchen.

I sighed with relief when I saw Auggie at the kitchen table, a crushed can of *Blue Moon* on the surface. He had another opened can which was tipped to his mouth, and a third which was still unopened.

"Hey, what are you doing up drinking alone?" I asked, swiping the unopened can and sitting across from him. "You should be in bed."

"So should you," he answered. "Declan knows you're up?"

I shook my head, wondering at how everyone had picked up that I had relinquished much control to Declan. Unknowingly, they deferred to him when it had something to do with me. *I must be even more submissive than I thought.* I didn't necessarily see it as a bad thing especially when Declan would never do anything to hurt me deliberately. It was nice having someone else calling the shots for a change. It was comforting to know he was there and would always be there.

"Dec's sleeping," I answered. "I didn't want to wake him with my tossing and turning. He deserves to have a good rest after staying up with me much of last night."

"If I had any doubts about him before..." Auggie stated, "...watching him take care of you through everything has completely changed the way I view him. I'm so glad you have him, Dad."

I smiled tiredly at him. "Thank you for that. He means so much more to me than you can even fathom."

"I think I have a pretty good idea," he answered, returning my exhausted smile. I hated that the last two days had taken a toll on him, just as it had done me. Auggie was always clean-shaven in the past, but his face now showed the signs of a beard forming. Like me, the boys grew facial hair rapidly, and I knew he took great care with his appearance to always keep things clean. I didn't have the patience to shave every day, so I let mine grow to an acceptable scruff and kept it neatly trimmed.

"I'm so worried about her, Dad," he said suddenly, his shoulders slumped. "I couldn't sleep because I felt so sick thinking about it all. Then I felt even worse, because all this time I've been thinking that she orchestrated this whole thing for a little attention and to have her way. I know she didn't take to Declan, and then this thing with James and Penny, it seems plausible that she would just get up and leave to escape us all for a few days, but now I'm not so certain. What if... what if—"

Something broke inside me, watching Auggie get all choked up worrying about his sister. He had been doing so well, keeping a brave front for everyone. He had watched me have a meltdown several times since Summer went missing, but now he had reached the threshold.

"Auggie." I got up from the table and went over to pull him into a hug. He clung to me, his breathing deep and wheezy as he fought to contain his tears. He lost the battle, sobbing into my shirt while I stroked his hair. God, it hurt listening to his pain. I had to put mine on hold to tend to him and be what he needed. Over the past couple of years, my relationship with my boys had quickly moved from only Dad to a confidant and friend, but he didn't need a friend right now.

He needed the father who had been there to reassure him Oscar would be alright when he'd smashed his finger into the door when they were six. He needed the father who had assured him that Oscar would get better when he'd fallen off his bike and broken his arm when they were twelve. The same father who he'd needed reassurance from when Oscar had rammed helmets with another guy playing football and had lost consciousness.

"It's going to be alright," I told him, having to believe

the words for myself so I could say them with conviction. "We'll find her. We have to believe that. We're going to find her."

After a few minutes of rocking him back and forth gently, he slumped against me. I brushed his hair back and prodded him to his feet. "Come on, you're exhausted. Let's get you back to bed."

He didn't protest, but followed me back to the living room. I knew he was emotionally and physically exhausted when he didn't balk at me tucking him in, just like old times when he was a kid. But thirteen, twenty-three, fifty-three— none of it mattered. I would gladly tuck him in if that was what he wanted.

"Will you stay with me until I fall asleep?" he asked, and *damn* if my heart didn't break.

"Yes, I'll stay."

He gave a long sigh. "I love you, Dad."

I was too choked up to respond, but he was asleep almost instantly anyway. I had the urge to call Oscar, find out if he was okay. He was more than likely already sleeping, but I couldn't stop myself. I needed to know he was alright.

I snagged the wireless phone from the corner table in the room and moved over to the sofa which I had pushed back earlier for the air mattress to fit into the living room. Before it could drive me crazy, I dialed Oscar's number. We didn't need to talk. I just needed to hear his voice. To know he was alright.

"Dad?" He answered the phone just when I thought it would go to voicemail. "Dad?" he said again in a stronger voice. "Is something wrong? My God, is it Summer? Have they found her?"

The fear in his voice was palpable, and I rushed to explain they hadn't found her, which was a good thing given what his tone implied.

"No, no, there's still no word. I just... I-I shouldn't have called. Go back to sleep, Oscar. Sorry for waking you."

"It's okay Dad," he said. "I understand. Is Auggie okay? I keep having this weird feeling."

They'd always had that bond when the other wasn't exactly happy. At first when they were younger, I would play it down, not believing them. As time moved on though, I had come to the realization that they had a bond not even I would be able to understand.

"He's worried about Summer too," I answered. "But he'll be fine. *We'll* be fine, and we'll find her. No matter how long it takes."

Arms slid around my waist as the couch sank beneath Declan's weight. I didn't even need to look to know he was the one holding me. He kissed the side of my face.

"She has to be okay," Oscar affirmed.

"Right. Now go back to sleep. Talk to you tomorrow."

"Alright, Dad. Good night."

"Night, Oscar."

I hung up the phone and sank back into Declan's chest. He tucked a hand beneath my shirt and caressed my abdomen. The comforting stroke was soothing— exactly what I needed.

"Checking up on your kids?" he murmured in my ear.

"I couldn't sleep. I found Auggie drinking in the kitchen. I think he was hoping to get drunk, so he didn't have to think about all this."

"That would only give him an illusion for a few hours."

I sighed, turning to bury my face into Declan's chest. "I watched him fall apart tonight, Declan. It was painful to watch, having to suppress my own worries to meet his emotional needs."

"He's lucky to have you." Declan kissed my hair. "They're all lucky to have you as their father."

And I'm lucky to have you. But I couldn't say the words because I was so choked up from all the tears.

"Dec, please hold me," I groaned, my shoulders shaking from the silent sobs that racked my body as I wondered when the hurt would stop.

9

DECLAN

S tanding just inside the living room, I watched Owen who was huddled over the computer, scrolling through Summer's social media accounts, trying to find clues that would lead him to his missing daughter. I noticed his share of the breakfast James had made us was still untouched on the computer desk, but his coffee cup was empty.

Again.

I hated seeing him like this, agonizing over Summer's whereabouts, but I didn't expect the situation to change until we had Summer safely back home. As though he sensed me watching, Owen turned his head, and smiled when he saw me. It wasn't the smile I was used to. Sure, the Owen I had come to know was there trapped inside him, suppressed by the fear and worry he was going through every minute Summer was missing. I worried he would be trapped forever if we didn't find her.

He held up his cup to me. "Hey, can I get another refill?"

I frowned, walking over to him. I plucked the cup from his hand. "How many cups have you had so far?"

He shrugged, his eyes glued to the computer screen, scrolling through Summer's posts. He continued even as he rubbed at his eyes, and I could tell he was wearing himself thin. His eyesight couldn't be the same as when he was younger, and he had been at the computer screen since the ass crack of dawn.

"I haven't been counting," he replied.

"I think you've had one too many to drink already, Owen," I told him gently, resting a hand on his shoulder. "You need to take a break from the computer as well. Your eyes must be tired."

He caught himself rubbing at them again. "I have to keep looking."

"And we will," I assured him. "But you can take a break from the computer for a minute. Remember, you wanted to go to Summer's apartment to look for clues in her belongings. Silas is here."

He sighed. "I guess I could come back to this later."

"I'll help you when we get back," I promised him.

He started to close the social media pages he had been perusing as he got up from the chair with a groan. "Shit. I think I've been sitting for too long."

I frowned with disapproval at him. I could appreciate us digging for clues as to where his daughter could have gone, but he was going to work himself to exhaustion if he continued pushing so hard.

"We're going to stop on the way to get you something

to eat," I told him, snatching up the cold breakfast that was still undisturbed.

"I'm not hungry."

"Think about what you want to eat so we can make the stop," I said, not giving him an option as I left him temporarily. I disposed of his breakfast, washed and put away the plate, before returning to the living room. Auggie had gone out for a walk, and James was with a client.

He had already shut down the computer by the time I returned to the living room, so we made our way out to the car. Owen greeted Silas, but this time it lacked the usual warmth between them. He stared off forlornly outside, mostly frowning until I asked him where he wanted to grab something to eat.

"I told you. I'm not hungry."

"You barely touched dinner last night," I reminded him. "And you didn't eat breakfast. It's almost noon, Owen. Either you make the choice, or I will make it for you."

I hated having to get into that Daddy mode right now, but I didn't know what else to do to get him out of his funk. When he didn't choose, I had Silas drop us off at one of those restaurant chains and ordered him a sandwich and orange juice. I figured he should be able to manage that even if he was too anxious to eat. The sandwich was as small as a bagel, easily downed in a few bites.

At Penny's apartment, she let us in. She only looked slightly better than the last time we had seen her. Her eyes were still red and puffy. I stood aside and allowed Owen to hug the girl to him as they shared in their moment of concern. From the interaction I had seen between them, Owen treated Penny almost like a daughter.

"How are you holding up?" he asked her.

"Horribly," she admitted. "I have to go back to work in a couple of days, and I don't know how I'm going to manage, to be honest."

"Oh Penny, you do what you have to do," Owen assured her. "It might be just the distraction you need."

"Summer's bedroom is down the hall to the left," she stated. "It's open, and I haven't touched anything. The police didn't find anything when they dropped by to take a look yesterday, but you know Summer better than anyone, so maybe you'll see something they missed."

I placed a hand on Owen's shoulder to stop him. "First, you eat."

He glanced at the bag that I'd gotten from the restaurant where we had stopped to get him something to eat. When he saw I wasn't backing down, he gave a sigh and walked over to the small table that had only two chairs. I hovered over him ensuring he ate every single bite and drank his orange juice.

"Happy now?" he asked, getting to his feet when he was done.

I smiled at him despite his sass. "Yes, very. I'm only looking out for your best interests."

His features softened, and he walked up to me. I knew that look on his face, when he was seeking comfort, so I pulled him to me in a warm embrace.

"I know you're being a mother hen because you care."

"I think Daddy cock is more suitable, don't you?"

Owen's bark of laughter was so sudden it startled even him. I brushed my thumb across his cheek. His first real laugh since Summer went missing.

"Hey, there's my Boy." I kissed him briefly. "I've missed that laugh and the light in your eyes."

He sighed. "I just can't be happy not knowing, Dec."

"I know." I kissed him softly on the lips. "Do you want to do this alone, or for me to be there with you?"

"I probably should do it alone," he said on a sigh. "I've been a crying fountain since Summer disappeared. I should spare you more tears."

"If that's your only qualm then I'm coming with you."

An hour later, Owen sat in the middle of the floor of Summer's bedroom, looking even more hopeless at the end of our search than when we'd started. I mostly comforted while he poked through his daughter's stuff, because I didn't feel at ease viewing her personal effects.

"I don't understand. There's not even a hint of why she would leave. Nothing!"

"Maybe it was a spur of the moment decision. You said it was after talking to her that she said she needed some time."

"So, it's my fault then."

"Owen, don't blame yourself for this."

"Then who should I blame?" he asked, exasperated.

"Nobody has to take the blame for something we don't understand yet."

"I know. It's so frustrating." He got to his feet and returned the little booklet he had found in Summer's drawer. He hadn't wanted to go through it, but it turned out to be appointments that she had been keeping a note of.

"Are you ready to go now?" I asked him.

"Why not? There's nothing else here."

His shoulders were so tense when I placed an arm around him. We found Penny in the kitchen washing up dishes, but her movements were so listless that she was just going through the motions. I wondered if the dishes had even been dirty in the first place. The stack she had on the counter to wash was surprisingly clean.

"Find anything?" she asked us.

"No, nothing," Owen answered. "We're about to go."

"Okay. Thanks for trying anyway."

Once more, we were back in the car and driving toward James's house. I wished we weren't staying with his ex, but Owen wanted to be close in the event of anything. He had assured me I could stay at the hotel where I had extended my reservations, but I refused to leave him by himself. He didn't even eat unless I forced him to. Last night, he'd slept fitfully, and he had been staring at the computer screen all day. He needed me to stay around.

"Did you notice they had separate bedrooms?" Owen asked me on the drive.

"I did." There was no way I could allow Owen to have a different bedroom when we moved in together officially. Given the way things were shaping up, it might take some time to put that plan into action. I still hadn't forgotten that I needed to talk to him about his book either, but how could I delve into that now with all that was going on?

"It's like I don't even know her," Owen said. "And that hurts. She's spoken to me before about problems with Penny. I sensed the move hadn't gone as smoothly as it should have, but I thought it would get better. She never made it seem like they were *big* problems. The more I learn about her, the more I'm convinced that she just left. Like James did."

For the first time I felt inadequate to reassure or help Owen, and it made me feel like crap. I couldn't imagine what he was going through. We rode in silence, and then it was another trek inside James's house to wait.

"You should get some rest, Owen," I told him as he made for the living room, me trailing him.

"I need to finish combing her social media posts first," he remarked, then came to a sudden halt inside the living room. I almost bumped into him, gripping his hip to regain my balance.

"Charles!" I said in surprise as my father jumped to his feet. Across from him, Auggie rose as well. "What are you doing here?"

Charles's face was red. I looked from him to Auggie who was observing anything but us. What the hell had Charles done now? He could be so offensive at times, and I hoped he hadn't done anything to upset Owen's kid.

"I thought I would lend some support," he answered, clearing his throat. "I mean you're dating Owen, so we're practically family. Right?" He glanced over at Auggie before dragging his eyes back to us.

"Uh, umm, thanks, I guess," Owen remarked, still

looking bewildered. "Although I'm not sure what anyone else can do, except wait for someone to call in information."

Charles gave me a quizzical look, and I shook my head slightly. Owen didn't know yet that I intended to hire a PI to look into Summer's disappearance. I had meant to hire the guy already, but Charles had taken some time to track him down. When he'd wanted to get out of his third marriage, Charles had used the guy to trace his ex's whereabouts. Even I had been impressed at the dirt the guy had come up with.

"Owen, give us a minute, will you? I'd like to talk to Charles."

"Okay. I'll be at the computer."

His intent solely on the task before him, he settled at the computer desk. I placed a hand on Charles's arm to lead him away, but he paused and turned to Auggie.

"Um, it was nice meeting you, August."

August? I'd never heard anyone mention him by his full name before. He obviously found it distasteful as his face heated uncomfortably, and he pushed his hands into his pockets.

"It was nice meeting you too, Charles."

I led Charles from the living room and outside to stand on the porch where we'd have privacy.

"What are you doing here?" I asked him again. I didn't trust what he'd said about being there for family. "I asked you to oversee things at the office, despite my better judgment, so I could stay on here with Owen."

"Despite what you want to believe, I really did visit to ensure you were alright," he said. "I know you care about this man, and if his daughter is missing, you'll be in the middle of it. Hell, you asked me to find a PI for you."

"Not so loud," I hissed at him. "I don't want Owen to know about this."

"You're keeping it a secret from him? You don't need me to tell you that's a bad idea."

"I'm doing what's best for him," I answered. "I don't want to get his hopes up that this PI will be able to find Summer. If we find her, we'll all be relieved, but for now this is just between us. Now where's the damn PI?"

10

OWEN

"Owen, I'll be back shortly."

"Oh, uh huh," I answered distractedly as I logged onto Auggie's *Facebook* account so I could continue my search from earlier. I didn't use social media, so I had no accounts with the popular ones. At one point, I had created a *Facebook* account to connect with my children, but they'd informed me back when they were teens that it was uncool to have their father as a friend. It didn't seem particularly useful outside of that, so I had deactivated the account.

Luckily, Auggie allowed me to access his profile since he was friends with Summer. From his page, I was able to check the posts Summer had made. There were a few that made me pause, but nothing alarming that stood out.

"Owen."

At my name on Declan's lips, I glanced away from

the computer and at him. He stood a couple of feet away from the chair where I was sitting, frowning at me.

"I'll be off with Charles for an hour maybe two," he stated, now that he had my undivided attention. "Promise me you won't spend the entire time on the computer while I'm away."

"I can't. I need to keep looking. I can't sit around here being idle, Dec."

With a sigh, he came over to me, and spun the chair so I faced him. With his hands braced on the arms, he crouched over me. My gaze flickered to the couch where Auggie sat, pretending that he wasn't hearing us.

"I'm not telling you to abandon your search," he said calmly. "I'd never tell you that, but, baby, you're going to run yourself down at this rate. You have to take care of yourself so we can all focus on Summer. Otherwise we'll all be busy worrying about you as well."

"Declan, I—"

"It's non-negotiable," he said softly. "You barely slept a wink last night, and your eyes are already bloodshot. Go up to the guestroom and get some sleep. Take a nap before you come back to the search. I bet you'll feel refreshed and more capable." He turned to gesture to Auggie. "I'm sure Auggie doesn't mind continuing the search while you take a nap."

Auggie rose to his feet. "I don't mind at all."

Declan nodded and touched my arm. "Come on. Let's get you up the stairs."

I wanted to fight him on this. A nap sounded like such a luxury when I had no idea what had happened to my daughter. Declan wouldn't stand for me saying no though. I saw it in the set of his jaw. So, with a sigh, I rose to my feet and took the hand he offered me.

"Good Boy," he said, when we were out of earshot of Auggie. Usually the praise would warm my insides, but I felt too dead.

Declan saw me to the guestroom and helped me with my shoes. "Promise me you'll take a nap," he said, when he finally coaxed me to lie down on top of the covers.

"Okay. Promise."

"I mean it, Owen. No sneaking down the stairs because you know I'm not around."

That was exactly what I had planned. I tried not to let the guilt show, but buried my head into the pillow as if I would do what he suggested.

I frowned at him. "Shouldn't you be back in Cincy minding the business? You know you don't have to hang around with me, right?"

He leaned over the bed to kiss me. His lips roved over mine, and I didn't respond at first, but it was hard to resist the lure of pleasure his lips promised. He broke off the kiss, then kissed my nose which I wrinkled at him. Always with the nose-kissing.

"I'm right where I want to be," he answered. "There's no way I can return to business as usual knowing you need me."

His words brooked no argument, so even though I wanted to protest, I didn't bother to waste words.

To be fair, I tried to follow his orders and take a nap, but I ended up tossing and turning for fifteen minutes before I gave up. I didn't bother to put my shoes back on, but padded downstairs, certain Declan had already left. I still found it strange, but sweet that Charles had traveled all the way from Cincy because he considered us family. I wasn't certain what to make of that. It didn't seem like the Charles I had come to know much about through Declan.

"You can go back to what you were doing," I announced to Auggie, who startled at my voice.

"My God, Dad, you scared the crap out of me!" he cried, spinning around to observe me. "I expected you to be in bed sleeping."

"I couldn't sleep," I told him.

"You've only been off the computer like fifteen minutes," he said, squinting at the time on the computer. "Seriously, Dad. Declan was right. You need to get some rest."

"I'll rest when we find out where Summer is. Now move over."

"Declan's not going to like this," Auggie argued, as he got up from the chair.

"And who's going to tell him?" I asked, going back to the computer.

A COUPLE OF HOURS LATER, I rocked back in the chair, my ass numb, my bladder burning a bit from the urge to use the bathroom which I had been ignoring, and my eyes blurry from staring at the computer screen. I had come up empty. Aside from some random posts she had made with sad faces, and one rant about people who believed they could walk back into your life after leaving, there was nothing there that raised an alarm.

Defeated, I paused over a recent live video of Penny's that Summer had been tagged in. Ignoring the sounds of Auggie and James somewhere about the house, I checked out the video. I had ignored every effort of theirs to get me to move from the computer. *Don't they know I need to keep busy?*

The video started with Summer walking ahead as though completely unaware she was being caught on camera. Her steps were jaunty, her curls bouncy as she walked along the greens. I couldn't tell where she was in the video, or who was behind the camera, but they looked to be at some park or another. Two teen girls jogged by minding their own business, but my focus was on my daughter.

"I'm so glad you talked me into going for a walk," Summer says, her hands going up above her head as she leans into the wind that rustles the leaves of the trees around them.

She spins, then stops, her laughter bubbly when she spots the camera. "Penny, you have to stop videoing me all the time."

"Don't pay me any mind, honey. You always look so good on camera."

Laughing, Summer strikes a pose, brushing her hair over one shoulder before giving her girlfriend a coy smile. "You're only wasting your phone storage."

"Shut up and look cute."

Summer's smile fade into a pout. "Don't be mean."

The camera wavers a bit before righting. "I'm not mean. I love you." The camera lowers to the grass as Summer's sandaled feet appear closer. It's as if they forget the camera is on them. "You really think I'm mean? Is that why you've been sad lately?"

Summer laughs. "I've not been sad."

The live footage ended, leaving me unsatisfied and even more conflicted. The two girls had obviously been facing issues in their relationship which had finally ruined what they had. It was such a pity too, because they were genuinely in love with each other. They didn't deserve to end this way.

"Did he get any sleep?"

The sound of Declan's voice jerked me back into the present. I didn't dare move as I waited for the response. Auggie would never betray me and tell Declan the truth —that I hadn't slept a wink since he had left.

"He was back down as soon as you left," I heard Auggie answer.

I groaned, closing the social media accounts as quickly as possible. Still, Declan reached me before I was able to completely shut down the computer. My hand trembled on the mouse. I could feel the energy bouncing off him, and for the first time since he left, I wondered what he had gone to do with Charles.

"I'm not a happy camper right now, Owen," he said, leaning close so his mouth was at my ear. "I gave you instructions which you clearly ignored."

I raised my head and reached out to stroke his arm that had come down on the chair. "I couldn't sleep, Declan. I *had* to do something."

He gripped me by the chin and tilted my head upward, his eyes roving my face. His features hardened. "You'll be good to no one if you've run yourself down,

Owen," he said. "Look at you. You need at least eight hours of sleep just to get rid of the bags under your eyes. Can't you see I'm worried about you?"

My heart ached for him, and for the first time in a long while, I wondered why he would want to waste his youthfulness on me. I felt immediately ashamed, because there was no doubt in my mind that Declan loved me. I didn't know what the hell I did to deserve such devotion from him, but I was selfish enough to never want to let him go.

"I'm sorry I worry you," I said on a whisper. "I just feel a little lost right now. I don't know how or when I'm going to snap out of it."

"Oh, baby, I'm so sorry we still haven't found her." He clung to my hands, bringing them up to his lips to kiss my knuckles. "I didn't want to say anything yet, because I don't want you to get your hopes up, but I've hired a Private Investigator to look into her disappearance."

I breathed hard through my mouth, and the breath trembled along my lips. "You have?"

He nodded. "Yes, I wanted him on the case since the day we found out, but we had a bit of trouble getting to him."

"We?"

"Yes, Charles and I."

My eyes widened. "So, he really *is* here to support us?"

"Yes. He's really trying to be a better person."

With a groan, I rose to my feet and threw my arms around Declan, hugging him.

"Thank you so much."

His hands slid around my waist to hold me to him. "I told you that I'd be more than willing to help you with your kids, Owen," he said softly, kissing my temple. "I meant every word of it, because your kids mean the world to you. If they're happy, you're happy. And I want you happy, because *you* mean the world to *me*. So, if you're happy, I'm over the fucking moon."

I swallowed the sob that bubbled into my throat. "I don't know what I ever did to deserve you, Declan. I really don't."

11

DECLAN

"Where's Dad?" Auggie asked, frowning when I sat down at the table to eat with him and James.

At the mention of Owen, my eyebrows furrowed with worry. I was concerned about him, and his refusal to eat, to sleep properly— his ability to do anything right now really. I didn't particularly want to be stern with him at this time, because I was trying to meet his emotional needs, but I couldn't decide if my approach was right or wrong. That bothered me greatly. I'd never had doubts before about caring for and doing what was right for someone, but I didn't want Owen to be the first person I let down.

"He's in the guestroom," I answered, recalling the ultimatum I had given him just fifteen minutes ago. Once again, he had insisted he wasn't hungry. I had given him two options, back to the bedroom or to have dinner with us. He had headed for the stairs without an argument.

"He's not going to eat with us?" James asked. "Maybe I should bring him something."

I frowned at James. "He doesn't want to be disturbed at this time. I'll take a plate up to him later and try to get him to eat something."

"Still, maybe he shouldn't be alone," James pressed.

"It's best for him right now." I leveled a more final look at James. "I know what's best for him, and right now he needs some time alone."

My gut was telling me Owen needed a firmer hand, but I hesitated, given the delicate nature of our current situation. He needed me to insist that he eat and to get off the computer, which was proving futile so far. And for him to sleep well, he needed sex. Hard enough to knock him out right after. He had all this pent-up energy that he wasn't using, and he needed to get rid of it to sleep comfortably. Perhaps even a bit of impact play to pull him out of his head. It had worked before.

Dinner with James and Auggie was a quiet affair. Unlike Owen, I cleared my plate, already determined that I would need my energy for the night. Once we were finished with dinner, I excused myself from the table and asked Auggie to make Owen a plate while I made some calls. Owen still kept my personal phone, but I was able to get by using my business one anyway.

The small house had very little privacy, so I made my way out on the porch to place the call. I hadn't called him in a long time before I had given in and made the call last week with regards to Ridge. Now the phone rang a couple of times before Heath answered.

"To what do I owe the pleasure this time, Declan?"

"Do you have a few minutes to talk?" I asked him, not wanting to interrupt him if he was in the middle of a scene.

"I have about ten minutes before I'm needed," he answered. "If it's going to need more time, I can put it off."

I closed my eyes and rubbed at my temple, relaxing under Heath's soothing tones. The man was usually so smooth. It was damn next to impossible for him to lose his cool which made him a fine Dungeon Master. A firm but caring one. He'd taken me under his wing when he saw my interest, but it hadn't been long after that he sat me down and explained where I fit into the scene. I wasn't a hardcore Dom. I could never be one, but he had seen something in me that made him declare me the perfect candidate to be some boy's Daddy.

He was right.

"Ten minutes should be good," I answered.

"Time's running. What's up?"

"I want to know about Ridge. How's he doing? Has he made any improvements? I would have called earlier, but my partner's dealing with something tough right now."

"Ridge is coming along," he answered. "Stubborn, but when is he ever anything but?"

"He's not refusing to kick the habit then?"

"Actually, he's been receptive to quitting the drugs. Lucky thing you caught him when you did. He'd just started up again."

"Do you know why?"

Heath's sigh was heavy. "That he won't talk about."

But he didn't need to talk about it. We all knew what his problem was. He'd fucked over Heath, the one man who cared about him more than I did, and that was saying a lot. He hadn't been able to forgive himself for it.

"You're not acting as his therapist, are you?" Heath was a clinical psychologist, but I didn't expect him to look after Ridge himself. He would know the right person to place in care of my friend.

"No, that wouldn't exactly be professional, would it?" When I didn't answer right away, he continued. "Ridge told me about this guy you were seeing. Sounds serious. Usually you'd be up my ass every day about Ridge's progress."

"I know he's in good hands."

"At least he will be in a few minutes," he answered. "I have to go. Ridge has a scene right now."

Surprise and concern filled me at the same time. "Heath, you know I didn't mean for things with Ridge to pick up right where you left off. Are you sure you want to be his Dom again?"

"I'm not," he answered, but even so I could hear the hurt and longing in his voice.

Dammit, I felt sorry for him.

"I'll just be overseeing that he gets the care and attention he needs. That he's taken care of in the right way."

"Fuck, Heath, you don't have to be a masochist and watch that. I know how you feel about Ridge. Watching him with another Dom is kind of extreme."

Heath's next breath was loud as he blew into the phone. "Don't worry, I have zero expectations this time. The last time I got feelings involved, and it damaged us.

This time I'm simply doing my duty by him, as I would for any other sub who's going a little haywire."

Heath's words were supposed to be comforting, but I still believed he was deluding himself. Ridge was his kryptonite, the only one who had been able to break Heath. Knowing how fickle my friend could be, I didn't wish him to lead Heath on again and break his heart. Heath had been devastated when Ridge had left him.

"If there's any trouble, I hope you know you can call me, Heath," I reminded him. "We haven't seen each other in a while, but my thoughts about you have not changed. You're good people."

"It would be nice to see you again. Ridge might like it too if you came around. How about stopping by one of these nights?"

"I'd like that. Well, I'll let you go. I've a lot to do tonight."

"Good luck, man. Talk soon."

Once Heath hung up, I felt re-energized. Earlier I had been so frustrated that nothing I tried was helping Owen, but hearing Heath talk so confidently about being there for Ridge reminded me that I had to give my Boy the care he needed. While I'd felt it in my heart that Owen possibly needed a swat on the behind and some rough fucking to rid him of all his anxious energy, I had been hesitant about doing anything that would hurt him or make him feel guilty after the act, but if I didn't do something, he would wallow in worry and make himself sick.

I re-entered the house and stopped at the kitchen to collect the plate I'd asked Auggie to make for his father.

He'd need to eat a bit of food for him to withstand tonight, but I already figured out how to get him to eat.

"Dad already brought it up," Auggie remarked.

I frowned and backed out of the kitchen. "Alright. Thanks. I'll go check on how he's doing."

"Declan."

At Auggie's voice, I paused and turned to him. "Yes?"

"Thank you... for being so concerned about him."

I nodded. "Any time."

Fully prepared to find Owen refusing to eat, I took the stairs two at a time and ran into James at the top of the stairs. He didn't look too happy as he remained in my way.

"What the hell have you done to him?" he demanded. "He's still refusing to eat, and he's sitting in a corner. He wouldn't move, and he refused to respond to my questions."

Fuck. I hadn't sent Owen in the corner. I had sent him to bed, hoping he would get some sleep while we were eating. If he had taken to putting himself in the corner, then my earlier hunch must be right, and he was begging for some intervention.

I assumed the responsibility of allowing Owen to disintegrate to this level where someone was now suspicious about our relationship, and while I wasn't ashamed of the roles we fulfilled in each other's lives, I was bound to shield him from any and all unwanted attention because of it. I wouldn't let anyone in our circle of trust without his permission.

"We'll be spending the night at my hotel," I told his ex, who was still glaring at me. "And perhaps for the rest of our stay in Columbus. Thanks for the hospitality, but we're going to need more privacy than we can get here."

I made to pass him without further explanation, when his hand shot out to clamp around my upper arm. "I've been observing you two, and I need to ask. Is—is he a little?"

I tried not to show my surprise at his question. The world was getting more open-minded, and alternative lifestyles were now more exposed than ever, but I wasn't expecting the question.

"Why would you ask that question?" I prompted then tugged at my arm which he released.

"It's kind of obvious. I've been watching you, and I've seen enough littles to know what they're like. It would explain the way he's always deferring to you and the orders you give him which to any regular person might sound like the norm. I hear the subtexts in every-thing you say and do for him."

"This time *you're wrong*," I assured him without further explanation. "What Owen and I share between us is strictly our business. All you need to know is that I've got him covered."

Before he could ask any more questions, I brushed by him to the guestroom. I understood Owen's desire to stay close, but the hotel was close enough. I needed to take better care of him where no one else would interfere. I could find that at the hotel, but not here.

I entered the bedroom, prepared for Owen's stub-bornness to shine through. I was prepared to demand an answer out of him of why he was in the corner. He didn't just dole out discipline when he wanted. *I* handled his discipline.

The second I saw him in the corner though, my heart ached, and there was nothing left inside me except the desire to find Summer for Owen. He sat with his head leaned backward onto the wall. His features, the slump in his shoulders, the listless way he watched me when I entered, weren't of someone who was coping. I needed to get him back on track.

12

OWEN

A s soon as my eyes focused on Declan inside the bedroom, I stuffed a hand into my mouth and bit down on the knuckles to avoid asking him for what I wanted. I was partly ashamed for the way I felt, but I didn't know what else to do. I could feel myself spiraling into despondency, slipping too fast down the slope, and he had the ability to pull me back up.

However, I was afraid to ask. I craved the comfort and the peace of mind that usually overcame me when Declan made love to me. This time was different though, or so I thought. What if he considered me insensitive to want to have sex when my daughter still had not been found? What if he didn't get the point of why I needed him inside me, to feel a part of him.

I watched Declan, tense with the uncertainty of what he would do. He had seemed frustrated earlier when I'd refused to eat, and he'd sent me to bed. I hadn't obeyed him though. Once inside the room, the corner had called to me. I needed the familiarity of corner time. This I could cope with. Summer's disappearance I couldn't.

Without a word, Declan came over to me. Instead of admonishing, he sat on the floor next to me with a grunt, his back against the wall. We were so close I could feel the outline of his thigh against mine. He reached over and rested a hand on my knee, but otherwise, he did nothing. He said nothing.

The seconds ticked by into minutes. Slowly the tension eased from my shoulders. *If he isn't upset at me, does this mean that he understands?* I leaned into him, my head resting on his shoulder. He slipped the hand from my knee around my shoulders and pulled me even closer into his body. He felt so good. The familiarity of his touch soothing me, comforting the ache in my heart. When he held me, he made me feel like everything would get better.

Declan turned his head and kissed my forehead. I closed my eyes, breathing deep and hard as he kissed down my nose and finally teased my lips apart. I opened up for him, his kiss so soft, so sweet, the exit for all the pain and weariness inside me. He cupped my cheek, and with his other hand guided me to move against him until I was straddling his lap, knees on either side of his hips.

"Oh baby Boy," he sighed against my lips. "I'm so sorry. Forgive me."

I pulled back slightly to stare at him in confusion. "Forgive you? For what?"

"For not seeing what you needed," he answered. "For letting you have to put yourself in a corner to get my attention. I swear I wanted to on several occasions when you refused to eat, but I wasn't sure if now was the right time."

I inched a hand under his shirt to stroke his hard abdomen, lightly brushing against the puckered flesh of his surgical wound. "I shouldn't want this so badly," I said unhappily. "What kind of father wants sex and craves discipline when his daughter is missing?"

With a groan, he gripped my chin hard. "You listen to me, Owen David Long, you're the best goddamn father I've ever come across."

"You think so?" I fretted, my shoulders slumping. "Because I can't help feeling I did a shitty job, and that's why Summer disappeared and why my own boys felt they couldn't talk to me about James."

"Baby, we talked about this before. You don't get to question the kind of father you are. You hear me, Owen? I'll spank you so hard you can't sit for a week if I hear you talking like that again. I'm not going to let you belittle what you've invested of yourself into taking care of your kids, and I'm sure they will be the first to agree with me."

"Maybe that's what I want," I said on a whisper, refusing to meet his eyes.

"What?" he demanded. "I want you to spell it out for me. Tell me how I can make this a little easier for you."

"I want you to spank me," I answered, heart beating harder. "And when my ass is so red I can't take it anymore, I want you to fuck me so hard I'll have no choice but to sleep after. I'm so tired, Declan, but every time I close my eyes, my brain goes off, thinking these crazy things about what might or might not happen to her."

"I'll find her if it's the last thing I do. I swear, I'll find her and bring her back home to you."

I smiled sadly at him. "You can't promise that. But there's something else you can promise?"

"What?"

Instead of answering, I showed him by kissing him. He understood perfectly well enough, to grip my waist and kiss me back. I was only too glad to give over control to him, free-falling because I knew he wouldn't let me hit the ground.

He broke the kiss. "Alright. We have a deal, but first you eat. You don't have to eat it all, but we need to get something into you. Then we need to leave and stay at my hotel. James is already curious enough about us, and I don't want him focusing on us at the moment. If and when we're ready to broaden our circle of trust beyond Silas, then we'll do so in our time. Not his."

I didn't really want to eat. I *was* hungry but thinking about the food made me nauseous. Still, I nodded because I needed what was at the end of that promise.

"Can I sit in the corner and eat?" I asked, because I didn't want to move. The corner was familiar, and I knew what always came after corner time. My aftercare.

"Sure, you can eat anywhere you want to."

I managed a few bites of the meal. Probably not enough to truly satisfy Declan, but he didn't push. Instead, he brought me to my feet and walked me to the bathroom, where he proceeded to wash all of me. *All* of me.

Freshly scrubbed and tickled pink, I was already feeling better when we descended the stairs. James wouldn't look at me. He seemed a little upset that I hadn't trusted him with the nature of my relationship with Declan. He'd asked me if I was a little, not that I knew what that was, and when I hadn't answered him, he'd left.

"You should return to your apartment as well, Auggie," I told my son when he walked us out of the house. "You being here won't solve anything. You and Oscar can be there for each other."

"But James..." he trailed off with a sigh, then tried again. "I don't want to leave him alone, you know."

I nodded. "I understand. He's worried about Summer too. We all are, but he's back on the job. He can't expect you to stay around forever, Auggie."

"I know. I'll stay a couple more days, then I'll go."

I nodded and hugged him. "Keep in touch. Please."

"Always, Dad."

He and Declan exchanged farewells, and then we got in Declan's car. He'd driven home, something he rarely did, because Silas was resting. He deserved it. He had been escorting Declan and me around through everything.

"You want me to drive?" I asked, falling back on what I was used to.

"No, you sit and relax."

The hotel wasn't far away, and I was surprised when Declan woke me. I was so tired that I had fallen asleep. He helped me out of the car, carrying all our things, because I was usually out of it when I just woke up. We rode the elevator to the suite I had been sharing with him when we got the news.

"You should try and rest," he said as soon as we entered, and he closed the door. "I wish I could have gotten you up to our room without having to wake you."

I smiled tiredly at him. "I guess I'm already feeling a little better."

"Good."

He helped me undress, shirt over my head, shoes and socks off. My jeans went next, and the covers pulled down the bed. I climbed in, but reached for his arm.

"Lie with me."

He undressed then snuggled me into his chest. His arms came around me, holding me tight against him, and I fell asleep without difficulty.

One minute I was sleeping and the next I was wrenched awake from a nightmare of being unable to find Summer. Gasping for air, I sat up in the bed, breathing hard, heart pounding in my chest, throat choked with grief.

"Owen," Declan called to me, sitting up beside me. He must have been sleeping as well. "What happened?"

"Bad dream," I answered. "Summer. I can't. Dec... please."

I wasn't speaking coherently, but he nodded, understanding, and I was relieved.

"Come here."

I went over to him, accepting his kiss. It was almost a note of apology for what he had to do. I accepted the apology, moving restlessly against him, and something shifted. I felt out of control, but I wanted to make the moves. I wanted to have purpose, to not feel so helpless.

I broke the kiss and stared down at him. "Dec."

"Hmm?"

"You said... you said to tell you what I want."

"Yeah?"

"I don't want you to spank me."

His eyebrows rose. "You don't?"

"No. I want to... to turn you on."

He chuckled. "Baby, you already do."

"I mean I want to kiss you all over. Almost like when you had me suck on your nipples. I found comfort in it that night. Is that alright?"

He brushed the side of my face. "If that's what you need to make you feel better, then yes. I'm sure I'll enjoy it."

"Thank you, Daddy."

Having a goal I could accomplish was a relief. I felt like a dangerous cocktail mix had hit my blood, and I was on a high no one could cut me down from. I straddled Declan's hips and kissed him, my hands wandering the corded strength in such slender shoulders. I trailed kisses down his neck, teasing him before I reached the sensitive points in his chest. He emitted a loud groan when my lips enclosed over his nipples.

"Oh God!" he gasped, when I flicked my tongue, and I began to feel in control of my emotions, like I could get something done.

Declan's fingers teased in my hair, tugging and releasing as he allowed me to stroke him to no end. He was poking me through the confines of his underwear, his cock hardening in very little time, and the thought flashed through my mind that I really had to talk him into getting his nipples pierced. Even more fun.

As the world and everything outside of the bedroom fell away, I focused on him, on pleasing him. His nipples became stiff points against my tongue, which I strummed until he was pushing my head from the sensitive buds. I released and shifted over him, pushing up his left arm to lick his pits. I wasn't kidding that I wanted to taste every bit of him, to have him so wild that when he was finally inside me, he would completely be out of control.

Like the rest of him, Declan's underarm was void of hair. Unlike me, he didn't sprout tufts of hair, which I did if I didn't shave regularly. I swiped my tongue over the expanse of his pit, licking and sucking on the flesh. I did the same to his other arm then kissed down his sides to his hipbone while shuffling down his body.

"Fuck! Jesus! What are you doing to me, Boy?" he growled, when I grasped his cock at the base.

I smoothed my hand down his length, lightly stroking him. I didn't immediately suck on his cock, but shoul-dered my way between his thighs to reach his balls.

"Hmm, so good," I murmured, licking down the seam of the twin jewels. I went to work, still stroking his cock while I sucked his balls into my mouth, reveling in their weight on my tongue. I was so caught up in the way he moved beneath me, that I fished my tongue lower, sliding over his taint, licking him over and over. The more he moaned, the more he groaned, this man of mine, usually in such control, the ache in my heart settled.

As my saliva ran down his taint, I chased after it greedily with my tongue, but felt him stiffen before I could reach his hole. He grasped me by the hair and held me back.

"Jesus, Owen! Stop."

Disappointed, I stopped and peered at him. His face was flushed, his chest moving hard from his breathing. He was blowing from his mouth, and I'd never seen him this way before, completely done in.

"You want me to stop?" I asked him. "You're not enjoying this?"

"Of course, I am," he answered, pinching the bridge of his nose with his free hand. He gave a nervous laugh. "This is just going too fast. I've never—"

To my surprise, his face turned even redder, and I understood. He wasn't joking in São Paulo when he told me his ass was off limits. I'd just thought that meant for other guys. I didn't expect to fuck him. Or maybe a time or two. But to deny himself even a rim job because he didn't want me near his ass after he'd plundered mine so many times, I was a bit disappointed.

"Fuck, don't give me those sad eyes, Boy," he growled at me. "You know our dynamic. Daddy fucks his boy, not the other way around?"

"Says who?" I challenged him.

"Says every Daddy Dom ever," he answered, frustrated, as if he didn't want to have this conversation with me.

"You don't know that for sure," I replied on a frown. "And it's just a rim job. Have you ever tried it before?"

"No, but I don't need to."

"How do you know you won't like it if you never try it?"

"Because…" He trailed off, frowning at me hard.

"We're us, Dec," I told him softly. "Sure, I adore calling you Daddy, and I am quite happy being your Boy, but we don't have to be like every other Daddy/Boy out there. We can do what feels right to us. That's all that matters, and I want my tongue inside you, making you feel what I do when you're eating my ass."

His head fell back against the pillow. "There are certain things I don't do, so you clearly know your role and I know mine. What if it changes things?"

I stared at him in disbelief. "Like what? If I eat your ass, I won't see you as Daddy anymore?"

When he didn't respond, I knew that was it. I'd hit the nail on the head. Sure, I liked bottoming. I liked when I was full of him, and I'd even be fine bottoming for him exclusively in our relationship, but I hated the reason he had for me doing this. It was so wrong.

"So, I'm just your Boy because you're the one fucking me in the ass?" I asked him.

"Of course not."

"That's exactly what it sounds like to me," I said, sitting up between his legs. "Do you think I only see you as Daddy because I'm always the one bottoming? It's way more than that, Dec. It's the way you make me feel in and outside the bedroom. It's the way you take care of me. The way you see to my needs without me having to ask. Whether I have your dick up my ass or mine up yours, it wouldn't change the way I see you."

He groaned and grasped my shoulders. "So, now you'll be mad at me if I don't allow you to rim me?"

"No, I'm not mad. Just disappointed."

"I told you before that I don't do ass play, Owen."

"You said it generally," I answered. "I didn't know that applied to us. I mean, what we have is different. At least, to me it is. I thought it was the same for you."

I made to move off the bed, but he was behind me, his legs going around my waist, trapping me. "We're not done talking about this."

I glanced back at him. "Aren't we? Haven't you already made up your mind? No one plays in your sandbox?"

He bit into my shoulder. "Calm down. The fact that I'm still here and not hightailing it out of the room should tell you something."

I paused and stopped struggling to get away from him. His tongue flicked over the place on my shoulder where he had bitten me.

"Are you saying that you've changed your mind?"

"I'm saying I'll think about it," he replied. "Give me time. This is new to me."

His honesty and the hint of uncertainty in his voice stripped away my anger. I really had no right trying to get him to do something he didn't want to. I wasn't even certain why I had gotten all hissy about it either, given my desire for being fucked by the man and not the other way. It would be nice though to know that it might not be something we would engage in all the time, but that the offer wasn't off the table. I might want to get my dick wet sometime too.

I bowed my head. "I'm sorry, Daddy."

He kissed my cheek. "It's fine. Come back to bed. Let Daddy take care of you."

Declan pulled me back to lie on the bed, and I went along with it. When he kissed me, his teeth sank into my bottom lip and a thrill ran through me. His hands gripped mine, holding them above my head, leaving me helpless and somewhat restless. I moved against him, tugging at my hands until he lifted his head.

"Remember we talked about safe words?" he asked, refusing to let go of my wrists.

"Yes," I answered. "Why?"

"Because you're fighting me right now," he answered. "And you need to let go or use it. I'm going to tie you to the bed. If you feel it's too much for you, use your safe word."

I bit my lip, not sure if I wanted to be tied up right now. I'd wanted to be the one with the power, not the one being controlled.

"Do you understand, Boy?"

His tone snapped me back into our zone, and I nodded. "Yes, I understand."

"Tell me what you understand."

"If I'm uncomfortable I use my safe word."

"Which is?"

"Jello."

He leaned forward and pressed his lips to mine. "Good Boy."

I watched him as he got my socks and one by one tied my hands to the bed with me facing the mattress. When I tugged, I was surprised to find that the ties held. He hadn't given me any leeway to let myself loose. There was no way I was getting free unless he untied me.

"You're all wound up so tight," he murmured, placing a kiss between my shoulder blades. "I'm going to teach you to let go. That I've got you."

"I know," I answered, glancing at him over my shoulder.

"I think you've forgotten, but that's fine. I am patient enough to remind you that you can always allow yourself to fall when you can't find your footing, because I'll catch you."

Kneeling behind me, Declan lay with his head between my legs, and with his hands on my hips guided me to lower my cock to his lips. I groaned when he took the tip into his mouth, taking more as he pulled my hips lower. He caressed my ass cheeks, squeezing them as he urged me with his hands to set a rhythm. I pushed forward carefully into his mouth, my head down as I watched him taking my cock deep into the back of his throat.

He aimed a slap at my ass cheeks every so often until I was blinded by my impending climax. He wouldn't allow it. He pulled at me until I reluctantly eased back my hips for him to release me. He shuffled from beneath my legs, kneeling behind me as he licked up my taint before toying with my hole. His tongue idled over my opening as he took his time doing to me exactly what I had wanted to do to him earlier. I pushed aside the thought and concentrated on what he was doing to my body.

He shifted away to retrieve the lube before settling

right back between my legs. He squirted the lube over my hole and started with two fingers inside me, pushing deep while I tugged on the socks because fuck I was trapped by all the feelings of pleasure that was rolling over me.

"Let go," he said, kissing my back. "Daddy will always be here for you. You don't have to do this alone. Trust me."

With a tortured cry, I let go, my hips moving as I fucked myself on his fingers.

"That's it," Declan soothed. "That's Daddy's good Boy. Take as much as you need."

He gave me another finger to work with as he stretched my ass until it burned, but I still wanted more.

"Please," I begged him. "Please, Daddy. More."

"You want my fist, Boy?" he asked.

I nodded so hard my vision blurred. "Yessss! Oh fuck, yes!"

"It's going to take some time to work you up to it."

"I don't care," I told him. "Do it, please. I need this."

He placed two kisses on my lower back just above the swell of my ass. "I know, baby. I know."

It did take just as long as he had remarked, but I loved every bit of the time it took. At one point, he left me to get a towel from the bathroom before returning to position it beneath me. Then he set to work, slobbering my ass with lube, stretching me with his fingers. It was amazing how much trouble the fourth gave in fitting even though the third had fit with much ease. By the time the fourth was in, I was gasping, my ass felt full, and I wasn't certain I could take anymore.

It wasn't uncomfortable at first, but the stretch felt

good. My cock was so hard I was leaking over the towe.
He kept kissing my thighs, soothing me, checking if I was
fine.

"Feels good?" he asked me.

"So fucking full," I whimpered.

"Safe word?"

I hesitated before shaking my head. "No, not yet.
Feels good."

"Hurts?" he questioned, slowly moving his four
fingers in and out of me.

"Yes," I gasped. "But still so fucking good. Don't stop,
please. Oh fuck, Daddy."

"Easy there, Boy." He stilled my hips when I tried
pushing back on his fingers to get more. "I'll know when
you're ready for more."

"Okay, Daddy."

I allowed him to lead, slowly working his final finger
inside. Just the thought of his hand inside my body was
enough. My torso on the bed, I closed my eyes, hissing,
and groaning into the sheet as he moved slowly, moving
in and out without dislodging his fingers. His tempo
increased gradually as he allowed my body the time it
needed to adjust to the new intrusion.

"Fuck!" he murmured when he removed his hand
and pushed my cheeks aside to peer at my ass. His thumb
rubbed around the circle, dipping inside before he rose
above me. "I'm going to fuck you now, Boy."

"Yes!"

"You like Daddy opening you up with his fist before
he fucks you, baby?" he asked as he pushed his cock
inside my body hard.

"Yes, Daddy!" I growled, hands clutching at the socks as he fucked me hard, pelvis punishing against my ass. Smack! Smack! He plunged inside me hard and deep, my ass relaxed enough for him to hold nothing back.

"Oh fuck," he muttered pulling out and pushing my cheeks apart. "Oh my God babe. Look at Daddy's pretty hole."

He returned to fisting me, hands moving faster, deeper inside my channel. I stopped trying to hold back. Arching my back, I clutched at the head of the bed, begging him to make me come. With his free hand, he reached beneath me, jerking on my dick. The intensity of his movements slowed somewhat, but the dual sensation of having my ass the fullest it had ever been, in addition to my cock being stimulated, wrung me out. I exploded onto the bedsheets, squeezing my eyes shut at the tightness of my ass cinching around his hand.

"That's it," he murmured, still pumping cock. "Get it all out. Daddy's got you. That's my good Boy. Daddy's got you."

I felt like I couldn't stop coming. There was so much of it. Tremors after tremors wracked my body. When I thought I was completely milked, my body defied me by spasming again before another squirt of cum puddled onto the bed. Declan continued to stroke me but more gently, soothing. He carefully removed his hand, and I felt him reach for the towel to wipe his hands.

As exhausted as I was, as trembly as my legs were, I remained on my knees because he wasn't finished yet. I needed the one final piece of him. I didn't even need to ask. Crouched over my ass, Declan stroked his cock, his slick hand moving smoothly over his girth. He didn't even last a minute before he was grunting, pushing my cheeks apart and stuffing his cock inside my entrance to feed me his cum. Only after receiving that from him did I allow myself to collapse onto the bed in exhaustion.

Vaguely I remembered Declan untying me while he kissed me, telling me how good I was. There was no way I could walk just yet, but I was functional enough to roll one way and the next with a little grimace as he tugged the sheet from the bed. Because of how little participation I could give, he made several trips to the bathroom, cleaning up the both of us.

He helped me into a fresh pair of underwear and by then there was a knock on the door. He had ordered room service—a platter of fruits, juice, and water. My ass smarted, but he helped me to sit up gingerly while he fed me the fruits and talked me into drinking the water. I turned down the juice. I was so tired I just wanted to roll over and sleep.

He finally allowed me to lie back onto the bed on my stomach, while he fussed over me.

"Need anything?" he asked leaning sideways to kiss my temple before going back to the apple he was crunching on. He had the television on, but the volume was so low I couldn't even hear what the people were saying.

"Like what?" I turned my head, giving him a smile because he looked worried like he thought he had broken me.

He shrugged. "I don't know. Ice cream? Tylenol? Diamonds? Or is that just a girl's best friend?"

I chuckled and stretched an arm around his waist. "I'm okay. You just broke my ass. No biggie."

He stilled. "You'll be sore a bit, but you'll feel better soon. Want me to run you a hot bath? It might help."

"I couldn't get to the bathroom in the first place," I told him, then grimaced. "Although I need to pee."

"Come on. I'll help you."

I needed to pee too badly to turn down his offer, so I allowed him to escort me to the bathroom. I did draw the line at him holding my dick while I peed, and for a second I did contemplate the Jacuzzi, but I was too tired. As soon as he brought me back to bed, I snuggled closer to him and yawned.

"It was worth it," I told him. "Thank you for knowing what I needed."

He brushed my hair from my forehead. "You're welcome. I don't always know though, Owen, so you've got to tell me if you need something and I can't figure it out."

"I'll try."

"Good Boy."

I smiled sleepily at him, and for the first time since Summer disappeared, I felt that everything would be alright. We would find her. It might not be tomorrow or even the day after, but I had to trust she would find her way back to us.

13

DECLAN

Long after Owen fell asleep trustingly in my arms, I lay awake, listening to his deep even breathing. Finally, after our vigorous lovemaking he was able to settle down into sleep without twisting and turning. Even as he'd napped on the short drive to the hotel, he had been groaning in his sleep as though in pain. I was relieved that our plan had worked, and I had worn him out to the point of exhaustion. I didn't anticipate him waking for a few hours. Maybe not for the rest of the night.

His heavy breathing gave way to light snoring and still I watched him, unable to sleep. He'd touched on a sore topic tonight that I never thought we'd discuss. Owen had made no qualms about the fact that he enjoyed bottoming for me. Damn, before tonight the last time we'd had sex, he'd begged me to take him over and over while denying him a climax. I never expected him to want to experiment with me.

I'd been sexually active for the past ten years, and I'd never bottomed for anyone before. I wasn't concerned about it hurting, especially for the first time. I was no stranger to pain. The thought of opening myself up for another man in such a manner just always left me feeling uneasy. I had always been in charge in my relationships. I didn't know how to let go and allow someone else to take the lead.

Was Owen right? Did I only see him as my Boy because he bottomed for me? No, I didn't believe that at all. It was more than in just the bedroom. I saw the vulnerability in him, his big heart, and the innocence that abounded inside him at his age. He didn't just allow me to take care of him in the bedroom either. I took care of him in every aspect of his life. It was more than just the sex.

Then why can't you give him what he wants?

After ten years of being in charge, I didn't see myself face down, ass upward being fucked by anyone. *Not even by Owen?* I gave it sincere thought, and I couldn't deny the curiosity that was there. I wasn't dead after all. I remembered the way he mellowed when I had my tongue deep inside his crack. He always looked so blissed after our lovemaking. Why would I turn him down if he wanted to do that to me as well?

The semi-hardness of my cock at my train of thought was a surprise. I buried my face in Owen's neck and kissed him. I'd do anything to make him happy for sure. And as long as it only happened once in a while. Then maybe…

THE NEXT MORNING when I woke up, showered and had coffee which I ordered for our room, Owen was still sleeping. Poor thing must have really been tired. He'd woken once in the middle of the night, stumbling to use the bathroom, and the second he crawled back into bed beside me, he'd been fast asleep again.

I was checking my work email on my phone when it vibrated in my hand, alerting me to an incoming call. Recognizing the number as belonging to Kieran Walker, the PI Charles had hooked me up with, I tried not to get overly excited.

"Hey Kieran," I answered the call, playing off as nonchalant when I was wound so tight, hoping it was good news. Owen could not survive any bad news about his daughter.

"Declan, I think we've got her," Kieran stated, his voice calm.

I squeezed my eyes shut. "You have? Where is she?"

"She's staying at a rundown motel across town," he answered. "Took a while to find her, because she hasn't once left her room, but I think we have her."

"You mean you've not seen her?" I asked in frustration.

"Like I said. She's staying low. I spoke to the people across from her, and they confirmed after a little bribery that she's there."

But what if they have lied to get the bribe money?

Technically I knew Kieran came highly recommended and would not have contacted me if he wasn't certain he had Summer, but I needed to know for myself. I'd feel crappy to get Owen's hopes up only for us to discover the person we had was only a lookalike.

"Where is she staying?" I asked him.

I scribbled down the address he gave me and thanked him before I rang Silas and asked him to get the car ready.

Once the calls were made, I debated leaving and hoping to get back before Owen woke up, but I didn't want to chance him awaking to find me gone. I went over to the bed where he was sprawled on the fitted sheets. He had on only his underwear, and in the light of the morning, I could make out just how hard I had fucked him last night. He had red marks all over his back and thighs.

"Owen?" I shook him gently.

He was a hard sleeper, so I wasn't surprised when he took forever and a day to wake. He blinked his eyes several times and frowned at me, as though trying to remember who I was. He was so adorable like this that I couldn't contain my smile, my apprehension about facing him after last night disappearing.

"Declan?" he said my name on a groan, then started to get up.

I held his shoulders and pressed him back to the bed which was so easy to do. If anyone wanted to manipulate this big guy, they could do it when he just woke. He never quite had all his faculties in working order until several minutes had passed.

"No, don't get up," I told him. "I just didn't want you to wake up and find me gone. I'll be stepping out for an hour or so."

His frown deepened. "You don't want me to come with you?"

I shook my head. "No. Go back to sleep. I know you're still sore from last night."

I kissed him between the eyes, and he sighed, closing his eyes. "Declan, about last night, I'm sorry if I—"

I pressed a finger to his lips. "You have nothing to apologize about. I told you that you could ask me anything, and I'm glad you did. It's a conversation for another time though. I promise we'll talk about it, okay? Just be patient."

He nodded. "Okay. I don't want to lose you because I was being stupid last night. It doesn't even matter if you don't want to. I'm fine with the way things are."

"We'll talk later. Stay in bed and get some rest."

"Okay." He snuggled into his pillow. "My ass *is* sore. I don't know why I still feel so tired though. Must be getting old."

I smiled at him. "Don't let Ocar hear you say that, or you'll never be able to live it down."

He grinned at me. "I know, right." He popped his eyes open, and they were serious. "Promise you're not mad about last night?"

"I promise. You still have my phone. Call me on my business number if you need anything."

With a nod, he went back to sleep. I ran a hand down the smooth expanse of his back as I straightened, then left him alone. He was so trusting he didn't even ask me where I was going. Hopefully, I would have a good surprise for him when I returned.

"You think it's her?" Silas asked, as we drove from the hotel.

"I hope so, Silas. For Owen's sake, I really hope so."

"It will be quite sad though if it is her. That she would leave like that without saying anything to her father."

"Yeah, it will suck for Owen for sure."

But I would help him through it, and I knew he would forgive his children anything anyway. He would just need some time before he could get over it because he loved those three.

"Silas, do you think sex helps to define a relationship?" I asked my driver.

When the words came out, I realized I perhaps should have left the question unsaid. I was beginning to use my driver as a sounding board, and he wasn't getting paid for that. At this rate, I would need to pay him the equivalent of a damn good therapist.

"Hmm, it depends," he answered. "Sex can make or break a relationship. It depends on the couple."

"And if you don't see eye to eye in the bedroom? What if there's something that one party wants that the other can't give?"

"Can't or *won't* give, sir?"

"Is there a difference?"

"It might make a difference to the other party involved," he answered. "It's like we take a lot for granted when it comes to sex, but when two people have the utmost trust in each other, they'll know the right thing to do for them. You go as far as you can trust."

Damn, he does deserve a bonus. He had hit the nail right

on the head. I didn't fully trust Owen not to look at me differently if I allowed him free rein with my person like he had wanted last night. How could I be vulnerable with him in such a way and expect him to see me as the strong protective kind of Daddy when it was morning?

"There are certain things about sex that can make us very vulnerable," I remarked, staring at the back of Silas's head. "Kissing for example. I find it to be more intimate than an actual fuck. I can count on one hand the number of guys I've kissed, and I've fucked a lot. It's not everyone you can show that vulnerability to."

"And you shouldn't," he answered. "But with the right person our vulnerable moments can turn into our greatest strengths. It can eradicate our fears, our inhibitions, and misgivings. When fears are driven away, there's nothing left but the perfection of love to bloom."

"Damn, Silas, you need a vacation," I told him on a chuckle. "You're getting too good at this. How does two months sound when we get back to Cincy?"

"What would I do with all that time, sir?"

"I'm sure you'll think of something. I insist." In fact, for going beyond the call of duty and for never batting an eye when I called him, especially for how long he had been with me, he deserved a vacation. Somewhere nice. He would like that.

We arrived at the long-staying motel where Summer supposedly had a room under a different name. I didn't like the looks of the place at all. There were no security features to the property. I could see peeling paint, and there was even loud music coming from a car parked at the other end of the lot.

The security was so lacking that I didn't even have to stop at the main office to request to speak with Summer. Silas simply parked the car out of sight of room 41. I immediately spotted the car Summer had been driving when she took Owen home that night. She was definitely here then.

I couldn't help feeling a bit pissed on Owen's behalf. He had been so worried about her when she was fine and hadn't contacted him.

It took great restraint to knock on the door instead of pounding the way I wanted to. I stood to the side, away from the peephole, because if she saw me, there was no way she would open up. She already hated my guts, and I wouldn't be her favorite person after this either.

"Who is it?"

At least she had the common sense not to just open the door.

I cleared my throat to disguise my voice. "Maintenance."

"Oh, I didn't call for maintenance," she said, at the same time I heard the bolt slide back, and she opened the door leaving the chain on. "You!" she shrieked when she saw me, and promptly slammed the door closed.

"Summer, I'm just here to talk," I stated, not too loudly to alert the neighbors. "Let me in, please. Your dad's worried about you."

"Go away!" she cried from the inside. "If you don't leave in the next five minutes, I'm calling the front desk to have you removed."

I decided to call her bluff by making a promise of my own.

"If you don't let me in, I have no other choice but to call your Dad and stake out your room to ensure you don't leave before he gets here. Come on, Summer, you don't have to like me, but we need to talk."

"Don't call my Dad!" she called out. "He'll only show up and try to fix things."

"And why is that such a bad thing?"

"Because he can't fix this. I just want to be alone for a while."

I took my phone out of my pocket. "Okay, then I have no other choice, but to call Owen. I hope you rehearse your explanation really good for why you've done this to him."

She must have been using the peephole, because at the first button I jammed on my phone, the door flew open again. She'd unhooked the chain, glaring at me as she opened the door. Before she could change her mind, I slipped into the motel room. She glanced around as though suspecting Owen was somewhere outside, before she closed the door and returned the chain to the hook.

"What are you doing here?" she demanded again, frustration coming off her in waves.

I ignored her question to check out her living situation. It was a cheap motel room, but at least it looked clean. The only furniture included a double bed which was unmade, two bedside tables, a dresser with a TV above it on the wall, and a small white plastic table across from the bed with two chairs. A kitchenette with a fridge and a cooktop was a few feet away from the bed and the bathroom was right off the kitchenette.

"I've seen the apartment you share with Penny," I

said, returning my eyes to where she stood next to the table, hugging her arms to her body. Hell, she was standing next to everything. That was how small the room was. "Why on Earth would you leave it for this?"

"I needed my space, okay," she answered. "You still haven't answered my question."

"You seriously think we wouldn't be searching for you?" I asked her. "Owen's worried sick about you. Of course, I'm going to have people search for you."

She groaned. "What don't you understand about wanting some time to myself to figure things out?"

"Had you said that to anyone, there wouldn't have been a need to have Owen freak out about your disappearance."

She rolled her eyes and crossed her arms over her chest. "It's hardly a disappearance. I sent Dad a voicemail that I would be away for a few days while I tried to gather my thoughts. He should understand this. He was the one who suggested I just needed some time to get used to the idea of things. The more I thought about it as I was driving home that night, the more it made sense. I couldn't think around Penny, because seeing her just hurt after we broke up."

"You sent your father a voicemail?" I asked her in disbelief.

"Yes, I did. Do you think I would be so heartless to leave without saying anything to him? I'd never do that to Dad."

Now that explained it. "Owen's phone broke," I answered. "He didn't get the message. Why didn't you answer the phone when we tried to call you?"

"Because after I sent Dad the message, I turned off all contact with the outside world," she replied with a frown. "I haven't even turned on the television. He didn't get the message?"

"No, he didn't. So imagine how freaked out your father has been about the whole thing. We even had the police called. Summer, there are missing person notices of you on electronic billboards!"

"Oh my God." She at least had the decency to look horrified. "I didn't mean to scare him. I swear I left the voicemail explaining everything about Penny breaking up with me, James, you. You don't know how crowded everything feels inside my head."

I sighed. "Then it's all a big misunderstanding, and we can bring you home."

She shook her head and stepped back from me. "No, I'm not ready to leave yet. I've finally been able to breathe and think while I've been here. Penny dumped me. She doesn't want me around. She doesn't love me. I'm having a hard time believing anybody does. Every-body just thinks I'm a downer."

I would have accused her of trying to play on my emotions, but her shoulders slumped in dejection, and her eyes filmed over with unshed tears. If this was acting, she could be nominated for an Oscar just for this perfor-mance alone.

"Summer, you know that's not true. Your dads, the twins, and even Penny. And you may not want to hear it, but I care too."

She scoffed. "You care? Give me a break. Why should you? You probably wanted me out of the way so you can have Dad all to yourself. He doesn't even call me daily like he used to, and I know it's because of you."

"If I wanted you gone, I wouldn't have hired a Private Investigator behind your Dad's back with the hopes of finding you."

"Why did you?"

"Because I love your Dad," I answered. "He's been miserable not knowing where you are."

"You can't make me go back," she said stubbornly, as she sat down at the table. "I won't. I'll just disappear again."

"And I'll find you again."

"Don't you get it?" she yelled at me, then started to sob. "I don't fit in! Everyone's okay with James. I'm the only one who has issues. Everyone's okay with you. I'm the only one who doesn't know if you're right for Dad. Everyone thought Penny and I were good together. I'm the one who screwed things up. I screw everything up! Everybody leaves! Now I'm losing Dad too, and it's your fault."

"Summer." Jesus, the kid was a mess. She really needed help with everything she was going through. She was processing everything differently from everyone else, and I felt at the heart of it were the abandonment issues she still hadn't worked out yet. I approached the table and took the other available seat. "Deep down you know that's not true. You know how your father and brothers feel about you. I've spent only a short time with Penny, and I can see that she's in love with you. She too is devastated by you leaving."

"Then why did she break up with me?"

"She said you had a rough patch. That you argued a lot, and you were having mood swings. You doubting her, always accusing her of wanting to leave you."

"And she did."

I reached over the table to touch her hand. "No, she didn't. You pushed her away." My heart broke for her, seeing her crying, so uncertain and vulnerable. Remembering how I had interpreted everything with Charles badly, I felt for her. "Listen, Summer, I kind of know what you're going through."

She scoffed but didn't pull her hand away. "I seriously doubt that."

"It's not necessarily the same thing," I admitted. "But I too lost my mom when I was only five. She died, so I grew up with very little knowledge of her. The difference between us is that you have a supportive father. My Dad couldn't even stand the sight of me. He handed me over to my grandfather to raise. The short of it is that it jaded me for a long time. I was gun-shy where people were concerned, not letting anyone get too close to me. But your father did, and now he's the best thing that's ever happened to me."

"Why are you telling me all this?"

"To let you know you're not alone. Your feelings are valid, and you don't have to think of yourself as weak or foolish for feeling the way you do."

She finally looked at me. "So, you won't tell Dad where I am?"

"I have to tell him," I answered. "How can I not?"

She rose to her feet and paced the pathetic distance between the table and the dresser. "You're not getting it!

You say you understand, but you don't. If you tell Dad where I am, he'll be here the next minute. You know that. He'll convince me to go back to Penny, or to return to Cincy. He'll want to control the situation and make me well. But this isn't about him, Declan. It's about *me. Not him.*"

"Summer, I can't hide this from him."

"You say you care. If you really do, then you won't say anything."

"Now that's not fair."

She stopped to stare at me. "I've been seeking help to sort through everything. I saw a therapist once, and she can accommodate me. I want to do it, and I want to do it alone."

I sighed, not certain what to do. I could see her anguish and that she truly desired the time alone, but how could I keep this from Owen? I couldn't. He would be devastated if he found out that I was keeping something like this from him.

"I can't leave and pretend that I've not been here."

"Then tell him that you know where I am, but I asked you not to share it with him."

I could see how *that* would turn out. "Summer, be honest with me. Are you trying to ruin our relationship?"

"This isn't about you! It's about *me* and what *I* need! Doesn't anybody *care* a-a-about th-th-that?"

"Okay, okay, don't cry. How about I tell him where you are, but I ensure he stays away?"

She gave me a blank stare. "You really think Dad's going to know where I am and not show up? If you believe that then you don't know him as well as you think you do."

Shit, she is completely right. Owen was protective of his kids, especially Summer, his last nester to leave the house. He would be here the next second if I told him where she was. And then what? She'd run off again? Maybe out of state the next time?

"Look, I have to tell your Dad I know where you are."

She didn't wait for me to finish, but flew over to the bedside table, grabbing random things. "Then you leave me with no choice but to leave."

"Is it such a bad idea for your Dad to talk to you about everything you're going through?"

"He doesn't understand how I feel! He thinks I should forgive James. I don't want to forgive James right now. I'm too mad. Too pissed off at him for leaving. This is nobody's problem to solve, but my own, and I want to work it out on my own."

"Fine! Fine!" I walked over to her and grasped her arm to stop her from throwing stuff on the bed.

"What do you mean *fine?*" she asked.

"I mean I won't disclose your location to him," I answered, hoping I could pull this off and not lose Owen. But if I didn't give in to her need, we would be back to square one if she went away again. At least I could attest to the fact that she was well. At least physically. She had a whole lot of work to do in therapy.

She eyed me suspiciously. "I don't believe you."

"It's not without its own price," I informed her.

"You're going to have to trust me with this, and I'll trust you that you'll keep your word not to disappear again."

"I don't know if I *can* trust you," she claimed.

"I don't know if I can trust *you* either," I returned. "But we have to trust each other in this. We have to, for the sake of your father. We want the best for you. We do, but Owen deserves to know that you are okay. Now the first thing you *are* going to do, is to call your father and reassure him that you are alright."

14

OWEN

Declan was gone when I came to. I couldn't exactly describe the feeling as waking up as it felt like I was rousing from a deep coma. At first, I was lethargic, not really wanting to get up out of bed, but staying in bed was no fun with just me there, so I gingerly rose and took care of my needs in the bathroom.

My body hummed a pleasant little reminder of Declan's hot abrasive lovemaking last night. It felt strange walking around the hotel at first, but eventually I didn't feel like I had a ball stuffed up my ass.

As I scrubbed myself, I relived every moment of his touch. I had impressions of his fingernails and tight grip on my neck, back, hips and ass, but when I walked by the mirror and saw them, I wasn't put off at the redness on various points of my body. Instead, a thrill ran through me at his unintentional marking of my person.

I patted my face with a towel, taking care to dry my beard which was a bit overgrown. Since I hadn't planned on staying in Columbus for so long, I hadn't brought my shaver. I stared at my face in the mirror above the vanity which clearly displayed a shock of gray. I had started going gray in my late thirties, but the strands had always been minimal. It was as though overnight I had sprung a head of silvery strands. They were mostly concentrated at my temples, and I couldn't decide how I felt about them.

I never thought about going gray before, but now I wondered if I should dye the silvery strands. Maybe people wouldn't think me too old for Declan if I did that. The idea sounded like a good one, but I was already certain Declan would object, which was just as well. I couldn't see myself visiting a salon every so often to touch up my roots. I'd watched Summer do the same for half a term of her sophomore year when she'd decided she wanted to be a ginger. I didn't have that kind of effort to waste on something so cosmetic.

But you will have all the time in the world if you quit your job.

I skipped over the thought, because I couldn't think about such a life-changing decision right now. First, to find Summer, ensure that she was fine, and *then* I could think about resigning.

Although I still worried about Summer, I felt much calmer than like a train wreck waiting to happen. I didn't bother to get dressed, but wearing a robe, ordered room service, because I was starving. I polished off the meal with nothing to spare and validated eating so much by reminding myself that I'd eaten very little over the last couple of days.

The room attendant returned to clear the breakfast

items and went away, leaving me to my thoughts and wondering when Declan would be back. I vaguely remembered him waking me up to let me know he was going out, but I couldn't even figure out how long ago that had been. I could have sworn that I recalled him promising to be gone for only an hour.

I was in bed, bored and flipping through the television when Declan's phone that he'd left behind rang. I swiped it from the bedside table and almost dropped it to the bed when I recognized the unsaved number displayed on the screen. I had assumed it would be Declan calling me from his business phone. I was wrong.

Summer.

Tears of relief clouded my vision as I swiped the screen with shaky hands, suddenly wishing Declan was here so I could lean on him for support. Summer's fair face appeared on the phone screen. She smiled tentatively, but my eyes were busy taking in everything. Her eyes were red as if she had been crying. Her nose was blotchy too.

"Summer, honey," I said, then choked up and started to cry. I couldn't get another word out. I could only stare at her beautiful face and allow my heart to rid itself of the fear I had been carrying since she had vanished. My tears only set her off, and then seeing her crying only made me cry more.

"I'm sorry, Dad," she kept apologizing. "I'm sorry. I'm so sorry."

"It's okay, sweetie," I tried to clamp down on my emotions to assure her. "It's okay. Whatever it is, it's okay. Just come home."

She sniffed and wiped her face with the sleeve of her shirt. "Oh, Dad, I can't. Not yet. I need more time."

"Summer, more time for what?" I asked her, ignoring the lump in my stomach. "Why did you leave? Is it because of Declan and me? Please, talk to me."

"It's not just that," she replied. "It's everything. My emotions are all over the place right now. I can't... I can't seem to get it together, even though I want to. I don't want to be upset that you're seeing Declan. I don't want to be upset that Penny broke up with me because I constantly made things hard for her. I don't want to be upset anymore about James leaving, but my heart's not listening to my brain, and I'm still so hurt and angry. But I... I'll get through it. I just need some time."

"I'll help you get through it," I told her. "I promise I will. Just come home. Tell me where you are, and I'll come get you. We've been so worried, not sure what happened to you."

"I sent you a voicemail when I decided to leave," she said on a sigh. "I didn't think you'd worry because I explained why I was leaving."

"I still don't get it, Summer. Why?"

"I know, and you probably won't, but I'm the one who has to listen to the voices in my head telling me I don't fit in, that I don't belong. I don't want to believe the lies anymore, so I'm seeking help."

"But why do you need to be away from us to seek help? Wouldn't it be better to have your family around, supporting you through it?"

"Because, there's so much going on right now and I just need to focus on me for a while. Everybody has their own thing going on, and I have mine. I swear, Dad, that's all it is. I'll be fine."

"So, what am I supposed to do, Summer?"

She smiled at me, her face a picture of innocence. "I'm an adult, Dad. I have to learn to handle tough situations, and right now I'm doing what is best for me. I'm sorry the way I had to go about doing it, but I promise I'll keep in touch with you every single day, like we used to. Will that make you feel better?"

I sighed, not liking this one bit. I didn't just want to see her on Face Time. I needed to see her in person—to hug her. I wanted back our movie nights, her stealing handfuls of popcorn from my bowl after demolishing hers.

However, with the exception of begging and cajoling, I had no idea how to get her to return home.

"At least let me know where you are," I begged her.

She shook her head. "I know you mean well, but you'll only be here the first chance you get. It's better this way. As I said, Dad, I'll call you, let you know about my progress. I'm not doing this to be cruel, or to make anyone worry. I really am not. I just need to work out some issues, and I'd rather work them out on my own. Can you understand that and not hate me for it, please?"

What choice did I have? If I pushed too hard, she might change her mind about calling me every day. At least I would have that to assure me that she was okay. Grudgingly, I nodded. "I can *never* hate you, but don't break your promise to me, Summer. I'll be expecting your call every single day. I don't like you being away from us, not knowing where you are, but you're right.

You're an adult. Just keep in touch or I'll worry. I'll still worry, but less."

She chuckled, but the sound came out as a sob. "I will, Dad. I have to go."

"I love you, Summer."

"I love you too, Dad."

She blew me a kiss then hung up, and I cried again, because it still hurt knowing she was not in danger, but not certain of where she was. She *wasn't* fine. My desire to go to my kids' rescue whenever they had a problem was innate to me and would never go away. I wanted them to be happy, and I'd do anything to achieve that.

I'm an adult, Dad. I have to learn to handle tough situations.

Yes, she was an adult. There was little I could do, but accept her calls every day and ensure she was progressing well. Hopefully, she would come around soon and get back to her life. It didn't sit well with me at all that my daughter was going through such emotional turmoil though, and I wondered if I could have done anything differently.

I was always positive that I had done a good job by them. Maybe I shouldn't have taken on extra shifts sometimes, or asked my neighbor Debbie to stay with Summer for me, but we'd needed the money. Auggie had needed braces and then later retainers. Summer had needed costumes for recitals. Oscar had needed new gear for sports. Three kids ate through your pocket fast.

When I'd composed myself, I washed my face in the bathroom, then started on the calls I had to make. Officer Pike answered his phone after the first call went to voicemail and I called him back. I relayed the information to him that I had heard from Summer who promised to keep in touch. He was empathetic throughout the whole thing, advising me not to hesitate to call him if I needed his assistance further. I was surprised at the offer, but then I remembered he'd had a private encounter with Declan.

It never ceased to amaze me how much my man could get done. While I was in a relationship with him because I loved him, I couldn't deny the privilege that came with being loved by a man of Declan's caliber.

After the police officer, I called the twins to relay the news to them. I couldn't get Oscar, so I left him a voice-mail, telling him to call me, or Auggie. I broke the news to Auggie who was surprisingly quiet. I thought he would be quite upset with Summer for leaving, but he only sighed and agreed to give her space while making himself available to her if she needed him.

Then he passed the phone to James, and it became complicated.

"Where is she?" he demanded impatiently.

"I don't know," I answered. "She said she was fine and needed a little time to sort through her feelings."

"And you believe her? What if she's lying?"

I couldn't blame him for thinking stuff I already contemplated. "She could be, but we can do nothing but trust her. She's not a child."

"Then why did she run away like one?"

Irritated, I snapped into the phone before thinking. "You mean why did she pull a James stunt?"

The other end of the line became silent. I closed my eyes tight and cursed myself on the inside for bringing him more pain than necessary. He already beat himself up so much about Summer. My words must have been a slap in the face.

"I should go," he stated. "Keep me updated on her progress if you can."

"James, don't go," I groaned into the phone. "I was out of line. I'm sorry."

"Sometimes I wonder if I should have stayed away from everyone," he said, his heart bleeding over the phone. "None of you will completely let me forget the terrible mistake I made, will you? I'll constantly have it thrown in my face, even though I already acknowledged how wrong I was for what I did. What must I do, Owen? I can't roll back time, but I'm trying to make up for it."

"I didn't mean to get upset," I answered. "I do believe you're genuinely sorry for all that happened. It's just that I expect you to be the one to empathize more with her, since you would have known what it's like to feel suffocated and needing the space. For the record, I don't like it either. I hate that she's out there somewhere, and I don't know how to get to her, but at the same time, she's asking me to trust her that she's okay. She's an adult, and I have to do just that. Trust her. Plus, she did promise to keep in touch with us. At this stage, all I want is for her to overcome whatever emotional struggles she is going through. If it means she needs some time to speak with somebody other than her family, I'm willing to give her that."

James's sigh was heavy. "You're right. You're so damn insightful about these things, Owen. And you know our kids so well. Will you keep me updated when she gets in touch with you?"

"Sure thing. I will. I should go now."

"Alright, Owen."

I hung up the phone and ran a hand over my face. I had spouted a lot at James, but it was just as much for me as it was for him. I needed to take my own advice and trust Summer, even when my instincts wanted me to search all of Columbus until I found her. I needed someone with whom to talk everything over, but Declan —always a great listener—was not around. He'd been gone for way longer than I had thought.

I realized then that he never mentioned where he was going when he'd left earlier.

15

DECLAN

"Are you sure there's nothing else I can do?" I asked Owen's daughter as we came to a halt at the door of her new fully furnished apartment. I was exhausted from all I'd had to do since I'd located her at the rundown motel. Regardless of how wealthy I was, it had still taken time to pull off moving Summer to a new apartment in less than twenty-four hours. There was no way I could have felt comfortable leaving her at the motel if I wanted to sleep well at night. Because she didn't want to face Penny, we'd gotten her new things to tide her over until she felt strong enough to encounter her ex and move out.

"I can't think of anything," Summer replied, her tone quiet. She had been subdued since she had called Owen and spoken to him earlier, while I'd done my best for it not to be obvious that I was listening in on the conversation. When Summer had broken down and started crying, my feet had itched to go over to her and take the phone out of her hands. I just knew Owen had been crying too, and the urge to comfort him was so strong.

"Well, you have my number," I told her. "If you think of anything, don't hesitate to call me."

She nodded and swallowed, but didn't comment. I was relieved our interaction had transcended her despising me. If ever I thought I had done the right thing, I was appeased by the grateful look in her eyes. She had tried opposing me finding her a new apartment at first, but then she had caved in when it had become one of the several conditions of me not telling Owen exactly where she was.

"And don't forget to call your father every single day," I stated, hoping she wouldn't prove me wrong. "He'll already be worried that he doesn't know your exact location, so give him that at least."

"I won't forget."

"Good. Take care, Summer. I do hope everything works out for you in therapy."

I turned to go, not waiting for a proper farewell from her, because I had been away from Owen all day, and I was dying to see him. I felt guilty for not explaining to him earlier where I was when I had called to inform him I would get to our suite later than I had planned. I still had no idea how I would break the news to him that I knew where Summer was staying, but I couldn't tell him. This was a recipe for disaster, a very foolish idea that could ruin our relationship. God knew I didn't want to lose Owen, but what could I have done? Forced her to reveal her location to Owen? That would not have helped her at all.

I was hoping Owen would come to understand why I had made the promises to Summer that I had. For him. Because his kids were his world, and he would want them to be safe and in good health. I was simply trying to do that for Summer.

Before I completely turned away, I was surprised to find Summer's arms thrown around me. I stiffened, the urge to push her away strong, because despite being affectionate to Owen and Ridge, I was not necessarily very receptive to others invading my space.

"Thank you, Declan," she said softly, her arms tightening before she let go and eased back. "I feel horrible for the way I've treated you. And yet, you did all this for me. Why?"

I patted her shoulder, not surprised to find affection in my heart for her. I already adored Owen's boys, but Summer had been difficult. Over the hours we had spent apartment hunting, however, and getting everything ready for her, I'd come to see bits and pieces of her that hadn't shone at all.

She was a funny girl with a dry sense of humor. Sharp-witted and sweet when she wasn't busy hating me. But she also had a profound sadness about her, and that was the reason I'd caved in to her demands. She hadn't done this just for attention. She really believed she had to work out her issues in therapy without the interference of her family.

"A large part of it has to do with your Dad," I answered. "I care about him so much, and seeing the way he broke down when we didn't know where you were, hurt. I promised him I'd look out for you guys, but not only that, I can see the younger version of myself in you at times."

"Well, thank you."

"You're welcome, Summer. Have a good evening."

Silas was waiting for me as usual. He had to be as tired as I felt, but he didn't even show it. At my approach, he got out of the car and held the door open for me. I smiled at him gratefully, because I was exhausted with everything I'd done to ensure Summer was in a safe place. And the worst part wasn't over yet. That would be facing Owen.

Not only had I leased Summer the apartment, but I had ensured her fridge was stocked with provisions she would need. I had thought about paying for her to stay at a hotel, but with her relationship having ended, she was heartbroken about living with her ex, and she needed a more stable living condition. I saw no good coming out of her going back to her apartment, tiptoeing around someone who was also a part of the reason she was hurting. I had no idea how long she would be in therapy either, so an apartment had seemed like the best bet. Even if she ended up returning to Penny, I couldn't count it as a loss, because I was thinking of her best interests.

I had wanted to change her therapist as well to someone who I knew to be of excellent repute, but she attested that she had enjoyed her previous session with the woman, so I conceded in letting her continue given I paid for the sessions. She had spaced out her next appointment because of the cost associated with each visit, but that would only delay her getting the help she needed to deal with her feelings of insecurity and her abandonment issues.

"Thanks, Silas," I told the man, squeezing his arm gratefully as I slipped into the backseat of the car.

I groaned, leaning into the comfortable seat as I checked the time on my phone. I had been gone for several hours, and it was almost eight at night. Poor Owen had to be wondering where I was, but other than calling him once, I'd given my full attention to Summer, ensuring that she had everything she would need while on her own.

As Silas drove us back to the hotel, I admitted to myself I had no idea if I had done the right thing or not. At one point, I convinced myself it was not too late to divulge Summer's location when I got face to face with Owen, but I already knew I couldn't. I had given Summer my word. There was no way I could have a better relationship with that girl if I broke her trust now.

"You think I did the right thing, Silas?" I asked the chauffeur, when he pulled up at the front of the hotel.

"There can be a thin line between right and wrong at times," he answered without giving a definite answer. "I mean, someone else looking on might say it's wrong not to let Owen know where she is, but your intention in all this matters. So the question is, why did you agree to keep this a secret?"

"Because, it seemed to be the last thing she had going for her," I answered tiredly. "It was the one thing that she could control, and I didn't want to take that away from her. I do believe she will work it out on her own. She's a smart girl."

"Are you prepared for Owen's reaction?"

I groaned. "Think it's going to be bad?"

Silas turned sideways to be better able to look at me. "That depends, sir."

"On what?" For some reason, tonight he seemed to be talking in riddles, when I wanted straightforward answers.

"On how much you trust each other," he answered. "How much faith you have in each other. I daresay this will test your relationship, probably far more than anything else has. It's important that you be frank with him about the why of it. Hopefully, he'll understand that you'd never do anything to hurt any of his kids and that you went into this with good intentions. Let's hope."

For once when Silas drove away and I entered the hotel, his words didn't offer me much comfort. I rode the elevator which reached our rooms quicker than I wanted. I stood outside, frowning at the door for about five minutes, before I finally caved in and decided there was no helping it.

Owen would understand. He had to. Summer was in a safe place. She had more than enough to tide her over. She was seeing someone about the turmoil of emotions she was experiencing, and she knew she could call me if she needed anything. She would also call Owen every single day. I had done the best I could while respecting her wishes.

And what about Owen's wish to find his daughter?

Shit, I was no longer positive about the right thing to have done.

You can still tell Owen where she is.

And break Summer's trust? I couldn't.

I unlocked the door and entered the room, closing it behind me with a soft thud. I found Owen on the bed, flipping through the channels while scowling at the big screen. When he spotted me, he dropped the remote to the bed and made to get up.

"No, don't get up," I said, walking over to the bed and sinking gratefully onto the mattress to sit.

"You look exhausted," he said, getting out of bed anyway. He was a sight for sore eyes, wearing only a pair of shorts that showed off his hairy muscled legs, and a T-shirt that did wonders to the width of his shoulders. My Boy was a walking advertisement for sex. And the damnedest thing about it was that he didn't even realize how attractive he was.

"I *am* exhausted," I said, glaring at my shoes as if they'd take themselves off my feet. "I think being bedridden while I recuperated from the surgery has made me soft. What do you say? Help me with my shoes?"

"Poor Daddy," he teased me as he reached for my right foot. "Where have you been all day? I know you called that you would be late, but I didn't know you would be *this* late. Hope you don't mind, but I had to eat dinner without you."

"That's fine. Something important came up."

He glanced up at me, the scowl he had on earlier completely gone. *I do that to him. I make him happy.* My heart squeezed at the thought of destroying that happiness with what I had to share with him.

"I've news to tell you," he said, beaming a smile at

me as he removed my shoe and sock. He reached for my left foot, his attention fully on my face while his hands moved. "You'll never guess who called me today."

"No? So why don't you tell me?" I hated playing into the game, but I wouldn't rob him of the joy of telling me he had heard from his daughter.

"Summer!"

My other shoe came off and then he was shifting my legs apart to wedge himself into the V of my thighs. With a laugh, he gripped my face and kissed me hard.

"She's okay! I mean, I still have no idea where she is. She doesn't want to tell me just yet, but she promises to keep in touch, and who knows? Maybe tomorrow or the day after she'll cave in and let me know where she is. I'm just so relieved she's fine."

He threw his arms around my shoulders and hugged me. I clung to him, squeezing him to my body, reveling in the solid mass of his frame leaning into me. I refused to believe this was the last time I would hold him. Regardless of how he reacted when I told him the truth, we would get through this. We had to.

"That's amazing," I murmured, and almost chickened out in keeping the secret from him. It would solve a whole lot. What was the use of telling him I knew where Summer was if I wasn't going to tell him her location? I would only be tormenting us both. But I didn't want to lie to him.

"It is," he murmured. "I wanted to tell you all day, but when you called me earlier you seemed to be in a rush, so I decided I'd wait until you returned."

"Yeah, about that." I ran my hands down his sides to

grip his narrow hips and eased him away from me to create space between us, but I didn't let go. "I need to talk to you about where I've been."

He scratched at the back of his head. "Do we have to? I don't really care as long as you're back."

I frowned at him. "Owen, where do you think I was?"

He shrugged. "I don't know. I tried not to think about it." His cheeks bloomed red with guilt. "I admit at first I thought it odd you were gone for so long. I surmised that maybe you, uh, were with someone, but then I realized how ridiculous that was. I trust you, and you'd never hurt me."

His words were that proverbial knife thrust into my heart. He trusted me never to hurt him, and here I was about to disturb the balance of our relationship.

"I'd never intentionally hurt you, Owen," I told him softly. "If I do, it would be because I have no other choice."

He frowned at me. "Why do I have the impression there's something you're not saying?"

"There is," I responded, and when he tried to step back, I kept my hold onto him until he stopped trying to get away.

"What is it?"

Before I responded, I stared into his anxious face, the way he clenched his jaw in anticipation of what I was about to say. He was trying to control his breathing, perhaps so I didn't realize how bothered he was by this conversation, but his hands were unsteady at his sides, and I hated that I was the cause of his dismay.

"Owen, you remember how I told you I'd be there for not just you, but also your kids?"

He frowned at me. "What does that have to do with anything?"

"Do you remember?" I prodded. "You said they weren't my concern, but I told you that they're a part of you, so they'll always be my concern as well."

"Yes, I remember. Declan—"

"Please, hear me out. Try not to react until you hear everything."

His hands gripped mine at his hips. "You're making me worry, Declan."

16

OWEN

Telling Declan he had me worried was an understatement of how I was feeling. I was clinging to the edge of my sanity, trying not to think the worst, but what the hell was I supposed to believe? He had been gone all day, and finally, he came home exhausted and making chit-chat about not intentionally hurting me. That sounded a lot like what you'd say to someone when you knew you had done something that *would* hurt them.

"I was there when Summer called you," he said.

I stared at him blankly, because I heard the words, but the meaning wasn't instantly clear.

"Remember I told you about the PI I had trying to find her? This morning I received a call from him that he thought he'd found her. I didn't want to tell you without being absolutely certain, so I left to check out this girl, and it turned out to be Summer."

"Ooooookay." I drew out the word as I tried to

understand what he was saying. "You mean, you know where Summer is?"

He nodded. "She was staying at a motel not too far from here. She mostly kept to herself, so she had no idea about the missing person report that's been floating around."

"But that's good news," I said, still bewildered at the somber look on his face. "That means we can go get her. I can help her to figure things out."

His groan filled the room. "Summer obviously knows her dad very well. She told me this would be your reaction."

"You found my daughter, Dec!" I cried, finally freeing myself from him. "Of course, I'm going to bring her back home. If she doesn't want to stay here in Columbus with Penny, she can always return home with us. I'll have to delay moving in with you, but I've got to ensure she's fine."

I moved toward the closet where I stored my carryon so I could change into something a bit more appropriate before we went back out to get Summer. When Declan didn't move, I stopped at the door of the closet and frowned at him.

"If you're too tired, you don't have to come. Get some rest. Silas will take me."

"Silas can't," he answered. "He's been out with me all day. He has to rest."

I shrugged. "Then I'll drive myself."

"Owen, come back here and talk to me."

"I can't. I need to find her before she leaves again."

I grabbed my bag and brought it over to the bed,

pulling out a pair of jeans. Declan got up and walked over to me. He took hold of the jeans. "Owen, let go."

"What? No. I need to get dressed."

"Owen, you're not going to get her."

My head snapped up to stare at him. "What do you mean I'm not going to get her?"

"I had a long chat with Summer today," he answered, his voice so soft I strained to hear him. "In fact, we spent all day together. I had to move her out of that motel room and ensure she had somewhere pleasant to stay while she worked out her issues—her depression, the abandonment issues."

My heart lurched in my chest before it thudded a sense of doom. His words replayed in my ears about not wanting to hurt me.

"Declan, I don't understand. Summer's not depressed."

"Maybe it's not as severe as it could be," he answered. "But it's there. Coupled with all the new changes that have been happening, she has asked for some space and some time to adjust, to work things out in her head."

Slowly, what Declan was trying to tell me sank in, and when it did, it sank far and heavy. I dropped the jeans and stared him in the eyes.

"What are you saying?"

"Baby, I'm sorry, but I can't tell you where she is," he answered, his voice low and gritty with something akin to pain. But it couldn't be that. I was the one who was hurt at his words.

"What do you mean you can't tell me where she is. You *have* to tell me!"

"I promised her," he answered, reaching out a hand to me, but I side-stepped him.

"Why would you *do* that? You know I've been worrying about her. Why are you keeping her whereabouts from me?"

"She had her mind all made up, Owen, that she wants to work things out on her own," he answered. "She was pretty sure you'd do this—want to be involved despite her wishes. I was afraid she would only disappear again. Given the situation, I worked out an agreement with her. I wouldn't disclose her location, but she has to get in touch with you every day, so you know she's fine. If she breaks her promise, then I can divulge the information."

Anger mounted inside me. "You had *no right* to make such a promise to her!" I thundered. "None! Why on Earth would you even agree to that? So, what are you going to do? Keep that information from me? For how long?"

"I don't know," he answered. "But I do know she's seeing someone, so hopefully she will be in a better frame of mind soon, Owen."

That wasn't what I wanted to hear. How could he seriously know where Summer was, but refused to tell me? Why would he do that to me?

"I don't get it," I said, my voice hoarse. "Why are you telling me this if you've already decided that you can't tell me? Why not hide it from me that you've spoken to her?"

"Because I don't plan on lying to you," he replied. "It

was never my intention to go into this and lie about it. When I promised I'd do whatever I could to help out your kids if they needed it, I never thought I'd be caught in the middle of things like this. What do you want me to do, Owen? Violate your daughter's trust and her wish to solve her problems herself? You've always told me that you raised them to be independent thinkers and for them to be able to handle themselves. Summer wants to demonstrate that. I couldn't take that away from her."

I inhaled a deep breath. "Dec, for the last time, where is Summer?" I didn't want to listen to his reasoning.

He shook his head. "I can't tell you, but I can say she has a nice apartment in a safe location. I ensured she had whatever she needed, which is why I was out all day. I couldn't get her to change her mind about doing this on her own, but I could make her comfortable. She will get in touch with you just as she promised, and she knows she can contact me if she needs anything."

Without a word to him, I stalked over to the bed and grasped my jeans from him. This time he didn't hold onto them, but allowed me to take them from him. Somehow it hurt even more that he no longer put up resistance. He no longer tried to stop me when I needed him to make me understand why he would do this.

I tugged off my shorts and got dressed in less than a minute. I couldn't stay with him right now. I couldn't look at him knowing he knew the whereabouts of my daughter, but refused to share it with me. I also felt betrayed that she had trusted Declan enough to talk him into secrecy while leaving me in the dark.

What happened to being partners and not hiding things from each other? He should *never* have made that promise to Summer. That made me pissed. That was not a promise he should have made to her. Knowing Declan as a man of his word, he would not tell me where she was without her consent.

"What are you doing?" Declan asked me.

I was too livid to answer him. He trailed me over to the bedside table where I took up his phone, my hands shaking as I rang Summer.

"Hello, Dad," she answered.

"Declan knows where you are?" I demanded over the phone. "Why? Why would you tell him and not me?"

"I didn't tell him," she replied. "He found me, and I had no choice then. Why? I should have known he wouldn't live up to his word and not tell you. I just thought he could be trusted since he went through all this trouble today to get me an apartment, food, and all. He's even paying for the therapist I want to see."

All the nice things she was telling me that Declan had done for her didn't register beyond the fact that Declan knew where she was and wouldn't tell me.

"He hasn't told me," I answered. "He refuses to. Tells me that you made a pact about you calling me every day in exchange for keeping your location unknown."

"He didn't tell you?" she asked, the surprise giving her tone a squeak.

"He refuses to."

"Wow. I can't believe he's kept his promise."

I felt hurt at her assessment of the situation. "Summer, how could you?"

"Dad, I tried explaining to you earlier. Don't blame Declan for not being able to tell you much. This is my choice not his, and today he's shown that he loves you. A lot. If he's keeping his end of the bargain, it's only because he loves you. There's no reason for you to be mad at him."

Except there were reasons.

I raised my head and stared at Declan who was standing in the same spot, listening to my end of the conversation. He didn't say a word, but his eyes were remorseful. I glanced away, because I didn't want him to cajole me into letting it all go.

"I don't even know what to say right now," I said softly in the phone. I felt like my heart was being ripped into two by these two people who I cared for so much.

"Oh please, Dad. I *will* call you, let you know what's going on. I promise I will."

But I was tired of the promises. That was the cause of everything. The promises and the leaving. The not knowing.

"There's nothing I can say or do to get you to change your mind about telling me where you are?"

"Nothing," she answered quickly. "Remember when I was twelve and sometimes Debbie from next door came over to watch me while you went out on a weekend? You didn't usually go out, but you did a few times, and now I understand you needed to get away. It might not have been for a long period of time, but it's the same. I just need some time. It doesn't mean I'll never tell you where I am. Just for now."

She had made up her mind, and I couldn't say

anything to sway her. We exchanged goodbyes, and seconds ticked by as I tried to process all this information. My daughter, not wanting me to know where she was, because she believed I would try to find her. Declan, the only person I'd allowed myself to be so wholly vulnerable with, wasn't sharing her location with me.

"Owen, I'm sorry," he said, but I still refused to look at him. "Please don't think badly of me because I'm trying to help your daughter. You know I'd never do anything to spitefully hurt you and your kids. *Nothing!* I love you."

Too bad I wasn't feeling it right then. If he loved me, he would give me the information I needed.

"I need to go for a walk," I said, pushing away from the bed to stalk toward the door. "I need to clear my head."

"I'll go with you," he stated. "Just give me a minute to put my shoes back on and to change my shirt. I've been wearing this all day."

"I'd rather go alone."

"It's late, Owen. I'm not letting you go walking on your own."

"But I'm trying to escape *you!*"

Declan blanched, and color rushed into his cheeks. His eyes went steely hard as they did when he was angry. The expression didn't last long, however. The anger was replaced by profound sadness. He made me feel guilty for what I'd said, even though I was still upset with him.

"Then I'll walk some distance behind you," he said, sitting on the bed and reaching for his shoes which I had helped him to take off just a few minutes ago. "I just need to know you're alright. You're upset, and I can even appreciate why. Truly. I didn't expect you to act otherwise. You love your kids. I get that. You just want to know they are okay."

I glanced at the door just a couple of feet away. I willed myself to leave, be alone and try to make sense of why Declan wouldn't tell me the truth. Did he expect us to continue our relationship as usual with this big secret between us?

But he told you he knows. That should count for something.

But not what mostly counted.

17

DECLAN

It took a lot for someone to hurt me. Usually I had to care first, and there were very few people I allowed close enough to hurt me in that regard. But Owen, had the potential to gut me, and his reaction to the news that I was aware of Summer's location did just that. I hated keeping the secret from him, but what choice did I have? I had promised Summer.

I thought he was coming around when he didn't argue with me going on his walk earlier. After walking with Owen—although 'with' was such a stretch given the distance he'd put between us—we'd returned to our suite where the tension swelled in the air around us. My attempts to get Owen to talk to me were all futile. Being on the other end of the silent treatment sucked, and now I understood why he hated when I did it to him.

While I had been in the shower, he had gone to bed, and when I slid in beside him, he'd shuffled over as far as he could go without falling over the end. Not wanting the space between us, I'd wrapped an arm around him just the same and kissed the back of his head, whispering to him once more that I was sorry. He hadn't answered, but remained stiff in my arms until he eventually relaxed as he fell asleep.

Waking up to an empty bed in the middle of the night was not what I expected from someone who had fallen asleep in my arms earlier. *Had he woken up and moved to the couch?*

"Owen?" I called softly, and when I heard no response, I climbed out of bed. I checked the bathroom first which was empty, so I took a leak before I went searching for him. There was no sign of him on the sofa, and the only other place to look was the balcony. If he wasn't there…

At the thought of Owen having left while I was sleeping, a cold dread overcame me. He couldn't give up on us so easily after everything we'd been through. He just couldn't.

My feet quickly ate up the distance to the balcony. The door was partially open, so I figured he was there, but I didn't feel relieved until I saw him for myself. He stood at the iron rail, just looking out at the panoramic view of the city at night.

I stared at him without making my presence known, contemplating how much of this scenario resembled the morning after we had slept apart due to Ridge's untimely presence in my home. He hadn't held onto his anger, and the whole thing had been resolved with relative ease, but it was perhaps too much to hope that this would turn out likewise.

"Owen." His back stiffened at my voice, and he made no attempt to turn and face me. I persisted. "Come back to bed. You need your rest."

Seconds ticked by without an answer from him. And then...

"It's useless. I can't sleep."

And it was my fault of course. I waited for him to add that part, but he didn't elaborate.

"Then at least lie with me," I suggested. "Let me hold you and whisper how sorry I am in your ears until you believe me."

"You don't need to apologize. You've done that enough already."

His words caught me by surprise. Apologizing was the only thing I knew how to do after my refusal to tell him Summer's location. If he didn't want that, what else was I supposed to do?

"How long have you been standing out here?" I asked, walking over to the lounge chair. I left enough space for him in case he felt like joining me. *Wishful thinking.*

He shrugged. "Two hours? More? I lost track of time."

"Why didn't you wake me? I would have stayed up with you."

His sigh cleared the distance between us. "You were tired. It wouldn't have been fair to you."

I sprang to my feet to know he had been looking out for me even though he was upset. Taking this as a good sign, I approached him to stand at the rail, but leaving a few inches between us.

"Are you still upset with me?" I questioned, needing to know what kind of mood he was in.

"No," he answered. "I'm not. I'm hurt and disappointed. In you. In Summer."

Somehow that hurt more than him being angry at me. His anger I could deal with. There was still passion in his displeasure, but what was I supposed to do with his disappointment? He seemed so lifeless, all the light, the spark in him, snuffed out because of a promise I wanted to keep to his daughter. But what was worse, having Summer disappointed in me or Owen?

"I understand I shouldn't have promised her something like that," I said, desperate for the spark to return to him. "If I could take it back I would."

He shook his head, glancing sideways at me, and the pain in his eyes hurt more than anything else I had ever experienced. Knowing I caused it, that hurt, that ache inside him. It ripped me apart seeing him that way. I was used to Owen being feisty, laughing, teasing. This was my doing, and I needed to fix it.

"Do you want to know what I've been thinking all this time I've been out here?" he asked, eyes locked with mine.

I wanted to look away when I heard the words, I was certain I would hate, but I couldn't seem to break our gaze.

"I kept thinking, when would you leave too?"

I stared at him blankly, not understanding what he meant at first, before his meaning sank in.

"You think—" I choked on the words, because I never even thought about him pondering so deeply. I turned to him, too concerned to be worried about whether or not he wanted me to touch him at this time. I placed a hand at the side of his neck, stroking the vein there. "Owen, you think I'm going to leave you?"

His eyes finally dropped. "I don't know what else to think. Why does everyone leave? James did for so long. I know I shouldn't be thinking this way, and I swear I don't hold anything against them, but the twins left too. They could have stayed in Cincy, but they opted to remain here. Now Summer's gone, and I don't know where. It's only logical for me to wonder when you'll leave too, right? When will you have enough of me?"

"Jesus!" I breathed hard, because every word he spoke hit me hard. "Is that what you really think?"

"What else am I supposed to think?"

"That I love you," I answered easily, stroking the side of his face. "That I'm only complete when I'm with you. That you've brought me the most joy I've had in my life for a very long time. I wouldn't give that up for the world, Owen. You have to tell me that you know that."

"I... I..." He gave a shake of his head as he grappled with what to say.

Anything. He could have believed anything else and I would be able to handle it, but I couldn't have him think that I'd leave him. I hated having to go against my word to Summer, but at this stage I was desperate.

"Alright." I gave in. "I can't have you doubting what we've been building together. If me keeping this a secret from you is going to affect us so much, then I'll tell you."

To my surprise he shook his head. "You can't tell me."

"What? Why not?"

He gave me a sad smile. "Because you're right. You didn't hear how betrayed she sounded when she thought you'd told me where she was. She extended an olive branch to you, and I'd be cruel to ruin that."

"But if this is going to make you upset, babe, and start questioning things between us, I'd rather have you know."

"I won't let you tell me," he reiterated. "Please don't break her trust in you, Declan. You got her to call me and that has to be enough for now. If you break her trust, you'll never get it back, and it's important to me that you get along with my kids."

"Owen, are you sure?" I asked him uncertainly. "Because I can live with Summer hating me, but I can't live with your indifference."

Owen took one step closer, his arms going around my waist. "I could never be indifferent to you."

Relief washed over me, and I clung to him. Forehead pressed to his, I closed my eyes and basked in the moment of having him forgive me.

"I swear I'll make it up to you."

When I opened my eyes, it was to find him smiling tiredly at me. "No need for that. Just promise me she's okay."

"She is," I answered. "I have pictures. Do you want to see?"

He nodded. "Please."

"Hang on." I kissed his lips hard, and he released me. I made the quick trip inside to grab my phone and returned to the balcony where he waited still by the rail. I held a hand out to him, needing further reassurance that he really had forgiven me.

He took the hand proffered to him and allowed me to pull him over to the lounge chair. I didn't have to coax him into my arms. He knew his rightful place, and he took it. I couldn't resist kissing his temple before opening my phone gallery to him.

He took the phone, and I held him as he scrolled through the photos I had taken that day. Most of them were of the cozy apartment where she now lived.

"This looks nice," he said in awe. "You were able to get her an apartment in a day?"

"There are perks to dating a billionaire," I teased him with a chuckle, that ended on an uff when his elbow connected with my stomach.

At my exaggerated groan of pain, he turned to regard me in horror. "Oh my God, did I get you in your wound?"

"I'm kidding. You got me nowhere near my wound. It's just nice knowing you don't want to gut me anymore."

"Don't be sure about that." He smirked at me. "There's more than one way to make you pay. Now how about that? Boy gets to put Daddy in the corner for a change."

I shifted uncomfortably, and he laughed, the sound I had been wondering if I would ever hear again.

"Is that what you want to do?" I asked him. "Punish me?"

He shook his head. "Of course not. I like to be the one on the receiving end of your punishment."

"Then what do you want from me? You don't want money or expensive things, then what?"

He glanced at me slyly, his gaze shifted over my torso. "You already know, but I'm willing to wait forever if I have to."

There was no mistaking what he was talking about this time. He couldn't have been clearer. He wanted me. *All* of me. And if he was trusting me enough to know where his daughter was when he didn't, then surely if there was ever a man who deserved my body without limitations, then it would be him. If he trusted me so explicitly, I should be able to trust him likewise.

"What if I told you there's no need to wait."

18

OWEN

I stared at Declan in surprise, trying to decide if he was being serious, or joking again. The night had been such a topsy-turvy emotional upheaval that I was undecided. The last time we had touched this topic he had promised to think about it, but I for one never thought to bring up it up again. I never expected him to agree to it either.

Declan bottoming for me would be the sweetest gift he could ever offer me, but I had to be certain he wasn't offering himself up as some sacrificial lamb because he thought it would make me feel better about our disagreement earlier. I had been livid about him keeping Summer's secret from me, but I'd also had the entire night to think on it while he slept.

If he betrayed Summer's trust, he would never be able to regain it. That wasn't the kind of relationship I wanted him to have with my kids. And so, even though it still bothered me that Summer preferred me not to know her location, I tried to see things from her perspective. She was at least right about one thing—if I knew where she was, I would have been there instantly. I couldn't help it. So *maybe* it was just as well I didn't know.

The part that had me coming around was accepting the fact that neither of us would have known where she was if he hadn't gotten involved and hired a PI. She would not have known I hadn't received her voicemail. She wouldn't have gotten in touch with me to let me know she was fine. She wouldn't have promised to get in touch with me every day.

Declan had done way more than I had given him credit for. The pictures he had shown me of the apartment where Summer was staying revealed the place was even nicer than where she'd been living with Penny. How could I stay mad at him for taking care of my child like a Dad?

"Are you telling me you won't mind bottoming?" I asked him for clarification.

"Let's think of it as my Boy taking care of my needs," he answered with a tentative smile. "You think you have what it takes to please your Daddy?"

"I know I do," I replied with a grin. "But how do I know you're not just agreeing now, because you want to make up for earlier?"

He curled his fingers into the hair at the back of my neck. "Honestly? I would be lying if I didn't admit that is a part of it. For one, I think for putting up with me after everything, you deserve a reward, and you've been clear you want to tap my ass. So why not allow you to have your heart's content?"

"Wow." I bit my lower lip, trying not to show my exuberance. "That's some reward."

"One you won't get every day, so I advise you to take it while the offer is on the table, baby Boy."

When he purred *baby Boy* in that way of his, sending shivers down my spine, I knew he was in the mood.

"As good as this sounds, I'm not sure your reason is good enough for doing something you don't really want to do."

"I wouldn't be offering if I didn't want to, Owen," he replied. He eased back against the lounger in a reclining position and pulled me on top of him. "The truth is, the way you decided to trust me with regards to Summer has reminded me that trust is a two-way street. Trusting me with your children, Owen, is for me, the ultimate truth of how much you love and believe in me. You deserve to have my complete trust and devotion in equal measure. This is me handing over to you the last piece of me that I had locked away with the intention of never giving to anyone. But I give it to you, Owen. *Only* you."

Holy hell. The man made sex sound so serious, and I was suddenly nervous about whether or not I wanted the responsibility of taking care of Declan in this regard. What if I turned him off bottoming for life?

"I still say we should sleep on it," I suggested, chickening out. "If tomorrow you still feel the same way then, yeah, I'm definitely not turning down the offer."

"I won't change my mind."

I pecked him on the lips and said with more confidence than I felt, "I hope you don't." I kissed him again, taking my time to explore his mouth. When he moaned, I released his lips and looked down on him. "Am I crushing you? I was thinking this is nice. Just lying out here, doing nothing, but make-out and drive ourselves crazy wanting to get off without actually getting off."

He groaned again, his hands going down my back to cup my ass. He nudged his hips upwards until our groins were pressed against each other. He was already semi-erect, but what could I say? So was I.

"You're the one into orgasm denial, not me," he remarked. "I'll hump your leg until I come. You can save yourself for tomorrow when we wake up and you finally fuck me. You can come inside me if you want."

I smiled down at him. Declan's needs and mine were different when it came to bottoming. I could already tell. I was greedy, wanting him to control my climax, my body and to do with me as he wanted. This wouldn't work for me topping him though. There would be no me dominating him. There would be me loving on his body and reveling in the fact that I could please him this way.

"Can't wait to *make love* to you, Daddy. I'll please you well. You'll see."

I lowered my head and kissed him again, over and over. I gave him a precursor of what would come if he still wanted me when we woke up. I was so hard my cock hurt to be released, but as he'd said, I loved being denied, and I could wait to get off. I didn't mind him humping my leg though. I even reached a hand down between us to help him to his climax. When I felt how close he was, I moved down his body and took his cock into my mouth, moaning around his hot seed that splattered my tongue.

I crawled back up to face him, and we shared a smile

before I shuffled to lie half-on top of him and on the lounger. He linked our fingers, and from time to time he would kiss my temple. It was so peaceful lying in his arms that it was little wonder I dozed off. I woke up to him gently setting me aside, and when I made to get up, he pushed me back down.

"No, don't get up. I'll get us a blanket."

He returned shortly after with the cover he had pulled from the bed. The maid had come by while he was away to bring us fresh linens. He fixed the cover over my frame before rejoining me. I snuggled into him, one arm around his waist as I fell into a deep sleep.

"Okay, it's morning, and I haven't changed my mind. Let's do this."

I blinked the sleep away from my eyes and focused on Declan who was staring back at me. He must have been awake for a while, because his expression was clear while I was trying to make sense of what he was talking about.

"It's too early," I moaned, snuggling my face into his warm crotch. "I need coffee before I can make sense of what you're talking about."

He ran his fingers through my hair. "You making love to me, Boy. Do you want to or not?"

I popped my head upward to gaze at him owlishly. "You mean now?"

"Yes, now. I'm in the mood. Somebody's been rubbing up on me all morning. Now I'm too stiff to function unless you take the edge off. So, are you going to do it?"

"I haven't even brushed my teeth yet," I protested. "I'm not going to let your first time be with morning breath. I was thinking of something special."

He scowled at me. "Special's for another time, Boy. On your knees."

He was serious. I'd never been fully awake so fast in my life. I sat up on the lounge chair then stood to stretch. Apparently, I had enjoyed rubbing subconsciously all over him too, because I had morning wood, all stiff and curving upward.

Noticing Declan's stare, I pushed down on my erection, fixing it into my shorts. "Just give me five minutes, and I'll be back."

"I'm counting down," he said, and I hurried through the door.

With some fast movements, I managed to pee, brush my teeth then grabbed what I needed from the nightstand and hurried back to the balcony. I skidded to a halt.

"Oh fuck."

Declan was completely naked, lying spread on his stomach, his feet slightly apart. He inclined his head to watch me.

"Did no one ever teach you it's impolite to stare?" he scolded. "Now come on over here and show Daddy what you want to do to him, Boy."

"You're fucking perfect," I said in reverence as I walked over to him, admiring the slope of his shoulders, the curve of his spine, the twin dimples above the swell of his ass. *And his ass*. Of course I had seen his ass before, but never in this light. Never as a place where I would take my pleasure. Round and firm, I could bounce quarters off that baby.

"Is there anything you don't want me to do?" I asked, coming to sit by his hip. The morning was light out, but not fully yet. The sun had just begun to peek out from the east, draping the sky in splashes of color.

"I can't think of anything," he answered. "I trust you more than anyone else in my life, Boy. You'll make Daddy proud in the way you handle your business. Won't you?"

My heart skipped a beat, because I was suddenly afraid of letting him down. *No, I won't let him down.*

"I promise, Daddy." I placed my index finger at the top of his spine and slowly drew down. I stared in awe at the goose pimples that broke out on his skin.

"My safe word is 'pineapple'," he said, which wasn't a surprise because he hated the fruit. "I say that word and you stop. No matter how good it feels. Got it?"

"Yes, Daddy."

"Good. You may proceed."

I couldn't help chuckling at his words. "You make this seem like some experiment."

"In some ways it is for me," he answered, his voice quiet. "Remember I've never done this before, so be gentle."

"You're in your Boy's hands," I reminded him. "I'll take care of you."

With that, I leaned forward and found his lips with mine. We kissed from our awkward position of his head turned to the side. After we broke apart, I kissed his cheek, the lobe of his ear and his shoulders.

I took my time kissing Declan's broad back, my hands reaching down to brush his naked ass as I kissed along his spine. His body mellowed under my caresses.

Licking and kissing the supple curves of his ass, I breathed a sigh of contentment that he was trusting me. When I spread him open, I felt the tremor that ran through his body. The small darker hue of his pucker pulsed in anticipation. I swooped down to claim my prize, concentrating on my licks at first.

"Fuck," he moaned, shifting beneath me.

Apprehensive that he had forgotten his safe word, I raised my head to ask him if he was still okay with this, only to end up with his hand in my hair, and my face smothered between his cheeks again.

"Don't stop," he growled at me.

At the need in his voice, I stopped doubting myself and took care of him, taking my time to pleasure him in a way that left him sweating, swearing, and moaning all into one. His ass at some point raised as he went on his knees, rocking back and forth on my skilled tongue. Yes, I took credit for the way he had transformed from unwilling to have anyone touch his ass, to pressing my head into his crack and demanding more.

Whether on the receiving or giving end, Daddy was still bossy, and I liked it.

With one last swipe of my tongue over his puckered entrance glistening with my saliva, I reached for the lube and coated him generously. Here came the hard part, ensuring he was prepped enough to take my cock with ease when it was time. Luckily, we weren't in a hurry to get to nowhere fast.

I played with Daddy's hole the way he instructed his Boy to. A finger into that tight rim that sucked in my knuckle, but protested against any more at first. I took great pleasure in opening him up, watching in fascination, placing a kiss on his back every so often or on his ass cheeks as his muscles loosened. I went from one to two fingers after several minutes. I never lost patience, intending to do this right. It was his first time. He had entrusted me with breaking in his ass, and I wouldn't disappoint.

"Boy, if you don't get inside me soon, I'm going to flip things around and bury my cock inside you," he gasped, when I had three fingers inside him.

With my other hand, I playfully slapped his ass. "Who's in charge?"

Declan glared at me over his shoulder. "I am. Don't forget that."

I chuckled at the fierceness of his tone which didn't match the look of pleasure on his face when I curled my fingers and hit his soft spot.

"Oh fuck," he grunted, eyes closing. "Do that again. But with your cock. Seriously, Boy, I'm already on the edge. Now help Daddy get over."

"With pleasure."

I removed my fingers and spread him open again to thrust my tongue snugly inside his body. I couldn't get enough of Declan. He was so sexy, so virile beneath me, lean muscles and all. If this was the one and only time I'd get to experience him trusting me this way, I'd never forget it.

All lubed up and playing it safe by squirting more inside him, I lined the head of my cock perfectly and pressed into him. I was satisfied that I had prepped him well enough that there was no undue hindrance as I slid inside his body. His tight heat enveloped around my cock, his rim pulling at my flesh, and I had to blink against the spots of color that exploded before my eyes.

"Sweet fuck!" I gasped. "Oh my God!"

Clinging to his cheeks, I pulled out slowly and slid right back into him, developing a rhythm that would get him used to the breadth of my cock inside his body. He reached back to rub a hand down my hairy leg, slapping me. "Harder. Fuck me, harder."

I laughed and kissed his back. "Greedy, bossy Daddy."

"Yeah, and you love it," he threw back at me. "You're loving Daddy's hole, aren't you, Boy?"

I thrust into him again, delighting in the tight bounce of his ass. "Yes!"

"Then show me how much. Really get in there, Owen."

With his permission, I pulled him to his knees so I could reach his cock while I pumped into him. He leaned back into my thrusts, head on my shoulder as I kissed his face.

"Oh fuck, Daddy," I groaned, caressing him. His hips were moving in tandem with mine, thrusting back eagerly. With my free hand, I caressed his body, his abdomen, finally getting to the stiff points of his nipples. And that was when Daddy went wild in my arms.

I released his dick and with both hands made work of his nipples the way he liked. Never letting go of the twin points, I canted my hips, working him hard and sweet with long then sharp strokes, keeping him guessing. He grasped his cock, blowing hard, our moans filling the balcony in the breaking of dawn.

"Fuck, I'm coming," he groaned, and I thrust into him harder, squeezing on his nipples. His body stiffened against me, his mouth open, gasping, desperately seeking air as he exploded over the lounger, his thigh, and his hand.

His hole became impossibly tight, clenching around my cock. I couldn't hold on. I was lost in him, and what he had given me today, despite his earlier misgivings. I contemplated pulling out of him and finishing on his ass, but there was a piece of me that wanted to have me inside him as he had been inside me countless times. To own all of him just as he owned me.

"Can I come inside you?" I gasped at his ear. "Please, Daddy."

He groaned. "Yes. Why waste what's mine, Boy?"

His words unraveled me. I leaned back, balancing on my arms so I could get a better view of my cock thrusting inside him. And then I was flying. *Holy fuck!* He blew my mind when he clenched his already tight muscles around me. With several sloppy thrusts that made no sense to any rhythm, I finally buried myself deep inside him as I came at last.

"Fuck. Fuck. Fuck," I repeated over and over, incoherent to say any other word, but it was enough.

It took a few seconds for me to come back to myself, lost as I was in him. I pulled out and wrapped my arms around him, my chest pressed to his back.

"Thank you. That was amazing. Did you enjoy it?"

He gave me a sly grin over his shoulder. "I'm not complaining. Yes, you were amazing."

"No regrets?"

"None. Boy, I don't remember asking you these many questions after we had sex."

"Do I get to do it again?" I asked.

He chuckled. "Now who's being greedy?" He pulled me down to lie with him on the lounge chair. He lay on his stomach and me on my back, our fingers intertwined. "Seriously, you want to do it again?"

I shrugged. "I would love to. Every now and then."

He leaned forward to kiss me, slowly, deeply, tenderly. "How about we turn it into some kind of reward—when you're a good Boy?"

"I'm always a good Boy," I said, with an incorrigible grin.

"Hmm. We'll see. Now be a good Boy and run me a bath. It will take me just a few to be in working order again. This time I'll fuck you in the shower, return the favor."

I shouldn't have been so turned on by his words given the climax I'd just had, but what the fuck, I was ready to have him inside me again. Watching myself claim him had just reminded me how beautiful it felt being on the receiving end.

"I'm on it."

19

DECLAN

"It's for you," I told Owen, when I checked my phone screen and identified the caller as his daughter. I smiled, feeling quite pleased that Summer was keeping to her word. We had spent the last two days relaxing after the scare of the days before, and also to ensure Summer upheld her part of the bargain. She had. She spoke to Owen every day and, surprisingly, me as well. The girl was starting to grow on me. She might be too old for me to play stepdad, but I was able to be a friend, and that I was.

"I can't believe she calls every day," Owen said in awe, as he took the phone from me.

"I'm glad she's sticking to her word."

Our bags at the front door, I left Owen talking to Summer to return to the car. Silas smiled at me, his arm resting on the window. He nodded to Owen. "See? Everything turned out fine. There's a lot of love and trust there."

I nodded my agreement. "That's for sure. I don't know what I would have done if he was less understanding."

"He has the heart of a father," Silas remarked. "One who is quick to forgive. One who thinks about the needs of everyone else and not just his own. I predict you two will go a long way."

"We couldn't have done it without you." I squeezed his arm affectionately. "In a lot of ways, Silas, you've been like a father to me. I can't thank you enough for that, but you deserve a vacation, and I won't hear a word of refusal from you. Owen and I will manage. We talked about it for quite some time last night, and we plan to send you on a cruise. Just tell me where and I'll make it happen."

"You've already made up your mind, haven't you?" he said, shaking his head at me. "In that case, sure I'll take the time off, but you don't have to send me on a cruise. I have some old friends I haven't seen in a while. It's probably time I pay them a visit and mend some fences that've been down for too long."

I gazed at Silas thoughtfully, taking in his slight frown and the somber look he wore. He was such a private person that I didn't know much about him in all the years we had been together. He was divorced. That much I was certain of, but I couldn't recall any relationships over the years, and it had been a lot of years.

"Need any help in that regards, you just name it," I told him.

"I may take you upon that. Do you need me to find you another driver in my absence?"

"I'll take care of it," I answered, shaking my head at him. "You go on home and enjoy the time away with your friends."

Of all the times Silas had seen me make out with Owen in the backseat like we were two horny high school kids desperate to lose our virginity, he'd never once blinked an eye. His face turned red however at my mention of his friends, confirming my suspicions that whoever he was referring to were way more.

"I'm sure I will. I may be out of town, though."

"Even better. Change of scenery and all. Good luck."

"Thanks."

He nodded his farewell and honked the car horn at Owen who waved at him. I watched Silas drive away, before returning to the porch and to Owen, who had wrapped up his conversation with Summer.

"That was a quick call," I stated, because they could talk for an hour sometimes when she called. "Everything okay?"

He grabbed my shirt front, and with a lazy grin pulled me to him. I went along with his sweet version of *manhandling* me. He teased a lot since I'd allowed him to top me, and I was grateful for the experience which had somehow brought us even closer. All our barriers seemed to have been lowered, leaving nothing standing in the way of our love for each other.

His kiss landed at the corner of my mouth. "Everything is awesome because of you." Another kiss landed directly on my mouth this time. I walked him into the door at his back and with him leaning heavily against it, I showed him how grateful I was for his understanding and forgiveness.

I broke the kiss, both of us panting lightly. "Welcome home."

His eyes widened. "This is home now, right?"

"Yes, for always."

His face split into a grin. "I feel like I should be taken over the threshold, to commemorate this moment, don't you?"

"Isn't that for brides?" I asked on a laugh, as the door opened behind his back to reveal David, who had been alerted to our arrival.

"Welcome home, sirs," David greeted us, standing aside for us to enter.

"Thanks, David," Owen and I said at the same time.

David grabbed our bags and walked ahead. Before Owen could follow suit, I stopped him with a hand on his arm. He turned to glance back at me. "Wha—! Declan, what are you doing?"

I wanted to laugh as I bent, grasped him around the knees and lifted, but needed all my breath to sweep him off his feet. He wanted to be brought over the threshold, I would indulge. He was heavy, but I could manage five seconds of lifting him. No biggie.

"You said to carry you over the threshold," I gasped. "I'm giving you your heart's desire."

"I didn't mean it, you crazy man!" He half-shouted and half-laughed.

At the commotion, David turned, and the butler, usually so stoic, burst into laughter. Owen grabbed onto my shoulders as though afraid we'd tumble to the floor, and as I had no intention of embarrassing myself that way, I walked us both into the house like I'd suddenly been gifted with the strength of Hercules.

"There!" I wheezed in triumph, carefully setting him back on his feet. "How's that?'

Owen was laughing so hard, tears spilled down his cheeks. "You're something else, you know. No wonder I'm crazy about you."

"Good. Now let me pretend my back didn't almost give out. That's just practice anyway for the day I do bring you over the threshold as my husband."

I watched him sputter, eyes wide as I walked by him. It took him a few seconds to process what I'd just said, and then he caught up with me.

He cleared his throat. "So should I move some of my stuff here or something?"

I hadn't even thought about that. I turned to him, making no move up the stairs, as I was certain there would be a ton of emails and phone calls for me to return. I'd left everything behind when I'd followed Owen to Columbus, and spent way longer than I had planned there, because of the mishap with Summer.

"Why not?" I shrugged, because it didn't matter.

He glanced around us. "I'm not sure my stuff will fit in with yours. They're pretty old and would look odd."

"They'll fit," I told him. "Just like we do. You'll see."

"It's too late to do that today. Maybe I'll get on it over the weekend?"

"Sounds good. If you need a moving truck let me know."

He nodded and inhaled deeply. "I can't believe this is officially home."

"Believe it, baby, because I never planned to let you go since you walked through the front door the first time." I laced his fingers through mine and rubbed at the fourth finger of his left hand. "I'll not stop until I make every bit of you mine." I sealed that promise with a quick kiss. "I'll probably be locked into my office for an hour or so answering my messages. You don't mind entertaining yourself, do you? Hmm, maybe I can get to them later."

He shook his head and stepped away. "I may go up and take a nap."

"Good. I'll check on you in a bit."

"You don't have to."

"But I want to."

"Okay."

I watched him ascend the stairs, torn between going after him, and taking care of the responsibilities I knew awaited me on my desk. David and Charles had kept me up to date on the different emergencies that needed my attention that I hadn't been able to check out. As much as I wanted to follow Owen, I knew I wouldn't be able to nap too with so much to do.

I stopped at the kitchen and grabbed a bottle of water along with a protein bar on the way to my home office. No telling when I would resurface, depending on how much I had to muck through.

Sorting through my messages alone took some time as I had to go through emergency calls that had to be made, those that could wait, and those that would go unanswered.

One of the calls was from Julia, the agent who had assessed Owen's manuscript. I had to tell him about that as reluctant as I was to do so, now that I knew the sort of effect it would have on him. I never intended to keep the secret for so long, but with not wanting to add to the recent troubles with his daughter, I had ended up keeping this from him for entirely too long. I had to come clean to him tonight and hope our fight was too recent for us to go through another.

I called back Julia and got her secretary who I advised that I still needed time to talk to Owen about her interest in his manuscript. After that call was made, instead of tackling the other ninety-nine things on my desk to do, I rocked back in my chair and tried to think of how to break the news gently to Owen about finding and reading his manuscript. In hindsight, I wish I'd exercised enough self-control and trusted that he would share it with me when he was ready. I'd robbed him of the opportunity to tell me himself.

Fuck. I scrubbed at my face. If I didn't get my shit together, I would royally screw up the best thing that had ever happened to me. I couldn't afford to let that happen.

Half an hour later, I had a plan that included a fine dining restaurant and a dish of truth served for a course, when a knock sounded on the office door.

"Come in."

I expected Owen to still be asleep, so when he entered the office, I was surprised. More so when I saw what he carried in his hands. It was the box with his manuscript. *Could he tell I had read each page not stopping until the last was read leaving me on a cliffhanger? Could he tell how*

*much I wanted to know of how Jack reacted when he saw Daniel
again?*

"I'm sorry if I'm disturbing you," he said, remaining
uncertainly at the door. "I wasn't so sure I'd still feel this
way later, so I thought to get it over and done with right
now."

"Yeah?" I couldn't keep my eyes off that damn box.
"It's okay. Come on in. Share what's on your mind."

He closed the door and approached my desk.
Walking around, he used his foot to push my chair back-
ward a bit, making room between the desk and myself.
He perched his ass at the edge of the desk.

"Remember when we talked about keeping secrets
from each other back in Columbus?"

Damn. This is it. He knows. "Yes?"

"You've opened up your heart and home to me," he
continued. "And you are right. There is something I am
keeping from you, and I don't want to keep it a secret
anymore."

"Okay."

"I was in your closet—"

"Our closet," I corrected him.

He smiled at that. "Yeah, *our* closet, and I saw the
way you rearranged everything to give me space. All that
space is mine, right?"

"Of course, it's yours."

He nodded. "Exactly what I thought. I have a space
in your heart and in your home. Thank you for that."

I placed my hands on his thighs and rubbed. "There's
no reason to say thanks. I'm the lucky one for having you

here. You could have turned down my offer to move in with me."

"I'd be crazy to do that. This is home. With you wherever you are."

"And your heart is my home," I answered, never once dreaming I'd say such things to someone. "And as long as I am there, everything is right with my world."

His gaze dropped to the box, and he removed the lid. He took out the sheaf of papers I'd neatly fixed the way I had found them. "When I got suspended from my job, you asked me if there's anything else I ever dreamed of becoming. The truth is that I do, but I've been partly afraid of being ridiculed, and I didn't want to have you laugh at my dreams. Some people may think it silly, so I've never talked about it to anyone before. I've always kept this part of me locked up. You're the first person I'll be sharing this with, although one day I hope I'll be able to share it with the rest of the world."

"Go on," I encouraged, knowing full-well I could stop him right there and tell him I already knew, but he seemed to have put a lot of thought into this, so I refused to take that away from him.

His gaze remained on the papers, and a worried frown marred his features. "I… the truth is that I write," he remarked. "I write totally sappy romantic stories of men falling in love with each other, and this is something I should have finished a long time ago, but I couldn't because then I'd have to face what to do with it. I still don't know what I'm going to do with it, but I'm going to finish it."

I tightened my right hand on his knee, pulling my chair closer to him. "Owen, look at me."

"You're not going to laugh, are you?"

"Look at me, and I'll answer your question." He finally raised his tortured, uncertain eyes. He really thought I would ridicule what he did. "Why do you think I'll laugh at your work?"

"I didn't just start to read after James left me," he answered. "I used to read a lot when I was a kid. I read my first romantic book when I was thirteen. My mom always had a shelf of romance books with those hot guys on the cover, bare-chested and gorgeous. At first, I was drawn to the books because of the cover, but then I read one, and I was hooked. They were het romances and still I read them. I loved them. I used to sneak a title or two up to my room to read. Then she caught me one day when I was sixteen. She was appalled that I was reading romance books. The next day she donated all the books on her shelf. I felt so ashamed I stopped reading, and then I rediscovered them when James left and I had free time."

"No disrespect meant, Owen, but your mother sounds like a piece of work to me," I told him. "She should have supported your love of reading."

"But they were books for women," he murmured. "Men aren't expected to be into that sort of thing."

"Says who? That's the worst case of bullshit I've ever heard. I'd never ridicule your writing. In fact, I found it downright sweet. There's a whole lot of heart in that book you wrote, Owen. I can't wait for you to write the ending."

His eyes widened in surprise. "What do you mean?"

I didn't have to say anything to him. I could have pretended this was news to me, but it was time for all the secrets to come out.

"That's the secret I alluded to in Columbus," I revealed. "When I was cleaning out the closet, I accidentally knocked over your box and the papers scattered to the floor. I had no intention of reading it when I saw what it was, but my curiosity got the best of me, and before I knew it, I was reading every single word."

Panic entered Owen's eyes, and I heard his sharp intake of breath before he let it out slowly, contained. "You read all of it?"

"I'm sorry. I know you're pissed. I probably should have stopped reading after the first few pages, but then I got hooked and couldn't stop. You're really good, baby."

He blinked a few times. "You read it and you *liked it*?"

"I loved it," I answered. "You write your guys with such passion and heart. I could see a lot of you in Jack."

He deflated, and the worry left his eyes. "I know somewhere in here I should be concerned you read it without my permission, but I'm so relieved someone likes it. I can't believe you read and liked it. You're not just saying that to make me feel good, are you?"

"Hell no. If it sucked, I would have said so, then taken you up to the bedroom and fucked the disappointment out of you."

He laughed which made me smile at his obvious delight. "You can still fuck all the happiness inside me." He placed the box onto the table on top of everything I had been working on, but I didn't care. He slid off the desk and into my lap, leaning forward to kiss me, but I averted my head.

"Before I get distracted, there's something else."

"What?" he asked. "Tell me fast, because you liking my book is doing crazy things to my insides right now. I'm so keyed up, I need you to get me down."

Oh hell yeah. I wanted to get him down alright, but first...

"I had your manuscript assessed by an agent," I told him.

Owen stiffened. "You did what, Dec? Noooo, why did you do that?"

I tightened my hold on him, afraid he would spring up any second now and walk out on me for overstepping the boundary. "I know I went a bit too far. Blame my habit of micromanaging everything, but I wanted to be able to give you good advice, and I'm not much of a reader as you already know, so I wanted someone professional who could pass on valuable feedback."

"I can't believe you *did* that," he remarked then groaned. "Who am I kidding? I *can* believe you did that."

"Don't be mad."

"I should be." He frowned at me. "It's just like my credit card all over again. I wish you hadn't done that, Dec. You had no idea what I planned for that story. Whatever you do, I don't want to know what the agent says when they contact you."

"She already has," I answered.

"I mean I— wait, *what?*" He shook his head. "No, I don't want to know. Whatever she said that is."

"Not even if you learn she loves it and wants to talk

to you about getting your novel out there when you're through with it?"

The annoyance he had worn only a second ago turned to wonder. "She wants my novel? She really does?"

I smiled at him. "Yes, she does. I told you it was good."

"And you're *not* paying her a ton of money for her to say that?" I scowled at him. "Hey, I know you, Dec. If you thought that would make me happy you would, so don't go scowling at me."

"Maybe I would, but I swear, not one penny crossed hands."

A dreamy smile came over his face. "So, she really liked it all on her own?"

I nodded. "She did."

"That's amazing." He had that dreamy look on his face for a few more seconds before he sobered. "But still, I can't accept whatever offer she has."

"What? Why now?"

"Because this is something I want to do on my own," he replied. "I know it's hard for you not to help out when you want to. And that's the only reason I'm not as upset as I should be, because I know you meant well. *However*, I don't want to have doubts about what I do, Dec, and if you're in the thick of things throwing your weight around, I won't know if I'm really good, or people are being accommodating because I'm in a relationship with the rich and powerful Declan Moore."

"Trust me, my name has nothing to do with her interest."

He shook his head. "That's the only way you get out of me being upset with you right now. I know you're a man of your word, and I want you to promise me that you'll not get involved. You'll allow me to go through the process. If I fail, you'll be there with lots of hugs, kisses, and comfort sex, but nothing else."

"But I can—"

He started to withdraw from my lap. "Comfort sex. That's the deal, Declan."

"Fine," I finally agreed. "I'll butt out of your writing career *unless* you ask for my help. How's that?"

He winked at me. "Good Daddy."

I scowled at him and pinched his ass. "The publishing industry can be pretty harsh, Owen. I don't want you to be hurt by insensitive people in the business."

He shuffled back up my lap to fit comfortably against me, my groin snugly nestled against his ass. He was rubbing himself slowly against me, almost as if he didn't know what he was doing to me.

"That's where the comfort sex comes in," he teased, before he took on a serious expression. "You'll be my support, my safe haven whenever I need to cry or let off any kind of steam."

"You'll at least use your card to take care of production costs such as editors and stuff?" I asked, reminding him that even though I wouldn't play an active role into him becoming a published author, I wasn't completely leaving him at the mercy of his meager purse strings.

"Sure. I will, but the publisher pays for that."

"Good. Then I'll butt out and let you handle it."

"Thank you for that. I know it won't be easy for you." I groaned. "No kidding, but rest assured, I won't do anything without talking to you." Owen lifted his ass slightly, then ground into my lap, further stimulating my semi. "Are you trying to tell me something, Boy?"

He wrapped his arms around my shoulders loosely, and leaned forward so his mouth was directly beside my ear. His hips continued a slow determined roll into my lap. "If I knew how to write it down in a mathematical formula for you, I would. But since I'm only good with words, here goes. I want you to fuck me, Daddy. First round. Don't make me come. Use me only for your climax."

I was only too happy to indulge the paradox that was my Boy. So sweet yet so hot. So calm and yet so spirited. By the time I bore him down on top of my desk, legs held apart as I fucked him, I prayed to God that the helpers had gone, because there was no quieting his moans. Most of all, I didn't give a damn. He had opted to let it go instead of being furious with me, which he had every right to be. Silas had been right that he had a big enough heart to accommodate the mistakes I made from time to time.

And as a note of apology, I gave him exactly what he wanted, to be used, worked rough by my cock, my jizz deep inside him while I denied him his own release. For now. I had every intention of making him explode later tonight after our dinner date.

20

OWEN

"I'm glad you're making progress, Summer," I told my daughter over the phone as I parked at the foot of the porch of our house. *Home.* The word felt strange in my thoughts, and I frowned at the two-story structure, wondering what it was about this place where I had lived for the past twenty-three years that had changed.

"It's a lot easier to breathe, and I finally feel like I'm figuring things out," she said, sounding every bit as contented as she claimed.

"That's awesome, honey."

"I... I'm supposed to invite James to the next session with me," she stated. "Umm, do you think he'll agree?"

Having kept in touch with James about Summer's therapy sessions, I was quite certain of my answer. "Pretty sure he'll only be too happy to. He wants to mend fences, but he's also willing to work at your pace this time instead of pushing. I'm sorry we tried to push you to accept things you weren't ready for."

"It's okay. I know everyone meant well." There was a lull in conversation, and I took the opportunity to get out of the car, closing the door gently.

"Everything okay with Penny?" I asked, because they had made up—of sorts.

"Yeah, we're going to catch a movie later. We're trying to take things slower this time. Perhaps it wasn't a good idea to move in together so soon."

"Well, there's no need to rush so take your time figuring things out."

She let out a loud sigh. "You've been so understanding about this. Are you… you're not still mad at Declan about knowing where I am, are you?"

"Truth? I do feel sad about it at times, but I'd rather him know than both of us be in the dark."

"Good. You shouldn't be mad at him. He's such an awesome guy."

I smiled on the way to the porch. "Yes, he is. I'm at the house to sort through the things I'll take with me, but I figure I'll be leaving most of the stuff for you guys to go through and decide if you need anything."

"It's funny how you say that."

"Say what?"

"The house. Normally you'd say home."

I paused at the front door. That was it. That was what seemed so different this time.

"Yeah, it doesn't feel much like home without you guys here with me," I answered. "You three were my home, but you're all gone to live your own lives, Declan's now my home."

She chuckled. "Being in love makes you sound weird, but I like it. I'm so happy for you. You deserve it more than anyone I know."

"Thanks, Summer." I closed my eyes and leaned my forehead against the door. These days I felt like everything had fallen into place. My kids were happy, Declan was happy, and *I* was ecstatic having picked my manuscript back up. I felt like I now had everything.

"I'll let you get to moving in with your boyfriend," she said on a snicker. "I have to go now anyway. Talk to you later."

"Will do. Love you."

"Love you too, Dad."

She hung up the phone, and with a big smile on my face, I entered the house. Everything was exactly the way I had left it, but it felt strange coming back here. Had it only been weeks since I had moved in with Declan to help take care of him? It felt longer. Our entire relationship felt like we had been together for years, but it had only been a few months.

My phone beeped, and I was surprised to see a text message from Summer given we just spoke to each other. Thinking it might be urgent, something she had forgotten to tell me, I opened the message and read it.

62 E Gray Street, Unit 3B

It took me re-reading that one line about six times before it finally made sense. Then came the overwhelming sense of wanting to see her in person. Every day we talked either by voice or video calls, but now I'd get to see her, touch her. I had Declan's car. What was to stop me from driving to Columbus and showing up at her door?

I didn't.

I suppressed the urge, understanding even more now than before why she wouldn't have Declan share her location with me. No powers on Earth would have kept me away from her if Declan had told me where she was the day he had found her. I could get crazy about my kids at times, especially Summer, but they were adults who would come to me when they needed me.

I smiled, sent her a quick acknowledgement then slid the phone back into my pocket. I felt ten thousand pounds lighter, because as much as I had gotten over Declan knowing her location, I was still a concerned dad, and a part of me remained on edge, wondering. Now I didn't have to wonder anymore.

I walked through the house, starting from upstairs, reminiscing about the good times and some bitter ones too that I had spent here. Every area of this house was characterized by the memory of my kids, trapped in every wall, the echo of their laughter, the tears, and the anger. Once upon a time, I would have never considered moving away from it all because of the nostalgia, and it was bittersweet running my hands over the surfaces of their things.

It was easier than I'd thought to decide what to take with me. It turned out that I didn't want much after all. The furniture and such weren't necessary, and the boys could have it. Otherwise, I'd just donate it to people who could find use for it.

I popped in the earbuds of the new cell phone Declan had bought. I found the audiobook I had started last night in bed while waiting on Declan to finish up in his office. I had to scrub the audio back a few chapters after realizing I had left the audio running when Declan had finally come to bed, and without a word, had pinned me to the mattress. He hadn't given me any time to pause the audiobook, and frankly, I'd been too into him to care.

It took me almost two hours to sort through everything upstairs. My bedroom took the bulk of the work as I went through all my clothes, piling them up into donations for Goodwill, and those I didn't mind taking with me. I had to throw out personal effects from the bathroom, clear out my dresser, the drawers of the night tables. Every now and then I would find something that made me pause and reminisce. Like the button the twins had given me one Father's Day, and the sorry pair of socks Summer had made for my birthday when she was ten.

When I finished with my bedroom, I stood back and stared at the lifelessness of it all. Everything had been stripped away, including the bed linens. All that remained were the furniture and rug. Closing the door felt so final, but it didn't hurt as much as I thought it would. Mostly I was excited about going home to Declan.

Home's really where the heart is.

Summer's room came next, but I didn't touch much, just some odds and ends of hers that I wanted to keep. The rest she would sort through when she got here my birthday weekend. The twins' rooms had less stuff since they had moved out years prior. They still kept enough for when they visited, however. I was claiming their high school framed pictures, putting them away in the box marked *Kids' Memories* when an arm came around me from behind.

I was so startled I dropped the box, but then I inhaled the familiar scent of Declan. With his other hand, he popped the earbuds out.

"I didn't mean to surprise you," he said. "Just how high did you have the volume anyway? I must have called to you a dozen times."

I turned in his arms to find myself pressed up against him. My favorite place to be. I smiled at him sheepishly.

"It wasn't too loud."

"I'll be the judge of that." He plucked the phone from my pocket and checked the volume. His mouth turned down in disapproval when he saw I had the volume at maximum. "Are you trying to damage your hearing?"

"I didn't think it was that loud," I murmured and tried to change the subject. "What are you doing here?"

He was dressed in one of his many power suits since he was supposed to be at the office. I had to say the suits worked well for attracting my interest.

"Do I need an excuse to see you?" he asked. "And don't think you can change the subject, either."

"I wasn't trying to change the subject."

He raised an eyebrow, and it was impressive how he only got one to obey. "You weren't?"

I flushed. "Okay. Maybe?"

Without another word, he cupped the back of my head and pulled me forward. I needed very little persuasion as I curled into his chest and allowed the wreckage that I had come to expect from his lips. He usually left me completely befuddled. I clung to the lapels of his jacket, gasps and sighs escaping me as he deepened the kiss and made me weak in the knees.

"You're lucky I find you so damn irresistible," he said, finally breaking the kiss. "But not so irresistible that I'll let you get away with harming yourself." A quick peck to my lips. "When we get home, I need a hundred-word short essay on why listening at full volume is bad for you."

I groaned in dismay. I'd been good for so long that he hadn't really needed to discipline me. "But I—"

"You argue and it's another hundred words."

I promptly shut up. "Fine. If you insist."

I sounded petulant, but he only smiled. "That's a good Boy." He glanced around the bedroom with the twin beds. "How's the official move going? Don't you need a moving truck?"

I shook my head. "No. I'm not really taking much. I'll have the kids check out the house and take what they need, then I'll donate the rest of the furniture and stuff to charity."

"You do know you can make room for them at our home, right?"

"I know, but none of these things really matter. I have the memories. They're important. There's just one thing I really want to keep."

He glanced at me. "Which is?"

"Summer's crib." He didn't say anything for a while. Just stood there staring at me, and I rushed to explain.

"It's not that I want to keep it out or anything. It will be disassembled."

He frowned at me. "Is this your way of telling me you want more kids?"

My mouth fell open. "What?" I exploded. "Hell no. Of course not. I've already raised three, and it's…" I trailed off now realizing how horrified I sounded at the thought of having more kids when Declan was young. What right did I have to take that away from him? "Dec, do you want kids?" Maybe I would for him, but… I couldn't see myself going through fatherhood again with an infant.

"No, I don't," he answered, still frowning.

I didn't know whether to believe him or not. "Are you certain? I mean, you're just twenty-five. You have enough time to change your mind."

"I'm pretty sure I don't want to have kids," he replied. "Unless they're furries. I'd adopt a dog or two, but that's it. I'm not into changing diapers and stuff like that. No, kids are definitely not in my future."

Thank fuck for that. "Just so we're clear, I'm not opposed to furries, but I'm certain I don't want more kids in my future. If you expect that you should be open about it with me. I don't want you to be stuck with a partner who doesn't want kids."

"You worry too much," he said, walking over to the TV in the boys' room. "It's not that I hate kids or anything. When you do have grandkids, as I'm sure will be in your future with your kids, I won't mind having them around. It's just the idea of having our own being around *all* the time that causes me to shudder."

"Okay. So, furries, but no human babies?"

"Yeah," he agreed with a chuckle. "Definitely furries." He nodded at the video game console the twins had left behind. They'd upgraded to a newer version so hadn't bothered to take this with them. It had been sitting there for quite some time. The last time they'd used it had been around Christmas when they spent the holidays with me. "You play?" he asked.

I shrugged. "The twins taught me, but can't say I'm any good. I'm quite rusty."

He stooped, the material of his pants stretching taut against his ass, and interest made itself known in my own. Unaware of the effect he had on me, he rifled through the boys' video game collections.

"I doubt they have anything good," I stated, clearing my throat. "They took the fun ones with them."

"Hmm, pretty sure we can find something." He continued shuffling for a few seconds, before he made a grunt of satisfaction and rose to his feet. "*Mortal Kombat.* What do you say? Want to battle it out? See who's topping who tonight?"

I narrowed my eyes at him and cocked my head to one side. The thought of topping him again sounded good, but I anticipated he made the offer full well knowing there was no way I could beat him. "Are you any good? I've never seen you play before."

"I used to play a lot back in high school," he answered with a shrug. "And then some in college, but you could say I got too busy so I'm a bit rusty."

"Do I have any chance of winning?" I asked.

He laughed, then leered at me, raking me over with a smoldering gaze. "Depends."

I swallowed hard. "On what?"

He approached me and when he was within arm's reach, dipped his hand between our bodies to cup my crotch. "Depends on how good of a distraction you can be. Want to test the theory out?"

21

DECLAN

"You know when I said you could distract me, I thought you'd be more subtle about it," I grumbled, trying to keep my attention focused on the screen as Owen sank his ass onto my lap, forcing me to let go of the controller with my left hand. I quickly wrapped my arm around him to grab at the controller, but he nudged my arm away with his elbow, laughing.

"Finish him!"

"You're cheating!" I accused Owen, as the computerized voice concluded my character's fatal demise.

"Die!" he crowed in delight, his fingers moving rapidly over the buttons—down, down, forward, square —to deliver the mortal blow that sent blood, guts, and gore spilling.

I didn't know what stunned me more—Owen's ability to deliver a fatal strike which meant he knew way more than he'd let on, or him crowing at the bloody mess that erupted on the screen. I'd had no idea he could be this brutal. Damn, he was being ruthless alright, his ass bouncing in my lap from his excitement on winning.

"Why do I feel like you hoodwinked me?" I asked him, groaning at the semi I now sported because of him. If he kept bouncing on my lap like that, our game would end prematurely.

He leaned back, a hand behind my head and kissed me too quickly for me to respond. The look on his face radiated such joy that I couldn't even be mad at him for setting me up. I'd walked right into it, being easy with him because I had no idea he knew his way that well around a gaming console.

"The twins did teach me how to play," he crowed smugly. "And I might have snuck in here one or two times when I was missing them just because. Auggie taught me the fatal moves, but not for all the. Just enough for me to put up more of a challenge."

"And you couldn't have explained that before we started? I spent almost half an hour explaining to you how the buttons work!"

"Well, you were being so sweet about it, I didn't want to interrupt your lesson lest I get additional punishment."

I gave him a mock glare. "Get your ass off my lap, Boy. I would have been gentle with you, but now I'll show no mercy."

How a grown man forty-six-years-old had perfected the wide-eyed innocent look was beyond me. He aimed it at me now, and if I didn't know better, I'd fall for it again.

"But Daddy's supposed to let his Boy win," he murmured.

I cocked an eyebrow at him. "Says who?"

"Says the Daddy Boy Handbook." He gasped, managing to look appalled. "You mean you haven't read it?"

He had the look down pat, and my chuckle became a full laugh. Now I no longer felt bad about shucking the work on my desk aside and deciding to join Owen here instead. It was totally worth it just to be beside him, sharing in nonsensical chatter and trying to beat him at videogames.

"I don't hear you complaining about my Daddy duties," I said, and when he couldn't think of anything, I added. "Exactly. Now move your ass."

When he refused to move, I boosted him out of my lap, and he spilled onto the bean bag chair in a heap laughing. I hid my smile, giving myself a pat on the back for making use of the opportunity that had presented itself to me to get Owen's mind off the move.

We hadn't really spoken about it, but in the same way I hadn't wanted to give up my childhood home that held so many memories of my mother, I figured he would find it hard to leave all this behind. He'd watched all his kids grow up within these walls, then he'd released them into the world. I couldn't completely forget the meltdown he'd had when he'd asked me when I would leave him too. I needed him to know I would be there until one of us drew our last breath. Even then my heart would completely belong to him.

"Aren't you supposed to be at work by the way?" he asked, righting himself as I selected a new character and allowed him to do the same.

"I spoke to Summer," I answered, thinking of the

earlier call between her and me. Since keeping her secret, she had taken me for a confidant. At first, I thought Owen would have minded, but he just shrugged it off and stated Summer could confide in whomever she wanted to.

"Oh? She told you she sent me her location?"

"Yeah, she did."

He paused to glance at me. "Is that why you came here? To prevent me from running off to Columbus?"

I flushed. "I would have tried talking you out of it, but I wouldn't have stopped you. I know you're concerned, and you have every right to be."

"I am, but I'm confident she's trying to be the best version of herself, and that's all I can ever hope for. I'll always love her whether it's a week, months or years before I see her."

"Your heart's so damn big. You know that?"

Owen ducked his head shyly, but I didn't miss his frown. "It's what we do as parents. Be there for our kids in whatever way they need or don't need us. The same for the people we love, really."

I ruffled the top of his head and leaned sideways to kiss his temple. "Ready to get screwed? Best of six rounds?"

He licked his lips and grinned at me. "Ooh yeah."

Before I could respond, he pressed play and the countdown of round one to our next challenge began. I easily won the next game which he professed to let me have, to even things up and make our game a little more interesting. I didn't believe him and won the third. By then he was on his knees, tongue peeking out at the corner of his mouth. It might not have been his intention to distract me, but he did. I couldn't stop thinking of plucking the controller from his hand and instructing him where to put his tongue. Swirling over the head of my cock.

"Now we're even," he said, pumping his fist into the air, and I caught a glimpse of what he must have been like in his youth. Carefree with all his guards down.

I couldn't help my actions. I tugged on his arm, and he tumbled into me, protesting until I had him pinned beneath me on the bean bag chair, with my mouth fastened to his. I just couldn't resist how infectious he was, how sweet and tempting when he was this happy and carefree.

He dropped the controller, and with a moan, secured his legs around my waist. I reached beneath him to grab onto his ass, but barely copped a feel before we slid to the floor in a tangle of arms and legs.

Our lips dislodged, and Owen placed his cheek against mine and laughed. "I don't think bean bag chairs were made for fucking."

"I thought we were gaming," I reminded him as I rolled off him.

"Hey, don't blame me this time. You kissed me."

"And you kissed me back."

He stared at me as he picked himself up off the ground. "Right. Next time I'll just keep my lips closed."

"When one hole closes, another one opens."

He flushed and stood, tugging down his shirt. "I'm calling a break. I need to cool off. I think there's still some water in the cupboards. Want one?"

"Sure."

"I'll order a pizza too," he added, bit his bottom lip, and asked. "How do you want it?"

I gave him a suspicious look. "If we're still talking about the pizza, then Pepperoni and black olives. If we're talking a blow job, then wet and sloppy."

He laughed, walking backward from the bedroom. "You already got the latter last night."

"That's almost twenty-four hours ago!"

"You let me win and you can have all the BJs your dick can take."

"Hmm."

He paused at the door, his mouth hanging open. "Ouch. That's my ego you just killed for having to think about that." He did an impressive spin and disappeared.

"Well, don't go. Prove me wrong!"

His head poked back inside the room. "Sorry, Daddy. I'm retiring my BJs for the unforeseeable future."

I snorted. *Yeah, right.* If I called him back right now, he would gratefully show me how much his BJ skills did *not* stink. Really. He gave good head, and I needed to stop thinking about it or we'd never finish our game.

By the time he returned with two bottles of water, I had my desire under control. He tossed me a bottle, before dragging a chair over to the TV this time, leaving the bean bag chair to me.

"No monkey business," he stated, taking up his controller. "Let's get this show started."

The next two games were played fair and square. It was hard when both of us were concentrating, but I won both although barely. I didn't crow at my victory, but played him another round before tossing aside the controller and crooking a finger at him.

"Are we done?" he asked.

"We're just starting," I answered, checking my watch. "Pizza should be here soon, but I'm sure we have enough time."

"For what?"

Instead of answering, I rose to my feet and held out my hand to him. He put down his controller, placed his hand in mine and allowed me to pull him to his feet. He moaned a little and rubbed at his lower back.

"You okay?" I walked him over to one of the twin beds in the room and sat, pulling him between my legs.

"Yeah, I'm fine."

His back was probably hurting from the way he'd leaned forward in his chair, but he wouldn't admit it. He could still get touchy about his age. Instead of forcing it out of him, I dropped my hands behind him and kneaded his lower back.

"Oh God!" he gasped, placing his arms on my shoulders and closing his eyes. "Don't stop. That feels so good."

The position was not the best, but I was able to see his face while I continued massaging his back. He relaxed into my touch, and I continued the motions until he was pliant in my arms. Only then did I bury my face into his stomach and kissed him through his shirt.

"Do you know what you do to me?" I asked him on a contented sigh. "Let me give you a hint, Owen. I've never skipped work before just for personal fulfillment. Never."

His hands tightened on my shoulders. "I know. I feel the same. I'm about to move in with you, Declan, after only being together for a couple of months."

I glanced up to look at him, my cheek still on his stomach. "Are you okay with that? Moving in on such short notice? I don't want to make you uncomfortable, so if you'd rather wait..."

He frowned down at me. "Are you sure that's not second thoughts on your part?"

"I'll never have second thoughts about you, babe. This is as good as it gets for me, and from where I'm sitting, I have it pretty damn good. I could never ask for a better man to spend the rest of my life with. You see my mistakes, my imperfections, and you don't hold them against me. You don't let them change what we have, and that's important to me, Owen."

He pushed my shoulders until I was lying on my back. Instead of following to lie on top of me, Owen lay next to me on his side. I turned and reached for his hand. We didn't say anything, just lay there smiling at each other. Utter fools in love.

I'd never felt more like *this is it*, in my entire life. We went from staring at each other to moving forward, and then we were kissing. It wasn't hot and heavy like our earlier gropes. It was a soft and gentle caress of lips that gradually grew in intensity. We didn't touch each other's bodies. Just my lips, opening his, commanding obedience which he granted without hesitance.

His submission was the foundation of our relationship, because if he had not submitted, I would not have had the opportunity to be the decisive figure he now craved.

I moved from his lips to kiss the side of his face even as the doorbell rang. I ignored it, kissing his cheek.

"That's the doorbell," he moaned.

"Yeah? I hadn't noticed."

"I think it's the pizza."

I groaned, but backed off when he pushed against my shoulder. "Okay. Go get it and come back here posthaste."

He rolled off the bed then patted his pocket. "Crap. I'll have to get my wallet out of the car."

I shook my head. "That's too much trouble. Here."

I expected him to argue when I reached for my wallet, giving him the money to pay for the pizza. When he didn't, I give him a quick kiss, because the person at the front door was really pressing into the buzzer. I lay back onto the bed, my feet dangling over the edge with a goofy smile on my face. I couldn't remember ever feeling this relaxed. I probably had a million and one things on my desk to work on, but they could wait until tomorrow. Right now, my time was all Owen's.

I frowned when several minutes passed and he still hadn't returned. I rolled off the bed and headed down the stairs to look for him. I found him in the living room, not talking to the delivery guy as I had assumed, but a woman close in age to him. She was a little plump with cheeks that reddened at the sight of me, and I couldn't decide what to make of her.

"Babe, everything okay?" I asked him as both turned to watch me approach.

I didn't miss the way the woman's eyes widened at the manner in which I had addressed Owen, whose cheeks turned red as well. He didn't shy away from me though, but motioned for me to come closer.

"This is my neighbor, Debbie Holden," he stated. "She used to help me sometimes with the kids when I had to be out. She saw the strange cars parked in the yard and was checking that everything was okay."

"I'm sorry, I didn't mean to intrude," the woman said on a rush. "I didn't know you were entertaining, Owen. I noticed you haven't been around, and I worried something suspicious was going on that you didn't know about. For a minute there I thought you had sold the house and I was about to meet the new owners."

"That's really neighborly of you," I remarked. I couldn't fathom what it was like having neighbors so close. There were so many acres of land between my house and the next.

"Debbie's wonderful," Owen said. "This is my partner, Declan."

It didn't escape me that Owen rarely ever introduced me by my full name, as if he didn't want people to know that he was in a relationship with one of the wealthiest men in the state.

"It's nice to meet you, Debbie."

She wasted no time in shaking my hand. "Nice to meet you too. This is a pleasant surprise. I thought something was odd with Owen not being here. He's usually a homebody."

"I still am," Owen replied. "Just from his—*our* home."

Her jaw slackened. "So, you *are* moving out and selling the house?"

"Moving out yes, but no plans to sell the house yet. We still have to decide what to do with the place."

"Have you two been together long?" Her question was innocent enough, and I glanced at Owen, giving him the lead on this one.

"For a few months," he answered. "It was quick. When you know you've found the one, waiting makes no difference except keeping us from each other."

"Does this have anything to do with your boss?" she blurted out. "He came by to visit you a few days ago, and I told him I hadn't seen you in a while. Maybe I shouldn't have said anything, but I thought I was helping since he's your boss and all."

Owen's frown matched my own.

Why on Earth had his asshole of a boss visited him? Since the guy suspended Owen for being with me, I didn't have much energy to waste on him and discussions of him.

Thankfully, the doorbell chose that moment to ring.

"Must be the pizza delivery man," Owen announced. "I'll go get it."

"I should go now I know everything is fine with you, Owen," Debbie added, moving behind Owen who walked the short distance to the door. "It was nice to meet you, Declan," she said to me. "Take care of our Owen. He's a good man."

"Debbie!" Owen scolded.

"What? You *do* need someone else to take care of you for a change."

22

OWEN

Frowning at the last paragraph I just re-read, I wasn't satisfied in the least. The feelings I wanted to evoke weren't coming across clearly. For the fifth time, I pressed backspace, erasing all the words I had spent most of the morning typing. I had to get it perfect, though, before I could move on. It was just the way I worked. Otherwise it would be a thorn in my side, always niggling me until I went back and fixed the error. Although these words weren't really an error, they were just far from the words I had anticipated writing.

A knock on the door sounded, but I was so focused on the computer before me that I barely acknowledged it.

"Owen, I need you a minute."

I glanced up at Declan's voice to find him at the entrance of the half-opened office door. His office which I had taken up residence in. At first, I thought he would have been upset that I had invaded his work area, but he hadn't minded in the least. After he came home from work too many times to find me at his desk, typing, he'd set up a little area all for me in his office. Now in the evening, we could be found working together before taking a break.

Usually I would be the one to have our meals prepared and had to remind Declan to pause all the work to join me, but now it was the opposite. I had already sent out query letters about my novel, including the requested sample chapters which meant I had to finish up the novel quickly in the event I was asked for the full manuscript. Not that I anticipated being so lucky as to get accepted on the first try. I already knew that I'd prob-ably be rejected dozens of times, but hopefully one day I'd get accepted. That was my dream.

I launched myself fully into the project, deciding that if I was going to be serious about publishing and quitting my job, then I needed to put in the work.

"Right now?" I asked him, frowning, because I loathed getting up from the computer without figuring out the right words to say, and not have Jack coming off as a complete jerk while trying to get his point across. "I'm kind of in the middle of an important scene."

He glanced at his watch, then back at me. "The applicants will be here in the next fifteen minutes. It's important to me that you show up as this affects you too. I don't want to choose someone you don't like."

I tried not to show how blank I was as I struggled to remember our earlier conversation while we were having breakfast. I couldn't for the life of me remember anything about applicants though.

"You don't remember," he said on a sigh. "When you

get caught up in your world, you're completely zoned out, aren't you?"

I couldn't decide if he was upset or teasing. He was right though, and I felt guilty about it. Since I'd picked up my manuscript, I'd felt a burst of inspiration, and now I was nearing the end, I found it difficult to be pulled away.

"I'm sorry if I've been a little distracted of late," I remarked, and rose to my feet to approach him. "It's just that I'm so close, and I'm excited about getting it done and having your opinion."

"You mean I shouldn't feel offended you prefer your book boyfriends to your actual boyfriend?"

My eyes widened. I thought he was joking, but I didn't want to take it for granted either. "Declan, is that how you feel?"

"I'm just joking," he replied on a chuckle. "Can you give me an hour of your time? The applicants for Silas's position will be here shortly."

It was my time to frown at him. "I don't know why you insist in looking for another chauffeur just for a few months. Silas will be back before you know it, and in the meantime, I can drive us anywhere that we need to go."

"Considering how I like to keep your hands busy in the backseat, we need someone else," he stated. "Besides, I have a feeling Silas might not be back."

"What? We're losing Silas?"

"It's just a hunch."

"I hope not. That sucks."

"If it's going to make him happy, then I'll wish him all the best."

I narrowed an eye at him. "Why do I have a feeling you know something you're not telling me?"

"I promise. It's all just a hunch." He cupped the back of my neck and smoothed his fingers down the skin. "So, is that a yes? Can you help me choose *our* chauffeur?"

"Sure," I answered. "I'll join you in fifteen."

"Good." A quick peck on the lips. "I have the breakfast room set up."

Declan returned downstairs while I went back to my book, adamant to get the last two paragraphs written.

I had every intention of joining Declan at the interviews. Given his comment about me preferring my book boyfriends—even if he was joking—I didn't want to disappoint him. It was just my luck to have a light bulb moment when I sat at the computer. Stepping away for a few minutes and returning to the manuscript seemed to be what I needed to identify the problem. I ended up deleting more than just the last two paragraphs. I deleted the entire chapter and started again.

In hindsight, I should have left the new chapter to later, but I wanted to get a head start. The next thing I knew I had the chapter all done, staring at the words *The End* and feeling a wave of accomplishment wash over me. It turned out that I also caught the time on the computer, and startled.

"Oh no!" I had done exactly what Declan had accused me of. I had become so caught up in my world that I hadn't remembered to join him for the interviews.

I saved my files, backing up to the cloud before I put the computer to sleep, because I didn't have the time to close out all the open browsers and documents I had been using. I pushed away from the desk, an apology ready on my lips as I hurried to find Declan.

When I entered the breakfast room, guilt eating me up, I came up short seeing an applicant with Declan. They were both standing and shaking hands as if they were either just about to start or wrap things up. The young man with him laughed, and I didn't know if my ears were deceiving me, but I could have sworn I heard a flirtatious note in there somewhere.

Tall and slenderly built like Declan, the guy was probably in his late twenties. He had dark hair in a pony-tail, that spilled over the collar of his shirt, which probably should have looked hippy on him, but instead turned out to add more charm to his already enigmatic face. He was good-looking. Damn attractive. And when he released Declan's hand, he said something and reached for Declan's shoulder.

It had been a long time since I'd got jealous over Declan, but there was no mistaking the overwhelming emotion that came over me. I was green with envy for this attractive man who had youth on his side. Just for a second, I wondered why Declan wouldn't favor him to me. What chance did I have when put next to someone like this?

I wasn't certain if Declan's side-step was deliberate, but he managed to elude the man's touch which was a bit satisfying to watch, considering he had no idea yet that I was inside the room with them. Spurred into action and not willing to watch anymore of this nonsense unfold, I stepped forward.

"Hey, babe." I *never* called Declan babe. That was an

endearment that he used, but I felt it was appropriate in *this* case. In the corner of my eye, I saw the other man observing me, unable to conceal his look of surprise.

Declan turned, his expression not betraying how he was feeling. I couldn't tell if he was pissed at me for showing up late, then giving him a pretentious *hey, babe.* I completed the trip toward him and gave him my best apologetic look. "Sorry I got a little carried away again," I said, then I slid my hand in the back of his hair and kissed him hard right there in front of the guy who was definitely *not* about to become our driver.

Declan's lips registered surprise at first, but then his arms slid around my waist and down to cup my ass. *Perfect.* When I moaned into his mouth, it wasn't pretentious at all.

The applicant cleared his throat, and I slowly ended the kiss, giving him a nip on his bottom lip that promised lots of naughty moments later. I'd have to make this up to him somehow.

Declan's eyes danced with humor as he pulled me into his side, one hand still gripping my butt possessively. Whether he realized the significance of that hold or not, to me it meant everything that smoothed my ruffled feathers of jealousy. He always knew so well what I needed.

"This is my partner who I mentioned earlier," Declan said, as if it wasn't evident by the show we had just put on. "You'd be driving for us both. *Babe,*"—my face flushed because he emphasized the word, clearly letting me know he was well aware of why I had used the endearment—"This is Miguel, one of the guys who applied to the position. He comes highly recommended."

I smiled in the direction of Miguel and extended a hand. "Nice to meet you, Miguel. I'm sorry I wasn't here sooner to make your acquaintance."

He looked uncomfortable as he shook my hand. "Nice to meet you too. It would be a pleasure to drive for you too."

His gaze lingered on Declan a little bit too long for my taste. *And with me there at that!* It was all I could do not to show him the door.

"Well, that's it, Miguel." Declan nodded to the man. "You'll hear from me soon once I've gone over everyone's profile again and made a decision. Let me walk you out."

"I'll do it," I volunteered. "It's the least I can do after missing everything."

Declan shrugged. "Okay."

He was reaching for a folder on the table when I walked out the applicant. The short trek to the front door was done in awkward silence. I held the door open for Miguel, and he turned to me.

"I'm sorry you didn't get to join us," he stated with a smile. Now he was eyeing me the way he had Declan. "If you do want to do this again so you can both get to know me a little better, I'm not opposed to the idea. You know, three can be a bit of fun."

I had no doubt that three could be fun for the right people, but that didn't include Declan and me. I'd never let anyone else get close enough to Declan to know how he reacted when he had his nipples sucked, or how soft his lips were on every inch of skin they trailed. His past passion was his own, but his present and future were mine.

"Ah, I wouldn't count on that," I answered. "But thanks for trying. Good luck with the job hunting."

I closed the door even though his mouth opened to respond. As far as I was concerned that conversation was done, and good riddance. The last thing I needed was help that tried to come between Declan and me. Silas had been perfect, and I hoped Declan was wrong about him not returning to his post.

He was no longer in the breakfast room, but I found him sitting on the long couch in the living room, a folder on his lap. He glanced up at me as he shuffled the paper on top to the bottom.

"What do you think?" he asked. "You missed all the other guys. There was a woman too, but Miguel has quite the experience for someone so young."

I scowled at him. I plucked the folder from his grasp and straddled his lap. He didn't say anything, but watched me as I skipped through the résumés. I hummed a little nonsensical tune as I located what I wanted. *Miguel Andres Johnson.*

"Ah here, you go." I handed him back the file and crushed the résumé into my fist. "I don't doubt he has a lot of experience, but not the kind we're going for."

"What? Why not? He comes highly recommended."

I tapped his nose. "You listen to me, Declan. I don't care if he comes with a seal of approval from the Queen of England. Just no."

He put down the folder on the arm of the couch and

brought his hands down to my backside. "You still haven't told me why."

"Because I have a feeling the ride he wants you to offer him is much more than a car," I answered on a frown.

"And?"

"And he's too damn pretty," I admitted.

I thought that he would laugh. At least a grin. I was fully aware how I sounded, petulant and jealous. He didn't do either though. Other than a patient smile and a gaze that melted my insides.

"I prefer your kind of pretty," he said softly.

I blinked at him and scoffed. "I'm not exactly what you'd call pretty."

"No? Because I find you pretty much everything. Pretty hot. Pretty sexy. Pretty lovable. Pretty. Will I have to make it your new nickname for you to believe me?"

As much as he pulled on every one of the strings of my heart with his words, there was no way I was going to have him go around calling me pretty. *Babe* was fine. *Baby* tolerable on some occasions, but *pretty* was definitely too much.

"Okay. Maybe I'm your kind of pretty." I leaned forward to place my head on his shoulder. "I'm sorry for messing up today and not being here on time. Would serve me right if you went ahead and hired him."

"Of course, I wouldn't. Trust me, I picked up on the flirtatious vibe, and I wouldn't condone that sort of nonsense coming between us. In case you missed it, I'm not too fond of anything that tries to create problems for us."

"I can't believe you're not upset. It's just that I was having difficulty earlier with the ending, and then it all fell into place, and I couldn't stop typing."

He pulled on my shoulders until my head was up and I was facing him again. "You're done?"

I nodded. "Yeah. I think so."

"Congrats. Now if you get a response from an agent you will be all ready to hit them with your manuscript."

I accepted his sweet kiss, and then blurted out with his lips still smashed against mine. "Do you want to read it?" However, with our lips together it came out garbled like an alien trying to speak human.

"What was that?" he asked, pulling away.

I took a deep breath. "I asked if you wanted to read it. I mean you don't have to if you don't want to. I'll understand, so don't go thinking you're going to hurt my feelings if—"

His hand covered my mouth, and I stopped talking.

"I'd be honored to be the first one to read your manuscript, Owen."

Tears sprang into my eyes, and I blinked them away. He removed his hand, giving me the opportunity to nod. "Okay. Thank you for not pushing, but allowing me to do this in my own time."

"Always. Now come on. I've got a surprise for you, although I'm not sure you deserve it now. You did make me wait after all."

I groaned as I got off his lap, and he stood. "I'll make it up to you, I promise. I want my surprise."

"Don't worry. You're about to. Wait for me, will you?"

H e was gone before I could respond. Curious as to what surprise he had for me, I stayed where I was. My birthday was coming up, and I knew he was planning to do something for me, although I had begged him not to go about anything extravagant. I was quite fine having him and my kids around. If he wanted to invite James too that was okay, and if he didn't feel comfortable with James being a part of the celebration, then that was fine too.

"I'll need to cover your eyes for a bit," he said with a grin, showing me the black blindfold, he carried when he returned.

I glanced at him nervously, because he'd never blindfolded me before having sex. He'd gagged me with different forms of our clothes. Like taking my underwear and stuffing it into my mouth when I got too loud. This was a new direction for us, but I was willing to try anything at least once, and then decide how I felt about it after.

"Okay," I agreed.

He came up to me, kissing my nose before securing the blindfold over my eyes. He adjusted the grip and checked that my nostrils weren't being hindered in any way.

"Not too tight?" he enquired.

"No. The fit is fine."

"Good. You remember our safe word?"

"Yeah. Jello?"

He didn't say anything. I didn't even sense him move until I felt his hot breath on my ear. "That's right. That's exactly what you're going to feel like when I'm through with you."

Nervous excitement zinged through my stomach. All the times he'd turned me into Jello, I'd had nothing to complain about. I was quite looking forward to this experience just as much.

His hands gripping my arm, Declan guided me from the living room. It helped a lot that I knew the layout of the house somewhat, but I hadn't been living here very long, so I wasn't certain of one of our turns. We did walk down several halls, a light flicked on somewhere, a door opened, and we were in a different section of the house. I sniffed the air, trying to make out where we were. The space felt different. Not like the fabric softeners and the fancy scents that hung around Declan's home. It was cooler, the air crisp and undisturbed.

"Have you figured it out yet?" he asked, speaking for

the first time, except for the instructions he'd given in when to step down or turn.

"I'm not really certain."

"You'll figure it out soon enough. Want to know what I'm going to do to you?"

He hadn't said anything about fucking me as yet. He hadn't even touched me sexually since we'd left the living room. Still my cock was pretty much stiff already in the confines of my sweatpants.

"Yes."

"Yes, what?"

"Yes, Daddy," I quickly amended.

"I'm going to undress you," he said. "Then I'll spank your ass for letting me do the interviews alone, even though you said you would be there."

My ass clenched in anticipation. Oh, how I missed being spanked. He did slap my ass from time to time when we had sex, but he'd not spanked me for discipline in a long while. Not since he figured out how much I loved it. He always gave me some other form of punishment to do.

Last week when I'd gotten caught up in my writing and hadn't eaten for a whole day, he had been livid. He'd disciplined me by having me wash up after we ate for the entire week—without using the dishwasher. Every evening I had to tell him why I was being disciplined, then he would kiss me and give me one of his *that's a good Boy* commendations.

Washing up the dishes was the one chore I really hated, and he had figured that out. The children had taken on that task when they were younger, dividing it amongst themselves. At least he had made it better by sitting with me. Once he had even snuck up behind me, pulled down my shorts and finger-fucked me. Each time I stopped washing he would stop moving his fingers, but as soon as I started washing again his fingers would be hitting that spot. When I was finished, he'd bent me over the table and fucked me. By then I had only been too grateful to release all the tension from him teasing me.

Declan was true to his words. He didn't completely undress me. He pulled down my sweatpants and underwear all the way down to my ankles.

"Don't," he ordered, when I made to step out of them.

He ran his hands beneath my shirt then down to cup my ass. "Pretty," he said, squeezing hard. "A nice shade of red is going to look quite pretty on your ass, don't you think?"

"Yes, Daddy."

He had me shuffle forward until I came upon something large and imposing. I swallowed my curiosity to ask him what it was, but I soon found out for myself. He took both my arms, and positioned me how he wanted me, draped over the hood of a car. We were in the garage then, and he meant to fuck me right there over the hood.

I let out a moan, and he chuckled. "Now you know where you are?"

"Yes, Daddy." And with my eyes covered, I felt more sensations than ever before. The coolness of the metal of the car that penetrated through the material of my T-shirt. The tight grip of his hands on my ass cheeks, his blunt nails digging into the flesh.

"Twenty?" He said it more like a question, and this was one of the reasons I loved him. He'd never hurt me, and even in knowing how much I enjoyed being spanked, he still wanted to confirm with me that this was what I wanted.

"Yes, please, Daddy," I moaned rubbing my crotch a little over the front of the car. "I deserve it."

"What are you being disciplined for?" he asked.

This sure as hell didn't feel like discipline, but pleasure. I quickly got my head from my dick. "For not keeping my promise to you," I answered. "I'm sorry."

The first few slaps were nothing besides warm up, but after the seventh, things started to get quite intense. He spanked harder and harder, alternating between cupping his hands and giving me his bare palm. The latter hurt worse than the former and left my ass stinging. I might have emitted a few groans and gasps, but deep inside I loved the way he owned every bit of my ass, especially when he stroked and rubbed. What I liked best though was the rhythm he now found, a sharp slap and grab. When he squeezed my burning ass cheeks it was a mixture of pleasure and hurt.

"Almost there, Boy," he said, his breathing shallow. "Just three more. Can you take it?"

"Yes, Daddy," I said on a moan, my legs already turned to the Jello he had promised earlier. If I wasn't well and truly draped over the hood of the car, I would have been a puddle on the floor of the garage.

The next spank was followed by a grab and spread. My cheeks went in opposite directions, and he hissed. "Fuck, that's a pretty pink hole all eager and ready for

Daddy's cock." He tapped a finger at my hole. "We fuck so much yet you're always so tight. You want me to ruin you again with my fist?"

Fuck. I couldn't explain why I craved it, but even after experiencing it for the first time, I still wanted it again. He had been so sweet and gentle the first time.

"Yes, Daddy," I said softly. "I want it so much."

"But not so soon again," he said. "Let's give your body some time. I don't want to hurt you."

"It's not hurting me if I want it," I said, passion making me say foolish things.

He spanked me, and I jumped. "It takes a lot for you to take my fist, Boy. Will you trust Daddy to tell you when you're ready again?"

"I trust you," I told him, because that was what it all boiled down to.

He didn't get to twenty. With a groan, he spread my ass cheeks again, and I gasped, working hard not to dig my nails into his car when his tongue swiped over my hole. He had to be kneeling between my legs. I tried to spread mine wider, but the damn clothes still around my ankles restricted me. It was maddeningly hot not to be able to move them apart for him.

"Fuck." He rubbed the pads of two fingers over my hole in circles, driving me crazy.

"Daddy," I huffed. "Please. I want."

"Tell me, what do you want?"

"I want your cock inside me," I begged shamelessly— I had none where he was concerned. Once I had given him my heart, everything that was me was also him.

I felt something wet hit my puckered hole followed by

his finger spreading the warm liquid around my rim then inside. A little more, two more fingers stretching me, my hips grinding to the movements, and I was shaking with want for him.

He didn't give me his cock right away. He spread one cheek apart, then poked at my hole with his cock, never quite penetrating me. The way he rubbed his dick around my hole then up and down had me closer to tears than his spanking had.

"Please," I cried hoarsely. "Oh please, Daddy. Please. Please."

And then he was pushing in, and I was no longer crying please, but telling him thanks. I babbled a whole lot of things that did not make sense. About me not deserving his cock because I had been bad, but I was so grateful he had decided to reward me anyway. I played into the scene, and he loved it. He gripped my hips and the sound of his pelvis slapping into my ass was music to my ears. I couldn't see him, but I heard every whispered, tortured breath of his. I felt the nip of his teeth wherever he bit me, the drip of his sweat on my skin when he tugged up my shirt to kiss my spine.

I was more aware of him than I'd ever been before. More aware of the aromatic scent of our coupling as he plunged into my ass over and over. Our pheromones wreaked havoc on our senses in that garage, and he fucked me as if both our lives depended on it. Like a gladiator whose freedom relied heavily on making me come.

I had asked him once before to use me, and use me he did. It was so strange how he used me, but made me feel like the most precious thing in the world. It was like plunging gold into fire, ruining it into to perfection.. That was exactly how I felt, lying there against the car, my hole being worked over good with hard thrusts.

Declan reached beneath my body for my cock and stroked me. "That's it," he murmured when my hips bucked into his touch. "That's it, my dearest Boy. Come for Daddy. Show Daddy how much you love when he plows you like this."

Usually I would be loud when I came, but today was different. A powerful wave of emotions rushed through my body, leaving me speechless. At the back of my mind, I was aware that this was a climax, but it transcended beyond something so simple to explain what was happening to me. Maybe it was being blindfolded which did the trick, but I was in tune with everything that was occurring inside and outside of my body.

I could hear Declan declaring how much he loved me, which he then alternated with how much he loved my body. His hands, calloused from working the gardens even though he didn't have to, rubbed over my back, gently scraping my sensitive flesh. I didn't only feel, but hear, the slide of his cock into my spasming ass, the tight grip that my rim had on the girth of his dick. I felt the tremor that ran through his body, the way he went completely out of control one minute, bucking his hips hard and fast in a manic almost desperate need, then the next minute he stilled, his body relaxing in harmony with mine, declaring a bond older than time, but new to our hearts.

"Holy fuck, babe," he groaned. Still inside me, he

pulled my torso up from the car. I fell back into his arms, legs still shackled by my own clothes, his cock still branding my ass, and I'd never felt more at home and safe than I did as he rained kisses over my cheek and neck.

"That was… beautiful," I said shakily on a laugh. "I don't think a hard fuck on the hood of your car is supposed to be beautiful, Dec, but you made it so."

He chuckled, squeezing me in his arms. "Not my car. Yours."

"Huh? What?" I couldn't resist any more. I yanked off the blindfold and was promptly robbed of speech. The brand new Bentley still had a shiny red and blue ribbon on top of the car. I had just jizzed on a car worth more than the value of everything I owned combined.

"Dec-lan," I choked out as he finally pulled out of me. He must have realized that I was of no use to myself, because he pulled up my clothes.

"It's yours," he said at my ear. "And before you turn it down, you need a car. Yours is pretty much wrecked, Owen."

I sucked in a deep breath. "But Declan. If someone needs a car, you don't go out and get them this. It's… oh my God. Declan, this costs a fortune."

"You know money is no object with me, Owen."

"But to me it is," I choked out. The car was tempting. I had been a chauffeur for years, driving around in other people's expensively comfortable cars. To be able to have one of my own was surreal, but how could I accept such an expensive gift?

He clutched my shoulders. "Listen to me, Owen. You

deserve this. You deserve to have your ass on a nice plush car seat after years of driving other people around. I swear I was going to buy you something more modest, but then I said 'to hell with it. This is the one I'm going to get him.' So I did, and it's yours. Do me the honor of accepting this gift."

I glanced back at the car. "It's beautiful."

"And it has your name on it paid in full. Come on. Let's check it out. I want to show you how I got the inside all custom-designed for you."

It was too tempting not to have my ass on seats that I would own for a few minutes. I was certain I would have him return the car, but when I sat in the driver's seat, and he showed me the custom-designed dashboard with the state of the art audio system that would make audiobooks double the fun for me, I was sold.

24

DECLAN

"This is silly," Owen grumbled as Charles headed for the jet, leaving us alone to have a quiet moment.

"What is?" I asked, fighting back my smile, because he was really making a fuss about me leaving for a business trip with my father over the weekend. I had even invited him, but he'd turned it down. I had backed off because meeting the people I rubbed elbows with for the first time could be overwhelming.

"That you had your new chauffeur drop us here at the airport when I could have driven you and your father in my car."

"I'll be away for the weekend so you can drive your heart out," I told him. "Now why don't you tell me the real reason why you're so cranky."

When I pulled him into me, he glanced around even as he came willingly. "What reason is that?"

"That you're going to miss me," I answered with a lazy smile. "Come on, admit it."

He sighed. "I *will* miss you, but you'll be back in two days." He groaned. "Two days of sleeping alone in our bed."

I snorted. "You won't even know I'm gone. You'll get caught up in the new book you've started."

He flushed, because last night I'd had to wake him up and bring him to bed after he'd fallen asleep at his desk. I liked seeing him so passionate about something, but he was neglecting to take care of himself at times.

"I won't spend *all* the time typing," he answered. "I'll have some alone time to do whatever I want."

"Good. I don't want you sitting at home alone. Go out and have fun."

It bothered me that he didn't have any friends. At least I had Ridge, and I could always call Heath. Owen's kids had been his friends, and they had their own lives.

"I'm thinking of going in to work and handing in my letter of resignation," he said.

That took me by surprise. "You are?"

"Yeah, I don't think I can go back through all the tension there, and it's just creepy that Trevor dropped by my house while I was out of town."

"Sure you're not doing it because you know it's what I want?" I asked on a frown. As much as I thought this was the best thing for him, I didn't want to make the decision for him.

"No, it's not you. I've been at that job for a long time, and you're right, there's no advancement. Plus, with

Trevor giving me shit on a daily basis, it's best for everyone."

"Then good for you." I kissed him briefly. "I have to go, but I'll see you soon."

He nodded, but didn't move. I hated him watching me walk away, but there was also a comfort that he didn't really want me to go, even though he knew I would be back. I would always be back for him. He still hadn't moved when I entered the jet and took a seat across from Charles, who already had two flutes of champagne poured. He was back to drinking then, but, so far, I'd not seen him drink as much as he used to.

"Bet you he doesn't leave until after we take off," Charles murmured, staring out the window with me and taking in Owen who just stood there, hands in his pockets, staring in our direction.

"We'll survive," I murmured, but inside I was hoping he would prove Charles wrong and leave. It *was* just a couple of days, and then we would be back in Cincy. He didn't have to make me feel guilty for leaving him behind.

Fifteen minutes later, we were up in the air, and the last glimpse I had of Owen was him still standing in the same position. I sent him a quick message that I would see him soon and a reminder to take care of himself until I could resume duties. He sent me back a sad face followed promptly by a heart emoji.

"To be honest, I didn't think it would work."

I glanced over at Charles. "You didn't think what would work?"

"The relationship between you and Owen," he

answered, and when I glared at him, he shrugged. "Come on, it was kind of far-fetched. I didn't say anything about it because it really wasn't my place, but I thought you were just experimenting with someone older. There was another older guy you were with once, but it didn't last long."

"What does that have to do with my current relationship?"

"Now don't get all huffy, I was just making an observation," Charles replied. "That day I first met him in your office as your boyfriend, I was confused as hell. You're one of the most eligible bachelors in the state. Hell, in the country. And you chose him."

My shoulders stiffened. "Our relationship has developed a lot over the past weeks, Charles. I actually think we can be more than business associates. I've been starting to see you as a friend. Don't ruin it with your baseless assumptions about Owen and me."

"But that's just it. I think I get it. I've never seen you this-this… *contented.* Yes, that's the right word. I've never seen you this contented and at peace before. He does that for you, so why would I even object? When you're together, I can feel how much you love him and how much he loves you. I-I had that with your mo-mother."

The anger drained from me when I heard the pain in his words. Sometimes I was so caught up in losing a mother that I forgot he had lost a wife too. I had convinced myself over the years that my pain was greater than his, but why did it have to be? Grief wasn't a competition.

"You know, I don't think I ever fully appreciated what

Mom's death did to you," I said now to his bowed head. "I've always thought about how growing up without a mother affected me. Having Owen in my life, I can now appreciate how her absence completely ripped you apart. I don't know what I'd do if I lost Owen. Just the thought of it makes me feel like I'm drowning."

His hand came down on my shoulder and he squeezed. "The damnedest thing about it is that one day it will hurt, and we know it will hurt, but we can't help loving them just the same, and pray to God we'll be able to survive the worst of it."

I curled my hands into fists, trying not to succumb to the panic the thought of losing Owen brought on. *Fuck, I hate thinking about stuff like this. Life.*

"If you'd known Mom was going to die as young as she did, would you still have pursued her?"

He chuckled, the sound starting off as humorous before ending on a sob. "First of all, your mom pursued me. She was so feisty and bossy. I couldn't help falling in love with her. I want to say that I would have avoided her had I known, but I don't believe that. I'd have loved her just the same, but I'd have made the days count more. I would have spent less time on business, more time with her, making sure she knew that I loved her."

"She knew," I said. "She died knowing how much we both loved her."

I was close to tears, and he wasn't far from it either, but we were both able to rein in our emotions, taking a few minutes to let the moment pass naturally rather than to force another topic to cover the fact that we were both hurting. For the first time, we shared in our mutual grief of a woman who had been taken away from us way too soon. And in that moment of grief, I found a comfort I never knew was possible.

"You should propose to him," Charles surprised me by saying.

"You think?"

"Unless you don't want to get married."

I leaned back in the seat and reached for the flute of champagne. "I do want to get married. I've been thinking about it a lot lately, but I'm not sure if Owen will be into it right now. Doesn't it seem a little too soon to you?"

Charles laughed. "The man moved into your house, Declan. I think you're both past the point of 'a little too soon'. Don't you think?"

"Well, that's true. But I'd like to talk to his kids first, get their blessing, you know. I think they won't mind. They know I love their dad, but I'd especially like the blessing of his daughter. She's been hearing everything second-hand, and she should feel better that I've talked to her about it."

Charles shuffled beside me. "If-if they're anything like the one I met, then I'd say you shouldn't have anything to worry about."

"You mean Auggie? I forgot you met him. What was your impression?"

"Yes, August. Fine young man."

I frowned at Charles, because he sounded strange there for a minute. "What is it? Did something happen when you two were together?"

His face paled. "Like what?"

"Like he said anything about Owen and me. He is comfortable with our relationship, isn't he?"

Charles rose to his feet. "Oh yeah. He seems fine with it." He bumped past me. "I need to take a leak. Bring up the Bacca file, will you? We can run through it once more before we land."

My eyes followed Charles as he made his way to the bathroom. He *was* acting strange at the mention of Auggie that I really began to believe the young man might not be as comfortable at the idea of his father and me as he had let on. But why wouldn't Charles mention it to me if that was the case? I wanted to dig some more and make Charles spill the truth, but today we'd bridged even more of the gap between us, and I didn't want to make a fuss, especially over something that could possibly be nothing more than my imagination.

Everything had seemed fine when Charles had met Auggie. There had been no hostility from either side. In fact, they had looked to be conversing when Owen and I had arrived at his ex's house. Deciding I was worrying about nothing, I shrugged it off and brought up the file Charles had requested. I already knew the contents like the back of my hand though, so instead, I removed my laptop and opened the file Owen had sent me of his book.

Soon I became enthralled in the love story of two men who were too different for a HEA to be in their future. That made the story even more intriguing, because I knew there was a satisfying one at the end. I had asked Owen about it when he'd sent it to me. After all, I didn't really care for a tragic ending. He'd looked at me as if I should have known better, then went on to explain to me that one of the key ingredients to a romance novel is the satisfying HEA that readers would expect.

What was truly impressive was knowing Owen had never done any formal training. He had just picked up on things after being such a romance lover. He exposed parts of himself in the book that were difficult to read, but made me understand even more than he probably would have wanted me to.

His main character bore a striking resemblance to himself— a tough exterior but all soft and warm with a heart of gold. It didn't escape me that his character wasn't just gay either. The main lead was bisexual like Owen and had lost his spouse, but instead of through abandonment, it had been through death. Regardless, the loneliness, fear, anger, and distrust in loving again were all there. In some ways, it was like reading about the tentative steps we had made at first, because he had been so distrustful of the connection between us.

Owen hadn't mentioned the book again since he'd emailed me his manuscript to read, but I knew he was waiting for me to give my assessment. I would have finished already if I hadn't decided to start over from the prologue. The truth was that I loved everything about his story, the imperfection of the characters, but especially the love between both men.

I could only hope that a HEA was written in the stars for Owen and me in the same way he had written one for the characters in his manuscript.

25

OWEN

While Declan was away, I did exactly what he told me not to do, but I was counting on David not to say anything about the long hours I spent in his office, working away at my computer. I'd pounded the keys so hard yesterday that I now had two dysfunctional buttons which made typing frustrating. I wished I had some kind of recording device when my fingers began to hurt from the repetitive activity, but I didn't, so I made do with what I had at my disposal.

I got lost in my writing because it was the only way I could forget that my manuscript was with a publishing house, and it would be six weeks to three months of torture before I got the rejection email. I anticipated that would happen, because everybody got the brush-off on their first attempt, right?

Even knowing the rate at which new authors were rejected, I still had a smidgen of hope which worried me. I shouldn't be banking so much on the publisher accepting my story right off the bat. I had gone for the biggest publisher out there which also accepted LGBTQIA+ content. Harver Press had a good reputation, and to be accepted by them would mean scoring big. The only problem was that they didn't accept simultaneous queries, so I couldn't query any other publisher until I heard from them.

I had to wait up to three months, which was maddeningly frustrating, but what to do? I started a new book, this one less angsty than the previous. One could say that Declan had made me a little mushy, and the guys I was currently writing kept me suitably entertained. I was having fun with my work, if not anything else, and that mattered to me. I felt like I was doing something I always wanted to, and that made up my mind for me about whether or not I wanted to quit.

Last night when Declan had called me before going to bed, he had explained that he would be home a day late. Something or another about the business he and his father had gone about was not going exactly the way they had planned. I no longer pretended to understand anything about their financial ventures, so I just accepted that he would be home late without question. We'd fucked over the phone, me jacking off really hard at the filthy things he'd whispered in my ear that he wanted me to do to him. He'd instructed me to fuck myself with the dildo and recount exactly how I felt.

It had been so hot. It was almost like the night he'd sat across from me and watched me while I pleasured myself however he instructed me.

I shook my head to clear the play-by-play feature

running through my mind of last night. My pants were getting snug in the crotch, and I had no desire to jerk off without Declan telling me to do so.

I was immersed in writing for God only knew how long when the office door opened. I didn't even realize until I heard David's voice.

"Owen, you're still here!"

I glanced up at him. "Oh yeah. I'm just getting some work done."

He checked his watch. "It's almost three in the afternoon. You mean you haven't left since you snuck in this morning at eight?"

I double-checked the time on the computer. "I think I used the bathroom once or twice."

"And look!" He pointed in horror at the untouched breakfast on my desk. "You still haven't eaten. This is not good at all. I can't lie to Mr. Moore when he calls me later to check up on you. He's going to be upset that you've gone without eating."

"Declan calls you to check up on me?"

He walked over to the desk and dropped a pile of envelopes then retrieved the tray with the cold scrambled eggs he'd brought me earlier.

"You have a letter or two in there," he said. "Place the rest on Mr. Moore's desk, will you? I'll go make you something else immediately. This won't do at all."

"You don't have to do that, David. I'm perfectly fine making myself something to eat."

"I don't trust you to remember. I won't bring it here, either, or you'll forget again. Take a break and come to the kitchen."

He was gone before I could say anything else. I couldn't even argue, because he was right, and my stomach was growling. Conceding that I'd done enough for the day, I shut down the laptop and sorted the mail. I placed Declan's letters on his desk before ripping the one from my credit card company open. Usually, it remained unopened until I felt like getting to it, but I needed to see if Declan had gone ahead with his promise.

Declan buying me a car had been an exciting moment for me. It definitely cost way more than my credit card bill. However, seeing the zero balance on my statement meant so much more to me. Feeling weak-kneed, I sat in his chair, my hands trembling as I read the statement.

Fully paid. Zero balance. At almost forty-seven years old, I was debt free. Most of my debt had come from taking care of my kids, and although I kept up with the payments, it had not been easy. Kids were expensive, and I'd had three to think about with no help at all from James. He was getting the best years of them when they no longer needed financial support or anything, and for just a split second, I felt the resentment that he had it so easy now.

I pushed the feelings away and located my phone. I rang Declan without thinking that maybe he was in a meeting. After all, that was the reason he wasn't coming home until tomorrow.

"Hey, everything okay?" he answered the call.

"I got it," I answered.

"What? You got what?"

"My credit card statement," I replied. "There's zero balance."

His sigh came clear across the phone. "Owen, I'm in a meeting. I told you I'd be doing this, and I don't really want to argue about it right now. At another time I'd indulge you to voice your disagreements, but it's been a stressful two days."

"I just wanted to say thanks, Declan."

Silence came over the phone. "Thanks? No 'you shouldn't have' behind it'?"

"No, none of that. Just thank you. It means a lot to be debt free."

"Then you're welcome. I told you I'd take care of you. Now I want you not to be so surprised when I do. Okay, love?"

"Okay. Sorry for interrupting your meeting."

"I needed the break anyway. How are you?"

"Honestly? I miss you, but I'm being patient."

"Are you eating okay?"

Guilty, I couldn't respond.

"Owen."

"I'm about to eat now," I answered.

"Good. I'll let you go then. I'll talk to you later."

After hanging up, I made my way to the kitchen, despite the lure of the computer. David had prepared me a plate to eat, and he hovered over me until I finished everything. I sheepishly told him thanks for looking out for me before I went upstairs and washed up. There was one task I had wanted to complete for the day, and I wasn't going to put it off anymore.

Forty-five minutes later, I was parked at the car depot

where I worked. I was supposed to return in a couple of days, but the closer the time got, the more my mind was made up that I couldn't return to work there. Maybe I wouldn't have if my relationship with Trevor hadn't soured. This place hadn't exactly been easy, but it had been home over the years, and it had helped me, and my children to stay afloat.

Resignation letter in hand, I realized my mistake when I saw my co-workers who were about gawking at my new car. I groaned, because my eagerness to take it out for a spin had clouded my better judgment. I should have driven my old car, but it had been giving me so much trouble of late that I hadn't even considered it.

To make matters worse, Trevor was also with the guys. *Shit.* I just knew what would go through his mind once I handed in my resignation letter. His face was rather stiff when he turned to watch me walk toward them.

"Damn, Long, did you hit the lottery or something?" Gray asked, moving closer to my car to inspect it. "This is one sweet ride. You've got to hook me up."

Trevor snorted. "I doubt his way is up your alley." He folded his arms across his chest. "What can I do for you, Owen? Your suspension is not up yet."

Instead of backing down at the contempt in his tone and the way my co-workers were eyeing us with unease, I squared my shoulders. "Can I speak to you in private?"

He shrugged. "Fine. Let's go to my office."

"Hey, can I go for a spin until you're ready?" Gray asked.

I laughed and shook my head. "Not this time. I see

the way you drive, Gray, and I don't think my car could survive you."

"Long!" Trevor snapped. "Quit wasting my time. You want to talk, follow me. Otherwise, you can take your shiny toy and get out of here."

Gray and Lance stared in surprise at Trevor's open hostility. I barely held onto my anger as I stiffly followed him.

"What's up his ass?" I heard Lance whisper behind our backs. Trevor, who had marched on ahead, couldn't have heard, but I had the same question. What the fuck was lodged so far up his ass that it hadn't come down in the time I had been away?

"Maybe jealous he can't afford a car like that," Gray said on a laugh.

Ignoring their comments, I curled my hands into fists at my sides as I walked down the hall and turned to enter Trevor's office. The son-of-a-bitch slammed the door in my face, leaving me to turn the knob to enter. He sat at his cluttered desk, looking bored as if he hadn't been serving me shit since the moment he saw me.

"Why are you here, Long?" he asked.

I could have shucked the envelope at him and walked out, but I didn't. I had to know.

"What the hell is your problem with me?" I demanded. "I've worked here for over ten years, and we've always gotten along. Now suddenly you treat me like a piece of gum stuck under your shoe."

"I don't know what you're talking about. Now what do you want?"

"Don't give me that bullshit!" I stalked over to his

desk. "It started when I got together with Declan. Why the hell does that bother you so much? Are you so homophobic that you'd treat me differently because I'm with someone of the same sex? That's discrimination, and that's against the law to demonstrate it in the workplace."

"Don't be obtuse. I'm not homophobic."

"Then what is your problem?"

He rose to his feet. "You wanna know what my problem is, Long? It's you! Plain and simple. You! For years you've been walking around here acting like something you're not."

I blinked in surprise at him as he came around the desk to stand before me. "What are you talking about? I've never once pretended to be something I'm not."

"Then why the fuck have you been masquerading as a straight man all these years when you know you're gay?"

"I'm not gay. I'm bi."

"Same difference. If I had known…"

He trailed off, chest heaving, eyes narrowed as though in pain. Our eyes met and held, and mine widened in understanding. *Holy fuck.* How had I missed this? My face flushed, and I stepped back away from him.

"Trevor, I-I didn't know. Why didn't you say something?"

"Would it have mattered?" he snapped. "Plus, I'm your boss. You don't have relations with the people you work for."

"Is that why you got upset with me for being with Declan? Because I worked for him?"

He stepped back from me. "Who says I'm upset? I

understand how these things work. You hit the Jackpot. You'd hardly let him go at this point."

The compassion I had begun to feel for him fizzled away. "I'm not with Declan for his money."

He made a grunt of disbelief. "This conversation is getting out of hand. What's your purpose here, Owen?"

Without a word, I placed the envelope on his desk.

"I guess that's your resignation letter?" he asked, reaching for the envelope. He tore it open and took out the sheet of paper, barely scanning it.

"Yes, I think you'll understand why I can't work here anymore."

He leaned back into his chair. "Why? Because he now owns your ass? He says to resign, so you resign? He says move out, so you move into his house?"

"How did you know I moved?"

"After trying to reach you several times without success, do you think it was hard to figure out where you were?" He stood and walked over to the filing cabinet in the corner of the room. Pulling out a drawer, he started thumbing through the files. "Look, it doesn't matter anymore. I think this is the best decision considering."

"But my contract says I'll have to give a month's notice."

He waved a hand at me. "Forget about it. We never enforce that around here anyway. Just leave. Thanks for your time with the company."

I nodded. "I'm sorry this couldn't be an amicable parting."

He didn't respond, and I took that as my cue to leave, so I did just that, still reeling with the shock of Trevor being into me. He had never once let on how he felt. Hell, I didn't even know the guy's sexual orientation. My whole world had been focused on my kids, so even if he had been hitting on me, it would have flown right over my head.

Several other co-workers were standing around my car, commenting on it, but I barely waved a hand to the guys. As I slid into the driver's seat, I heard the comment.

"Damn, who knew an old piece of ass could be worth so much."

The comment left me with an acrid taste in my mouth and bile rising in my throat. Was that what everyone who knew me before would think of me, because I was with Declan? I hated the speculation of why I was with him, but I had known this would inevitably happen.

I put on an audiobook even though I was too distracted to follow the narrator's voice, but it calmed me down the more I listened. I was almost home when a car in front of me slowed down, the backdoor opened and a sack was thrown out to the sidewalk. At first, I thought the person was dumping garbage, and I honked my car horn which only resulted in the driver picking up speed.

"Son of a bitch," I muttered at the littering scumbags. I was all for catching the license plate number, but I wasn't as good with numbers as Declan. And movement in the bag that now lay on the side of the road caught my attention.

I slowed down given the light traffic and pulled up to the shoulder of the road where I wouldn't impede other drivers. Getting out of the car, I hesitated about what to do. Not knowing what was in the bag was killing me, but at the same time, that squirming would not let me leave, knowing it was something alive. And then I heard it—the pitiful yelps of a wounded dog.

I knew how risky it was since I had no idea if the animal was vicious or not, but how could I leave it there? The end of the bag was tied, and there was no way that animal was going to get free. The damn driver hadn't even punched holes in the bag for the animal to breathe properly.

A mixture of rage and empathy had me deciding to move with caution, but going to free the animal. I spoke in soothing tones as I crouched at the bag, working the knot loose. The whimpering continued, but I was terribly alarmed by the lack of movement from the dog when the mouth of the bag was finally opened. It was as if the animal preferred the safety of being in that bag than being in the open, and that ripped at my heart like you'd never believe.

Carefully, I peeled back the bag to reveal more of the dog. An Italian Greyhound, with the most pitiful eyes I had ever seen, stared back at me. Their left leg went up to cover their face as if deflecting, and I noticed the scars their dirty coat could not hide.

"My God, you poor thing," I crooned to the animal. "I'm not going to hurt you."

It took me damn near an hour to coax the dog out of the bag and into my arms. I was hell-bent not to force them out though, but to let them leave on their own accord.

26

DECLAN

Arriving home earlier than planned to find Owen not home was a mixture of relief and disappointment. He was expecting me tomorrow, but I hadn't been able to wait any longer. The ink hadn't even dried on the deal Charles and I had made when I'd been heading for the private airstrip to get on the jet and fly out of D.C. Talking to Owen at night wasn't enough. It had felt strange going to bed without him beside me.

With Owen absent, I had the driver and David help me to take the equipment I had bought for Owen's birthday into the room I kept locked from him. He had no idea what I had planned, and I wanted to keep it that way. Over the next couple of days, I would have to distract him while the interior decorator came by to do the transformation like we had talked about.

I couldn't wait to see the look on Owen's face when I revealed the room to him. Everything so far was all planned to perfection. His kids had all confirmed they wouldn't miss his forty-seventh birthday for the world. The one thing I hadn't been sure about was whether or not to invite James. In the end, I did invite him, because it would make his kids happy to see us all together. It was also a good way of showing everyone that I understood quite well that James would forever be a part of our family, and I was okay with this.

Our driver, Barry left, and I made for my office. The new driver Owen and I had settled on was in his mid-thirties, spoke very little, but was pleasant whenever addressed. I didn't mind if we never had that kind of relationship that Silas and I had enjoyed. Silas was one of a kind, and I didn't anticipate having another driver like that man.

On my desk, I found a pile of mail and shuffled through it until I saw one that was rather interesting. It was addressed to me and stamped by the Ohio Cancer Research Institute.

Curious as to what the letter was about, and because this meant more to me than some realized, I ripped open the envelope and took out the letter.

Dear Mr. Declan Moore,

The Ohio Cancer Research Institute will be hosting their bi-annual Awards and recognition dinner on Saturday July 28th. The Board of Committee would like to recognize your unwavering support of stem-cell research and other new technologies for fighting cancer.

It is with great honor that we will be using this function as a means to highlight the achievements we have made thanks to your

*charity and foundation. We have enclosed tickets to the event, and
we hope that you will be there to accept this award.*

I re-read the letter and took note of the signature
before replacing the letter in the envelope and pushing it
under a book. For years I had been supporting the
research institute through the charity set up in my mother's honor. I didn't need any recognition for it, however.
The initiative had been Charles's, and although he had
slacked off, I had picked up the reins and ensured that we
gave millions in donations every year. It was one way of
remaining close to my mother.

Pushing the award from my mind, I walked out of
the office in search of David. I found him in the kitchen,
closing the refrigerator. When I entered, he turned to
acknowledge me.

"Have any idea where Owen went?" I asked.

"I'm not so sure, sir," David answered. "He's been
gone a long time, though. I expected him back already,
given I had to drag him away from the computer because
he wasn't eating."

"What do you mean he wasn't eating?" I asked,
alarmed. "Is he sick?"

David groaned. "I wasn't supposed to let that slip.
I've only been able to get him to eat because he thinks
you call me to check up on him."

I frowned. "He's been holed up in my office again,
writing himself weary to the bone?"

"I'm afraid you've unleashed a passion that's been
locked up inside him for a rather long time," he
responded. "I'm pretty sure it's nothing to worry about,

and that as soon as he's let some steam off, he will slow down a little."

"Hmm. Maybe I should have thought of something else for a birthday gift. This will only encourage him."

"But he'll be so excited, sir."

Yes, he would, and even though I thought it, I knew I would do anything to support Owen's dreams rather than put him down. This was his moment to shine, and I would help him get all the way to the top if he would let me. He had turned down my offer to get him published, but I could do other related stuff to still be involved in his work. If he was hell-bent spending the rest of his years writing, then I would see to it that he had the right environment for his comfort.

I just had to trust him that he wouldn't get lost in his work and forget all about me.

"I'd like your opinion on something, David," I told him, fishing into my pocket for the flat black velvet box.

Rather than to risk Owen finding out about the proposal beforehand, I had used my time in D.C to visit a jeweler and gotten a ring I thought suitable for an engagement. Charles had helped me to choose, and that had been another bonding experience for us. It turned out the old man did have some useful opinions on rings and what suited Owen. I'd had no idea he'd studied my soon-to-be-fiancé so intently, but he had quickly assured me that he would give the same treatment to any man I was serious about. I couldn't have called him out on it, because I'd never been this serious about anyone before.

David gasped when I popped open the box. "Why,

sir? I never thought you felt this way about me. What will Owen think?"

"He'll never believe it." I laughed at his teasing tone as he took the box to inspect the ring—a simple milgrained ring in white gold. Seven small diamonds shone from the channel setting in the band.

"This is breathtaking," the butler remarked. "He will simply love it."

"I guess the big question isn't if he will love it, but if he will say yes to wearing it."

David gave me a wide-eyed look as he handed me back the box. "Is there any other response but yes?"

"I hope not. He'd break my heart if he said no, but maybe it's too soon."

"Your heart will tell you if it's too soon." He frowned, creases forming in the center of his forehead. He opened his mouth to add something, then closed it.

"What is it?"

"Umm, nothing, sir."

"No, it's something," I persisted. "You were going to say something just now. You *do* think it's too soon."

"Oh no, not that, sir. I was simply going to ask to permit me to help in the planning of the wedding."

I eyed my butler as if I was seeing him for the first time. The color in his cheeks was higher than usual. "You want to help plan my wedding?"

He shrugged. "It was stupid of me to suggest. I know you probably have some well-known wedding planner in mind already. It's just that, it's something I've always wanted to continue doing. I planned my sister's wedding, and it was stunning. I've always regretted not finishing my training in events planning."

He was right that I had already picked out the wedding planner who had helped me to plan Charles's last wedding. I was leaving nothing to chance. Yet, there was so much hope in his eyes that I thought I at least owed him to show us what he was capable of.

"Okay," I agreed. "If Owen says yes, then you can show us what you've got planned and we'll tell you if it's up our alley."

His eyes brimmed with tears. "Oh my God, I'm going to plan your wedding."

I chuckled at his enthusiasm. "*If* Owen says yes."

"If Owen says yes to what?"

At Owen's voice, I quickly pocketed the jewelry box and turned to face him. My smile of greeting fell away when I saw how tired he looked. He had dirt on his clothes, and he was holding a dog in a blanket like a baby.

"Owen, what the hell happened?" I asked, marching toward him, but the Italian Greyhound in his arms squirmed and started to howl a pitiful sound. Owen stepped back from me.

"Don't come closer. He's still skittish of other people. It took me an hour to get him out of the bag and another hour to get him into the car with me. We spent all afternoon at the vet."

I shook my head, trying to make sense of what he was saying. "You picked up a stray?" This time I kept my voice low as Owen rubbed the dog's head.

He turned sad eyes toward me. "He's not a stray.

Some cruel piece of shit just threw him out on the sidewalk in a bag. The poor thing seemed to be used to that sort of treatment. He shows signs of terrible neglect. His front left paw is useless. He had a fracture that never healed properly, and the vet says he'll never use that leg again."

"That's horrible!" David cried. "The poor thing was probably cast aside because he can no longer perform in races. It's such a widespread problem here that I wish something more could be done for them."

Owen nodded sadly. "That's what the vet says. So many are discarded or sent to the pound when deemed unfit for racing. I'm glad I was there to rescue this little one. It makes me so angry that someone can treat them like this. I wish I had gotten the license plate number of that car."

"There are shelters around Cincy that try to rescue Greyhounds," I said, unable to tear my eyes away from the dog in Owen's arms. The mutt was trembling. It was a wonder he had allowed Owen to get close to him, but then my man could be rather patient and loving. The IG could not have encountered a better person.

"I don't want to take him to a shelter," Owen said, eyes imploring. "I don't think I could give him up after all we've been through today. It was so sad seeing the way he reacted to the vet at first. Can we keep him, please?"

"Owen I—"

"No, listen. You don't have to do a thing for him," he rushed to add. "I'll be a hundred percent responsible for him. I'll ensure he gets walked every day, and the vet believes he's properly trained. He's had all his shots, and all he needs is a little love and a home. He doesn't deserve to be cast aside simply because he's no longer in his prime." His eyes bored into mine. "You of all people understand that, don't you, Dec?"

Of course, I understood. Owen saw himself in that dog, and there was no way in hell he would be happy without knowing firsthand his new pet was okay. I could appreciate him not wanting to give up on the animal. It was kind of the way I didn't care that people would say that Owen was past his prime. He didn't hold any lesser value for me.

"Of course, you can keep him," I told him softly, walking slowly toward him so I didn't startle the new addition to our family. The dog whimpered, but didn't let out that howling sound that he had earlier. A hand on Owen's shoulder, I kissed him. "We'll take care of him. Alright?"

He bit into his bottom lip, worried. "You won't change your mind later if he makes a mess or chews on your couch or something?"

That wasn't something I was looking forward to, but if it did happen, it wouldn't cause me to throw the dog out. "I won't change my mind."

Owen's shoulders slumped in relief. "Thank God. It's been a horrible day. First quitting my job, finding out the reason Trevor hated me all of a sudden, and rescuing the dog. Plus, I don't think I slept enough last night. I'm feeling extremely tired."

"I'll help you find a place to make him comfortable," David offered. "I think we have a laundry basket large enough that we can pad with some towels. I'll also get him a bowl."

Owen smiled at David. "Thank you."

I rubbed his back, feeling the tension in his muscles. He wasn't lying about the day he'd had. It hadn't escaped me either that he'd mentioned quitting his job, and his supervisor Trevor, but we would get to that later after the dog was settled.

"I'll run you a bath for you to wind down," I told him as David left to find all the things he'd mentioned. "Are you hungry?"

"A little," he admitted. "Just something light. Don't think I could eat anything heavy right now."

"Good. I'll get you something."

"Are you going to make it yourself?" he asked, and for the first time since he'd come home, he smiled.

"No, smartass," I replied. "But if I did, you'd eat it and love it too."

"Of course, I would. I love you so much right now for letting me keep him."

"I wouldn't have it any other way, Owen."

David returned with the basket, and they brought the items upstairs to our bedroom to set up in the corner, because Owen didn't want the dog to be out of sight. While they went about padding the interior, I ordered us a soup and salad meal from the restaurant that usually catered to our needs when I had food delivered. Then when David left and Owen tried to get the dog to stay in the basket instead of following him everywhere, I went through to our bathroom and prepared a bath for him, setting up scented candles that would soothe him.

I was about to get him when he entered the bathroom wearing nothing but his boxers. He paused at the entrance and took in the softly lit bathroom, smiling at me.

"I should be doing this for you since you've been away from home."

I walked over to him at the door and pulled him inside while reaching for his boxers to get him fully undressed. "I'll take a rain check on that. You need it more than I do right now."

He sighed, stepping out of his boxers. "I'm sorry, but I'm too tired for sex right now."

I frowned at him. "That's fine. I'm not expecting sex from you, Boy. Now stop thinking so much. Get into the bath, and stay there until I get you."

He stared at the door. "But if he wakes up…"

"Don't worry, I'll sit with him. Just get in and stay in."

Instead of moving to the Jacuzzi, he wound his arms around my neck. "Dec, I swear if I didn't love you already, I'd fall in love with you now. I don't know what the fuck I did to deserve you, but I won't question it. I'll just love you back as best as I can."

I dropped a kiss on his lips. Nothing more because I could indeed see how tired he was. I ensured he was situated in the warm bath first, hearing his contented sigh, before I left him alone while I went to sit with *our* dog.

27

OWEN

Tomorrow would be my birthday, but as I glared at the computer screen, all I could think about was how much I sucked. And not even in the good way, like sucking on Declan's cock or something. I meant that I genuinely *sucked.* That was how I felt, as I acknowledged that I had no idea where I was going with this new story.

Who the hell said I could be a writer anyway?

I had been riding the waves of euphoria ever since I finished my novel and sent it off to the agent of my first choice of publishing house. And even though Declan had assured me that night I had brought our dog Lucky home that he loved my book, now I wondered if he was only being polite. What did I expect anyway? We were sleeping together, and he wouldn't want to crush my feelings. He didn't read a lot either, so maybe he thought it was good, but it really was crap.

Oh God, what if I had sent a crappy manuscript to an agent?

What if they were right now laughing at me thinking I could be a writer?

Forcing such thoughts from my mind, I scratched Lucky's head and tried to return to my writing. Hands planted on random keys, I typed, and gibberish came out. None of it made sense, and I had no idea what to do. I had no idea what the next step should be.

"Hey, you okay over there?" Declan asked.

I had completely forgotten that he was at his own desk working. "I'm fine," I said, lying through the skin of my teeth. "Just a bit tired."

"You've been at it all day," he replied. "Why don't you give it a break? You don't want to get burned out."

Burned out on my second book? Maybe I didn't have it in me at all. "I don't think I can do this," I confessed, staring at the dog sleeping at my feet. Lucky had become attached to me, and even followed Declan around as well. It was so good to see him gaining health, and Declan was talking about him getting the surgery to correct his damaged leg to increase the probability of him using it again.

"Owen, leave the computer and come here."

I didn't want to. He would try to make me all better, and I wasn't sure I deserved to feel better right now. I just wanted to wallow for a minute in my incompetence.

"Well, don't keep me waiting, Boy."

And when he got *that* way, I couldn't say no. With a sigh, I rose to my feet. The sudden movement had Lucky raising his head.

"It's okay, Lucky. I'm not leaving."

The dog watched me walk over to Declan, and when

he was satisfied I hadn't gone far, he rested his head onto the floor and went back to sleep, ignoring us. I walked around Declan's desk and stood beside him. He pushed back his chair and motioned for me to sit on his desk.

"Now why don't you tell me the truth? What's wrong? You must have sighed a dozen times in the last half an hour."

"I don't think I'm good at this," I answered.

"At this what?"

"Writing," I answered. "What if I'm just deluding myself, Declan, and I really suck. What if nobody likes the stuff I write? What if they think—"

"What if they think your book is awesome like I do?" he interrupted. "What then? Owen, I told you that it's good. You had an agent already express interest in getting her hands on this book. If my own opinion doesn't count for much, then at least consider hers."

"But she knows you. What if she's being polite?"

"And what if she's not?" he countered easily. "Owen, do you enjoy writing?"

I nodded. "Of course, I do."

"Then that's the reason you should continue. Not the thousand *what ifs* that your mind can come up with."

"And if nobody reads my work?"

He took both my hands. "You already have a fan. I'll read anything you write." He kissed my hands and rose to his feet. "I think you need a distraction. Tomorrow is your birthday. I need you in the best mood possible for your big day."

I let out a contented sigh. "What kind of distraction?"

"I'll tell you in just a minute. I'll have to make a call first. Why don't you go up to the bathroom and take a shower? I'll lay out something for you to wear."

I was too curious to press the issue, so I got off his desk. "Okay. Will you be joining me?"

"Soon. Go."

Lucky trotted after me, and I scooped him up to make the walk up the stairs easier for him with only three functioning legs. Once in the bedroom, he hopped over to his bedding and curled up, completely forgetting about me. I stripped and hurried into the bathroom, expecting Declan to join me, but he didn't.

Disappointed, I eventually exited the shower and toweled off my body carefully. I had even taken the time to cleanse myself as best as possible for him, making myself ready for anything he had in mind. I entered the bedroom naked to find him waiting for me, a leather outfit on the bed.

This was about to get kinky.

"I called Heath," he stated. "When you agreed to us going to a dungeon to satisfy your curiosity, I hope you meant it, and it wasn't a joke."

I stared at him, numb. Sure, I had meant it at the time, but I didn't really think we would go. Not that I didn't want to. Hell, yes, I wanted to, if just to eliminate that curiosity from my mind.

"Did you mean it?" he asked.

"Uh, will I have to do anything?" I asked, because from the little that I knew, I wasn't certain I would be able to get involved in the scenes.

"No. We'll be there to hang out with a friend of mine

and for you to observe," he answered. "Heath runs a very safe and consensual club. He's very particular about who gets in, and once you're banned, it's for life. No one dares to cross him."

"Sounds intense."

"It can be." He sat on the bed, observing me. "I know you've been curious. I love that about you. If you'd like to go, we'll do so tonight."

Tomorrow I would be forty-seven. I had never experienced anything of the sort before. I nodded. "Sure, let's go."

"Good. But sit here a minute." He patted the bed beside him. "I need to explain the rules to you before we go. Heath's my very trusted friend, and I do not want to unleash you unprepared in a dungeon. Things will be very different. Some things you might never have fathomed. Mostly we'll be watching the stage where the exhibitionists usually are."

I went over to the bed to sit beside him, because I didn't want to be the newbie at the club either. It was way more information than expected as he explained the reason for the leather outfit he had placed on the bed for me, to what I would do once I was at the club—which was really nothing—and how to keep my emotions in check, not disturbing a scene and so on.

It was a lot to remember.

"Basically, follow my lead," he ended. "And it's important to remember, regardless of what you see happening, everything at the dungeon is consensual and negotiated before play happens."

"Okay."

He cupped the side of my face. "I don't mean to scare you, babe, but this is serious. It's a safe place for members of the community to express their desires, and Heath works damn hard to keep it that way. He's very respected in the BDSM community."

Got it. Don't do anything to piss off Heath. Follow Declan's lead, and everything will be okay.

"Still sure you want to do this?" he asked again.

"Yes, I'm certain."

"And you remember your safe word? If any time you're feeling uncomfortable, just say the word, and I'll get you out of there."

And just like that he had me at ease again. "Okay."

"Good." He got to his feet and tugged off his shirt. "Get dressed in the outfit on the bed then wait for me downstairs. I'll be with you in an hour or so."

It took me close to half an hour to get on the skin-tight leather pants and boots. At least he had gotten me a matching leather vest that covered much of my hairy chest. He loved my fuzz, but not everyone would feel the same.

I brought the dog outside to do his business, since he would be left alone, before we returned to the house. I didn't have any worry of Lucky remaining at home by himself. He was a quiet animal who slept a lot. The vet had said he was still recuperating and until then he would be a bit sluggish. His bowls were filled with water and food, although he shouldn't be hungry before we returned.

I settled in the living room and brought out my phone which I would have to leave in the car. According to Declan, phones were prohibited in the dungeon to maintain the privacy of the members.

I opened the group chat I had with my kids and initiated conversation with them until Declan was ready. They responded immediately wanting to know what the plan was for my birthday. They still refused to confirm whether or not they were coming to Cincy, but they couldn't fool me for a minute. I knew Declan had a party planned. I had even told him that I didn't want a fancy do. Just him and my kids, and my heart would be content.

Auggie had just left the group chat with a vague excuse that he had to go when I felt Declan's presence enter the living room. I glanced up with a smile which fell from my lips.

"Oh fuck."

Declan grinned at me, and I couldn't help staring at him in his leather gear. *And I thought my pants were skintight.* His seemed painted on him accentuating his lean muscles. His leather pants had a flap at the front that did very little to hide the flaccid bulge beneath. When aroused, he would be a sight to behold behind that flap. His chest was bare except for the chest harness held together with a silver ring in the center. Two tight leather strips were around his biceps, and to complete his outfit he had on black gloves and a hat that resembled the shape of a police hat.

"I take it that I pass," he stated.

"Can we just stay home and have fun instead?" I asked breathlessly.

With a chuckle, Declan walked over to me and

gripped my chin. He leaned my head back and kissed me hard, tongue wrapping around mine as he pressed me back into the couch. I opened up for him, ready to give him whatever he wanted.

He pulled back. "Heath's expecting us. I got these outfits when I was in DC, hoping we'd get to use them, so we're going to show off a little tonight. We don't have to stay long. Just give me a chance to check on how he's been treating Ridge. Are you ready to go?"

I nodded and bit my tongue, because if I spoke, I would be asking him to cancel our outing. But I really wanted to see what all the fuss was about when it came to dungeons. Declan had been there and done that. Light BDSM was okay with him, but I already knew he wasn't into the heavy stuff which was okay with me. I just wanted to *know*.

28

DECLAN

As I parked the car in front of the gray building, I noticed that there were quite a number of vehicles already parked. I hadn't been to the club in a while, but from the class of cars I was seeing, Heath's clientele had caught the interest of some very wealthy people living in Cincy. Although, Heath did travel around, visiting various BDSM clubs in different cities to teach safe practices and host shows.

I glanced over at Owen and couldn't tell if he had stopped breathing. He looked like it. He was peering out the window, taking in his surroundings. I'd tried to keep things light on the drive to the club, but when I had announced five minutes ago that we were approaching the club, he had gone silent and tense.

"Think Lucky will truly be okay on his own?" he asked, turning his head to me as I removed the key from the ignition.

"He usually sleeps well at night," I reminded him.

"His bowls are full if he needs anything. I think he'll still be fast asleep when we get home. We won't be out for long anyway. Just hang around enough to give you a tour, catch up with Ridge and Heath, and then I get to take you home and you tell me which new kink you want to try."

At least that brought on a smile from him. He gave a small laugh. "I'm sorry I come across as freaking out. I just don't know what to expect."

"It will be fine. Now stay put. Let me get the door for you."

He didn't argue which showed how occupied his mind was. Even though he allowed me to open doors for him, he would grumble that he could get it himself. He was so nervous he hadn't even removed his seatbelt when I opened up his door.

"Sorry," he apologized and reached for it, but I brushed his hands aside and gave him a smile.

"It's okay. I'll do it." I unbuckled him from his seat, but didn't move back for him to leave the car. I rubbed his thighs in the tight leather he wore. "Hey, if you don't want to do this, we can always come back some other night. Or better yet, use the internet to satisfy your curiosity."

"Oh no. We're already here. We're doing this."

"Good Boy. Now give Daddy a kiss to show him how grateful you are that he's brought you here."

He leaned forward and just before his lips touched mine, he whispered, "Thank you, Daddy."

His kiss was soft and sweet. It didn't last long either, but I was completely fine with that. I helped him from the car and together we headed for the almost hidden glass front door. Heath didn't want his dungeon to resemble a back alley of shame, and I wouldn't have brought Owen any other place but here to experience this for his first time.

"If it eases your mind, Heath's a clinical psychologist," I told him. "He knows what he's doing, and once you enter through these doors, he has your best interests at heart. You will see dungeon monitors moving silently around to ensure everything stays the way Heath wants it. Safe for everyone involved."

"Wait." He clutched my arm. "Heath is a psychologist?"

I grinned at him. "Yeah. What did you think? That he rides a motorcycle, wears leather all day and keeps a sub at his feet at all times? Nah, that part of him comes out when he breaks down his cuffs and removes his tie."

"Wow. My mind is blown. I can't wait to meet this man."

I wrapped an arm around his waist from behind and caught the lobe of his ear with my teeth. "You're mine, Owen. I know this won't happen, but if anyone touches you while we're here, you can count this your one and only experience at a dungeon."

At my growl, he grinned at me. "You know you're so good for my ego. You make me feel like I'll catch the eyes of other men around when I doubt that will happen."

"Hmm. Remember the club on the Fourth? You're damn desirable, Owen. You just don't see it, but the rest of us do."

At the door, I pressed the buzzer and a few seconds

passed before the door was opened. The large guy who stood at the entrance was bald with a tattoo running over his scalp. He wore leather similar to mine.

"Friends of Heath," I told the guy. I was pleased when I glanced at Owen to find he wasn't gawking at the nipple rings the man had in, nor the multitude of piercings.

"I need names," security answered, tapping away at his phone.

"Declan Moore."

He paused and glanced up at me. "ID?"

I showed him my ID, and only then did he crack a smile and opened the door wider for us to enter.

"Heath told me to expect you and your companion," he stated. "Let me notify him that you're here. I know he wanted to greet you himself."

"Thank you."

The man walked away giving us a healthy view of his naked ass, because the back of his leather pants didn't have a seat.

"You okay, Owen?" I asked, reaching for his hand to squeeze.

"Yup, totally fine."

I grinned at him trying to appear nonchalant about what he'd just witnessed. We were barely inside the club, and there was really nothing to see here in the hall where we waited. A few lewd sketches were on the wall which was a surprise. I had expected Heath to get rid of them, but knowing the man, he probably kept them around as a mechanism to get over the hurt of what Ridge had done to him.

Owen pointed out one of the paintings of an orgy in exaggerated form. "We should hang one of those in our bedroom."

"Sure. I'll ask Ridge if he's up to drawing another."

His mouth fell open. "Ridge drew that?"

Before I could answer, a familiar man materialized from behind the thick curtains that hid what lay just beyond the entrance. Heath. Something moved inside me. Happiness I supposed. I hadn't seen him in quite some time since I'd had to split my loyalty from him to help Ridge deal with their breakup.

He didn't seem to have aged any at all. Even though I never quite knew his age, he had to be pushing fifty or pretty close. The silver in his hair was quite pronounced and his body was just as solid as ever. Dressed in black boots, tight leather pants and matching leather jacket, he could resemble anyone from the leather community, but he didn't. Heath sucked the breath out of a room—in a good way. You felt him whenever he entered a room. You stared at him, and I was damned proud of Owen for not having his jaw on the floor.

With the leather jacket he wore hanging open, the myriad of tattoos along his chest were revealed. As he stepped forward, the material parted flashing us with the nipple rings he wore. They were medium-sized rings that would be perfect for nipple play and reminded me of Owen suggesting I should get my nipples pierced.

His nipples weren't the only thing pierced, and I wasn't even referring to the rings he had lining his cock. Heath's tongue was pierced in two places, and he had in a hoop for his septum piercing.

Heath grinned when he saw me. "Well goddammit, if you're not a sight for sore eyes! My little pup has grown into a man."

I snorted at his antics as I met him halfway, and we embraced. This man had given me a solid foundation and molded me into the Daddy I was for Owen today. He clapped me heartily on the back, almost dislodging my spine—the strength of the brute. It was what Ridge had liked about him at first. He used to go on and on about how Daddy Heath could easily lift him and throw his back into the wall while they fucked. Back when they had been happy together.

"I've missed you too, Master Heath," I said, respectfully using his title since we were in his establishment. This was his scene that I wished to be a part of for a short time, but for as long as we were here, we would follow protocol. "If you let me go, I'll introduce my partner to you."

"No introduction necessary," Heath replied, letting me go and approaching Owen. He held out a hand. "I'm Master Heath, and you owe me a whole lot of gratitude for teaching Daddy Declan everything he knows."

Owen's cheeks turned red, but he remembered to shake Heath's hand. "It's nice to meet you, Master Heath. I'm Owen—" he pointed at me, "—his Boy."

His response was perfect. Still he glanced at me, seeking my assurance, and I nodded at him, smiling with all the affection I felt for him.

"You've trained him well," Heath remarked, releasing Owen's hand. "And he seems perfect for you. Are you ready to go in?"

I returned to Owen's side. "Sure. Let's. Owen's been dying to see what your lifestyle is about."

Heath smiled ruefully as he led us beyond the curtains. "Hope I didn't disappoint in what you expected."

"Umm, actually I had no idea what to think," Owen admitted. "Daddy's been quite tight-lipped about you, Master Heath."

I couldn't be any more pleased with Owen. I wasn't certain he had processed all I had said, but he was setting the scene for himself to get comfortable, and he'd picked up that one way to do that was to use our titles.

"So how have you been all these years?" Heath asked, as we walked down a long narrow hall.

"Working away as usual," I replied. "Taking care of Ridge and hosting bachelor parties. Speaking of Ridge, is he here? How is he?"

"He'll get there." We came to a stop at another door that Heath opened with a swipe card. He paused to glance back at us. "Need to use the locker rooms?"

"No, we're just here to observe," I answered quickly even as Owen gripped my hand tight. He relaxed his hold at my words.

"Such a shame," Heath replied with a chuckle. "But then you never did like to share, did you, Daddy Declan?"

"I don't share," I said, reiterating what he already knew. "I won't even pretend that I do."

"Your Boy feels the same?"

"Damn right he does," I answered, but I left the bite

out of my words, because this touched too close to home for Heath.

We entered the main area where a lot was happening. Heath had redesigned since the last time I had visited. The stage was bigger. To the right was a setup like a bar, but I knew that couldn't be, because Heath vehemently refused to serve an ounce of liquor in his dungeon. He was dead set against the practice, which was understandable. Some of the practices indulged in the dungeon could turn lethal if not handled with care.

My gaze skimmed over the various people who were seated around the main stage area. Owen was busy taking in as much as he could from the suspensions hanging from the ceilings to the various toys that were either in use or not. Subs knelt or sat at the feet of their Doms, who were busy socializing with each other.

Owen startled, and I turned to find out what had caught his attention. I smiled in amusement at the sub who had his head and hands trapped in a ventilated isolation box that hung from the ceiling. The box resembled a smaller version of a coffin, so I could see how that seemed strange to him.

I leaned over to him. "Remember, don't gawk."

He glanced away quickly. "Right. Sorry."

"Looking won't get you into trouble," Heath said, overhearing our conversation. "We have quite a number of exhibitionists here who don't mind you looking and enjoying at their expense. It's one of the reasons I made this stage. We get to watch the Doms and their subs at play."

"Apart from this main hall," I added, to explain to

Owen, "if you follow those thick curtains around, they lead to different rooms for various activities. There are special rooms for penetrative play, right, Heath?"

"That's right. Can I get you two something to drink?"

I stared at him in surprise. "You serve liquor now?"

He frowned. "No, not liquor. You know my stance when it comes to that. However, we do provide energy drinks, bottles of water, and fruit juices so everyone can replenish regularly."

"Just water will be fine," I answered, at the same time I checked with Owen, who nodded.

"Great." Heath pointed to a scattering of seats closer to the front of the room. "Have a seat, and I'll be back."

29

OWEN

As Declan and I made our way over to the section Heath had pointed out, I could feel curious eyes on us. If Declan was right, Heath ran a tight operation so it made sense a couple of strange faces would garner so much attention. I tried not to gawk or react in any way that made me stand out more as a newbie on the scene, but I was certain I didn't always hide my shock. Like finding that man standing with his head in a box that lowered from the ceiling by chains. Or seeing the other man staring back at me from a cage on the floor that didn't look big enough to fit me. He couldn't stretch out comfortably there, but he didn't seem to have a problem with it. In fact, he looked rather content just being there.

The dungeon did have a dark and depraved feeling to it. The lights were low guaranteeing intimacy, even when knowing dozens of eyes were on you. When Declan sat, I paused, not sure what to do. *Did he want me at his feet like I saw happening with other subs who were sitting?* He took the decision out of my hands by patting the seat next to me.

"Come curl up next to Daddy."

I hoped my relief didn't show when I curled up into Declan's side like he suggested. Now this I preferred to being at his feet. I had no problem with the subs sitting by their Doms' feet looking happy about it, but that wasn't the kind of relationship Declan and I had.

A man wearing boots with painful looking studs walked by us tugging on a leash. My eyes widened at the sight of his sub, completely naked except for a harness with a long horse-like tail. His face was disguised by the matching horse hood over his head. His legs were encased in boots with fur and his hands covered in…hooves?

Declan kissed the side of my face. "Ever heard of pony play?"

I shook my head. "No, Daddy."

"You're in for such a treat tonight, Boy. Daddy can't wait to show you all the depraved things you get to choose from later."

I swallowed hard, and my dick swelled in the tight confines of the leather. "I can't wait, Daddy."

While he stroked my warm skin, I continued my observation of the room, really taking note of the things I would like to be done to me. If not later, then sometime in the future. I was fascinated by the young man bound in rope suspended from the ceiling. Not something I'd be into for fear that I'd pass out even before all the knots were fastened, but it was nonetheless intriguing.

Now the guy sitting on a chair having his ass eaten

looked right up my alley. The chair was specially designed with a cut-out. His legs were spread, and the other man servicing him was lying on the floor on his back, his face beneath the chair.

I tugged on Declan's arm. "Can we have one of those?" I whispered so no one else could hear.

He chuckled, the eyes he trained on me full of patience. "We can have anything your heart desires, baby Boy. Maybe I should have gotten you a pen and paper to jot it all down?" he teased.

Before I could respond, Heath returned with our drinks, but didn't stay, stating there was a scene he needed to check on before he could settle in with us. He disappeared, leaving Declan and me to sip our water and continue our observation of the room. Apparently, the guy pretending to be a pony wasn't the only furry around. One section of the room was set up like a kennel with plates and dog cages. One guy lay on his back contentedly while his master scratched him all over.

"Want to check out the other rooms?" Declan asked me after a while. "There are some that are open to everyone's viewing and others are restricted."

I nodded. "Okay."

He stood and helped me to my feet. Again, the eyes were on us. I shrugged off the feeling of being watched, and focused on enjoying the night and broadening my knowledge.

As he led me past a huge man who tipped his bottle of water toward me, Declan shifted me in front of him. I wasn't surprised at the possessive hold of his hand on my ass from then on. I didn't mind either. He was definitely a catch from tonight's picking, and he was *my* catch. I felt damn lucky. And stupidly in love.

Never in a million years would I have agreed to this before I met him, but here I was opening my mind and seeing the myriad of possibilities to enhance our sex life, which was amazing, but there was always room to try new things, and I was down for trying stuff at least once. At least some things.

We left the main sitting and display area to move through another curtain. This corridor was darker, and goosebumps washed over my skin when I heard the moans, groans, whispering, screams and whimpers. I must have startled, because Declan stopped to eye me.

"Remember, you just have to say you're ready to go and we're out of here."

"Okay, Daddy."

I loved the way he always checked up on me, ensuring I was okay with every little thing. He took nothing for granted. That showed me how much he cared. It was these little things over time that had convinced me that this young man saw me as the love of his life.

We didn't really stop for long at any of the rooms. The first had more than one couple engaged in swapping partners. We barely spent a couple of seconds there. As hot as it looked seeing all the naked flesh, it didn't really whet my appetite, mostly because I couldn't ever see myself sharing Declan with anyone else.

The second room had a Do Not Disturb sign, so we went by it. The third seemed more fun, but another poly play with a naked sub lying on a round table that spun. We entered the room for a few minutes, silently observing the scene without disrupting them. The sub was brought right around the circle of people who did all kinds of things to him, from spanking to having him suck on their condom-clad cocks.

With just a silent raise of his eyebrows, Declan communicated that he was ready to move on, so we did. The door to the next room was already wide open, and another couple was inside watching the scene that was taking place. I smiled when I noticed Heath with the couple. He waved us over, and I still tried not to stare too hard at him. Age had never looked so good on a person in my opinion. Heath was the epitome of what Declan had casually teased me about being—a silver fox. It wasn't hard to see the intelligence and experience in his eyes.

"You may be interested in this," he said quietly. He had been cheerful earlier when we'd met, but he had a grim look about him now. "He's been begging for this again, so I'm giving it to him."

"Heath," Declan started, staring at the sub who was moaning as if in pain. He was spread out on a cross, his welted back to us. There was something familiar about him.

"It has to be done," Heath returned.

"But you don't have to watch," Declan replied.

"I can't *not* watch. I have to ensure he's fine after."

It was their conversation that had me figuring it all out. Ridge. The young man bound to the cross was Ridge. I wasn't sure how I felt about watching someone I knew. I had been aware that he would probably be about, but I didn't expect him to be involved in a scene.

I reached out to touch Declan to ask that we move on, but my hand froze midair as the Dom who was punishing Ridge came into view. Dressed like I'd never seen him before in leather just like the rest of us, I almost passed out to recognize Auggie.

No, that can't be, I tried to reason, even as I watched the Auggie lookalike take a flogger to Ridge's back. *Auggie's in Columbus. He should be traveling to Cincy tomorrow with his brother for my party.*

"Fuck!" Declan muttered beside me when he recognized Auggie. "What is *he* doing here?"

I made to move forward. It was more of a self-conscious movement, but Declan's hand clamped on my arm to stall me.

"I know you're shaken up, but you can't interrupt the scene," he said in a hushed tone that was so low I doubted anyone else could hear. "He needs to cater to the needs of his sub."

Nooooooooooooooooo!

I still found it rather difficult to believe the man who flogged Ridge with such precise and practiced strokes was my son. This was a side of Auggie I had never seen before. Fuck, a side of him I wished I *hadn't* seen. If he had come out and told me what he liked, I would have been able to cope with it, but seeing him in action was so personal. I could never un-see it.

He was so controlled, so masterful, I couldn't tear my eyes away. I should have probably left once I identified him, but I was rooted to the spot, watching one of my babies demonstrate how much he had grown. How much he wasn't a little boy. I couldn't decide whether I was proud or appalled.

Declan came up behind me, his body as rigid as mine. He spoke into my ear. "Do you want to go?"

The word *yes* stuck in my throat. I should go. My son was whipping Ridge into shape. Over and over the flogger lashed Ridge's flesh, never in the same place one behind the other. Ridge's muffled grunts turned to pants and cries of pain. *I should really go.*

I shook my head. "No," I answered hoarsely.

The other couple who were in the room with us moved on. Heath let out a frustrated sound, and I turned my attention away from Auggie and Ridge to the man who was watching his lover being flogged by someone else. *Why isn't he doing it himself?* As much as he tried to hide it, he flinched each time Auggie struck Ridge. He was breathing harder, deeper, but not in an aroused manner either. He seemed upset.

"Fuck, Ridge, say the safe word already," Heath growled beneath his breath. "Fucking say it."

Auggie approached Ridge, his hands going into the man's hair to stroke him. His lips were close to Ridge's head as they spoke earnestly. Auggie was so deep into the scene that he hadn't once turned toward us. His whole focus was on Ridge and each reaction he got out of the sub's body.

"He's not going to code red," Declan said, his voice so sad that I wrapped an arm around his waist. The comfort wasn't for him alone. Something felt different in the room all of a sudden. I was uneasy, and it wasn't just me either. I didn't think Auggie pausing the scene to talk to Ridge was a part of the script. I didn't think the way Declan and Heath tried not to show their concern was usual. Something was off, and my son was involved. I wanted to go to him, but I also knew that would have been a big mistake.

"He has to for Master August to stop," Heath remarked. "It's what he asked for. That no matter how bad it got, not to stop until he used the color code."

Declan released me to grab Heath's arm and they backed out of the room. I wandered after them, but remained in the doorway so I could still see in the room where Auggie continued to reason with the bound man. Ridge kept shaking his head even as his back heaved. He was clearly in pain.

"You listen to me, Heath," Declan replied. "Ridge fucked up when he walked out on you. He's been beating himself up about it all these years. Don't you get it? Don't you see what's happening? He's letting himself be punished for it. He doesn't think he deserves your forgiveness. I'm telling you, he won't stop until August has him just a few inches away from death, and I'm not about to let the kid go that far."

"Kid?" Heath asked on a frown. "I've mentored Master August since his college days."

I paled. "Since college?"

"Why do I get the feeling something else is going on here?" Heath demanded.

"He's m-my son," I stammered. "August is my son."

Heath blinked at me, just as surprised as I had been when I spotted Auggie for the first time. "You're the father who's having a birthday tomorrow? He told me that was the reason he was in town, but decided to drop in a day early to check out the club."

Before he could say anything else, a figure materialized before us.

"Auggie?" I said his name softly.

He didn't acknowledge me, but thrust the flogger in his hand toward Heath.

"What's wrong?" Heath demanded, eyes going back inside the room. I tore my eyes away from Auggie inside as well to find Ridge sobbing. His lithe body jerked against the restraints at his hands and ankles.

"I call code red," Auggie replied, sounding strange and distant. "I can't do it—what he wants. His body's had enough, but he's still not satisfied. It would be abuse to continue. I'm sorry, but I can't Master Heath. I've let you down."

"Auggie, you've not—"

Auggie walked off, and I moved to follow after him, to make sure he's fine, but Heath grabbed me by the arm.

"No." He nodded at Declan. "I don't like the mood he's in. You go to him, Declan. He knows to go to the aftercare rooms, and I'm counting on you to make sure he's okay. That he knows he did not let me down. Tell him I'm proud of him, and I'm sorry for letting him do what I was too much of a coward to do. I'll stay with Ridge."

"I need to go to him," I insisted, pulling away from Heath. "He's my son."

"You know why his father can't be the one to go to

him right now," Heath told Declan as he inched inside the room. He turned to me. "Do you trust your Daddy, Owen?"

Confused, I glanced from him to the serious expression on Declan's face. "Yes, but—"

"There's no *but* about it," Heath replied, his voice so stern it made my spine straight. "It's either you trust him, or you don't. Which is it?"

"I trust him with my life," I said without missing a heartbeat.

"But will you trust him with your kid's?" Heath asked. "You're a sub. You're too new to this to understand, but what he needs right now is comfort and reassurance from another Dom who understands. Someone on his level. Daddy Declan can give him that. Let him."

30

OWEN

Declan was gone for a long time, and I worried. I still didn't understand what was happening with Auggie, but both Heath and Declan were concerned enough for me to worry. It was hard to go against my instincts to seek out my son and comfort him, but Declan was far more knowledgeable than me in these affairs. I decided to trust the man I loved with another kid of mine.

Declan gave me a swift kiss before he took after Auggie, but only after asking Heath to assign a monitor to me. I didn't bother to advise him that I didn't need a monitor. Now was definitely not the time to argue about such mundane details when my son was somewhere in this club hurting. And why? Because he believed he had failed the sub?

I caught a brief sight of Heath going to a still sobbing Ridge before the same man who had let us into the club led me away. I loathed going with a stranger, but I had no other option, so I didn't kick up a fuss. He brought me back to a quiet room that looked like an office with a small refrigerator.

"Want something to drink?" he asked. "It might be a long wait. No one can rightly say how long these things usually last."

I wanted to ask him what these things were, he spoke of, but I didn't want him to explain it to me. I shook my head and prepared for as long as it would take Declan and Auggie to resurface.

The monitor was right. It took forever. An entire hour passed with me alternating between sitting, standing, and pacing the small office area. In the end, I accepted a drink because my mouth got dry. I conjured up all sorts of things that could be happening between Declan and Auggie. What if they were wrong and Declan couldn't snap Auggie out of whatever mood he had been in?

"Your first time at a dungeon?" the monitor guy asked me, his tone sympathetic enough that I believed he was striking up conversation just to be polite.

I glanced up at him sitting across from me. "What gave it away? The way I've been gawking at everything?"

He chuckled. "A combination of a few things. I'm sorry the experience didn't go better, but this is a great dungeon for first timers."

"It was all going fine," I answered. "Until I saw my son. I had no idea. He's never said anything before."

He snorted. "It doesn't have to be weird, you know? My old man and I went to the same BDSM clubs until he found out I was gay and he disowned me. It didn't stop me from being involved in the leather community. I just started to frequent gay establishments."

"Oh." I frowned at him. "I'm sorry about that. I don't talk to my parents either. They don't like that I'm gay, and my kids are also queer, so to make everyone comfortable I took my kids out of that toxic surrounding."

"That's good. You know the best thing you can do for your son is to be supportive," he remarked. "In this day and age, there are some people who still see us as a sick and twisted community the city should shut down. Don't make a big deal over it."

We fell silent again and time went by without me knowing how much. I was getting restless when Heath appeared, his face grim. I rose to my feet, expecting Declan and Auggie to be behind him, but they weren't.

"Where are they?" I demanded. "Are they okay?"

"He will be fine," Heath answered. "It took some time, but your Daddy's got it under control. He's at the car, and he's expecting you." He motioned to the monitor. "Fraser, walk him out and ensure he's safely delivered into his Daddy's waiting arms, will you?"

Fraser got to his feet to lead me out, but I paused and turned to Heath. "How's Ridge? Will he be okay?"

He gazed over my shoulder, unwilling to meet my eyes. "I don't know. I keep thinking I'm doing what's best for him, but I'm not so sure now. He's really fucked up."

"But you'll take care of him? Declan will never forgive himself if anything happens to him."

He gave me a tired smile. "Declan's a good friend,

and a good Daddy. He doesn't have to worry. I'm committed to seeing this through. To ensuring Ridge is well."

I wished him a good night, then followed Fraser from the office. We took a different exit that spat us out at the back of the building where Declan's car was parked. He was standing at the hood, waiting for me. When I saw him and the car, it took everything out of me not to run to him. Instead, I shook the dungeon monitor's hand and thanked him for sitting with me.

Declan's arms opened when I was close enough to him. I walked into them, and he buried his face into my neck. I wrapped my arms around him, holding onto him tight.

"Where is he?" I asked. "Is he okay?"

"He's in the car," he answered. "We'll take him home and ensure he's okay throughout the night."

I pulled away to peer into the car, and right as rain, Auggie was in the backseat bundled into a large towel. He was slumped as though sleeping, but his eyes were half-mast.

"Can I go talk to him?" I asked.

"We need to talk about that," he replied, cupping my chin. "Just the condensed version so we don't have to delay getting him home. Auggie experienced what we call a top drop. I'll go into details later, but know that right now he's kind of feeling low from the pain he believes he inflicted on Ridge. We're going to take him home and give him a whole lot of love and care to turn around his mood."

I couldn't lie that I wasn't scared about not understanding what was happening to Auggie, but Declan said he would explain later, and it seemed urgent that we got Auggie home.

"Okay. Let's do this."

He kissed my forehead. "You're an amazing father, Owen. I'll sit in the back with Auggie. I hope you're up to driving?"

I was still a little shaky from all that had happened tonight, but after all he and Auggie had been through, I was determined to handle at least this. I could be competent at something.

We climbed into the car with Declan and Auggie in the backseat. I decided I didn't need to speak to Auggie after all. Just having him in my sight was enough. I didn't know what to say to him anyway when he was in this mood that I still didn't understand. He hadn't responded to me earlier when I had addressed him as a father did. At the same time, I couldn't bring myself to call my son Master August as Heath had done.

I decided to give Declan the lead on this one. He'd done a wonderful job with Summer, and she was even visiting tomorrow for my birthday.

For the drive home, I was aware of Auggie's hanging head and the way Declan kept talking to him in hushed tones. I couldn't make out what was being said between them even when I tried my damnedest to listen shamelessly. But when Auggie laughed even though the sound was restrained, I relaxed for the first time since I'd discovered him flogging Ridge.

The drive home was uneventful. Declan had me leave him and Auggie at the front door while I parked the car.

"I'll be with you in a few," he told me.

I watched them as they entered the house before I parked. My phone which I had left in the car rang. Oscar.

"Hey, son, it's rather late to be calling isn't it?" I asked him. "Is something wrong?"

"I don't know," he answered, his tone worried. "I have this bad gut feeling. Umm, Auggie went out tonight, and I can't get through to him. I'm afraid the feelings I have are in relation to him, but how will I know if he's not answering his phone?"

I sighed. "You can drop the pretense, Oscar. I know Auggie's right here in Cincy."

"Uh, I don't know what you're talking about."

"I think you do," I replied. "Are you in Cincy already as well?"

"Yeah, I kind of drove us here," he answered reluctantly. "I'm sorry, Dad, but he-he wanted to get here early for an engagement of his. The house is empty, so we decided to stay there."

"And then pretend tomorrow that you only got into town?" I asked him.

"I know. I'm sorry, but if we'd told you we were here early, you'd want to know why, and then we'd have to explain."

"Are you one too?" I asked him. "A Dom."

He groaned. "How'd you find out?"

"It doesn't matter," I replied. "Auggie is fine. He's spending the night with Dec and me. I have to say that I don't really appreciate all this lying from my kids, and we're going to have to talk about this tomorrow. You're all grown, and you can be straight with me even if you think I won't like it."

"You're right. We should stop trying to protect you from things. It only makes matters worse especially since you always find out anyway."

"Exactly. So, no more lying going forward."

"Okay, Dad. Have Auggie call me when he can."

"I'll see if he's up to it. See you tomorrow, Oscar."

"You too, Dad. Night."

Declan hadn't turned on the lights inside the house. Just the one in the hall which cast sufficient light on the stairs for me to make my way up the stairs. I suddenly felt so tired. I still didn't know what to make of the night. I'd definitely seen some interesting things, and I'd learned the little spanks Declan gave me were nothing in comparison to some other impact play like what Auggie had done to Ridge. I couldn't imagine being lashed so many times and not bowing out at the pain.

I had my hand on the doorknob when one of the guest bedroom doors opened and Declan came out.

"Everything okay?" I asked him as he advanced toward me.

"Just hold me a minute, will you? I forgot how draining this can be."

I hugged him, feeling the tension in his body slowly ease. "Is there anything I can do?" I asked him. "Do you need to take some time off and tend to him? Just tell me what to do, and I'll get it done."

He eased back and cupped my face. "I know how

tough this is for you—me not allowing you access to him, but we've made progress, and the last thing I want is for him to get back into that black mood I had to pull him out of. It's best right now if I take care of him."

I nodded. "Okay. I trust you." I did.

His lips pressed to mine, and he kissed me, backing me into the door. I clung to his shoulders and allowed myself to get lost in him and this newfound trust I had in him. It was infinite.

"I find the way you trust me so incredibly sexy," he said with a grin. "Now get undressed, check on Lucky and get into bed. Try to get some sleep."

I frowned at him. "You won't be coming to bed?"

"I need to stay up with Auggie," he answered. "I'm going to get him something to eat, then I'll see what he's in the mood for. If I can get him to do stuff, take his mind off what just happened, he will be better sooner."

I nodded. "Okay, I'll try to wait up."

"Don't. There's no telling when I'll get to bed."

I squeezed his hand and watched him head for the stairs, loving him so much I had the strangest urge to cry. Him being there for my kids had crumbled the last of my walls. I had no reason to keep the already half-crumbled wall erect. He had proven himself time and time again. He was here to stay. He was here for the long haul. It was with calm that I accepted it. Warmth spread throughout my being, reminding me I didn't have to do this alone. I had Declan now.

I might have done it alone for over fifteen years, and he could have easily decided my kids were adults and so were none of his concern. Instead, he had done his best to get to know them, to befriend them and to take care of them when I was unable.

And it felt damn good to know that I didn't need to have all the answers.

31

DECLAN

My eyes popped open at someone shaking me. Frowning irritably, my vision slowly cleared, and the image of Auggie, his hands on my shoulders surfaced to my brain. I immediately straightened, groaning from the ache in my neck since I had unintentionally fallen asleep in the chair. I had meant only to sit with him for a few minutes while he was sleeping to ensure that he was really out for the night. I must have fallen asleep shortly after as well.

"Sorry for waking you," he said, dropping his hands and sitting on the bed. "I didn't want to, but you looked so uncomfortable in the chair. Pretty sure you'd be better snuggling next to Dad. He thinks I wasn't aware, but he must have checked on us half a dozen times."

I chuckled hoarsely as I rose to my feet and stretched the kinks out of my body. "He's been worried about you. He doesn't understand, but he was willing to give us the space for you to come around."

He rubbed a hand over the back of his neck. "Yeah, he's an awesome Dad like that. How am I going to explain all of this to him?"

I placed a hand on his shoulder and squeezed. "Don't worry about it. I'll talk to him. Your Dad's pretty open-minded, more than most, and I'm sure he'll understand. Or did it escape you that *he* was at the dungeon too?"

"That *was* a surprise," Auggie admitted, then frowned. "Does that mean you're his Dom?"

"Hmm, think of it as a lighter side of a Dom/sub relationship," I answered. "I care for him."

He nodded. "I know. I think it's wonderful you came into all our lives. Summer told me what you did for her, and I never got to say thanks for being there for our sis. And now what you've done for me tonight... Man, Dad sure is lucky to have you. We all are."

I smiled at him. "I'm just glad you're okay." I glanced at the door longingly. I had barely spoken to Owen since I'd gone after Auggie to help him with his Dom drop. His had been a bit more severe, and he had taken a while to snap out of it, which was the reason I had decided to stay with him.

As someone who had experienced Dom drop often when in training with Heath, I could appreciate how he felt and help him get over the dark depressing mood that could follow the spike of adrenaline rush a Dom felt during a scene. Given the way his scene with Ridge had ended abruptly, he'd had less of a time to let his emotions ebb back to normalcy. That significant drop could be detrimental to the mental health of a Dom.

"You know you have nothing to be ashamed of,

right?" I said to him. "Ridge is a very special case, and personally, I'm glad you were able to read into the situation and put a stop to it before it got out of hand. That's the marking of a good Dom right there."

"Right. I'm not a failure."

"No, you're not," I agreed. "Everyone tries to make these rules and tells you what's supposed to happen, but when you and your sub are in that scene, it all boils down to trust between you two. You could not trust your sub to be honest with you about when he'd had enough, so you did the right thing.

"And even if you did make a mistake, which you didn't, it's important to know that we're all human. We'll make mistakes. With experience, we'll make less of them. God knows I've made quite a few with your father, but he's still here, and I'm still learning. And because he loves me and he knows I love him, when I make shitty decisions, he understands it's not with the intention of hurting him. He forgives me and we move on.

"The dynamic won't be the same for you and Ridge, because really, Ridge belongs to Heath, as much as they're both skirting around it. When you do find that person though, love, trust, and forgiveness will make the difference."

He rubbed a hand over his face and gave a nervous laugh. "Damn, this is heavy for a 2 a.m. conversation, isn't it?"

I couldn't help laughing. "Possibly."

The bedroom door cracked a bit, and I could see Owen peeking in. Auggie noticed as well, but I left the decision up to him.

"You can come in, Dad."

The door widened, and Owen tentatively entered the room. "I didn't mean to intrude. I heard sounds, and just wanted to check everything is okay."

"I'm okay now, Dad," Auggie replied, his cheeks blooming with color.

I stifled my chuckle, because I couldn't imagine what it would be like to bump into Charles at a gay dungeon. I didn't suppose that would happen since Charles was straight anyway.

"Really?" Owen asked. "You're not just saying that for me not to worry because I've been worrying all night."

"Declan handled it."

Owen sighed but his smile was reassuring. "Thank God. I'm going back to bed then."

"Wait!" Auggie cried. "Take Declan with you. He's done enough tonight, and he snores. I need to get some decent sleep."

I snorted as I walked away from the bed toward Owen. "I can tell when I'm no longer wanted. Sleep well, Auggie."

"Yeah, you too," he replied, slipping back under the covers. "Sleep, I mean."

I laughed at the waggling of his eyebrows. Good, he was definitely feeling better. I wrapped an arm around Owen's waist and pulled him from the room, closing the door behind us.

"He's really feeling better?" he asked as we entered our bedroom.

"Yes, I wouldn't have left him otherwise."

With his features going all soft, Owen walked over to me and placed his hands on my chest. "I really lucked out with you, didn't I?"

I pecked him on the lips. "I could say the same thing about you. Help me out of this leather, will you? I feel like it may never come off."

He laughed. "But Daddy, you look so hot in it."

"Yeah?"

"Hell yeah. It would be a shame to let it all go to waste."

I stopped tugging at my harness and quirked an eyebrow at him. "Are you saying what I think you are?"

"That I've wanted you to fuck me since you came down the stairs earlier in that leather?"

He got down on his knees before me and reached for the flap at the front of the leather pants. He ripped it apart and moaned at the sight of my semi.

"Oh shit, had I known you were going commando beneath this leather."

"What would you have done?" I asked.

His answer was to lick the head of my cock, circling his tongue just beneath the soft glands. With the friction of his lips, he claimed all of me, one inch at a time. By the time he had me fully into his mouth, my legs were tense from the effort it took out of me not to thrust. The feeling of my cock at the back of his throat, especially when he swallowed around me was way too good.

"I'm going to fuck your face," I whispered to him.

The look in his eyes challenged me to do it. I slid my fingers into his hair and gripped gently as I pulled back then worked my cock back between his lips. Slowly, I fucked him, hissing each time I retreated, and he let his tongue come out to play. I thrust deeper, quicker, but mindful not to gag him.

He kept up with me, never once backing away, and when I closed my eyes, completely basking in the moment, I could still see his face so full of fucking love. A shiver ran through my body, and my hips bucked in desperation. He ran his hands up my chest until he found my nipples, brushing them into painful points.

"Oh fuck, baby," I moaned, gasping.

He squeezed my nipples, and I was done for. With a grunt, my eyes flew open, and I pulled out of his mouth. His lips opened in anticipation; his tongue thrust out to collect the dew he so desperately sought. I stroked from base to tip twice and choked out a cry as ropes of cum hit his greedy tongue.

"Fuck, Owen!" I wasn't nearly done. Another stripe landed on his cheek and yet another dripped from his chin. When the last spasm left my body, I was depleted.

"Hmm," he moaned. "That was good."

I grinned at him. "But you missed a couple."

I scooped the mess from his chin and cheek, feeding it to him. He latched onto my finger, moaning around it, and I smiled at him. It *didn't* actually taste as great as he was letting on, but his enthusiasm was endearing.

I tilted his chin and leaned down to kiss him. "Happy birthday, baby."

His eyes widened. "I suppose it *is* my birthday."

"You supposed right." I turned him toward the bathroom. "Let's go to bed so we can wake up and start the day off right."

"I'd say we started it off right already. Why are you pushing me toward the bathroom?"

"Because I intend to kiss you some more before I fall asleep, and my cum doesn't exactly taste like whipcream. Don't know how you can stand the stuff, but hey, I'm not complaining."

Owen gave a burst of laughter which he tempered down when Lucky raised his head and yipped at us in annoyance from his corner. We really ought to get him settled in another room of the house since he was now doing so well. That dog had seen more than he probably should.

"It's not so bad," he said. "Maybe it's an acquired taste, and I can say for sure I've gotten quite acquired to it."

He disappeared into the bathroom, and I worked on getting the leather off my body. Sexy or not, it wasn't necessarily the most comfortable outfit at all. I would have ditched it sooner if I hadn't been too worried about Auggie to think about it.

Owen was leaving the bathroom when I stepped in. I copped a feel of his ass, because how could I resist? I took care to brush my teeth then joined him in bed. He was practically lying on my side.

"Hey, didn't you claim that other side?" I asked him.

He shuffled over a bit. "But you always pull me over to your side anyway."

"True."

He turned to face me, and I pulled the covers over us, leaning forward to kiss him. I wasn't kidding about kissing him several times before we both fell asleep. It had been a trying night and kissing him wound me down in a pleasant way.

When our lips parted, he smiled at me. "You've been very patient with Auggie tonight," I remarked. "I know it wasn't easy for you."

"Does this mean you'll finally tell me what happened?"

"There's a lot that goes on when a Dom and a sub initiate a scene," I answered, stroking his leg that was thrown over mine. "One of the reasons I asked you not to interrupt any scene you found at the dungeon is because it takes a lot to get into a scene. Everyone reacts differently, and some are able to get in and out of a scene quickly. Others need time to wind down, and interrupting can be jarring for both parties involved."

"Okay, I understand that."

"Remember what you felt the first time I spanked your ass, even though you enjoyed it? You fought it at first."

"Yeah, I felt odd that I liked it. Like I wasn't supposed to enjoy it."

"A sub or Dom drop can be like that, but multiply the feeling by let's say ten. For Auggie, he had a Dom drop which is usually being moody, aloof, a sense of depression. It can get quite bad, Owen. Like really bad. I would always have a Dom drop after an intense scene."

He peered up at me. "Is that why you abandoned hardcore BDSM?"

"A part of the reason. It's really not in me to be a masochist. Not that there's anything wrong, but we all have to find out where we fit, and I've decided where I do."

"Which is?"

I squeezed his thigh. "I fit as your Daddy, Boy."

He sighed and snuggled closer to me. "Yes, you do."

At his confirmation, I kissed the top of his head. "Good. Now sleep. We have only a few hours before the rest of your kids descend on us, and we have things to do before they get here."

He planted a kiss at the side of my neck. "Dec?"

"Hmm?"

Another kiss on my neck. "Thank you."

"No thanks are required, Owen."

"No, seriously. Thank you for not only taking care of me, but my kids as well. Thanks for taking care of us."

"You can count on me to be there for you all."

He tilted his head back and our eyes held. His was serious, and he brought a finger up to brush my bottom lip.

"We'll be there for you too," he said softly. "I swear we will."

I was touched at his words. All my life I'd felt mostly alone, and now I had a family of my own. I nipped at his finger on my lip.

"Go to sleep, birthday boy."

He sighed and closed his eyes, his body relaxing against me. "Okay, Daddy. Can't wait to spend the day with you and my kids."

32

OWEN

"Hey, Dec, what are we doing here?" I asked the man beside me when Barry pulled into the parking lot of a tattoo parlor. This morning was great, and I was still riding the wave of spending the morning having breakfast with Dec, Auggie, and Oscar. The three men in my life had made my birthday special so far, showering me with more gifts than I thought necessary.

Summer had called to wish me a happy birthday as well, but she was still in transit from Columbus. She had informed me that she was traveling alone and reassured me she and Penny were fine.

"It's a tattoo parlor," Declan answered as he opened the car door and got out.

I didn't wait for him to get the door for me, but got out on my own, which earned me a proper scowl. "I know, but what are we doing here?" I repeated nervously.

"You'll see. Come on."

I reluctantly caught up with him and together we entered the tattoo shop. There was a woman at the front desk with a chin-length bob and her neck covered in colorful tattoos. She popped the gum she was blowing when she saw us and smiled.

"Hi, welcome to Tats Central!" she greeted. "What are we having done today?"

"Hi, I called to set up an appointment at eleven with Pierce," Declan answered. "The name's Declan Moore."

She opened a book on the desk and blew another bubble. "Ah yeah, here it is. You're not related to the fancy Moores of Cincy, are you?"

"No," Declan lied.

She laughed. "Right. What would he be doing here? Anyway, Pierce is down the hall, two doors down on your right. The guys all have their own private booths where they work."

"Nice. Thank you."

"And maybe you can check out some tats to go with that nipple piercing you're going for."

I gaped at Declan. "You're getting what?"

"Thanks. I'll think about it," Declan answered the woman, before moving down the hall just as he had been instructed.

I hurried to catch up with him. "Declan, you're piercing your nipples?"

He gave me a blank stare and pointed behind him with his thumb. "That's what she said."

"Oh my God. Declan!"

He paused at the second door which was half-opened. "This is what you wanted, isn't it? I remember you going on and on about how I should get my nipples pierced so you could have more fun with them that way. Well, happy birthday."

"But you already gave me a birthday gift," I said in awe, thinking about the day passes the kids and I had to spend at Declan's country club. I hadn't even known he belonged, because we'd never been before. He never mentioned it either, but apparently his father was more of the regular member who kept up Declan's membership there.

"And there's more to come," he teased. "This is one."

I swallowed around the excitement that caused my mouth to go dry at the thought of Declan's pierced nipples.

"You're not doing this for me, are you?" I asked him.

"Hell, I'll be on the receiving end of the pleasure when your lips are teasing those bars."

The door opened and a presence filled the doorway. We both glanced up into the amused eyes of a man in his late twenties. He was slender, with stylish black hair sporting blond highlights. I kept thinking he couldn't be the nipple piercer since I could only see one piercing displayed on him—the right corner of his bottom lip.

"As interesting as this conversation's getting," the guy said, with a grin. "I have another appointment soon, so we need to get this show on the road." He leveled his eyes on Declan. "You're Moore, right?"

They shook hands. "Yes. This is my partner, Owen."

He shook my hand and looked me up and down. I blushed because Oscar had brought me a shirt with the graphic *Birthday Boy* and a cake on the front that he had begged me to wear. Now I wished I had on something a bit more grownup.

"I'm Pierce," the guy stated. "Come on in. I'll explain what's about to happen and give you a second to decide if you still want to go through with this."

The room didn't look as scary as I thought it would. It was well lit, for one, with a nice comfortable brown couch set on one side of the wall. The room consisted of a black reclining chair, a padded table much like what you'd find at the hospital, a showcase of jewelry, and a stainless-steel counter with all sorts of equipment. The final piece was the standing mirror that was mounted on one wall. It reminded me of the mirror Declan and I had in our bedroom which we used when we wanted to see everything as we fucked.

"On the phone you said you wanted nipple piercings," Pierce stated. "Just one or both?"

Declan glanced at me. "It's your choice."

My cheeks turned red as two pairs of eyes turned toward me. "Both," I answered.

Pierce grinned, clearly having too much fun with this. "Awesome. And that will be all? Either of you interested in getting your dicks pierced or something?"

I gawked at him. "You do that here?"

He laughed. "Yeah. Not often, but sure, if you want your partner here to get a Prince Albert, I can help with that."

"A what?"

Declan scowled at Pierce. "Let's stick with the nipples for now. One pain at a time. I'm not even sure I'll get through both."

"I'll hold your hand," I volunteered.

Pierce guffawed. "Well, that's sweet. Let's talk about the healing process before I have you pick out the jewelry of your choice."

Pierce went through the boring stuff, but I paid attention especially to the healing time and the aftercare. It seemed awfully long to have such a small wound heal to the point that I started to question why bother, but Declan was adamant about giving *us* this birthday present.

"You choose," Declan told me when Pierce brought us over to the showcase with jewelry.

I groaned. "Why did it have to be my birthday? I don't know what to choose."

"Let me help you out there a little," Pierce replied then started asking questions such as preferred stone and color, before going to the lengths of explaining why Declan should start with a simple barbell fourteen gauge. "After six months, you can come back and get the gauges tightened, but right now we want to give you a little room on either side to accommodate the healing process."

We ended up going with a fourteen gauge diamond nipple barbell ring which was a bit expensive in my view, but I wasn't about to argue the price. In the little time we'd been at the tattoo parlor, the idea of seeing Declan's nipples with those gauges had taken root. My kinky heart couldn't wait for the wounds to heal so I could pay them attention.

"How long will it take?" I asked as Declan lay on his back and Pierce started prepping each nipple. As sensitive as Declan was to his nipples being touched, they peaked, and Pierce replaced the hold of his fingers with a scissor-looking instrument before marking the area on both sides with a marker.

"Hmm, less than half a minute on each," Pierce replied.

I would never admit it to Declan, but when Pierce turned with the needle in hand, I averted my head. I couldn't watch. Nerves upended in my belly, making my knees weak.

"That's it. First one's done," Pierce announced.

I glanced at Declan's chest. "Holy shit." He hadn't even grunted in pain. The diamond studs on either end glittered. Holy shit was right. I'd have to keep my hands —my mouth—off him for a while, but when those bad boys were healed… they were so mine.

Even knowing Declan took to the pain well, I couldn't convince myself to look while the other was being pierced either. I waited until Pierce made the second announcement that he was done, and then I took a deep breath.

"What do you think?" Declan asked me as Pierce cleaned the wound and checked his work.

"How soon before I'll be able to play with them?" I asked Pierce, and the two men laughed.

"We don't want to irritate the wound too much," Pierce replied. "Give it some time when he comes to get those bells tightened. Then we'll see if you're ready for nipple play again."

Declan sat up and rubbed his hand over his chest, around the area but not touching it. He rose to his feet and walked over to the mirror to check out his piercings.

"Not bad," he said with a grin at Pierce. "And the pain wasn't so bad either. Hmm, maybe I'll think about that Prince Albert for another time. I think you'll like that."

"Will someone explain to me what a Prince Albert is?" I asked, my curiosity well and truly hooked.

"I think seeing it works best." Chuckling, Prince walked over to the coffee table in one corner of the room. He found a magazine, flipped a few pages then handed it to me without a word. I stared at the dick in front of my face with the pierced tip. It looked painful. Yet so hot. My eyes raised to Declan.

Amused, he snatched the magazine from my hand and handed it back to Pierce. "We need to get out of here before you give Owen any more ideas."

"But imagine the attention I could pay to a little detail like that," I murmured.

"Anyone ever tell you just how comically sweet you guys are?" Pierce asked as he led us out of the room to the front desk. "It's refreshing to see. The next piercing is on me."

Declan settled his bill and we accepted a business card from Pierce before we left. Once we got into the car, I leaned sideways and kissed him so hard he tried to pull me onto his lap. I evaded him and released his lips.

"Thanks for doing that. I can't wait for them to heal."

"I'm looking forward to it," he said.

Our next stop was the country club. Charles and Auggie were waiting for us in the lobby chatting. I couldn't remember ever seeing Charles smile, but he was at Auggie, and I was relieved they were getting along. I so wanted our families to blend well with as little fuss as possible.

As soon as they saw us, I watched Charles shut down a little. He became all serious and businesslike.

"Hey, where's Oscar?" I asked.

Just then he rounded a corner and came into view, Summer at his side. My day picked up immensely at seeing the bounce in my daughter's step. I hadn't seen her smiling so genuinely and being so openly relaxed since she went off to Cincy.

"Dad!" she flew into my arms, and I hugged her to me, forgetting the members who were eyeing us. I didn't care. It was so good to have my little girl back.

"I'm so glad you made it!" I nearly squeezed the life out of her until she laughed and squirmed away.

"Dad, I can't breathe."

I loosened my grip and brushed at her curls. "How are you?"

"I'm doing great," she answered. "Happy birthday! How has it been?"

"So far amazing," I answered, releasing her and staring at all the faces that made this day the best of my life. "Now that you're all here, I feel truly happy."

"Good. I won't feel so guilty about having to leave you here then."

I glanced at Declan. "What? You're leaving?"

He came over to me with a couple of strides and took my hands. "This is for you and your kids. You don't get to see them often enough. The facilities at this club are amazing, and Charles will ensure you're all well taken care of while you're here."

I nodded, because it wasn't as if I didn't already suspect he was planning something for later. I squeezed his hands and let go. "Alright. I'll be the most spoiled that I can be while I'm here."

He grinned. "Good. Take care till later." He turned to Charles. "You'll be able to stay, right?"

Charles glanced at Auggie before returning his attention to Declan. "Don't worry. I won't let you down."

33

DECLAN

"**A**re you going?"

I glanced up at Charles as I packed the bucket of ice to dip the champagne in and carry out back to the poolside where everyone else was waiting. At least everyone except the man of the hour who would be here any minute now shepherded by his sons.

"Going where?" I asked, utterly confused as to what Charles was asking me.

"To the award ceremony," he answered and when I continued to stare blankly at him. "I know you got an invitation to the Cancer Research's appreciation ceremony. I also received one, and when you didn't RSVP, the director of the board called me to find out whether or not you were coming."

I looked away from him and returned to my task. "I don't want to talk about it."

"Come on, Declan. This is an honor. You can't

decide not to go."

"I guess this means you're going," I stated.

"I have to. I go to every event. For your mother."

"Then good for you, but I'm not going." Satisfied that there was enough ice in the bucket, I reached for the champagne, but Charles snatched it.

"Please, Declan. You have to go. If not for you, do it for your mother. She would have been so proud of you and all you've contributed to cancer research."

"But that's the thing, Charles. I didn't do it for recognition. I just did it because it needed to be done."

"All the more reason you deserve this."

I sighed. "I know you mean well, but this is hardly the time to talk about it. Owen and his sons will be here any minute. This is his party, and I want everything to be perfect."

"Does *he* know about the letter?"

"I didn't think it necessary to show him."

"Because you know he'll agree with me."

Frustrated, I glared at Charles. "Look, Dad, I—"

We both froze. I stared at him in horror. We didn't both speak but stared at each other. I couldn't decide which of us was more shocked. I couldn't remember the last time I'd called Charles 'Dad', but the word slipped out now. All I could think of was Owen's kids calling him Dad while I was around and the word just kind of got stuck. That was the only explanation I had. It couldn't be the way Charles seemed to be playing the Dad role of late better than he'd ever done before.

Today he'd carried out his part in my plans perfectly. He'd gotten Owen and his kids passes to the country club where they had spent the day relaxing, giving me the opportunity to get his party prepared for tonight. I'd spoken to Auggie afterward who confirmed Charles had ensured they had been treated well while they were there. Outsiders could sometimes be frowned upon, but Charles had connections, and his pockets were deep enough for him to hold enough sway there.

"I didn't mean to call you that," I said, but the apology felt wrong. "I know how much you hate it."

"I don't hate it," he stated on a sigh. "I just never thought I deserved the title. Every time you said it when you were younger it felt like a mockery, reminding me how shitty I really was as a father. I didn't have to go through that when you called me Charles."

I was about to respond, though I had no idea of the exact words I would say, when Summer appeared. She smiled, looking elegant in a short yellow wrap-around dress that had made me frown when she had come down to help me with last minute arrangements. She had taken one look at my disapproval before laughingly patting my cheek and teasing me that I was already acting like her Dad.

"I think you have guests at the door," she announced, looking from me to Charles. "Didn't you hear the door-bell ring?"

Charles pushed away from the island before I could. "I'll go get it."

One of the members of the waitstaff, who came along with the catering company, appeared and retrieved the bucket with the champagne, leaving Summer and me alone.

"Everything okay with your father?" she asked. "Things looked quite intense between you."

"It's fine," I answered, then retrieved a bottle of wine from the fridge that Owen and I had pulled a few nights ago. "Want some?" I asked.

"Nah. I'm a lightweight. I'll wait till Dad gets here."

I poured myself half a glass and drank a little before turning to her. I had to get this out before my courage fled.

"Summer, what would you say if I asked your dad to marry me?" When she didn't react, I rushed to explain. "I know you always say that you're the last to know things, and this time I want you to be the first person in on this."

Her face burst into a grin. "I'd say, thank fuck. If Dad didn't snatch you up, I would. He deserves all this that you've provided for him, but more importantly, he deserves someone who cares about him the way you do."

I let out the breath I had been holding on a whoosh. "Good, because I plan to propose to him tonight. Now to pull the twins to one side so I can get their blessings beforehand."

She let out a squeal and hugged me. "I'm so excited. Now I have three Dads. How about that?"

That was how Charles found us when he returned to the kitchen with Silas in tow. The chauffeur looked damn good, his eyes more vibrant than I'd ever seen them.

"Silas, you made it!" I released Summer to embrace the man who had become more than an employee of mine. He was a dear friend.

"I wouldn't miss Owen's birthday for the world," he

answered, patting me heartily on the back.

"How have you been?" I asked, stepping back to take him in. He looked like a new man—not physically, but he seemed more relaxed.

"Good," he answered, tight-lipped as usual when it came to his personal affairs. "You and Owen?"

I glanced at Charles and Summer who were watching us. "Good."

He chuckled. "Touché."

Summer and Silas were catching up when my phone message alert went off. I quickly removed the device from my pocket to check.

"Okay everyone, that's Auggie. They are pulling up right now. Everyone around to the pool area."

Charles and Silas turned to do just that while Summer and I went to get the door. It had been Oscar's idea to keep Owen at his former home with them rather than have him here to make setting up the party more difficult. Owen probably had a good idea that I was planning something for him, but hopefully he would be surprised when he saw how special I had made everything. From catering to decorating, and inviting the people he cared about to share in the moment with us. At the last minute, James had decided not to come, but he had sent a personal greeting for Owen.

"Nervous?" Summer asked, when we were at the door.

"It's that obvious?" It was the damn proposal that did it. One minute I had no doubt Owen would say yes, and then another I wasn't so sure. What if he wanted to date some more?

"Yes. I don't even know why you're nervous. It's obvious Dad will say yes. Fifteen years, Declan, and I've never seen him like this with anyone else."

I gave her a smile. "Thank you."

I opened the door, and we waited for Owen and the twins to join us. He smiled when he saw me, walking faster so he was ahead of his sons.

"Okay, you guys have made it super obvious you have something planned," he said with a smug smile. "The twins went so far as to argue over what I should wear. What do you think?"

After his complete turn, showing off his slacks and new dress shirt, I tugged him toward me and kissed him hard. "You look amazing as usual. I hope you're hungry. We're going to have dinner at the poolside."

"All of us?" Owen asked.

"I thought it would be nice for us all to spend the evening entertaining you. That's fine, right?"

He smiled. "Sounds good. I mean, who else would I rather spend my birthday with?"

Oscar snickered, and as I led Owen into the house, I gave him a warning look. I didn't need to because as I did, I witnessed Auggie sticking him in the ribs with his elbow.

"Dad, you should tell Declan what we decided about the house," Auggie remarked.

"Yes, please tell."

As we walked toward the pool area, I listened to Owen explain that the boys wanted to keep the house. Auggie was thinking of moving back to Cincy as the company he worked with was expanding here. It was more of a surprise that Oscar wasn't moving back with him since they were so close.

"Moving back is a tough decision," I commented to Auggie, wondering if his access to Heath's dungeon was a motivator.

"Hmm, I think he's met someone here he might be interested in," Oscar answered. "And the fact that I've asked and he's remained tight-lipped shows me how close to the truth I am."

Both Owen and I regarded Auggie with surprise. From the way he was scowling blackly at Oscar, I would say his twin was close to the truth. I glanced at Owen, and he shrugged, so he was just as clueless as me.

The little conversation was a good distraction, but as we approached the glass sliding doors, there was no way I could hide what we had been up to. Owen gasped as he took in the transformation of the pool deck. David, who had taken charge of the event, to my delight, had outdone himself. Now I had no doubt that if—when Owen said yes—he would be planning our wedding.

The external lights were off, and the pool area illuminated by candlelight, around the poolside, on top of the tables, and even the surface of the pool. The one lighted area was where the catering staff had set up, but otherwise there was nothing but the intimate glow of candlelight.

"This is…" Owen struggled for words, and I slid open the glass doors, urging him to step out. When he did, our friends materialized all singing *For He's a Jolly Good Fellow*. I watched Owen as he grew overwhelmed, laughing and crying at the same time.

I was grateful to every single person who had accepted our invitation and made it to the party. We were only a handful, but they were people Owen would be thankful to share the experience with. I had even managed to invite a couple of the guys he used to work with who he always talked about favorably.

I couldn't say that was all unselfish motives, though, as I had hoped to send a message to his former boss that Owen was happy and well taken care of. I hadn't made a fuss over Owen telling me why his boss had been nasty to him, but I didn't particularly like the way he had found out things. Right when he was in a relationship already was hardly the best time to talk to him about having a romantic interest in him.

His neighbor was also here, and Pierce from the tattoo shop had left such a mark on me that I'd asked him if he wanted to drop by too. He seemed outgoing, friendly, and he wasn't too much older than Owen's twins. I might have been trying my hand at matchmaking when I invited him. I'd thought he would suit for Auggie, but if Oscar was to be believed, his twin already had his sights set on someone else.

To round up the party, were David and Bailly. Then there was Charles who smoothed his fingers through his hair when he saw us. For some reason, his color was higher than usual.

Owen laughed when they sang the last line, clapping his hands to his mouth as he turned to me. "You told me this was just us," he stated before turning back to our guests. "Well this is truly a surprise. I can't believe you all came. Thank you for the delightful surprise."

34

OWEN

I took a while for me to process that all my friends and family were together in one place to help me celebrate my birthday. I had truly been hood-winked by my own children who had led me to believe we were just having dinner together that night. Since Declan knew my aversion to big crowds—not that I knew many people anyway—I had believed him that he had kept the celebration to just us. Not that a dozen people were a lot, but still it was way more than I had imagined.

I hadn't wanted to make a big deal about my birth-day, because at this age, what was left to celebrate? They had proven me wrong. My children and Declan's thoughtfulness for the entire day left me feeling grateful to have a family like them.

They had planned out the day perfectly. After drop-ping me off at the country club, Charles had ensured we had access to the facilities. At first, I thought I would have been disappointed because Declan didn't spend the day with me, but what he'd done in the morning was enough to tide me over.

Being with my kids all day had been good for all of us. Auggie and I hadn't spoken about last night, and seeing him laughing and over his drop made my day. As usual, Oscar had all of us laughing, and seeing Summer's genuine smile instead of that miserable look she usually had on her face lately were perfect birthday gifts.

But my partner was Declan Moore, and he always had something else up his sleeve.

I got caught up interacting with one person after another, giving me insufficient time to properly thank Declan for organizing the event. Everyone seemed genuinely happy to be present, even the two guys from Cush, Gray and Lance, who were in attendance. Seeing them, everything fell into place of Declan asking me one night casually after sex about the people I was closest to at that job.

"Nice party," Silas stated, coming up to me when I found myself unexpectedly alone for the first time since we walked out onto the pool deck.

"I can't take any credit for it," I replied, aware that my grin was possibly a little bit too wide, but unable to help it. I gave in to the urge and hugged him. "I'm so glad you're here. We've missed having you around."

"Missed me so much you already hired my replacement?"

Horrified, my eyes wandered over the pool area, seeking out Barry. "We could never replace you. He's just here until you get back." I returned my attention to him. "Although Declan doesn't think you'll be returning. You wouldn't have any idea why he thinks that way, would you?"

He tugged at the top button of his shirt. "That's what he says?"

"Yeah." I really studied him and the way he hesitated in correcting me. "He's right, isn't he?"

"I've been with Declan for the longest while," he answered, staring across the pool. "I've watched him grow from a boy into a man. Now we both have a different path to take. His is with you."

"And yours?" I asked him.

He gave me a smile I couldn't quite interpret. *Wistful?* "I'm still trying to find it, but if there's one thing I've learned from watching you letting down your guard with Declan, is that it's never too late for love." He placed an arm on my shoulder and steered me to a table to sit. "It's your birthday. Let's change the subject."

We snagged cocktails from the waitstaff as well as the finger foods that were being served. We chatted for quite some time before I noticed Charles had stepped away to a little corner and was talking into his cell phone. He looked pissed, and his posture was the opposite of the relaxed man I had witnessed earlier.

When his call ended, Charles punched the air aggressively and ran his fingers into his hair. I glanced around for Declan, hoping he would intervene to check on his father, but he wasn't anywhere around.

"I need to go check on Charles," I told Silas, rising to my feet. "Something seems to have upset him, and he's been having such a good relationship with Declan of late, I don't want this to change things."

"Sure. Go ahead. I'll be around."

Charles spun toward the side of the house, and I followed, moving quickly to catch up with him. He was walking too fast as though trying to get away.

"Hey, Charles, wait up!" I called to him.

He spun around and frowned at me. "What? Is something wrong?"

I came to a halt before him. "I don't know. That's why I'm here. I couldn't help noticing how upset you were at that call you received. You're not leaving upset, are you?"

"It's fine," he said although his tone was clipped and anything but. "Go back to your party. Declan spent a lot of time getting everything perfect the way he thought you'd want it. This is your night, and I'm not going to ruin it."

"You're not ruining anything, Charles," I told him. "We're a family. We look out for each other, and I don't like you driving when it's clear you're upset. If you don't want to talk about it, at least come back to the party until you cool down a little. I can call your driver for you or even take you where you want to go."

He scoffed. "Declan would never forgive me for that." He groaned and ran his fingers through his hair again. "What a fucking mess!"

I raised an eyebrow in his direction, challenging him to try me with his problem.

"It's Poppy," he continued. "My wife. She's making everything difficult. I thought the divorce would be easy, but she's doing everything she can to hold up the process. In one breath she's insisting the baby is mine even though we both know the truth to that, but she's smearing my name. I refuse to be thought of as a negligent father for a second time! I wouldn't do that to a child again."

"I'm sure you have lawyers who can fight this thing. You can easily prove the child isn't yours."

He lowered his head. "The truth is that I'm still concerned about the baby. Poppy is so irresponsible."

"You're worried she might get rid of it?" I asked in surprise. "Why? Do *you* want the baby?"

"No. Yes. Damn, I don't know. I don't know."

"Look, Charles. This is clearly something that's not going to change overnight. I'm not going to let you drive like this, so come on. You can even stay in one of the guest rooms if you want."

Only after the words came from my lips did I realize in horror what I had done. Inviting the man into a home he had shared with a wife and his child. It felt a bit presumptuous.

"It's okay if you don't want to," I hastened to add, "But stay awhile. Perhaps talk to Dec about the issue with Poppy. He always knows what to do."

Charles chuckled despite his frustration. "You caught on to that, huh? He always knew how to get me out of my predicaments, but I can't intrude. He has you in his life now."

I frowned at him. "Charles, you do know that even though I'm in his life, I can never replace you, right? Look at me. I love Declan something fierce, but my kids are still very much an active part of my life. You're no different."

Charles shook his head. "You see things so simply. I can't."

"We see things how we want to make them," I answered.

He stared at me as seconds ticked by, before he sighed. "I'll stay awhile, but there's something I should tell you."

"What is it?"

Side by side we headed back toward the poolside, walking slowly across the lawn.

"I started a foundation a couple of years after Declan's mother passed," he replied. "It was to aid in providing funds for cancer research. Declan took it over as soon as he was eighteen, and the foundation has thrived because of him. He doesn't need to do consultation work, because he stands to inherit everything, but he takes that money and pumps it into the foundation. Not only that, it's a condition for the companies he works with. If they turn a profit after he's handled the business, the owners contribute a percentage to cancer research. Millions of dollars have been invested in stem cell research and the latest technologies to fight cancer as a result."

Listening to Charles speak about Declan's generosity and commitment to cancer research made me so proud of him. He was an all-around nice guy. I wasn't even upset that he hadn't told me about the foundation. For something of this nature, he would want to keep quiet about it, wanting his contributions to go unnoticed.

"The Cancer Research Society of Ohio would like to present him with an award for the role he's played in helping them," Charles continued. "He's their biggest donor, Owen, and he's being recognized for it. The problem is that he doesn't plan to show up."

I groaned. "That's so like him."

Charles stopped me with a hand on my arm. "You have to get him to change his mind."

I stared at where his hand was, unrelenting. "I don't know, Charles. This is Declan we're talking about. Did you know that he sent the kids of the maids to college? I wouldn't have known about it if one didn't mention it to me. Declan doesn't like accolades for charity work."

"I understand, and that's admirable, but this is different," he remarked. "This is something that can help him feel closer to his mother. One of the reasons I had such a tough time dealing with his mother's death was because I felt helpless. I felt that everything was futile even when I contributed to the foundation, but what Declan has continued has changed lives. They will have survivors who have benefitted from the research and treatments talking about their experiences. He needs this for further closure."

Did I think Declan would change his mind about going to the appreciation ceremony? I strongly doubted it, but I also could appreciate Charles's reasoning. Additionally, Declan's closeness to the society would only keep his mother's spirit alive.

"I'll try to talk to him," I answered. "But I can't guarantee what his response will be. When is it?"

"Tomorrow night."

"What? But that hardly gives me any time to bring up the subject!"

"Owen, if there's anyone who can get Declan to change his mind, it's you. He listens to you."

The earnest way he was looking at me made my stomach queasy. He obviously thought Declan would change his mind if I asked him to reconsider. He had more faith in me than I even had in this regard. I didn't want to coerce Declan into doing anything he was dead set against. As much as I would love him to go, I'd have to support him if he preferred not to be recognized for his charity work.

"Charles I—"

"Dad!" Summer cried, appearing before us and taking my other arm. "Where have you been? Declan's been waiting."

She tugged, but Charles didn't exactly let me go which left me in limbo.

"You'll talk to him?" he asked, refusing to relent.

"I'll try," I told him. "But I can't guarantee what he'll do."

He looked as if he was about to argue, but then he released my hand and nodded. "I guess that will have to do."

Summer tugged me across the pool deck. "What was that about?"

"Something I need to talk to Dec about later," I answered. "Nothing to worry about. Now why have you been hunting me down?"

"Because it's time to cut the cake," she answered.

I glanced up to find everyone on either side of a table that had been wheeled out onto the deck. In the center of the table was a four layered cake that was shaped out into a mountain with a road running from the bottom to the top. Instead of the top of the cake, the number 47 candle was halfway up the mountain road. The road sign at the bottom of the cake contained the customary *Happy Birthday Owen.*

"This looks fantastic!" It did. It was almost sinful to think about cutting it. The cake looked more like a display that should only be admired, but a knife was passed to me to stick in the bottom tier.

"I couldn't decide from your kids, so they'll all do the honors with you," Declan told me with a smile.

As I returned his smile, I couldn't stop thinking about what Charles had informed me. He really should go and collect that award. He would know his mother's death had not been in vain. He had turned her death into a positive impact for other cancer victims.

"Actually, Declan," Auggie said, pulling me out of my thoughts. "We talked about it, and we've decided it's your turn."

I was touched at my kids' gesture and from the look of astonishment he wore, Declan hadn't anticipated it either. "Are you sure?"

"Yes, dude," Oscar replied. "It's our way of telling you we're cool with you and our Dad."

"You already told me that," Declan replied.

I frowned from my kids to Declan. "What? When did you talk about this?"

Declan moved closer to me and took my arm. "Later. Let's get into this cake."

There was something he wasn't telling me, but with our guests watching our interaction, I nodded and decided we could talk about it later. Declan placed his hand on top of mine, and only he knew of the tremor that speared through me as he came closer behind me. He held me intimately to him with his left hand on my hip. What followed next was a countdown before the slightest pressure of his hand on mine sent the knife slicing through the layer of the cake.

The kids would not let up until we exchanged the first bite of cake, and I couldn't help thinking how wedding-like this was as Declan slipped a small slice into my mouth. I shamelessly sucked his fingers into my mouth to the delight of those watching us. These people were our safe zone. We could be ourselves around them, and I hadn't gotten the chance to really be with him tonight. He'd been too busy ensuring everything went according to his plan.

We had barely swallowed the cake when Oscar handed us two glasses filled with champagne.

"I'd like to make a toast to our dad," he said, and I swallowed my groan, hoping he didn't start goofing off. "My brother, sister and I are all unique individuals. Blame our dad for that. He taught us to be nothing but ourselves since we were kids, even if that meant he had to rush from my soccer practice to Auggie's academic competition, and then Summer's rehearsal. By the way he did all that in a day. But what we all have in common is a father who has always been there for us. Now that we're grown, we look back and wonder how he did it all. Alone. So, on behalf of Auggie, Summer, and myself, we wish you a happy birthday, Dad."

I blinked away the tears that had sprung into my eyes

the second he started talking. "Thank you. I'm so glad you could make it."

"We'd not be anywhere else but here for your birthday, Dad," Auggie added. "I do believe Oscar forgot to say the word, so I will. Cheers everyone."

We all tipped our glasses before I drank from my glass. Declan was unbelievably quiet. I glanced at him to find him watching me rather than drinking from his glass.

"Something wrong?" I asked, about to place the rest of the champagne onto the table.

"Nope, nothing," he answered, but proceeded to tug at his shirt, his face getting unexpectedly red.

"Dad, you going to finish that champagne?" Summer asked.

I glanced at the glass I still held. "I'm already giddy from all the excitement. I think I can do without all this drinking."

"Seriously, Dad, you should finish that," Auggie seconded.

"Why are we acting so weird?" I asked them, turning to Declan. "You too. Why are you so flushed?"

Declan swore beneath his breath and took the wine glass from me. "The wait is killing me."

I watched bewildered as he fished into the glass with his index finger. Even when he brought out the ring, I was still confused. Until he handed the glass to Summer and went down on one knee. I forgot how to breathe. He had made comments before about tying the knot, but I was not expecting this. Not now. Not so soon. I always thought when—if—we decided to make our relationship legal, we'd talk about it together, yet here he was proposing before our friends and family.

"Let me get any doubt out of the way first," he said, staring up at me, and I couldn't help thinking that kneeling right there on the pool deck was probably not very comfortable. "I know the first thing that's popping up in your mind right now is that we've not been together long enough. But is enough really about time? Shouldn't it be about loving you enough and you loving me back the same? Because I love you more than enough, Owen, and I plan to spend the rest of my life with you. I'd like to make it official, and not with a long drawn out engagement either. I'd like to officially bind us together with vows, because I know we'll honor them. Will you marry me, Owen?"

Maybe if he had just asked me to marry him, I would have said yes, and that would be that. After that perfect little speech though, about me being enough for him, I did the damnedest thing and cried. They were not quiet little sniffles either that could be looked on as just a bit of emotion. I was completely blinded by the embarrassing tears that would become an essential part in the retelling of our proposal story—of how I lost my shit.

I was at a loss for words, and Declan became alarmed. I tried to tell him that I was fine really, just surprised and needed a moment to breathe, but no sounds came. He eventually took me by the shoulders and steered me in the direction of the house while the kids tried to distract our guests.

In the living room, Declan sat on the couch, and I still held onto him, placing my head on his shoulder while I tried to regain my composure. *Dammit, Owen, after this he may just change his mind about marrying you!*

"I'm sorry," I said on a deep breath, then when he stiffened realized he probably thought I was turning down his proposal. I rushed to add, "About the crying! I don't know where it came from. I'm sorry about that. Not the proposal." I leaned back so I could see his face.

"Maybe I should have done this later in private," he said, sounding so uncertain.

"No, that was perfect."

"Except you still haven't given me an answer yet, so you kind of have me by the balls here, Owen."

"Of course, yes!" I told him. "Was there any doubt what the answer would be? The day I moved in here was the day I sealed my fate with you, Declan. You're right. Our love is enough, and nothing else matters."

"Thank God!" He took hold of my face and pulled me closer so he could kiss me. I clung to him, mindful not to press too near to his chest and irritate his newly pierced nipples. Remembering our trip this morning, I kissed him harder, thanking him for everything.

"He said yes!" I heard Oscar shout in the distance, and my lips curved against Declan's as he chuckled.

"Good grief, I'm going to be step-dad to Oscar."

I laughed while extending my left hand to his. "Too late for you to change your mind. Plus, the other two will make up for Oscar's peculiar ways."

Taking my hand in his, Declan slid the gorgeous band onto my ring finger, gently pushing the metal over my knuckle. It fit perfectly. I couldn't stop staring.

"It's so beautiful," I breathed in awe then glanced up

at him. "Did you mean it? No long engagement? Because I'm down for that. Just a small affair like—why are you grinning like that?"

"You didn't just say yes because I proposed to you in front of our family and friends," he answered. "You're already talking about our wedding, so I know you really want this too."

"Of course, I want this, Dec. I want the whole experience with you."

"Good, because you're about to become Owen Moore."

35

DECLAN

"**A**re you sure you wouldn't rather stay with us?" I asked as Owen's kids piled into Auggie's car.

"Maybe some other time," Oscar replied for them. "I'm sure Dad's night is just about to turn interesting, and we don't want to be around when all that goes down."

"Damn, Oscar, do you always have to say what's on your mind?" Owen asked on a scowl.

The younger twin shrugged. "I just tell it like it is, because you two are too polite to tell us to beat it, so I'll do it for you." He turned to Auggie. "Get the car started, Auggie. We'll be here for another day before we head off to Columbus, so we'll see you again before we leave."

"Good. Have a safe journey."

All our other guests had already left, and Owen curled into my side as we watched Auggie back out of the driveway. I wrapped an arm about his shoulders and together we watched until the taillights disappeared.

"You okay?" I asked him.

"Never been better. Thank you for tonight. It was wonderful."

I caught him checking out the ring on his left hand again. He did it every so often when he thought I wasn't looking. Like he still found it unbelievable that we were engaged to be married. The sooner I got him to the altar the better. I couldn't wait to be able to refer to him as my husband.

"You're welcome," I told him, then led him back inside the house. "Are you sleepy?"

"Not particularly. Why? Have something in mind?"

I pretended to contemplate. "I can't think of a single thing."

"Well, I've been wondering if sex will still be the same now that we're engaged," he said teasingly. "You know, will you still fuck me, or will it all be soft and sweet from now on? Is this where the romance ends, and the dry spell begins?"

I snorted at that. "In a few minutes when I take you to our bed and arrange you the way I want you, I'll ask for your assessment after. Husband or not, Daddy will fuck you like he knows you crave it, Boy, and you know what?"

"What?"

"You'll love it. You'll beg for more."

He let out a moan. "Are we going to the bedroom now to make me beg, because I've gotten really good at begging?"

I chuckled at his eagerness. "Not quite. There's one last thing I have for you."

He stopped walking. "Declan, you've already given me so much!"

"It's your birthday. I'm allowed to pamper you. It's the one day you can't complain."

He groaned but followed me down the hall and past my office. I brought us to a halt at the door I had closed off from him since I had this idea. Holding his hand, I turned to him.

"I know you said I shouldn't interfere with your writing. That you want to do it on your own. I admit, it's hard not to step in so I turned my attention otherwise and hope you'll find this to be my own little way of letting you know I fully support you and your dreams."

He laughed uneasily. "I've been wondering why this door is locked. You don't have an agent tied down to a chair inside, do you?"

I grinned at him. "See for yourself."

I produced the key from my pocket and unlocked the door. I opened up and stepped aside, feeling extremely proud of the room that I had turned into a writer's den for Owen.

"Oh my God!" he exclaimed, striding further into the room. He came to a stop and took in everything in the room. I didn't have the slightest idea what to do when I came up with the idea, so I'd joined one of those writers' support groups on social media. Except this group wasn't for writers but their spouses. I had received a lot of suggestions from them about how to arrange Owen's space to maximize comfort and productivity.

"I can't believe you did this," Owen murmured, "All this is for me?"

"I already have an office," I told him, "though I may be forced to move in here if you never resurface from this space."

He glanced at me. "Oh, I'll resurface. I need my daily dose of Daddy to get through the day."

He moved even closer to the long desk laid out as the central feature of the room. Not one, but three LED monitors ensured he didn't have to move back and forth between files and open web pages. He had the best voice to text recognition software known to man, with a micro-phone system I had been assured could be surpassed by none.

I had outfitted him with a complete set of Apple products, MacBook, iPad, iPod, headphones, watch, and even another iPhone just for business. Because I was concerned about him forgetting to eat at times, he had a mini refrigerator so he could at least keep hydrated.

Another side of the room was arranged as a sitting/relaxation corner. A long sofa bed where he could lounge if he wanted to take breaks in between writing. He didn't have to trudge up the stairs just to take a nap. He could cross the room and have his own mini suite. And if that wasn't enough, Lucky even had his own little nook, so he could be within reach of his favorite person.

"You like it?" I asked him. I had spent a lot of time organizing this room for him, and it meant the most to me from today's affairs—next to our engagement. He would spend much of his time in this room, and I had taken that into consideration when I lovingly chose every piece of furniture and appliance for him. Everything was selected for his comfort.

"Oh, Dec, this is too much."

"There's nothing that's too much to give to you," I assured him. "I plan to encourage your dreams until you believe in you as much as I do."

He sucked in a deep breath, and his eyes widened. His nostrils flared. "Oh God, what if I'm in way over my head, Dec? You've made all this so real. What if—"

"You're so successful you become wealthier than me?" I finished for him.

His jaw dropped open. "I doubt that will happen, but that would be something, wouldn't it? You'd have no need to take care of me then."

I walked over to him and wrapped my arms loosely around his waist. "Wrong. I'll still be taking care of you then. Get used to it."

He leaned into me, turned his head and kissed me. "Thank you, for everything. Tonight surpassed anything I could have dreamed of."

"And it's just about to get better. Now it's time for the begging you're so fond of. You can test out your new office tomorrow."

Since we had already closed up for the night after the caterers left, Owen and I headed upstairs to our bedroom. I teased him just enough to whet his appetite, my hand cupping his shoulders, sliding down his back, feeling the play of muscles there before dipping to grab his ass. By the time we entered the room and I closed the door behind us, his heavy breathing was audible.

"So, you wanted to know if the sex would change?" I hummed, backing him toward the bed. "Are you ready to find out?"

"Oh yeah," he answered. "I'm always ready when you are, Daddy."

"Good." I didn't come to a halt until he had no choice but to sit back hard onto the bed. "Because it's your birthday, you get a special treat."

He blinked several times. "Yeah? What is it?"

"You get to choose something from our assortment of toys to use tonight," I told him. "What do you crave? A, my hand against your naked ass? B, the shiny new butt plug I bought you so you can keep my seed inside you longer? C, the fat dildo you picked out from that sex website? What is it going to be, Boy?" I reached for his crotch to cup him, squeezing his erection hard. Dirty Boy that he was, he hadn't even needed much to be turned on.

"I choose D," he panted.

I smiled at him, amused. "There's no D, Boy."

"Yeah, there is. All of the above."

"Declan," Owen said later as he settled back against me, and his voice was so serious that I opened my eyes. We had truly explored option D, and the experience had left us both mellow. After the rough rounds of sex, I now held him tenderly to me, stroking him affectionately.

"Hmm?"

"Tonight was perfect in every way," he answered. "And I hope I'm not about to mess it up, but I promised your Dad I'd at least talk to you."

"Talk to me? About what?" No sooner than the

words came out of my mouth than I figured out the direction this conversation was heading. "Owen, Charles and I already spoke about my feelings with regards to this."

He pressed a hand to my shoulder. "I know, and I don't want you to get upset about it, but having him explain why it meant so much to him, I really think you should go."

"Why?" I demanded. "To take credit for doing exactly what? Thousands of people are still being diagnosed with cancer and are dying from it every day. There's nothing for us to celebrate."

He gasped and sat up in bed. "Is that what you really think? Because that's not true. Yes, people are still being diagnosed and people are still dying from cancer at an alarming rate, but there are survivors. The technology is developing, and lives have been saved. I know it looks grim from where we are standing, but if the help you've given has saved even one life, that's nothing to scoff at."

"One life out of thousands? Hundreds of thousands?"

"Declan." He sighed my name and reached over to stroke my face. "To someone, one person might mean the world. Think about it. If I was in that position, and someone else's assistance made it possible for me to be a survivor, how would that make you feel? My kids? One survivor is still enough, and I'm sure there are more than just one. Your father says many aided by the treatment options now available to them through your funding will be there. Your mother's death was *not* in vain."

I drew in a painful breath, seeing my mother's gaunt

face clearly for the first time in a long while. "I don't know, Owen."

He shuffled down to lie beside me again, shifting on his side to observe what he could of my face in the room. "What is it that you're really afraid of Dec?"

"Nothing," I replied quickly. Too quickly.

Owen didn't respond, just lay there beside me, waiting. I could have pretended he had fallen asleep or that I had, but when I'd opened my heart and home to this man, I had given him access to everything.

"I've always donated but never attended their events," I confessed, throat tightening as I sought to explain. When I took too long to continue, his hand searched for mine. He laced our fingers together, and feeling the metal of his engagement ring was what gave me the words. "Humility only has a small part to play in it. Truth is that I'm not sure how I will react being at a function that will bring back so many memories, seeing the survivors and wondering why my mother couldn't be among them. Why did she have to be one of the unlucky ones? And that thinking would just be wrong, you know?"

He sighed and squeezed my hand. "There's nothing wrong with the way you feel. It's a natural reaction, and it shouldn't stop you from growing. Declan, your mother would be so proud of you. You know that, don't you? I mean, I'm just your lover, and I am so damn proud of you."

As Owen's words seeped into my consciousness, I believed them. They weren't words I heard often. I knew I'd had success in business, and I'd done a whole lot of good that no one else knew about, but I was rarely ever told those words. *I'm proud of you.* To hear them from Owen made me feel like I could brave going to this function. I could accept that award and give an acceptance speech about what it meant to me. I could, because he would be there with me.

"I don't want to force you to do anything you don't want to," he said softly. "But I want you to give it some thought and decide again in the morning." He leaned forward and kissed me, missing my mouth and landing somewhere on my chin. "I love you, Declan."

It didn't take him long to fall asleep then, but I had too much on my mind to be as easily carried away into oblivion.

36

OWEN

"Told you the little guy would take to me," Oscar mumbled, as Lucky pawed his lap before settling down with his head on my son's thigh. I was amazed at how much healing Lucky had done, considering the abuse he had received, but it only showed me he was a loveable dog who had been desperately in need of attention. Declan and I spoiled him rotten. The maids thought he was adorable, and he was always following David around when he got bored of sitting beside me while I worked

I grinned as I thought about having my own space now and not having to distract Declan, or be distracted by him from working so closely together. I had felt like a king this morning as I sat in my writing cave. Declan had snapped pictures of me just before he went off to work.

"Don't forget to walk him out," I said, shifting my attention back to Oscar who had volunteered to pet sit for us.

"Yeah, you look like you could use some walking too," Auggie commented, patting his twin's stomach. "You're going a little soft around the middle, aren't you?"

"Go fuck yourself!" Oscar cried, slapping away Auggie's hand.

I rolled my eyes, not bothering to tell him to watch his language. I knew full well not to come between them when they were goofing off or fighting. They could easily both turn on anyone who interfered.

"Will you two grow up?" Summer growled at them. She looked absolutely stunning in a fancy red dress with gold trimmings at the waistline. Her gold shoes, handbag and necklace completed her outfit. She looked like royalty, and my heart swelled with pride.

Auggie straightened next to her, wearing a brand new tux. He looked so grown up. With what I now knew of him, I loved him just the same and also had a newfound respect for him and the lifestyle he had chosen. My only desire for him was to find a sub of his own who would leave him fulfilled the way I felt about Declan.

"Yes, please," I remarked nervously. "Tonight is supposed to be special, so stop horsing around. We're here to support Declan."

I had woken up this morning to find Declan wide awake and staring at me. He always seemed to think better at night when he was supposed to be sleeping. He had agreed to attend the appreciation ceremony after all, and I had been thrilled. What he didn't know however, was that Charles and I had organized to have our own little cheering section. Declan had received an invitation only for a plus one, but Charles had produced two more for Auggie and Summer. There would have been a third, but Oscar had volunteered to stay with Lucky for the night.

Declan had no idea yet that my kids were going with us. He'd heard them come in, but just thought they were all kicking back at our place until we got home. It was their last night in Cincy anyway before they returned to Columbus tomorrow, and within a week or two Auggie would be back to stay permanently. He had made the decision look easy, but I knew it was a big move for him and Oscar. Those two, disagreements and all, though different as night and day, were thick as thieves. They had always been within close reach of each other.

"Owen!" Declan called, as I imagined he was descending the stairs. "I think I've made us late, and you know how much I hate— oh!" He came to a sudden halt just inside the living room and swept his gaze across us before his bewildered stare landed on me. "What's going on here?"

"Now don't freak out," I answered, walking over to him because he looked too damn sharp in his tux for me not to touch him.

"Why would I freak out?" he asked, but he was.

I didn't expect tonight to go without a hitch, but that was the reason I brought back up. "No reason," I answered, brushing imaginary lint from his perfect shoulders. "There's absolutely no reason for you to freak out that my kids—minus Oscar—are coming with us tonight to lend their support."

"They are?" Declan's surprised look landed on Auggie and Summer, this time, taking in the way they were dressed. "Jesus, I'm so touched, but you guys didn't have to go through all this trouble. I hope Owen didn't make you."

"I didn't make them," I replied. "I asked, because what's the harm in asking? They said yes."

"Yeah, but it's kind of hard to say no to you, love," Declan pointed out.

"Well, we said yes all on our own," Summer stated. "Deal with it. You have your personal fan club going with you."

Oscar snorted. "Yeah, party of three, and the fun one's not even included."

"Party of six," I corrected. "We're picking up Charles on the way. Plus, Heath and Ridge said they will be there too."

Declan swallowed hard. "When did you have time to plan this?"

"It was quite easy. There's very little the people in your life wouldn't do for you. Now come on. Car's here, and we're already going to be late."

"Fashionably late *is* a thing, you know," Summer stated.

"Declan loathes being late for anything," I explained, and his eyes caught mine as we remembered the first spanking he'd ever given me.

Oscar walked us to the door, and I reminded him once more to let out Lucky before following the others to the limousine that Charles had provided for the night. I could tell Declan was more nervous than he let on, but thankfully Auggie engaged him in conversation about business to take his mind off the purpose of the function we were attending.

We picked up Charles on the way which reminded me that this was the first time I was seeing his house. He was dressed already and came outside as soon as we drove up, so I didn't have the chance to take a peek inside, but from the exterior alone, it was quite lovely and screamed affluence and luxury. The house was more modern than the one we lived in with wall to ceiling glass all around.

"Hey everyone," he greeted as he joined us, sitting next to Auggie. Sometimes it was hard to imagine Charles as the same man I had initially met that first day in Declan's office. He was calmer, a whole lot friendlier these days, and he got along okay with my children.

"You could have informed me I was going to be ambushed tonight," Declan told his father after we all greeted him back.

"That's not on me," Charles protested, leaning back in his seat. "All I did was ask your fiancé to help persuade you to show up. He did everything else on his own. I just facilitated him."

I liked the way Charles referred to me as Declan's fiancé. I fiddled with the ring on my finger, feeling all warm and happy that we were able to do this for Declan.

"Well, thank you for having Owen talk me into going," he answered. "You were right. I shouldn't pass up this opportunity."

Charles nodded but didn't respond, and I didn't miss the sheen of tears in his eyes before he glanced away. I felt sorry for him sometimes. He was desperately trying to make up for lost time, but he had lost all of Declan's childhood. He couldn't get those days back. He'd lived nothing but a shallow existence for years, and now that he had a soul again, he had to be struggling. He was on the verge of a divorce that didn't seem to be going smoothly at all, and although Declan had been willing to help him, he had refused.

The drive lasted a total of twenty minutes to the Golden Circle Golf Club where the event was being held. Heath and Ridge had already arrived before us and had been seated. As a result of RSVPing late, however, we were unable to all sit together. Declan, Summer, and I were brought to a table at the front where the other awardees for the night were seated. Auggie and Charles sat two tables away with Heath and Ridge, but other guests sat in between them.

Although we arrived a few minutes late, the function didn't start on time which afforded acquaintances of Declan to come over to our table to stop by our table. Declan whispered to me that they were mostly Charles's golf buddies and business associates, not close friends, but that hardly set my mind at ease when they kept stealing glances at me.

Finally, one man, with thinning hair and considerable girth around his middle eyed me as he spoke to Declan. "Heard congratulations are in order because you got engaged."

Declan smiled easily at me. "Sure did, to this wonderful man right here."

I smiled politely and shook the other man's hand. He didn't do a good job of hiding his shock.

"Hello there, I'm Owen," I greeted. "Nice to meet you."

He mumbled something I didn't quite catch before he suddenly remembered he had something to do.

"Jackass," Summer muttered, and I chuckled.

"We're in polite company," I reminded her.

Declan squeezed my thigh. "No, I'm inclined to agree. Jackass." He leaned sideways and kissed my cheek. "Don't let them get to you tonight. These high society types can be full of themselves, but they are usually painfully polite. If anyone crosses the line with you, do let me know so I can set them straight."

I had no intention of doing anything of the sort, but I nodded. Thankfully the event commenced shortly after. It started out as a long drawn out affair, with addresses by different sponsors of the event in addition to the mayor who was in attendance. The most fascinating parts were from a member of the Cancer Research Society who gave a presentation of what they had been working on over the years and the breakthroughs they had so far. Afterward, there was another slideshow presentation of cancer patients who the research had helped.

I tried to keep in tune with Declan's emotions, taking his hand in mine as we watched the proceedings unfold. I was deeply humbled at the experience of being there and learning about the illness that had caused the love of my life to lose his mother. Eventually, he allowed himself to relax which placed me at ease to enjoy the night's activities.

At one point, I excused myself to use the restroom. I wasn't even gone that long, but by the time I returned to my seat, I was surprised to find Declan gone. Summer was looking toward the exit, her face full of worry.

"Where is he?" I whispered.

"He went through that door." She pointed to the door at the back of the room where the function was being held. "They were showing pictures of those who had succumbed to cancer this year, and he bolted. You have to get him back. He's up soon."

I went after Declan, hoping he hadn't disappeared on me like he had done the night he'd been terribly ill at my home. I wound my way through the tables until I reached the exit. I came to a halt out in the hall and breathed a sigh of relief when I spotted him pacing back and forth. Thank God I didn't have to go searching for him, because I had no idea how to make my way around the golf club.

Declan stopped when he saw me. His shoulders were straight, his eyes panicky. "I can't do this." He waved a leaf of paper on which he had jotted down his thank you speech. I had scanned the speech for him, so I knew it was pretty good, short and to the point.

"Declan," I said his name with empathy, approaching him and when I was close enough, I drew him to me, not caring who saw us. We were engaged anyway, and even if we weren't, it was nobody's business. I pulled his head onto my shoulder, keeping him there with my hand at the back of his neck. He sighed into me, his right arm coming around my waist as he made use of my support.

"It's confronting it all over again," he whispered hoarsely. "It's been so long, Owen. Why am I not over it yet?"

"You lost your mother when you were young, Dec," I reminded him. "Nobody's going to hold it against you if you still miss her. You don't have to play tough in there. Just be you."

"If I am myself right now, I'll not be strong enough to make it through the speech."

"Do you want me to go up there with you?" I volunteered, even though I hated being the center of anyone else's attention other than Declan's.

"You'd do that?" he asked, raising his head.

"Of course, I would."

That made him smile. "That's alright. I think I can manage it by myself. I'll be inside in a few. Just need a few minutes of fresh air."

I nodded my understanding. "Okay. I'll be inside waiting."

37

DECLAN

I watched fondly as Owen walked back into the room, the lighting setting off the gray in his hair. Since we were together, I had showered him with gifts, but none held as much significance of what he had done for me tonight. Not only had he persuaded me to be present at the event, but he had organized, in such a short time, to have my friends and our family here for support.

He tried to make it seem like it wasn't a big deal, but I had some idea. For one, I doubted his kids had brought formal attire with them from Columbus, which meant they had spent the day trying to find something to wear to the function. Heath and Ridge had even left their kinky club to present themselves in *polite* company, and I knew Heath preferred his leather to the formal attire he was dressed in.

I was just about to follow back inside when Charles stepped out of the room. He looked miserable, his eyes red, as if he had been crying. He paused when he saw me, his throat working hard with each swallow.

"You okay?" I asked him, breaking the silence.

"Yeah, been thinking maybe I shouldn't have pushed you to come tonight," he answered. "I didn't expect it to be so tough. I come every year, and they've never done the acknowledgment of those who passed away the previous year."

"It's okay. I'm still glad that I am here."

"I know it was tough to watch," he stated. "God, I was so wrong for telling you before to get over it when I'm still living every day with the ache in my heart."

"Do you suppose it will ever go away?"

"It has gotten better," he replied. "It's just a slow process."

I nodded, about to inform him that we should get back inside when Auggie appeared. He glanced between me and Charles, but his gaze quickly landed and settled back on Charles.

"Declan, they just announced you," he told me. "You need some time?"

"No, I'll be fine."

The hum of chatter that had started in the room dwindled and heads swiveled in my direction as I took to the side to walk up to the large stage where I would be required to collect an award that meant very little to me personally.

"Ladies and gentlemen, as he makes his way to us, let's give a round of applause to Mr. Declan Moore," the MC announced my appearance. "Mr. Moore has been a staunch supporter of the cancer research initiative for close to seven years, donating millions of dollars each year toward research and also in the payment of treatment for cancer patients who are unable to afford the care needed. For his commitment and dedication, we have opted to award Mr. Moore tonight."

By this time, I was on the stage, slowly walking toward the other man who continued speaking.

"I'm going to ask the Mayor to assist us in making the presentation."

I had been the subject of too many functions to be nervous about standing there before the hundred or so guests in attendance. I shook the Mayor's hand, collected a glass pyramid looking award with words inscribed on the front. The guests cheered, and I could swear I heard Summer's jubilant cry somewhere in there. A couple of pictures later then came the hardest part—the speech.

"I wasn't sure that I would be in attendance tonight," I started, as I took out the little speech I had written that Owen had gone over for me. He was good with words. I was good with numbers, so it only made sense. I glanced over the room of people, my eyes first landing on Owen's smiling face. He looked so proud, his attention completely riveted on me. Beside him, Summer leaned against her father, also smiling. At their table, Heath had an arm around Ridge, but for once they weren't sucked into each other, and Auggie and Charles were just as focused on the stage. Charles looked pale, his mouth was set in a grim line and on top of the table, Auggie had a hand covering his in support.

My family. All of them. They gave me the courage, the peace of mind and comfort to be here tonight.

Just be you.

I folded up the paper of the carefully written words. "I wrote some words that I thought would be safe. Words that touch on the surface and get the job done, but not the words that adequately express what this award means to me tonight.

"I'm not even certain that I deserve this award. When kindness is extended, it's not to be done with the expectation of receiving anything back, so I was hesitant in coming here today, but my wonderful fiancé reminded me of what all this truly means."

I glanced at Owen whose face turned a shade of red as heads swiveled, following my stare to land on him. Beside him, Summer beamed. God she was gorgeous in the way she supported us.

"You see, when I was five years old, the most tragic thing happened to me," I continued, regaining their attention. This time I passed my gaze over the table where the cancer survivors in attendance were seated. "I lost someone very important to me to cancer. My mother." I expected the tightness in my chest, the stinging in my eyes and nostrils, but this time the symptoms of my grief didn't manifest itself. "For a long time, I was devastated, and as soon as I got the opportunity, there was no question about supporting the initiative of the Cancer Research Institute. I kept thinking that I'd do everything I could to help beat this ugly disease that rips our loved ones away from us way too soon.

"As my fiancé reminded me yesterday, that some good came out of my mother's death. The lives that have been saved because of the continuation of research and the funding of treatments for those who generally wouldn't be able to afford it. And it's in her memory that I continue to pledge my support for this worthy cause.

"And before I go, there's one individual who deserves a mention." I rested my gaze on Charles who stared back at me. My eyes misted when I saw him making no effort to hide the tears that shamelessly rolled down his cheeks. "If I could choose anyone to pass this award to, it would be my father, Charles Moore, who did everything in his power to give my mother one more day. He is the epitome of how we should care for a loved one who has been diagnosed with this monster we all dread. With care, a fighting spirit and willing to go the extra mile to give our loved one, one more day. One more day of love. One more day of laughter.

"Charles—my father started this foundation, and despite the pain he endured over the years of losing a wife he loved very much, he continued to contribute to the cancer society. He did it silently and without fanfare, but that he did, paving the way for the man I am today, with a likeminded desire to see more cancer survivors and playing a part in giving others one more day.

"So from my family to yours, let's continue to support this amazing initiative that has been working to improve and prolong the lives of cancer patients. Thank you."

The shakes started only after I stepped back and walked off the stage. There was applause, and everyone stood, but I only had eyes on reaching Charles. Auggie's hand dropped from Charles's back as I handed him the award I had been given.

He shook his head. "No, I can't. It's yours. They gave it to you, because you deserve it."

"And I pass it on to you, because you deserve it too," I told him, pressing the award in his hand. "It's from me to you. For Mom and everything you did for her while she fought. For always fighting to give me one more day with her."

Charles crushed me in a hug, clinging to me, his cries turned to sobs. I had never seen him let his guard down like this before, and it moved me to tears. Drunk I had seen him several times. Never like this.

"I'm so sorry I couldn't give you more," he gasped. "So sorry you didn't grow up to see just how wonderful she was as a mother, a wife, a friend, and a decent human being."

"I know. I know."

THE REST of the function was uneventful. As soon as I sat back in my seat, Owen kissed me and told me how moved he was by my speech. At one point, Charles got up, still apparently distraught, and I made to go after him, but I didn't need to. Auggie followed him within a couple of seconds, and I trusted Owen's son to look out for him, because he was a good kid. When they returned, Charles looked better, calmer, and I nodded in approval. Auggie had the sensitive spirit of a knowledgeable Dom that no doubt helped in the way he handled Charles's breakdown.

At the end of the event, we spent another thirty

minutes talking with various people who stopped us on the way out. It was a relief when we finally made it outside to wait on the driver to bring the limousine around. We waited in silence, words not needed. Summer was yawning, and her head rested on Owen's shoulder.

I was thinking about how pleased I was that I had decided to come after all when I felt a tap on my shoulder.

"Excuse me, Mr. Moore, may I speak with you, please?"

I turned, suppressing my sigh that yet another person wanted to comment on my beautiful speech that my mother would have been proud of. I was in for a surprise though. A young man not a day over twenty was trying to gain my attention.

I mustered up a smile. "Hello, sure I have a minute to spare until our ride gets here."

The boy's nervous smile turned wide with relief. "I won't be long, I promise. I just—I had to say thank you in person. Your speech really moved me about that one day, you know. You gave me several more of those one days with my family."

"Excuse me?"

"I'm one of the many who benefitted from better treatment options because of your contributions," he answered. "I don't know how much you know of what goes on behind the organization of the cancer society, but we have the option of knowing who sponsors our treatment. I've known since I was fifteen when I was first diagnosed with Hodgkin's lymphoma, and I've always hoped to one day meet you in person. I'm so glad you showed up tonight."

Stunned, I stared at the young man who was bursting with energy. My first thought was that he looked nothing like my mother. He looked healthy and happy, his eyes full of grit and courage. There was knowing that I helped someone beat this awful disease, and then there was *knowing*.

"You're welcome," I stated, shaking his extended hand. "I'm so glad you are able to get the best treatment possible."

"It's just been a year of no treatments," he continued. "But I feel confident. Thanks to you, I'll be able to start college soon." He peeked at Owen, color rising in his cheeks. "I'm able to see a clearer future with my boyfriend."

That made me smile. "Good for you, kid. All the best with college and the boyfriend."

"You too. Both you and your fiancé."

The limousine rolled to a stop, and the others, except for Owen who stayed with me, headed toward the vehicle. On a whim, I reached into my pocket for my wallet and removed a business card. I handed it to the young man. "I never got your name. What is it?"

"Taylor. Taylor Vickers."

"Well, Taylor, it was nice to meet you. Do me a favor and keep in touch, will you? Just drop me a line every now and then that you're okay. If you need anything, you can also give me a call."

He stared up at me, his eyes wide. He took the card from me then threw his arms around me in a quick hug before pulling away, embarrassed. "I-I'm sorry. Thank you. I promise I'll keep in touch."

"Good. Take care."

Taking Owen's hand, we turned toward the waiting limousine. Owen squeezed my hand, and I glanced at him to find him smiling at me, wearing his heart on his sleeve.

"What?" I asked, my face heating up.

He shook his head. "Nothing. Just thinking how much I love you right now."

38

OWEN

"I forgot how much I love cake," I groaned as Declan and I piled into the car along with David. We had just been to the cake tasting to decide which we wanted for our wedding. David was taking our wedding seriously, even when Declan and I tried to goof off. He kept us on track, and I couldn't believe the wedding was going to take place in just two weeks. Two weeks until we said I do and he would be legally mine.

"I think everyone knows that now," Declan snorted beside me. "You insisted in tasting everything even when we'd already decided on the winner."

"I just had to make sure," I replied, but he was right. The maple, pecan, and pecan praline flavor and filling had been quite perfect. It had been an instant hit for all three of us. Declan apparently had more expertise in this than me, because of his father's many weddings, and he was able to guide me into agreeing with an arrangement for our cake. A blue and white three tier cake, with each tier wrapped in a bow of the colors of the Pride flag. The edible inked phrase *All We Need is Love* topped off the finishing.

"The cake is just perfect," David added, flipping through the tablet he had on his lap. Declan had gifted his butler—our wedding planner— with the device to help him better organize our wedding instead of the thick folder he had which only got bigger and bigger.

"And next up is…?" I asked.

"Fitting your tuxes but that's a couple of days away," David answered. "I'd say that we're pretty much on track. We should be closing our guest list any day now. There are just a few people who have not RSVP'd to confirm as yet."

I fell silent because some of those people were my own family members. I had no idea why I had even bothered to send them invitations, because it wasn't like I anticipated them showing up. They'd all made it clear before how they felt about my lifestyle and that of my kids. I had reached out to them once more though, because this was their opportunity to show me that over the years they had changed.

I should have known better.

On the ride home, we decided on party favors for our guests, turned down a registry since we hardly needed anything and went through our track list for the wedding reception. David had already taken care of the officiant, the floral arrangements— most things really. I was amazed at how efficient he already was for a guy who hadn't finished his diploma in events planning. He definitely had a knack for it.

"And since you decided not to recite the traditional vows," David told us as our driver parked before our home. "Don't wait until the last minute to write your own."

"We have to *write* the vows?" Declan asked. "Shouldn't we be able to speak freely on the spot?"

"A wedding can be so overwhelming that the words don't come the way we'd want them. Picture Owen walking down the aisle, and all your thoughts have scattered, because you're finally marrying the man of your dreams. Do you trust yourself to remember exactly what to say?"

With that, David got out of the car and headed for the house. Declan turned to me with an amused expression.

"I bet you didn't write vows for your first wedding, did you?"

"Nope. We used traditional vows. You should listen to David and write yours. I do plan to rob you of speech that day."

"If you do, I won't be able to read the speech anyway," he said on a small laugh. "I'm telling you, I don't need to write down my vows to you."

"Alright then. It'll just be you and me and our fifty or so guests. I thought we'd have twenty-five max, but you and Charles know a lot of people."

"And half of them haven't even made it on the guest list," he reminded me. "See, we're keeping it small and intimate the way you wanted."

"Hmm." I reached out a hand to tug at his tie a little. He was due back at work and had only taken a couple of hours off to go cake tasting with me. Even though I had told him I could do it on my own, he had insisted on being there.

"What's that sound for?" he asked. "Are we doing something wrong with this wedding that you don't want?"

"Oh no. Not that," I quickly assured him. "David is rather good at this, don't you think?"

"He is. Now will you tell me what's wrong?"

I sighed. "My parents haven't called to confirm whether they will be coming or not. I guess that's safe to say they aren't coming, isn't it?"

His hand covered mine. "Give me the address, and I'll get them here."

I chuckled. "That's not the way it works. You can't *make* them come."

"Want to bet?"

"Well, they should *want* to come. I don't want you coercing them."

He squeezed my hand. "I'm sorry if they let you down."

"Yeah, me too. I'm thinking of calling them, you know. I mean why should they get to turn me down so easily by not responding?"

"You think it's worth the trouble of getting hurt?"

"It's going to stink either way. I might as well get it over with rather than to wonder if the invitations got lost in the mail or something."

Declan raised his eyebrows in disbelief. Yeah, I didn't believe that for a minute either.

"Okay, just keep me posted." He kissed me swiftly. "I

need to get back to work. I have a consultation in the next hour that I need to prepare for."

"Sure I can't entice you inside for—"

Declan slapped his hand over my mouth to muffle the words as he glared at me. "Don't even go there. I can't be late for this meeting. But tonight. I promise."

I nodded, and he released my mouth. "Okay. I'll make us dinner."

I watched him go and when the car had disappeared from view, I entered the house slowly. Lucky, hearing me come in, trotted up, barking and wagging his tail. I reached down to scratch behind his ear while avoiding his licks.

"Hey there, boy, wanna play?"

He yipped, chasing his tail which made me laugh. He was such a comical dog, and we loved him to bits.

"I guess that's a yes. Just give me a minute, and I'll come play with you."

I patted his head before heading for my writing cave, Lucky in step beside me. Once I entered the office, I took up my business phone because the last thing I wanted was for mother to recognize my number and deliberately not answer the call.

Even though I hadn't called home in quite a while, I still remembered the number. I sat in my chair scooping Lucky onto my lap for comfort and to ease the tension while I waited for someone to answer the phone. It rang three times before it was picked up.

"Hello?" Mother's disgruntled voice came over the line. She sounded rushed as if she was in the middle of something.

"Hi Ma', I hope I didn't catch you at a bad time," I replied. "How are you?"

Silence came from the other end of the line, and for a while I thought she wouldn't respond.

"Owen, what are you doing calling here?"

I closed my eyes against the pain I shouldn't even feel anymore. I knew they were this way, but I had hoped they would have changed given the time that had passed between us. Times had changed. Even people who were once opposers were now supporters. What would it take for them to still love the only child they had?

"I wanted to know how you and Pop are doing, Ma."

She snorted. "Is that so? Because I think this is about that abomination we received in the mail a week ago. Thank God I threw it away before your father saw it."

"I guess this means you're not coming to the wedding?"

"Are you marrying a woman?" she countered.

I sighed. "No, Ma. I fell in love with a guy. He's pretty awesome, and the kids all love him. If you would just give him a chance too, you'd love him. His name is—"

"Declan Moore," she said before I could finish. "I know. Your cousin Percy looked him up and apparently knows a little bit about this guy. So the money is the reason you're doing this? You'd sell your soul because he can buy you expensive things?"

Bile rose into my throat. "Didn't you hear what I said Ma? I love him. He loves me. Isn't that the reason people get married?"

"You can't love somebody of the same sex. That's just wrong."

"Why?" I challenged, my voice hardening.

"Because that's not the way it's supposed to be. And see what happened? You and that wife of yours are being punished for your abominable lifestyle. Isn't that the reason all your kids are… are like that? All my beautiful grandbabies ruined because of the parents they have."

Fool. I was such a fool to think time would have changed anything. "My kids are beautiful because of *who they are*," I stated in a cold voice. "I thought to extend an olive branch, hoping this would be the opportunity for our family to come together, but apparently I hoped for too much."

"As far as we are concerned, we don't have a son," she declared before hanging up in my ear.

I blinked away the angry tears, because they didn't deserve them. It was time to stop revisiting that train station hoping for the train to pull up. If they wanted to reconnect from now on, they would have to reach out themselves. I would make a life with my newly reconstructed family, and to hell with anyone who disagreed with how and why we loved.

"Come on, boy." I boosted Lucky from my lap and took him outside with his favorite ball. We played, him doing most of the work, but it made me feel good about myself watching how happy he was despite everything he had been through.

I had a manuscript to get back to, but I spent a lot of time with our dog, and when he was tired, I went for a swim in the pool. By then I had shaken off the disap-

pointment of the call I had made to my parents. I had
Declan. I had my kids and new friends. When Declan
and I had returned to the tattoo parlor to check out
tattoos he could get in remembrance of his mother, we'd
gotten around to talking to Pierce again. We'd been so
caught up in the moment that we'd even invited him to
the wedding. Another friend in the making, That was
enough for me. We would take care of us.

After swimming, I left Lucky to wander the property
as he liked to do from time to time. One of the doors
remained open, and he always knew to come in via that
means when he was ready.

Dressed in dry clothes, I returned to my office and
sank into my seat, turning the computer on. It had taken
me a while to get used to having so many devices to
choose from, but now I loved the ease and luxury of writing. Being in my office also made me feel so much more
valid as an author even though I had nothing published.
It was almost a month and still no word from the
publishing company.

While my computer booted, I took up my cell phone
to text Declan that my parents would be a no show for
the wedding. What I found were six missed calls from a
number that wasn't familiar and a voicemail. With my
three kids living in a different location, I couldn't ignore
the unfamiliar number. I first checked the voicemail.

"Mr. Long?" A masculine voice came through the
recording. "This is Editor in Chief Max Trellis calling
from Harver Press. We sent you an email, but we also
wanted to reach out to you in person. We'd love to talk to
you more about your manuscript. We were quite

impressed with the details. Please give us a call as soon as you can."

Completely stunned, I missed the extension I was told to use once I called the number and ended up listening to the message again because I could hardly believe it. My first submission, and I got accepted. They hadn't said it in so many words, but they wouldn't want to discuss more about my manuscript if they hated it.

I couldn't decide whether to laugh or to cry and I ended up doing a little bit of both.

39

DECLAN

O wen's little teasing remark that I had stopped before he had gotten it all out remained with me throughout the day. I was surprised I made it through the meeting, and after it ended, I forced myself to remain in my office working. Owen had fast become an addiction, but I had to remind myself that this was our normal. I didn't have to rush on home because he would be there when I got back. He had nowhere else to go but in my bed.

Regardless of using these thoughts to keep me going throughout the day, when the clock struck five, I was ready to leave. I had my computer off and was stuffing papers into my briefcase to take home with me before changing my mind. I didn't want to bring home any work today. Owen and I were getting married in two weeks, and I wanted to spend some alone time with him without the distraction of work in the background.

More than likely if I brought them home anyway,

they would remain untouched. There was a whole other kind of touching that I was looking forward to doing. Touching that was way more pleasurable.

I had just ended the call to my driver to bring the car around when there was a knock on my office door. I glanced at the clock, hoping I wasn't about to get some task to do that would require a lot of my time.

"Come in!" I called.

Charles entered the office, looking sharp even though it was the end of the day. He was always impeccably dressed. While his attitude had improved a lot, when it came to his appearance, he was quite anal about it. God forbid anyone saw him looking anything but at his best.

Something about his appearance worried me though. He had some confused bewilderment about him the last few days he'd been to my office. He had assured me he was handling his divorce with Poppy, but I wasn't certain he was doing a good job of it. He looked wanner these days, more pensive and secretive. Charles wasn't usually the secretive type. He lived out his flamboyant affairs and laid-back lifestyle in the open for everyone to see, so this side of him had me concerned.

"You're leaving," he stated, without closing the door, and because I heard the disappointment in his tone, I stopped packing.

"About to," I answered. "Is something wrong? Close the door, and let's talk. How's the divorce going?"

He closed the door, his face set in a grimace as he came over to sit on the chair directly in front of my desk. He carefully arranged his jacket without even realizing what he was doing.

"To be honest, the divorce is anything but smooth," he answered with a sigh. "And she's convinced the judge at the last hearing that she's in a fragile state and unable to handle a divorce at this stage, so they pushed back the hearing until *after* the baby has safely entered the world."

"Poor unsuspecting child," I empathized. Nobody deserved a manipulating mother like that. What kind of life would that baby have?

"She's definitely not fit to raise the child after carrying that baby girl into the world."

"It's a girl?" I asked.

He nodded with a smile. "She called me up a few days ago, asking me for help to take her to her appointment. She isn't supposed to be driving, and because I didn't want her to attempt it and endanger the baby, I took her."

I frowned at the wistfulness in his tone. "Charles, you're not thinking about dropping the divorce and trying to make your relationship work with Poppy, are you? Because I'm telling you that you don't have to prove anything to me."

"It's not that."

"Then what is it?"

He sighed and shook his head. "It's stupid."

"Well, I've seen you do stupid things for a long time. I'm used to it, so tell me."

"I want the child," he said, managing to shock me. "Now hear me out. I am not going to do anything to claim her child. It's just how I've felt since she told me about the baby and tried to convince me it was mine. It didn't matter to me then, and it doesn't matter to me now, but I know if I make my interest known, she will constantly use the baby against me."

"Yes," I agreed. "That she would."

"And besides, with the way everything is going, what would I do with a child anyway? I never had the touch your mother did."

"I don't necessarily agree," I said. "I remember you being pretty damn good at being a father up until everything fell apart."

That got me a little smile from him. "Thanks for trying to make me feel better."

"I'm not. It's just the truth."

"Okay." He slid down in the chair and stared at his shoes. "That's not exactly why I came to talk to you."

"No?"

He pinched the bridge of his nose and stared at his shoes still. "No. Umm, it's just a delicate matter. I don't want to offend you. I'm just curious and a bit confused right now."

I straightened up in my chair, preparing for whatever it was that I wasn't intended to like based on his tone. "Just tell me and we'll decide how offended I am after."

"Umm, how—how did you know you were gay?"

I blinked at him, then stared, because his question took me by surprise. "What?"

"It's a valid question," he said. "I mean how could you be certain?"

He sounded serious about the whole thing, so I pushed down my bewilderment at where the question was coming from and tried to answer. "Umm, well, uh, I guess I pretty much knew it even before I *knew* it. I mean, girls never did anything at all for me. Sure, I could see when they were cute back then, but all I could think about was kissing some boy I liked back in middle school. I pretty much knew then."

"Oh." His frown deepened. "I guess it's more complicated if you like both, right? I mean, how can you be sure?"

"You don't *have to* choose," I replied. "I mean Owen's bi. It's either you have feelings for men and women both or you don't, but why are you asking me this now?"

"I explored in college," he started to answer even before I finished the question. "Since lately I've been thinking about Terry Allen, my roommate. Terry was gay."

"It's okay, Dad. Many people experiment in college."

"You don't understand. Back then things were more complicated. We didn't have this support of equal rights as you do now. Terry wanted more. I backed off and chalked it down to experimenting. And I fell in love with your mom, I didn't want anyone else."

After my mind went around in several circles, I believed I stumbled upon my father's dilemma. "Are you telling me that…"

"I don't know," he answered. "That's why I ask how do you know? I… uh… there's this guy I've been having these weird feelings about, and nothing will come of it because I know how wrong it is, but the feelings are there."

I frowned at him. "Dad, it's not wrong to have feelings for another man."

"I know *that*. It's just that it would be so wrong to get involved with *him*. So, so wrong."

"Why?"

"Because…" He trailed off then got to his feet. "It doesn't matter. Forget I said anything. I'm clearly out of it. Of course I am not bisexual. I would have known by now."

"Unless you've been in denial," I said gently.

He grinned at me, but I saw the panic in his eyes. "Nope. No denial here. We know how much I love pussy, right?"

I scowled at him. "What the fuck, Charles. You don't have to prove anything to me by deliberately being crude."

He scrubbed at his face. "Shit, you're right. I know. Look, just drop this. Are you planning a bachelor party?"

I didn't want to drop the subject, but for now I agreed. I needed the time to think about what Charles had revealed today, and he needed more time to come to terms with his new self-discovery.

"No, we don't want a bachelor's party. I've seen too many, remember?"

"It doesn't have to include strippers," he replied. "You've held so many bachelor parties for me. I have to throw one for you."

"We've already decided, Charles. No party. Owen and I will spend that time together. We'll have our rehearsal dinner, and that's enough."

"Fine. Do you need me to help with anything for the wedding?"

I snapped my briefcase shut. "Nope. David has everything taken care of. He's like a one man show that can't be stopped."

"I still think you should have hired a professional to plan your wedding."

I didn't even take offence to him. "David is doing a great job. I bet after seeing ours, you'll want him to plan your next."

Charles's scowl was priceless, and I laughed as we walked out of my office.

"I'm never marrying again," he professed as I locked up.

"Uh huh. Let's see if that guy you don't want to mention feels the same."

I felt the daggers of Charles's eyes boring into me as I headed for the elevator. It felt so good to tease him good-naturedly. It reminded me of the relationship Owen had with his children.

The car was already parked at the front of the building. It was mostly a quiet drive home as usual which had become my new normal. No more chatting like I did with Silas. I didn't mind though, because the new driver was at least polite and did his job well. It wasn't his fault he couldn't morph into Silas, and from what I could tell of my former driver from Owen's birthday party, he was enjoying his vacation. I was quite positive he wouldn't be back any time soon.

I found Lucky napping outside, and I tried to tip-toe by him, so I didn't disturb his beauty sleep, but his nose twitched, his eyes opened, and then he was up on his three good legs. He crashed into me, barking, and I laughed. Our little guy had definitely brought color into our lives.

He mouthed the ball Owen had left out and nudged it toward me. "At least let me get out of all these stuffy clothes first," I told him.

He wasn't patient though, and with a sigh, I placed my briefcase on the paved ground and grasped the ball. "Okay. Just a couple of rounds then I must go smooch your master."

The look on the dog's face was utter disgust, although that was probably my imagination. I threw the ball, and he ran after it, impeded by his bad leg, but it didn't stop him at all. Owen and I were looking into the pros and cons of having him go through surgery to correct the problem with his leg. I dropped to my haunches when he had the ball and patted my thighs. "Bring it here. Good boy!"

"You could at least change first," Owen said, walking toward us from the side door he would have left open for Lucky to come in and out as his heart pleased.

I smiled at him walking toward me wearing faded jeans and a tank top.

"I tried to bargain with him," I answered, throwing the ball. "He wouldn't let me."

While Lucky ran after the ball, Owen walked right into my arms for the customary greeting kiss we exchanged whenever I got home from work. It was the same kiss I dropped on his lips when I left home in the morning as well and he was still sleeping.

He had a tendency to sneak down to his office in the middle of the night and crawl back into bed late which meant he was barely lucid when I went to work in the morning. After spanking him three days in a row for leaving our bed in the night, I had given up and accepted he enjoyed working at night without me distracting him. I had just asked him to come back to bed sooner as I worried about him not getting enough sleep.

Owen's hands curled into my shirt, and he brushed his thumbs lightly over my nipples. I moaned into his mouth. My nipples would still need more healing time, but they were less tender, and he had fun touching them every now and then. I couldn't wait for them to be completely healed so he could get to toying with them.

"Hmm," I moaned in between his kisses. "I like where this is going."

He kissed me deeply. "I have good news. Really, really good news."

I eased back to peer into his face. His eyes were shining with excitement he could barely contain. "Your parents are coming to our wedding?"

He shook his head, his smile failing just a tad. "Umm, no. They're still not coming. My mother practically told me that they no longer have a son, so that's that."

I cupped his face. "I'm so sorry about that."

"It's honestly their loss. I have an amazing family in you guys, and if they can't accept that, then we don't need them anyway."

"I know, but it's still tough."

"Yeah, but you guys are my everything. *That's* all I really need."

At the sudden silence around me, I realized we had been ignoring Lucky who now walked away affronted.

"What's your good news?" I pressed. "We're getting married tomorrow instead of waiting for two weeks?"

He slapped my stomach lightly. "No! The wedding date stays, but I heard from the publishing company."

"Wow. That's quick. Congrats, babe."

"I didn't even say I got in."

"You don't need to say it. You look it."

He laughed. "Well, yeah. I can't believe I got in on the first try, but it's even better. They want to meet with me in person."

"Is that customary?"

"No, but they said they wanted to talk to me about a future with their company."

"Sounds serious." And out of the ordinary which made me immediately suspicious, but I didn't mention it to him. He hadn't asked for my opinion, and since he'd asked me to stay out of this, he would be meeting this publisher alone.

"Exactly what I thought," he answered. "It's a bit nerve-wracking."

"When and where do you have to go?" I asked him.

"Over the weekend," he replied. "Their headquarters is in New York City. They're paying for the hotel, airfare and everything."

Now that made me even more wary. "And this company is legit, right?"

He nodded. "As legit as they come. They're one of the Big Six Publishing Houses. Now you know why I'm so excited that they obviously thought so well of my story that they gave me a personal call."

"Then we should celebrate tonight." Despite my

misgivings, I would support him just as he had asked and hoped the best for him. I kissed him hard. "I'm so proud of you."

And I was. I wouldn't have my over critical mind try to pick holes into this publishing house and why their deal with him had to be done in person.

40

OWEN

Pressing a hand to my knees to stop them from shaking, I sat out in the waiting area of the publisher's office building, waiting to be admitted to see my party. Everything here in New York City was so much bigger. The people seemed larger than life, and even the building seemed to have taken a life of its own.

I smiled as I remembered Declan lecturing me last night about the dangers that lurked in the Big Apple. He didn't care how old I was. I had never been to New York City before, and he wanted to drill into my head that the city was different. As far as he was from me, he had insisted that I called him if anything went wrong or if I was in a situation where I didn't feel comfortable.

The man had forgotten that I had been taking care of myself long before he came along. Seeing how worried he was, I had listened dutifully though. The way he had made love to me afterward desperately, was almost as if I wasn't returning. It was sweet that he felt the same way I did when he had gone off with Charles to his conference.

I had landed at JFK Airport four hours ago, but Declan had discarded the accommodation the publishing house had set up for me. He hadn't been satisfied with the less than stellar accommodation, so he had found me a driver—apparently from contacting a business associate —who had met me at the airport and taken me to the Sheraton. I had taken a quick nap before waking up to get dressed for my meeting.

In hindsight, I probably should have arrived in NYC yesterday at least to give myself some time to relax, but my wedding was approximately one week away, and I didn't want to spend more time than necessary away from Declan. David hadn't liked it either that I was going to be away for a day at the last minute.

A message came in on my phone, reminding me that I hadn't deactivated the ring tone. I quickly switched it to silent before I tapped open the message from Declan.

Declan: *I think writing is similar to show biz so I'll say, break a leg.*

Smiling I sent him a quick response.

Owen: *Maybe if they were broken they wouldn't be shaking so badly. I'm nervous. Why am I doing this on my own again? You should be here.*

He sent a smiley face.

Declan: *You admit you need me.*

Owen: *I always need you.*

Declan: *I shouldn't admit this, but you don't*

need me, babe. You got this. Call me with the good news once you're done."

Owen: *Okay, Daddy.*

I grinned at my last message because his didn't come in right away like the others. I pictured him sitting there in his office getting all hot and bothered.

Declan: *Later I'll make you say Daddy while I watch you take care of yourself. How about that?"*

"Mr. Long, Mr. Trellis will see you now."

I jumped at the unexpected voice and quickly exited the message application. I slipped my phone in the inside pocket of my jacket and rose to my feet to address the slender blonde who smiled at me. She reminded me of the Barbie dolls Summer used to play with.

"Thank you," I answered and followed her down a hall to a door boasting the plate of Editor in Chief. She knocked once, opened the door and announced me.

"Come on in," came the same voice that had left me the voicemail. I had listened to the voicemail so many times that I would have been able to pick out the voice anywhere.

I entered the office, and the door was promptly closed behind me. I was surprised to find three pairs of eyes on me. Two males, one closer in age to me, the other in his early thirties and a woman with gray streaks in her hair. For a minute, I felt myself panicking because I wasn't prepared for this. How could I be? I was a chauffeur who thought he could write books.

"Mr. Long," the older of the two men said, rising to

his feet with his hand extended. "We spoke on the phone."

I closed the distance between us and shook his hand. "Right. You must be Max Trellis."

"That's right. I'm so pleased you were able to take us up on our offer to be present in person today," he stated, walking me over to the table in the room where the other two members of his team were. "We have lots to discuss with you today, but first allow me to introduce you to two of our team members here at the publishing house. This is Marie Snowden, one of our Literary Agents, and Glenn Forbes, our Marketing Manager."

"Nice to meet you." I shook their hands before taking the seat they indicated. The room felt lopsided with me on one side of the table, Max at the head and Marie and Glenn on the other side. I suddenly wished I had brought Declan with me, but he was right. He trusted me to be able to make sound decisions where my writing career was concerned, and I would show him that I could.

Max made small talk, asking me about my flight and my hotel. Was I comfortable here and if there was anything they could do for me? Did I want a tour of the city before I returned to Cincinnati? As much as I appreciated the small talk, it only left me in suspension, confused as to why I really was here. Why wasn't an email good enough? Why would a publishing house spend money to pay for airfare and hotel just to see me, an unpublished author?

"I'm sure you've been wondering why we asked you to come here?" Max asked.

"The question has crossed my mind," I replied honestly.

Max chuckled. "We are very much interested in your story, Owen. May I call you Owen?"

"Sure. Owen is fine."

"Good, because I believe we're all about to become very good friends, Owen."

It was at that point that I started to feel uneasy. I couldn't put my finger on it, but the niceties seemed overdone. As much as I didn't have any understanding of how publishing worked, the way these three were looking at me like I was under a microscope didn't sit well with me at all.

"For a very long time our publishing house has been a traditional one." This time it was Marie who spoke, her speech slow and even as though she deliberately took the time to enunciate each word. "We've been toying with the idea of venturing into a less traditional path, and your story caught our eyes."

"You see we think you would be perfect for a launch of our new rainbow house which we will be launching soon," Glenn added. "We read your biography that we request each aspiring author send us, and we were fascinated with your family. You describe you all as one big queer family. May we ask you to elaborate?"

My head was spinning with information. I was flattered at them opening a rainbow house and wanting my manuscript apparently to be a part of their launch. At the same time, they made no mention of my manuscript itself. I found them more interested in my family and me.

"I'm not sure what you want me to elaborate on," I

answered, my grip tightening on the chair arms which I clutched.

"What do you mean by your family is one big queer family?" Max remarked. "You have twin boys and a daughter, right?"

A shiver ran down my spine. "I never mentioned any of that. How did you know that?"

"Oh, it's common procedure," Max replied with a smile. "No big deal. We usually check up on potential authors to ensure they are who they claim to be. When you've been in this business for as long as we have, you learn that it pays to be cautious."

"That makes sense," I supposed. "I don't wish to dig into my children's sexuality, however. I talked about my family as a whole, not for them to be dissected."

"Oh no, you must not think of it in such a manner," the Marketing Manager replied. "Let's give you an idea of what's at stake here, Owen, and you can decide if you want to be a part of our transformation. We are a big company, one of the biggest names you'll find in publishing. Yes, we have published gay content before, but they've never been the main focus of what we do. As the world becomes more open and accepting, we see a market to explore and give the people what they want. However, this type of content from 'own voice' authors is quite rare, and that's where you come in. With your sexual orientation, you can be the face of our rainbow house. With your big queer family, you will be the author with an authentic voice. Readers will love it."

Stunned, I stared at the three faces focused on me, eagerly awaiting some response out of me. This was bigger than anything I could have possibly come up with. On the one hand I felt flattered they could see me as the face of anything. On the other, I felt off, like this was wrong. Or not necessarily wrong, but at least not moral. They didn't want me for my book. They wanted me because they thought I was gay and my family was queer.

"Is that an engagement ring?" Marie asked, pointing at the ring on my left hand, and I didn't even realize before then that I had placed both my hands on the table. "This is so exciting. When's the wedding? We would want to feature you and your prospective husband on our website. We'll get people talking about you long before your book is even launched. Now *that's* effective marketing."

"I'm not gay," I blurted out. It was the only thing that I could force out amongst their excited chatter of having a gay author to use to lure readers to their new gay literature line.

"What?" Max asked. "Of course, you're gay. You're engaged to a man, right?"

"Yes, but I'm not gay. I'm bisexual," I answered. "My fiancé is gay, but I'm not. My sons—one is bisexual and the other is pan. My daughter is a lesbian. To dismiss their sexuality and mine by highlighting only one color of the rainbow is wrong. It's not who I am."

Silence filled the room, and I could hear my breathing hot and heavy. My vision went dark for a few seconds as the enormity of what was happening here struck me. They just wanted to exploit who I was for financial gain. That was all. I could have understood if they had genuine interest in my book, and the fact that I was bisexual could be a selling factor, but when they were only interested in my sexuality, I had to call bullshit where I saw it.

Marie recovered the fastest and gave a laugh that was brittle. "Being gay or bisexual? What difference does it make since you're marrying a man? Surely it doesn't matter now to say you're bisexual?"

I gaped at her and how dense she was. I struggled to my feet unable to hear anymore. "I suggest that you brush up on what you know of the LGBTQIA+ community before you get too hasty and start your rainbow house. By the way, had you read my manuscript at all, you would have noticed that my character isn't gay. He is bisexual."

"Don't be ridiculous. Of course, we read your manuscript," Max said, getting to his feet as well. "We just believe we'd gain more traction marketing your character as gay instead of bisexual. I mean, in the book, he's with a man the entire time, so what difference does it make to the story?"

Horror filled me as I stepped back toward the door. "My character so happens to fall in love with another man. This doesn't mean that he's any less likely to be with a woman should he lose his partner or something? You want to know why I am touchy about this subject? Because I'm tired of us bi people having to justify ourselves to everyone." Like my parents. Maybe that was the reason I had written one of guys as bi instead of gay. My parents never understood why I would want to be with a man if I swung both ways. Since I did, why not pick a nice woman to marry then? They had felt the same about James, always badmouthing him. Why hadn't he been satisfied to stay married to a man? Why had he needed the women too? It was like telling me my twins weren't valid.

I fucking hated it.

"If you'd just listen to our reasoning, you'd find that it's more profitable to have a gay character than a bi one," Glenn announced, chiming into the discussion. "All the numbers say so. We're the experts in this. If you'd just sit calmly and let's go over the numbers with you then you'll see that we have a point. It serves absolutely no purpose to market your character as bi."

I nodded to them. "You may have your financial reasoning for thinking so, but my book means more to me than dollars and cents. By all means, if you want to publish gay fiction only then do so, but you have no right to change my character to suit *your* needs. You have no right to want *me* to change who I am to fit in with your marketing ideas. Simply from what I can see here, you're just not the publisher I'm looking for. I wish you luck in your endeavors."

Of course, I didn't wish them luck. I had no problem with them wanting to publish only one spectrum of the rainbow, but when they wanted me to lie about who I was to deceive the public for financial gain, this was where I drew the line. Disappointed, I wished I'd never taken that flight to New York. I wished my manuscript hadn't left the saved folder on my computer.

41

DECLAN

The sight of Owen's crestfallen face and drooping shoulders hurt more than it should have, like whatever rejection he had received today had been aimed at me personally. He hadn't told me what was wrong when he'd called me earlier, and I had rushed out of an important meeting to get him home.

"Hey, how did it go?" I asked him, standing in my private office bathroom since I had excused myself from a web-meeting the second I saw my phone ringing and Owen was on the other end of the line. He had called me way quicker than I'd expected, and I had no idea if that was a good or a bad thing.

"It was horrible," he replied, talking so fast I didn't hear what he said after.

"Baby, slow down, I can't understand a thing. What's wrong?"

"I just want to come home," he replied, his tone so distraught that it alarmed me.

"Do you want me to come for you?" I asked him.

He let out a loud breath. "It's ridiculous to ask you to do that. I'll just stay in my hotel room until my original flight is due tomorrow anyway. A few hours in the city won't change how horribly today went."

"That's it. Get your stuff together. I'm coming for you."

"Declan, don't."

"I don't like the way you sound hurt," I answered. "Once I'm there, the hotel will call you that a car is waiting for you out front. It will take you to a private airstrip to meet me. I'm coming for you."

When he hadn't protested any more than that, I knew it was bad. I stood as he made his way inside the jet. He looked relieved when he saw me, and I reached for him, pulling him into me. Owen clung to my shoulders, burying his face into my neck. Shudders ran through him, and I ran my arms down his back, alarmed that something bad had really happened to him.

"Did someone hurt you?" I asked, my voice sharper than I intended because it was one thing not to offer him a contract, but it was another thing altogether to hurt this man.

He shook his head. "No, but it didn't make it any less painful."

"Come here." I pulled him toward the seats, sitting with him next to me. "I couldn't get a word out of you on the phone. Tell Daddy what's wrong. Whose toes will I need to step on?"

He took a deep breath and spilled everything that happened to him once he had the meeting with the publishing company. I listened, anger boiling, at the way they had only been interested in using Owen for their financial gain. He was clearly devastated at the reason they had been interested in him, then wanting him to claim a false identity as a marketing ploy.

If they even knew the man a little before they made those ridiculous propositions, they would have known it was a waste of everybody's time. Owen was an honest man, and he was a good writer too. It sucked that his first attempt at having his manuscript published was nothing more than an advertisement and money scheme for the publishing house.

"They even wanted to know more about my kids!" Owen ended, just as angry as me. "I can't believe the real reason they were interested in me, and they had the guts to want me to lie and deceive readers. That's despicable."

"It is," I agreed. "And thank God you're a man of integrity. I have no doubt they will find someone gullible enough to accept their offer."

"They'll probably even be successful too for doing it!" Owen cried in frustration. "That's immoral."

"Do you want me to do something about it?" I asked him calmly.

He stopped ranting and stared at me. "You can?"

"Pretty sure if I dig deep enough, I can get some heads rolling in that place. I've worked with a lot of people over the years, Owen."

He chewed on his bottom lip then gave a sigh and deflated. "I want to say yes. I wish I could, but I don't want to be involved in anything at all with that company. For sure they'll get their comeuppance."

"Are you certain?"

He smiled at me, the bright spots of red from anger

fading from his face. "Yes, I'm sure, but you're incredibly sweet for offering."

And because I knew his weakness, I teased him. "If you knew my thoughts right now, you wouldn't call me sweet."

That smile I loved so much widened with mischief, but before he could say anything it was announced for us to secure our seatbelts for takeoff. We complied, but he reached for my hand and relaxed in my presence as we taxied the runway before taking off.

"I'm so disappointed," he said on a sigh. "This trip was such a waste of my time."

I squeezed his hand. "Don't think of it that way. File it away as experience. Now you'll be more cautious with the next publisher I am sure."

"What next publisher?" he said on a groan. "I'll never send another manuscript to anyone else."

"Bullshit!" I protested.

He turned his head to me. "I know I said I didn't need your help before but maybe——"

I shook my head, cutting him off. "Nope. You and I know that you've got to do this on your own... I'll still be here to hold your hand through the rejections and share in the joys of your success, but this is something you have to do on your own or you'll never be sure if it's you or me that's responsible for your success."

"At this rate, what success?"

I gave him a blank stare. "You're being dramatic, babe, but I understand you're not feeling your best right now. I have something that might cheer you up."

The words were hardly out of my mouth before

Owen had his seatbelt undone and plopped his ass into my lap.

"Damn, Boy, safety first," I told him just as the light on the seatbelt switched to green. He looked appeased as he bowed his head until his lips hovered over mine.

"You were saying?"

My dear predictable Boy could so easily be turned on. I knew he was still pissed about wasting the day chasing after an opportunity that had been an utter disappointment. He was still burning with adrenaline from the experience which he was able to convert into sexual energy. He was ravenous, his lips roving mine aggressively while he shifted restlessly in my lap, his ass doing that sexy thing in which he rubbed it all over my aching cock.

"Fuck," I gasped, tearing my lips away from his. "I don't have any lube, Boy."

"We'll come up with a substitute," he murmured.

I reclined the seat all the wall back to a slope then pushed at his hips while teasing him. "You sure you want to do this?" I asked him. "We don't have to do anything but cuddle all the way back to Cincy."

Sliding off me to his feet, Owen made quick work of his belt, undid his pants button, unzipped and tugged down his pants to show his erect cock which he took in hand, massaging his length.

"I'm sure of what I want, Daddy, and it's not just a cuddle. Maybe a cuddle afterward."

"Then completely undress and come here."

I undressed, sitting in the chair and watching him. I kicked off my shoes, pulled off my pants and my shirt followed suit. Owen's eyes hungrily wandered to my nipples. I lightly grazed them with my hands, and he sucked in a deep breath.

"Daddy, can't I play with them?" he moaned.

"Not yet," I told him. "They're still a lot sensitive. I know something you can play with though."

He regretfully tore his eyes away from my nipples to my crotch. His disappointment didn't last for long. He licked his lips, "Fuck, Daddy, you going to make a man out of me?"

"Does the sex feel any different yet?" I asked him.

He laughed. "No, but perhaps when we get married. It's just nine days away."

"Can't wait to prove you wrong. Bring that ass over here, Boy. Daddy wants to snack."

"Yes, Daddy."

I reclined the chair some more and indicated how I wanted him. He turned with his back to me straddling my waist then inching down the chair to lie with his head positioned in the direction of my feet. His lovely thick ass was just what I had ordered. I spread the cheeks, adjusted him a bit closer before I set my tongue to work.

Gripping my thighs for purchase, Owen licked me, rolling his tongue over the tip of my cock. His moan as I continued pleasuring him reverberated through me.

"Fuck," I moaned, coating his hole with saliva before leaning backward and using my thumbs to stretch that pretty pink rim. He didn't stop sucking as much of me as he could while I fingered his ass, ensuring he was well stretched. When I was satisfied, I went back to licking, the muscles in my neck straining with each lift of my head to get to my prize.

I slapped his ass hard, the sound echoing in the cabin. My fingers printed out on his skin and I squeezed, gripping the flesh hard until he squirmed.

"Let's go to the bed," I told him.

With one last suck of my cock, he released me, and we went through to the bedroom. My legs were shaky, and I was only too glad to sink down onto the bed.

"Come and sit on my face, Boy. I'm not done with you yet."

"Oh God, Daddy," he moaned as he straddled my shoulders and settled himself down gingerly over my face.

"Ride my tongue."

And ride my tongue he did. He backed that sexy ass up and down my tongue, reaching back to pry his cheeks apart while he was at it. His sighs and moans filled the cabin. Every now and again, I aimed a slap at his ass just the way he liked it. It set him off even more until I clamped my arms down his thighs and pulled him fully back to smother my face with his cheeks. I sucked at his puckered opening.

"Oh Daddy, I can't wait much longer," he moaned, wrapping a hand around my length. "Please."

With a little nudge from me, he slid to his side on the bed. I leaned over him, kissing him and the minx couldn't resist lightly brushing the nipple rings.

"Don't move," I told him.

I hurried to the bathroom, quickly checking the supplies on hand. Not one goddamn thing. The conditioner was the only thing I saw as suitable. I checked and found it was an organic brand. Good enough. I returned to Owen to find that he had moved. From the look on his face, he was begging for it.

I dropped the conditioner to the bed. "Didn't I tell you not to move?"

"I was getting impatient," he answered flippantly. I had left him on his side, but he was on his abdomen, and as I watched him, his ass rose off the bed, begging for my hand. Usually I withheld the punishment when he demanded it, but I knew he probably needed it more right now. Something familiar that he could relate to after his disappointment earlier.

"Come down to the edge of the bed," I instructed him.

He shuffled down without arguing. "Like this, Daddy?" The bottom of his feet hung over the edge of the bed and his ass was poised perfectly within the reach of my hands. I caressed his backside.

"Perfect. Eight hard spanks. I want you to count them aloud for me. Do you understand?"

"Please, twelve Daddy," he begged.

I pinched his ass and two red spots formed. "Now we're down to six. You want to argue with Daddy?"

"No, Daddy," he moaned. "I'd like six spanks, please." He turned wide innocent eyes toward me. "Six on each side."

He was too good at this. Damn, he arched his back into the first slap.

"One!"

The second slap echoed in the room, but he moaned, spreading his legs so wide to tempt me with his hole.

"Two!"

I gave him his heart's desire, because I couldn't resist him. Six slaps on each cheek left his ass red with finger-prints. I soothed my hands over the flesh, and he whimpered into the sheets he had stuffed in his mouth.

"Are you ready to take me inside now, Boy?" I asked him.

"Yes, Daddy," he answered. "Will you give it to me hard, Daddy? Punish me for disobeying you. Please."

Damn, he is really into the scene today. I coated us both carefully with the conditioner and lined up with his puck-ered ass that spread so freely like a lotus when I entered him. I didn't plan to enter him all at once, but I went in with such ease that I couldn't stop myself until I was buried to the hilt inside his tight warm crevice.

I pulled out, and he groaned. I slid back inside him with a slow thrust, testing to ensure that we were both slick enough. The last thing I needed was to hurt him.

Satisfied that we were both adequately 'lubed', I clutched his sides, pulled out and thrust hard. The shift of muscles in his back was amazing. He pressed his torso to the bed, content to do very little but to have me use him. Over and over like a vessel meant to house my cum, I thrust inside my Boy's ass. He couldn't stay passive for long though. He threw back his ass into each thrust, rolling his hips as I sheathed myself inside his body.

Pulling his torso up, I wrapped a hand across his chest going up around his other shoulder into a loose choke hold. I kissed the side of his face as I fucked him.

His back grazed my nipples sending goosebumps down my spine.

My climax hit me out of the blue. I didn't expect it or I would have been taking care of him as well. I could do nothing but cling to him, grinding into his ass as though I wanted to crawl into his skin, become the pigments of his flesh.

"Fuck. Fuck." I shuddered against him. "Fuck, baby. I couldn't hold back."

He gasped, laughing in amusement. "Now that's the way to give a compliment."

I pulled out and a drip of my cum followed. I caught it with my finger and fed it back inside him. He clenched his ass to keep my seed, and I wished I had his favorite butt plug to keep his insides all cummy the way he liked it.

"I'll help you get off," I told him.

He turned over onto his back and fisted his dick. "I can handle it. You can watch if you want to."

So I sat back on my haunches, and I watched my Boy sliding his fist over his cock, stroking himself. Just eyeing him was a turn on, but it was taking him a while to get there.

I reached for the conditioner. "Here, let me help."

"How?" he asked.

I didn't answer but allowed him to watch me as I fingered my ass with the substituted slick. His breath hitched when he noticed my intentions. I worked a finger inside my still so tightly clenched hole. Sometimes when we had sex, he would stick a finger up my ass, but since the first time he fucked me, he hadn't asked again, and I hadn't volunteered. Not that it was unpleasant, but fuck, I'd rather be inside him, and he preferred it anyway. I wasn't inflexible though, and he would get off more with me clenching on him.

"Daddy, you don't have to," he said when I reached for his cock to coat him as well.

"You didn't enjoy it the first time?" I asked, pausing.

"Of course, I did. You're so fucking tight, Daddy. Just thinking about it makes me want to nut so hard."

"Good. Then this won't take long."

With Owen lying on his back, I straddled him, reaching down to kiss him before I grasped his cock and tried to get him in. It was a fucking tight stretch of my ring, but when I lowered myself until I was fully seated, the sensation was breathtaking. I felt stretched to the limit.

"Oh fuck, Daddy," he moaned when I began to move, riding my Boy slowly at first. He gripped the sheets, hips bucking upward each time my ass snapped down into his pelvis. I increased my tempo, riding him harder as I loosened up for him. The play of emotions on his face was everything. His chest heaved, he keened loud, he swore, and then he claimed he was fucking dying. But death felt good if this was what it was.

I watched as I resurrected him, his eyes flying open. I rode him even harder, my hands pressed into his chest as I slammed my ass down over and over. When he couldn't take anymore, his hands clamped down onto my waist, holding me flush against him as he raised his hips, grinding even deeper inside me.

When his climax subsided, he fell back against the

bed, breathing as hard as me. We stared at each other, and I saw the same wonder in his eyes that I was sure was in mine. How the hell did sex with him get better every time?

Carefully, I lifted off him, trying to hide my wince of discomfort now that the endorphins were wearing off. I could feel the ache in my ass. I'd probably be walking funny when we got off the jet, but I couldn't even bring myself to care.

"How are you feeling now?" I asked him, lying on my tummy while he still remained on his back.

"About sex?"

I bit his shoulder playfully. "I already can tell how you feel about that. I mean the way everything turned out today."

"Still disappointed," he answered. "But someone knows how to cheer me up, so I'm too mellow right now to think about it. Later I can go back to being pissed."

"Works like a charm every time."

42

OWEN

As it turned out, I was too busy helping with everything we needed to do on the last minute for our wedding to dwell much about not getting a contract with the publishing house of my first choice. At times when I wasn't busy and there was a lull in my day, I would remember how everything turned out. I even got really sad about it once, but then Declan sat me down and reminded me that I *had* gotten an offer. I had just turned it down. Regardless of the greater why of it, they must have at least liked my manuscript to take me on as the face of their rainbow house. I immediately felt better.

I didn't send my manuscript to another publisher. I didn't want to focus on anything apart from my wedding. After our honeymoon to God knew where since Declan wanted it to be a surprise, then I could return home with renewed focus and energy to start over. I reminded myself of the number of times some popular books had been turned down by publishers before being accepted. I was willing to wade through all the rejections to find the right publisher that fit with my style.

Declan and I were late in taking our engagement photos, but made a day of it, and we loved the result. I spent some time perfecting my vows to him and when I believed I had them down pat, I memorized them but still kept a cue card with the words in the event I forgot my lines. I still had no idea how I would react on the day itself. I was surprisingly calmer than Declan about it, but he had never been married before. I had been, so I was over the initial overwhelming feeling of it all.

Four days to go from our wedding, and the kids had all come to Cincy. Auggie moved back into the house, having no intentions of returning to Columbus with his twin. We had our rehearsal dinner which David had booked for us at a family-run Italian restaurant. We hadn't been sure of the place, but David had asked us to trust him, so we had, and we weren't disappointed.

The rustic trattoria interior design was appealing and made us all feel at home. The food was delicious and the company for the night was good. Everyone in our wedding party arrived. Heath and Ridge joined us, though they looked to be more distant than the last time we had seen them at the appreciation ceremony held by the cancer society. Even Silas had attended. Alone. We had included a plus two in his invitation for him in the event Declan was right and he had two men in his life. I would have been satisfied with at least one for him. Silas was too nice a guy not to experience the love I had with Declan.

With everything Declan and I ended up doing during the day, we didn't have time to have sex at night. We would fall asleep in each other's arms, exhausted from that day's activities. The night we arrived home from the rehearsal dinner, I teased him that we were already the couple who were too tired to have sex. To prove otherwise, he had indicated for me to get on the bed. He had fucked me right in front of the mirror where I watched the whole thing unfold with fascination.

Declan and I were having breakfast the day before our wedding when my kids visited. We had been seeing them a lot because of the wedding preparations, but today we had nothing planned. David had insisted in Declan and I resting up for the big day, and that was exactly what we had planned, to laze the day away by the poolside.

While I glared at them when they took seats around the table without being asked, Declan looked on in amusement. My kids really needed to learn boundaries, but Declan didn't seem to mind.

"What are you guys doing here so early?" I asked.

"We're splitting you up for the day," Summer replied with a big smile.

"What?" I frowned at their grinning faces.

"It's the day before your wedding," Oscar explained. "We can at least get you for the day before you shackle yourself to this guy."

"But we have plans," I protested.

"What plans?" Auggie asked. "I'm sure I heard David say to take the day off."

I flushed and glanced at Declan for help, but he

shrugged. "Well, we wanted to spend the day together, before you know, the big day."

"I guess you'll have to change your plans then," Auggie said for the first time since he arrived. "You don't mind, do you, Declan? Charles should be here to entertain you for the day."

"What if we don't agree with this plan?" I protested. After the hectic preparations of the last few days, I was looking forward to spending the day with my fiancé. "Whose idea was this anyway?"

"We all thought of it," Summer replied. "Come on. You two have to humor us. Think how much better it will be tomorrow when you see each other after spending the day apart."

"Declan, do something!" I begged him when they persisted, because three against me was so wrong. I couldn't tell them no on my own.

"I don't think we can stop them," Declan replied with a grin in my direction, and I wondered if he had been a part of this plan. "Plus, I think what they are really trying to say is that they'd like to spend the day with you before giving you away tomorrow.

I frowned at him. "And what will you be doing with Charles?"

He shrugged. "I'm not sure what he has planned. This is as much news to me as it is to you."

"I bet he's going to want to throw you that bachelor party," I groaned. "If he does——"

"I won't look at any of the strippers," Declan said on a laugh. "Cross my heart."

"I'm not worried about strippers," I said, getting to my feet.

"No?" Declan raised an eyebrow, his lips twitching. "Why not?"

"Because you know better," I answered. "And since you really want to marry me…" I trailed off leaving the rest to his imagination.

Declan laughed. "You're right. The only stripper in my future is you."

"And I'll give you a good show too," I told him, ignoring my kids' shocked faces, as if they couldn't believe the conversation Declan and I were having in their hearing.

"Shame on you." Oscar wagged a finger between Declan and me. "Don't you see that kids are present? Dad, go grab an overnight bag and let's go. You'll see Declan tomorrow."

"Hold up!" Declan finally protested. "What do you mean tomorrow?"

"Oh yeah!" Summer piped in. "We're following tradition. We're not letting you see the groom before he walks down the aisle, so no sleeping in the same bed tonight."

"I never agreed to this," Declan said on a frown.

I grinned at him. Earlier he had been fine with me being gone for a day while he spent the time with his father doing God knew what.

"It's fine, *babe*," I told him. "It will be just for a night. I'll make it to the wedding on time."

"You'd better. You don't want to be tardy."

Or maybe I do if it means a spanking on my honeymoon.

Half an hour later, I returned downstairs, freshly showered and packed to go. We got everything I would need to get dressed for the wedding tomorrow, and Declan walked us out to Auggie's car. The kids got in, but Declan held me to him, a hand going around my waist then down to grip my ass discreetly. At least I thought it was discreetly until I heard Oscar's mutter.

"Oh gross."

I ignored him and kissed Declan deeply. After all, I wouldn't see him for the rest of the day. The next time I laid eyes on him, we would be joined together as husbands. I clung to him, one hand tangling in the hair at the back of his head, my excitement mounting at the thought of being his husband.

"Time's up, guys!" Summer cried, knocking on the window with her knuckles. "Let's go, Dad. Stop grossing out the kids."

Declan grinned at me. "Want to gross them out some more?"

I pushed his hands away from my ass. "I would, but they might leave me behind, and I'm starting to like the idea of not seeing you for a day before we get hitched."

He sighed and opened the car door for me. "Alright. I'll see you at the ceremony promptly at one." He turned to Auggie and leveled him with a stare. "You guys asked for him for the day. Please bring him to the ceremony the same way I'm sending him off. Healthy and happy. That is all."

"Dad's forty-seven you know!" Oscar muttered. "Pretty capable of taking care of himself."

"Oscar!" Auggie growled at his twin before nodding at Declan. "He'll be fine. We'll see you tomorrow."

"And be on time!"

I waved at Declan and for the hell of it blew him a kiss. His smile, relaxed posture, and the way he looked at me with all the love in his heart made my kids' teasing worth it.

"Has anyone ever told you guys that you're gag-worthy?" Oscar asked, craning his head to stare at me from the front seat.

"Remember that time I came home from work early and caught you half-naked in my bed with that girl?" I returned, reaching out to ruffle his hair as he cringed. "Think of this as payback. At least Dec and I didn't do anything in your bed. Maybe."

"You wouldn't!"

43

DECLAN

Owen was late, and I was pretty certain it was all a part of his plan. I kept glancing at my watch, tracking the time while I stood with Charles, Ridge, and Silas who were all acting as groomsmen. Our wedding was taking place on the rooftop of the Palais Royale Hotel, and even though I had gone through everything David planned for the event, I was still blown away with his arrangement of the décor.

The simplistic arrangement of the colors ivory and gold that we had chosen gave the wedding a classy feel. The flooring of the rooftop was covered with faux lawn, and flowers played an integral part of the decorations as we had requested. They were all around, transforming the rooftop into a garden, completely relaxed and natural.

Everything was perfect. Except it was twenty minutes past the hour and Owen was still not here.

"It's completely fine," Charles whispered from where he stood. "It's customary to keep the groom waiting."

I glared at Charles, not comforted in the least by his attempt to be encouraging, and he backed off. Ridge grinned at me, delighting in my discomfort. I scowled at him and wished Heath's wrath on him, fully knowing from the way Heath was staring at him in adoration now that it wasn't likely to happen. Ridge would love it anyway.

"What are you grinning about?" I asked him.

"Watching you squirm over someone," Ridge answered. "I never thought I'd see the day. You, my friend, are well and truly caught."

"If you're trying to cheer me up, Ridge, it isn't working."

At that moment, I caught sight of David hurrying down the aisle, and I didn't like the frown he wore. I let Owen out of sight for twenty-four hours, entrusting they would get him to our wedding on time and this happened!

"They're on their way," David said, coming to a stop beside me. "There was a hiccup with their ride, but they should get here soon."

"I need my phone," I growled to no one in particular. David had confiscated it from me to keep me from badgering Owen.

"Just relax, sir. Everything will be fine."

I turned away from David to Charles. "Give me your phone."

Charles glanced between me and David as if trying

to figure out what to do. "Uh, David said they'll be here soon."

"Give me the damn phone, Charles."

Twenty-four hours and no word out of Owen. I needed to at least hear his voice.

Charles handed me his phone without another word. I punched in Owen's phone number, and it rang unanswered. After ringing him three times, I glared at Charles like it was his fault.

"Did you try calling one of his sons?" he asked me.

"I don't know their numbers off the top of my head," I growled.

He tugged at his bow tie. "Um, well, I think I have August's number somewhere in my phone. Let me search for it."

I frowned at him as he took the phone and searched for Auggie's number. I was too worried though to ask him why he had my soon-to-be step-son's number. I was too grateful when he handed me the phone.

"Declan, we're on our way," Auggie answered on the second ring. "We just had to make a quick stop at the hospital."

"What?" My bellow was loud enough to startle our guests, but I didn't care. "Why? Is something wrong with Owen?"

"No, not Dad. It's the driver. He was feeling sick and passed out. We had to take him to A & E."

"Is everything fine?"

"Yes, the doctor says he will be fine. Something about the heat and dehydration."

"Where are you now?"

"On the way. Dad's driving the limousine."

"Can I talk to him?"

The line went silent for a few seconds before Auggie came back on the line. "He says he'll be there in five."

"Five minutes, Auggie!" I stated, before hanging up and handing the phone back to Charles.

Fuck, as if I wasn't already nervous as it was. Standing and twiddling my thumbs just made it worse, but I could do it for five minutes. No longer.

They got here in four. I glimpsed Owen at the back entrance to the roof deck although he was partially blocked by Auggie, Oscar, and Summer. Auggie and Oscar wore matching tuxes, and Summer was simply stunning in the gold lamé dress she wore.

"They're about to begin," Charles whispered beside me, as if I couldn't see for myself.

I couldn't tear my eyes away from Owen as he made down the aisle to our wedding march of choice, Elle Henderson's *Yours*. He was... beautiful, lips relaxed in a smile. He looked neither left nor right to our guests but kept his eyes locked on mine. Summer walked beside him, and the twins flanked him on either side. If anyone had a reason to protest us getting married today it was definitely not going to be one of these three.

My eyes misted. Not something I would have imagined happening, but I was staring into the eyes of my forever. A year ago, I would have never dreamed to be so in love with someone else. The most I would have dared hope for was a willing body that satisfied me, but Owen was so much more. He was the more of everything I had been too afraid to hope for.

Owen joined me before the officiator, and I linked our fingers, just continuing to stare at him while the question was asked about who gave this man to be married. The twins and Summer echoed that they did which prompted laughter from the guests.

"Sorry for getting him here late," Auggie apologized as he fit into the space next to Charles.

"I'm sure he wasn't worried," Owen murmured.

Ridge snickered, and I shook my head. "Not at all."

Owen raised his eyebrows, but before he could say anything, the officiator cleared his throat and commenced the ceremony.

It all happened faster than I had anticipated, the ceremony flowing smoothly, and then we were asked to recite our wedding vows to each other. Owen took out a piece of paper from his pocket and read with ease. Each word that he spoke, I found myself panicking. I hadn't written my vows. His were so sweet, and I could see some of our guests dabbing at their eyes.

"Declan," the officiator prompted me when Owen was done. My heart pounded in my chest as Owen stared at me expectantly to hear my declaration of love. I was at a loss for words.

"You didn't write the vows, did you?" he asked in amusement as he watched me sweat in front of our guests.

"Oh God, he's going to choke," I heard Ridge say.

"I'm not going to choke." *I was seriously choking, but I wasn't going to admit it. Not over my dead body.* "You take my breath away."

Owen's quiet chuckle filled the air. "I told you I would. Go on."

He'd never let me forget it if I messed up my vows, so I took a deep breath and pulled myself together. "From the moment I met you I knew there was something different about you," I said and mentally patted myself on the back for a good restart. "At the time, I had no idea just how much you would come into my life and mess up the order of things. In a good way. First getting me to fall in love with you, giving me the strength to leave certain things in the past, and the courage to forgive. You've taught me patience, and you've taught me what it means to truly love someone, because I've been on the receiving end of your love for me. I've made mistakes, and I can't promise I won't make more, but it will never be with the intention of hurting you. I'll always protect you, cherish you, love you, take care of you. I'll take care of us. Always. Till death do us part."

Silent tears cruised Owen's cheeks. Playfully, I should have teased him about it as I would come to do later, but in that moment, I was just humbled by this man agreeing to be my husband.

"That was beautiful," he said as I plucked the pocket square from my breast pocket to gently wipe his face. "It's not fair. I'm the writer in the family."

That made me laugh and set me at ease. The fifty or so guests we had were only privileged to share in this moment with us, but this was about *us*. Our forever.

We exchanged matching rings, and seeing the physical evidence of our vows to each other, sealed and approved legally, I eagerly pulled him to me when I was finally told I could kiss my husband. The cheers faded into the background, along with Oscar's teasing. Something fluttered around us, landing on us, but I ignored it for the sole purpose of marking my husband before our witnesses.

"I love you," he murmured against my lips, his arms winding around my waist.

"I'm crazy about you now even more than I was when I first met you," I told him. Musical cords struck up in the background, but I still didn't have enough of him yet. I doubted I ever would.

The next time our lips parted, we finally turned to our guests who rose to their feet and cheered. We had confetti in our hair and on our clothes. As we walked down the aisle, I brushed the ones from Owen's hair.

"Tell me," he said. "Where are we going for our honeymoon?"

I hadn't planned to tell him until we got there, but he was dying to know. I couldn't deny him anything.

"We're going to Greece," I replied, pleased at his slack-jawed look when I revealed our destination after our reception. "We'll spend two weeks taking care of us, then when we get back, we work on getting your manuscript published. How about that?"

In the middle of the aisle, Owen stopped me to grab me by the back of the neck. "Sounds like a good plan."

He kissed me hard, my arms went around him to secure my husband to me. The only real plan I needed was loving Owen as we had promised in our vows.

EPILOGUE

"**N**ervous?" Declan asked, coming up behind me to massage my tense shoulders. He was wearing the shirt he had insisted in making solely for the event *Proud Husband of a Romance Author.*

"More like dying," I answered, leaning into his touch. Ever since the launch of my debut novel four months ago, I had been anticipating this day. My publisher had set up my first official book signing event, and it was nerve-wracking.

In the end, turning down Harver Press had been the best decision I had made as an author. Not long after Declan and I had returned home from our honeymoon in Greece, we had discovered the company embroiled in a lawsuit with an author claiming their work had been discriminated against.

Apparently, the publishing house had willingly accepted gay books to be a part of their publication, but the books didn't stand a chance as they didn't invest as heavily in the titles as they did books geared toward the het market. Their mad dash to start a rainbow line had been with the intention of disputing the lawsuit and not because they had a genuine interest in publishing authors of LGBTQIA+ content.

While it had taken me over a year to get my book published, I was pleased by the result. I had been rejected by a total of eight publishers when I was finally accepted by Bliss Books Publishing House. Though a smaller entity, the company had all the qualities that made me decide to accept their contract. They had been true to their word, fulfilling every promise made and exceeding my expectations in their launch of my book.

The majority of the public loved my book. I remembered reading the first set of bad reviews and feeling horrible about it, but like he had promised, Declan had always been there for comfort. He didn't interfere, but he was a moral support, always by my side, attending interviews with me and flying with me wherever I needed to be.

Having sold a quarter of a million books to the public, my debut could be described as a success, and my publisher had organized a series of book tours across the different states. Today was the official launch of my first book signing, and my gut twisted with nerves because I had no idea how it would go.

Declan leaned sideways to kiss my cheek. "You'll be wonderful. Regardless of what happens, you know I'll always be your number one fan."

I tilted my head up for him to kiss me properly, and when he did, I still got butterflies in my stomach. He was right that marriage had definitely not watered down the quality of our sex life.

"I just realized something," I said, when he broke the kiss.

"What?"

I snatched up one of the books from the table and grabbed the *Sharpie* marker I had bought for this purpose. As he watched, I made out my first autographed book to him right on the dedication page that read:

To my husband, Declan, for believing in me and supporting my dream. You've given me the happy ever after I thought I would only get from books.

Love, Owen.

"It's not like I'm famous or anything," I said, marking the date and handing him the copy of the book. "But maybe one day my autograph will be worth something."

"Thanks, love." He accepted my gift, tracing the words lightly with his fingers. I remembered the way he had gotten emotional when I had shown him the dedication page.

"No, thank you for all you've done for me," I told him. "Even if no one comes today to the book signing and I'd be disappointed, it will always be better because I have you."

"Well, that's not going to happen today, Owen," my agent Sophia remarked, coming up to my table with a bright smile. "You should see the number of people lined up outside waiting for us to begin. I'm not worried one bit about you not having fans here today. I'm worried you won't be able to see everyone who will be here."

My eyes widened in surprise. "Really?"

She laughed and glanced at Declan. "Have you not convinced him how good he is yet?"

Declan shrugged. "I try, but what can I say? My husband's determined to be modest."

"You ready to meet your first fans, Owen?" Sophia asked.

I didn't think I could ever be ready, but I nodded, and she moved on to have the venue opened up. Behind me, Declan's hands rested on my shoulders in support. He squeezed me gently and leaned forward to whisper into my left ear.

"Daddy will be here for you, Boy. You don't have to worry about a thing. Now be a good Boy and there's a treat waiting for you back at our hotel when we're through."

I perked up at the mention of a treat. Declan's treats kept getting better and better, and now I made every effort to earn them.

"And we're ready for action!" Sophia announced just as loud chattering reached my ears followed by a mass of people heading toward me.

Despite trying to be prepared mentally for the event, my heart was beating hard in my chest, and the sharpie marker slipped from my fingers nervously.

Then I saw who headed the line, and the nervousness ebbed away.

"Hi, we're your biggest fans and would like to get signed copies of your books, please!" Summer chirped, her fiancée Penny beside her.

Behind the couple, Auggie and Charles followed, their baby girl in Auggie's arms. Oscar was next, chatting to Ridge and Heath who were married a couple of months ago. James, though he came alone, was smiling, and I was pleased he had fallen in love as hard as I had. He was much happier and had forgiven himself like the rest of us had done. His guy fit right in with us. Pierce and David, who had surprised everybody by hooking up at our wedding, were now inseparable. The kid who had warmed his way into my life almost like a son, Harper, the cancer survivor and his fiancé. Then there was Silas rounding up the family with the two men who had won his heart all over again.

And if I never saw another person walk into the venue, I would be happy because I had my family. Those by blood, and others by choice.

Want to find out how David and Pierce hooked up at Owen and Declan's wedding? Sign up to my newsletter to get this juicy bit!

AUTHOR'S NOTE

Dear Reader,

Thanks so much for reading the Taking Care series. When I started this series, it was to fill a void in the daddy kink romance world by having an older man being the boy and the younger man the Daddy. Declan and Owen's story transcended beyond that. I never saw three books coming out of them, but in writing this last book, they just would not stop. I eventually had to declare them done, although I heard much grumbling from them. It's my hope that you will see them again in the little specials I usually write. I am thinking of one for Halloween, maybe Thanksgiving, and Christmas—definitely the latter, if nothing else.

Declan and Owen's story touched on some very important themes that make this story one of my favorites. Family and friendship. In writing their story, it didn't touch on just them, but the role their family and friends play in their relationship. Owen's family became like my own, finding a place in my heart.

It is my intention to carry on this series with spin-off standalone novels for the couples mentioned at the end of the epilogue. I hope you have as much interest in them as I have. Don't forget to sign up to my newsletter to get regular updates from me. You can sign up here.

Take care
  Gianni

COMING SOON

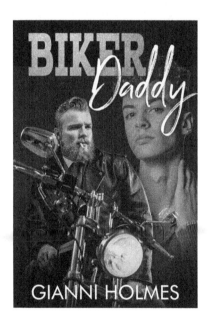

*The story of the President of an Outlaw Motorcycle Club
and the son of the chief of police who swears to marry*

him when he's older. First published through Prolific Words as an unedited short story. Will be expanded to a novel.

The story of a boy who leaves his town in shame but returns a man. Falling in love with his best friend's dad was never in his plans. But this time it doesn't feel wrong. It feels oh so right.

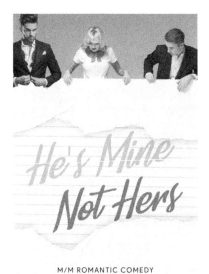

M/M ROMANTIC COMEDY
GIANNI HOLMES

What happens when best friends who so happens to be mother and son fall for the same guy? Neither intends to let the other have the prize, but one must concede.

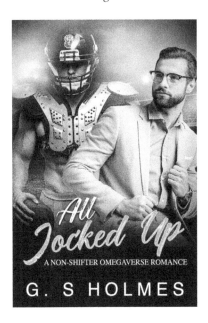

Will this omega Professor be able to hide who he is for long when sleeps with his student and discovers nature's way of telling him he's been claimed?

FREEBIES ON PROLIFIC WORKS

Biker Daddy (Unedited Novella)
Lemonade & Loose Lips (New Series For Subscribers
Only)
Mr. Hopper (Roleplay)
Of Thunder & Trickery (Loki & Thor fan-fic)
The Pick-Up

ALSO BY GIANNI HOLMES

Taking Care Series (Daddy Kink)

Take Care of You

Take Care of Me

Take Care of Us

Mother's Day Special

Father's Day Special

Till There Was You series (Hurt/Comfort)

Easy Does It Twice

Ollie on the Out

All Hearts on Deck

The Pick-Up (coming soon)

Corporate Pride Series (White Collar)

Falling for Mr. Corporate

My Dear Mr. Corporate

Corporate Bondage

Topped (a short story)

The Runway Project series (May/December)

Unwrapping Ainsley

Where There's a Will

ABOUT THE AUTHOR

Gianni Holmes is a high school Spanish teacher by day and a naughty but nice writer by night. She loves to watch romantic comedies especially old sitcoms such as Everybody Loves Raymond and The Andy Griffith Show. She spends much of her time writing or impersonating her characters. Apart from her love of superheroes, she also enjoys cartoons and watches them regularly. She is a single mother who lives with her five-year-old daughter in the Caribbean.

If you would like, you can write to her a gianni-holmes@gmail.com or join her Facebook group Gianni's Gems.

- facebook.com/gianniholmesbooks
- instagram.com/gianniholmes
- bookbub.com/authors/gianni-holmes

Made in the USA
Monee, IL
01 November 2020